Tori Haroldson had to admit she was impressed with the man standing before her. Their initial meeting had come apart at the seams. In retrospect, she realized McGann was completely unaware of who she was. His responses had been genuine, given the circumstances. She had put him on a defensive track, irritable now with herself for her own lack of patience. She rubbed her thumb and forefinger together, a nervous habit acquired from childhood.

There seemed to be two Bryson McGanns. One who had been capable of killing, automated and accurate. No thought, just action as demanded by the circumstances laid out before him. A man who was no stranger to situations like the one they faced together this morning. Death had played its hand and McGann rose up to meet the challenge. His actions were instinctual as much as they were initiated by training. Tori Haroldson believed that Bryson McGann acted not only out of the need to protect themselves, but also, out of the responsibility to respond because of his ability to do so. She realized that anything else would have been far less than his being demanded.

Tori Haroldson also sensed there was another side to this man standing before her. She had seen it in his eyes after the day's events had played out. Something burned deeply within him that led McGann to walk a line of deep conviction in doing what he believed was right. Although she had known him briefly, she considered herself a good read of character. He was a man of honest intent. He lived his life fully. Bryson McGann was a man capable of great passion.

Dr Lynn

You are always a bright spot in my day

Thanks for your friendship!

Enjoy the novel...

Fondly

Walter Deck

A Bryson McGann Novel

RED 7

By
WILLIAM BECK

WESTVIEW BOOK PUBLISHING, INC., NASHVILLE, TENNESSEE

First Perfect Bound Edition December 2007

Printed in the United States of America on Acid-Free Paper.

ISBN 1-933912-77-4

Page Layout by Mary Catharine Nelson and Tracy Lucas

Cover design by Landon Earps

Pre-press by Westview Publishing Co., Inc.

WESTVIEW BOOK PUBLISHING, INC.
P.O. Box 210183
Nashville, TN 37221
www.westviewpublishing.com

To Rebecca –

My love, my life, my very reason for every breath…

Characters

The Vikings
Gunnar Bergfinn
Astrid - Gunnar's Wife
Rolvag Thorstien
Sigurd Ormsmon

NESSA Employees
Bryson McGann - Assistant Projects Director
Joe "T.C." Canton - Assistant Projects Director
Randall Sumner - Director
Red O'Brien - Assistant Director of Offshore Operations
"*The Four Horsemen*"- Assistant Directors
Scott Freeman
Kate Harper
Noel Johnson
Carl Steitzer
John Beech – Pilot
Pat Evans - Pilot

U.S.S. John C. Stennis CVN-74
Lieutenant J.G Kendall Stevens
Lieutenant Commander Ron "Black Dog" Wood
Lieutenant Casey "Spiderman" Slater
Captain Harold Culpepper

Namibia
Peter Oduru - Discoverer of the Oduru diamond
Sarah Oduru - Wife

The Villains
Stephan Kholos – "The Greek"
Solange
Sabrah
Sahtay

Newlyweds
Becca and Alex Ramsey

NESSA Guest Lecturer
Tori Haroldson

Washington D.C.
Richard Simon - President
Benjamin Wolcott - Advisor
Andrea Buckler - Wolcott's friend
Senator Jason Ramsey
Olivia Ramsey - Wife
Foster Hughes - Chief Justice
Martin Boggs - Carlton Trust CEO
Stan Reynolds - Secret Service

NSA
Ashlyn Sanders - Canton's fiancée

AGSI
Skiddy Pete - Research Scientist
Ryan Wyborn - Narissa's Captain
John Busby - Helicopter Pilot
Larry Sully - Nerita's captain

Amsterdam
Abram Mossel - Diamond cutter

G- 8 Leaders
Henri Becque
Geoffrey Haines
Giovanni Bertoluzzo

Surgical team
Mick Henke - Plastic Surgeon
Noi Lin - Surgical Nurse

Acknowledgements

Writing is a mistress of disproportionate jealousy and love. Completing a novel demands constant attention and sacrifice, and it is only brought to life by the pure love of creating. It is that joy that carries me onward in this journey. It is one I have been blessed with by God, and am grateful for beyond words.

No one person writes a novel. There are a myriad of people responsible for getting a book published; faces behind the scenes whose names are unknown, and too often forgotten. Those people who gladly listened, gave a smile, or just a pat on the back. Friends who simply cared enough to ask. My readers, who continue to believe enough in my abilities as a storyteller, for me to keep bringing Bryson McGann to life. To each of you I give my thanks…

There are some very special individuals who helped bring RED 7 to print. Their thoughts, words, guidance, and ideas were invaluable.

-My parents, Donald Bryson and Margot, whose guidance in life set the compass rose of my life's journey.

-Donald, my brother, whose understanding of my ideas, his wisdom, and poignant questioning, helped keep this book on course. I hold you in my deepest love and respect.

-Fred, my brother-in-law, whose patented inventions continue to inspire ideas within the pages of Bryson McGann novels. A round to friendship and laughter – 12:45.

-My family members whom I love dearly; Danny, Rae, Rick, and Sidney, Linda, James, Mercia, Suzanne, Mary, Mark, and Jackie, of course, all the nieces and nephews too. Thanks for your caring and support which is beyond measure. You are treasured.

-Hugh Daniel, my editor, thank you for your friendship, insight, and multiple talents. They are priceless. Westview's talented staff, my thanks!

-Tom and Janie, I cannot thank you enough for your assistance and friendship. You cared about my passion, and willingly continue to offer your gracious support. The dinners and stories have been great!

-Author Eric Wilson. My thanks for your invaluable time and kind words about RED 7.
-Jennifer, your words of encouragement and friendship continue to mean so much. L.T.D.
-The Purple Hat Gang, just know your friendship is invaluable.
-Most of all, Rebecca, you are beyond any words I could ever write. Your presence in my life and continued belief in me, compares to nothing imaginable. My endless love.

William Beck

"Every gun that is made, every warship that is launched, every rocket fired signifies, in a final sense, a theft from those who hunger and are not fed, those who are cold and are not clothed. This world in arms is not spending money alone. It is spending the sweat of its laborers, the genius of its scientists, the hopes of its children… This is not a way of life at all in any true sense. Under the cloud of war, it is humanity hanging on a cross of iron."

- Dwight D. Eisenhower, April 16, 1953

"The one true inevitability is change. It is what we do with change that impacts the world, and potentially offers hope to all mankind."

- William MacMichael, June 9, 2007

Prologue – Greenland 997A.D.

A THICKENING CLOAK OF FOG enveloped the others searching the wooded thicket, until their silhouettes were swallowed in the cold, gray veil. Gunnar Bergfinn stood silent in the autumn morning, curiously prodding the moist, loamy soil with his sword. He concluded that this mound of dampened sod had once been the resting spot of someone from long ago, until hands unseen had desecrated the gravesite. Oddly, Bergfinn felt the steel of his sword strike a hard, metallic object. Dropping to his knees, powerful hands clawed the earth until a gleaming copper ingot revealed itself to him.

He eyed the metal intensely before scooping it up. The object, nearly the size of his palm, possessed a barren coldness unlike anything the man had known. Superstitious and unwilling to chance bad fortune, he quickly prayed to Odin for protection. Still, the heavy copper captured Bergfinn's fascination and he tucked it into the leather pouch on his belt.

Over a year had passed since his fingers dug the gleaming metal from its resting place and even longer since his journey began. Now, on another autumn morning, stiffening breezes played through the trees, tugging at burnished leaves. A circling raven's lonesome cry echoed from a seemingly distant place. Chilling wet drops fell upon his craggy face, soaking his beard, while he attempted to blink away the rain.

The startling reality that Gunnar Bergfinn was not dreaming washed over him in an inescapable drama. Clouded memories from these last eighteen months flashed before Bergfinn's eyes, with the advent of his impending death.

Howling winds of the ferocious gale ripped across the rocky terrain in a valiant effort to plague the treeless landscape in one final act before passing across Greenland's coast. Cold, black slabs of stone rose up steeply from the sea below, standing in muted defiance as they had done for eons against the harsh weather of the North Atlantic. Angry seas swollen from the storm's onslaught raced headlong, crashing violently into the face of the vertical cliffs. The thunderous pounding launched plumes of foamy, white spray skyward in raging fury.

Occasional glimpses of feeble sunlight peered momentarily from the heavens, quickly disappearing in the leaden skies. Only now did the tempest's grip begin to wane as the weather system tore itself apart over the land it attacked so brutally.

An image of a man materialized in the midst of the rainstorm. Shoulders hunched against the deafening winds, Gunnar Bergfinn pulled the gray woolen cloak tighter across his thick chest. Heavy socks wrapped in leather boots protected the stout legs pushing onward to the cliff's edge. The man's coarse red beard hung limply below his chin, as strands of wind-tossed, wet hair seemingly possessed a life of its own underneath his leather headpiece. Anger clouded the Greenlander's face while a knotted brow gathered above blue eyes, roaming the sky and sea below.

Months of preparation had left the Viking impatient. The fleet should have sailed by now, and still it would be days before the seas quieted and presented them their opportunity. Tales of Bjarni Herjolfsson's ill-fated voyage over a decade before played repeatedly in his mind. Caught in a violent gale after leaving Iceland, Herjolfsson's fleet had been thrown far off course. Unfavorable winds pushed them westward to strange lands. Weeks passed before they were able to sail back to the shelter of Greenland's coast. It was the vision of Herjolfsson's saga that continually haunted his thoughts, rekindling Bergfinn's restless spirit.

Years before, a young, red-haired maiden with a fiery temper quelled that spirit. His marriage to Astrid Egilsdatter changed his life dramatically. She had pushed the Viking into giving up his ways as a seafarer and trader for a new life in Greenland.

But it was her friendship with Thjohild, Erik the Red's wife, that troubled him most. He held no particular love for the man or his wife. Yet that same friendship precipitated their move from Iceland. Thjohild's constant meddling finally persuaded Astrid to convert to Christianity. Turning away from the Norse gods left him terribly unsettled. Superstitious by nature, Bergfinn needed no bad fortune from worshipping the wrong gods. Admittedly though, he loved his wife in spite of all these things.

No longer content to simply raise sheep, his wandering spirit reemerged. Bergfinn finally convinced Astrid to embark upon a journey with him. Long time friends, Sigurd Ormsmon and Rolvag Thorstien, took little encouragement when asked to lead an expedition beyond the lands Bjarni Herjolffson had seen. Their Viking hearts pounded with thoughts of adventure and the unknown.

Skilled seafarers in their own right, Ormsmon would captain one boat and Thorstien the other, chronicling the journey. Wealth, gathered from their days as traders along the European coastline, provided ample funding for the undertaking that lay ahead. Putting together the crews and finding two more pilots offered little difficulty, since rumors of their plans had spread some time before. New opportunities and destiny awaited the two hundred and thirty-four men, women, and children willing to make the arduous journey.

Much of his life had taken place on the seas. The crisp breeze and salt air brought back a flood of memories. The Viking leader once again felt at home upon the open water, with the sun and stars to guide him. Careful not to let Astrid hear him, Gunnar Bergfinn mumbled thanks to Odin for the return of fair weather. Now running under a full sail woven from the fleece of Norse sheep, the blue-striped material billowed, pushing the fleet of Viking knarrs on a westerly tack.

These carefully constructed boats made from strong oak timbers, nimbly skirted the waves, being far superior to any vessel of their day. Master craftsmen designed overlapping sideboards riveted together with iron, and woolen rope dipped in tar was pushed between the cracks to keep out the water. Outfitted with a rotating sail and an oar for steering, the boats could easily maneuver in any direction. Each boat also possessed long oars, needed when winds were slack, or for extra speed. Intricate carvings adorned the swan-necked bows and sterns rising as much as fifteen feet above the decks. Images of serpents, dragons, and other creatures sat atop the prow to chase away evil spirits.

Gunnar Bergfinn smiled knowingly at Astrid as her gaze lifted to the four other boats in the small fleet. Greenland's coast soon became a faint silhouette, slowly retreating beyond the horizon. Surely, only good fortune lay ahead.

Eleven days of hard sailing brought them to the cold and forbidding shores Herjolffson had described, later known as Baffin Island. They had followed his course in reverse, and now the small fleet took a more southerly tack. The wind and currents became more favorable and the seaworthy knarrs increased their speed. Two more weeks passed. The group of seafarers found themselves navigating the inside passage between a large island and the new continent off their starboard beam. During the night, the group continued on a westward heading, searching for a place to make landfall.

Pale orange sunlight struggled to peek through a misty dawn. The new day's offering brought with it the outline of a distant shore. A cry went up, and the decks erupted with life. Men and women awakened, crawling out from underneath their protective covering of animal skins. All eyes strained ahead while Bergfinn quickly noticed the change in the water's characteristics. The vessels had left behind the open sea and moved into the calmer waters of a vast river. By mid-morning, sails were furled and oars beat the water with powerful strokes. Drawing the boats closer to a rocky coast, the Greenlanders took note of the tall, thick stands of spruce looming ahead along the shoreline. Once the knarrs were beached, Bergfinn ordered guards placed at strategic points on the rocky bluffs overlooking the newly established camp. The Viking leader was taking no chances with the group's safety. All the members of the expedition were on alert, ready at a moment's notice to repel any invaders in case they were attacked.

Two days after landing, a group of strange looking men clothed in animal skins materialized from the forest, their features unlike anything the newcomers had seen before. Thick dark hair covered their heads. Black eyes, perched above high cheekbones, invited caution. This group of skraeling, a Norse epithet for those of low respect, showed indifference to the larger numbers from the long boats.

Tensions ran high with this first meeting until it was apparent they came only to barter for goods. The *Omamiwinini*, known also as the Algonquin, drew pictures and spoke of great waters many days journey to the west along the mighty river. Thorstien listened and memorized each drawing so he could scribe it onto the stone slabs he used for his chronicle. The skraeling also warned of fierce warriors who lived to the south, with whom they had done battle on numerous occasions.

Bergfinn eyed Ormsmon for his reaction. His glance elicited a smile from his friend of many years. He knew his decision was already made. They would follow the sun along the great river.

Several more days passed and as the Vikings prepared to continue their journey, the group of natives gathered once again. The skraeling leader eyed Bergfinn with a piercing gaze, saying nothing. Reaching into a pouch, his fingers pulled out a handful of reddish-colored beads with a quality unlike any the Viking had ever seen. Bergfinn held out a calloused hand, accepting the offer. Carefully, he placed the beads into a leather pouch at his waist and pulled the silver cloak pin from his garment. The intricate design of a serpent fascinated the native leader, as a brief smile washed across his face. He spoke a few words and the group turned, leaving the Vikings alone on the shore.

The boats stopped only as needed for provisions while sailing westward. Their journey halted when a thunderous roar brought them below a set of magnificent falls the skraeling had spoken of. The expedition's three leaders came to a decision. Gunnar Bergfinn and Rolvag Thorstien would take fifty men while the rest of the group remained behind.

Heavily forested land provided ample timber to build a small knarr. Numerous hands worked the wood, completing the keel, ribs, and decking in several weeks. With a borrowed sail from the Viking leader's boat, the small band of explorers departed, leaving the task of temporary shelter for the others.

Clear, blue water swept beneath the keel as the boat dipped into large troughs between the waves. Bow-spray shot skyward and over the gunnels. This strange creature with the head of a snake, adorned with painted wooden shields of fifty warriors, made an imposing site. News spread quickly along the lakes of an evil spirit holding bearded men in its belly. Days passed, as the group made its way along their journey following the sun. Occasional storms hampered the crew, yet they paled in comparison with those witnessed upon the oceans.

Months elapsed. Late fall's chilling winds found the men skirting the western edges of the largest of the five lakes they had explored. Enshrouded in the morning's mist, an island appeared before them.

Bergfinn gave the order and strong backs pulled at the oars until the rocky bottom grated along the wooden hull.

An eerie stillness clung heavily with a profound foreboding. Something disturbing tore at Gunnar Bergfinn. However, the sounds of men wading ashore quickly cancelled his thoughts. A deep forest, nearly devoid of summer's once green leaves, lay before them. The Vikings found no sign of life, only areas of strange diggings and an earthen mound buried under damp leaves.

Bergfinn had let himself be caught off guard, not listening to his instincts. The copper ingot had been an omen. Finding it had brought bad luck, and now ill fortune hovered menacingly around the small group of men as winter's vengeance struck without warning. Frigid temperatures and wicked snows brought storms that whipped the water into an unimaginable frenzy. Vast sheets of ice spread quickly across the lake's surface and passage soon became impossible. The small band of men found themselves marooned on the island. Deer and other small game were plentiful so they had no worry of starving to death. Illness and confinement in close quarters did little to quell the tempers of the increasingly restless men. Six succumbed to fevers and three more died at the hands of their feuding shipmates.

Spring could not come soon enough for Gunnar Bergfinn and his crew. Winter's passing brought warmer days and preparations were made for their return voyage. The men's grumbling finally ceased with the melting ice. Each day passed with agonizing slowness as the weary Greenlanders continued their journey through the lakes. Anxious to be reunited with those they had not seen for many months, the haggard men finally retraced their course back to the Viking encampment.

A blow from the Norse god Thor's mighty hammer could not have struck them harder. Shouts of joy turned to sorrow at the realization no life existed in the settlement. The warriors, predecessors of the Huron they had been warned about, somehow had surprised and massacred the Greenlanders. Gruesome findings of decomposed bodies brought tears of anguish and bellows of sorrow as broken men fell to their knees.

Bergfinn swallowed hard, unprepared for the sight of his beloved Astrid. In her fist, a dagger caked with the crust of dried blood told part of the story. He knew someone had paid dearly for their heinous acts. A necklace with a delicate silver cross lay silently in matted blood upon her cheek. Drawing in a ragged breath, he averted his eyes from the discolored skin and lifeless form, considering the cruel irony. In Astrid's struggle with death, her newfound Christian God had done no more to help than the Norse gods she abandoned.

The Norse explorers solemnly gathered the lifeless bodies of their family and comrades. Words filled with anguish were spoken to their gods, while some men wept. Bergfinn wished to have no memories of Astrid and the others who had been so violently butchered. He ordered their bodies placed aboard the decks of the knarrs, set afire and cast off. In the growing twilight, the blazing flotilla drifted slowly from the shoreline, its fiery glow illuminating the men's somber faces. The still waters reflected the haunting image of the funeral pyre in the eyes of each Norseman. There was no doubt as to the decisions needing to be made, and the stark reality of each Viking's own mortality.

Loathing captured Gunnar Bergfinn. He refused to grieve. Intense hatred filled the men and their sorrows brewed into a raging maelstrom. Now with little reason to live, the forty-one survivors vowed to fight to the last man.

Thorstien scribed the continuing saga as the ferocious Vikings followed the murderous warriors, hunting them unmercifully. The group's only reason for living lay in the satisfaction of killing as many of the *skraeling* as possible before they themselves lay bloodied and dying.

Summer's long days past, and the knarr turned on a southerly course leaving behind the great river. Brisk winds pushed the few remaining souls, who had cheated death, along a narrow waterway until it eventually carried them into a vast lake of clear, blue water. Mountains rose up along the western shore, and towards the east, several tall peaks watched over them silently under blue skies.

Now only eight men remained, sitting alone with their thoughts, consumed by their ardent scorn. Faded memories of better days filled Bergfinn's mind, yet his resolve did not weaken. There could be only death.

Farther to the south, the warriors waited in ambush for the weary survivors. The Vikings' need for food brought them to the shoreline, as the serpent-headed boat drifted underneath a canopy of autumn leaves. Hungry and near exhaustion, the men prepared to wade ashore in search of food, when a hail of arrows rained down upon the unsuspecting Vikings. Two of the men died instantly. Bergfinn managed to turn the sail while the others pulled at the oars, carrying the knarr into the current. Undaunted, the attackers ran into the waist-high waters, climbing over the gunnels. Bergfinn tied the steering oar off in the direction he wanted the boat to sail and with a rallying scream of defiance, joined his men in battle.

Rolvag Thorstien had been the only other survivor of the initial attack. Together, they hurriedly threw the dead bodies over the gunnels as the boat limped into deeper water. Bergfinn's friend had turned to speak when another volley of arrows struck. He pitched forward over the side of the knarr, a bloodied arrow protruding from his ravaged neck. Rolvag stared blankly into the horrified eyes of Gunnar Bergfinn. Bitterly, he watched his friend's lifeless body sink into the river's dark waters. Several more of the barbarous enemy clamored aboard and the lone Viking fought them off, killing the last with his bare hands.

☙ ❧

Overhead, a circling raven's lonesome cry echoed from a seemingly distant place.

Chilling wet drops fell upon Bergfinn's craggy face, arousing him while he attempted to blink away the rain from his eyes. He had no recollection of how long he had been unconscious, or how far his boat had drifted in the current.

Pain and fever wracked his body. Bloody wounds from a knife were crusted over and festering. He knew the arrow in his side would kill him long before the infection. The Viking's raspy breathing now came in labored gasps, as life's end hovered imminently. Peering up through dull, vacant eyes, an unknown blackness suddenly enveloped the boat. Gunnar Bergfinn, the last of the Greenlanders, knew with certainty that soon he would be joining his men in the halls of Valhalla.

Chapter One

Eurus - Southwestern Pacific: 2008

BECCA RAMSEY'S CAPABLE HANDS firmly gripped the helm, almost as if they possessed knowledge all their own. She sailed precipitously close to the wind, heeling the Eurus well to port. A spray of white foam rocketed skyward and over the deck as the keen-edged bow parted the blue Pacific waters. Intuitively, Becca held steady to the prescribed course following the charted rhumbline, and rarely casting an eye at the binnacle. The black dial of the compass hovered silently, encased in its glass housing and barely moving from the ascribed heading.

She had grown up on the water. Her father, a veteran and winner of two coveted Whitbread races, provided Becca with her knowledge of winds and currents and a deep respect for the sea. By the age of twenty, she was competing professionally and her skills surpassed many a seasoned competitor. Now twenty-eight, her life had changed dramatically.

The Eurus had been a gift, actually a wedding present from her husband Alex's family. Becca protested. The Ramseys insisted. They could well afford it.

Their success and fortune was no secret. The family history was alive with politicians, ambassadors, and men of prestige down through the years. Her father-in-law, Jason Ramsey, and his wife, Olivia, were well known in and out of D.C. circles. His status as a respected member of Congress and his reputation for steel-walled honesty sat well with his constituents. The former Becca Chase could have done much worse.

Alex had allowed her to name the vessel and she chose the Greek term for the East wind. It was a fitting name. Sixty feet along the waterline, the Eurus offered all the comforts of home. She was the epitome of luxury with air-conditioned suites and a gourmet kitchen. Fully computerized controls, auto-guidance, all the latest radar technology, satellite communication, and entertainment options completed the package.

More importantly, she was built for endurance and able to take most anything the ocean could throw at her. The Eurus' knife-like bow and hull were coated with a material to reduce friction and increase speed. The Kevlar sails billowing from the masts were able to withstand extreme winds. Her designers even considered the worst. In the event the boat capsized, she possessed the ability to right herself, if fully buttoned up.

Automatically, Becca scanned the waves to the horizon and back, basking under blue skies and feeling the kiss of the warm breeze. Perfect conditions. The long, brown ponytail pulled to the right side of her head, weaved and bobbed at the wind's calling. It was her signature. Becca was wearing it that way when she first met Alex, or more correctly, when her team had beaten the esteemed senator's son and a cadre of twenty-seven other boats in the San Francisco to San Diego run. Odd, Becca thought, as she lifted the long billed cap from her head, how life played out its tangled web. She slipped easily into the memory.

Winds stiffened and seas ran high at the start of the race. From there, the weather worsened. A series of storms pummeled the boats, tremendously straining equipment and taxing sailors to their limits. Twelve of the competitor's boats never finished. They gave in to the elements long before the finish, seeking the shelter of the closest harbor. Alex Ramsey's team fought desperately to take the lead, yet their best was over an hour behind Becca's crew when the race ended.

The senator's son had caught her attention as she tended to the racing boat's cleanup. Dark, deep-set eyes peered at her above a full smile that spread slowly as he stepped aboard. Becca Chase was instantly taken when he offered his hand in a sincere gesture. Alex Ramsey's charm went beyond his portrayal in the magazine article she had read. He was even more handsome than the camera could capture. That had been over two years ago. The couple had married and were now cruising the Pacific on their honeymoon.

Becca's daydreaming ended, jolting her back to reality with the sharp, snapping gunshot of fluttering sails. Plowing heavily into the crystal blue troughs, the sixty-foot sailboat quickly lost speed. The comely brunette tossed back her head, laughing at herself for the momentary loss of concentration. It had been years since she had allowed a boat to sail into the wind causing the sails to luff. In one swift motion, Becca engaged the winch controls, pulling in the sheet and expertly turning the wheel to bring the Eurus back on course.

"Just how long you been sailing, lady?" a voice called out from below.

An upturned bow formed quickly on her tanned face. "I can still beat the pants off you," she replied.

Alex Ramsey popped out from the hatch and moved agilely across the teak deck taking a seat next to his wife. He kissed her quickly on the lips, handing her a bottle of Evian. His fingers stroked the touch screen controls of the Eurus' command center, entering a new course. Almost immediately the computer adjusted steering onto the new heading while simultaneously trimming the sails.

"You take all the fun out of sailing," Becca chided, relinquishing the helm.

"Actually, I'll put some fun back into it for you," her husband replied.

"Oh?" an impish grin imparted.

Alex worked the screen, pulling up a map of their current location. Another keystroke and the details enlarged. "I've plotted a new course that will take us right here. Take a look," he answered, pointing to a small island on the computer screen.

Arching an eyebrow, her eyes darted to the screen. "And where exactly is here?" she asked, taking a long pull from the bottle.

"That, my dear, is where we're spending the night. Thought it'd be nice to take a break and relax. How does a candlelight dinner and a bottle of Pinot Gris sound to you?" He kissed the back of her neck, tasting the slightly salty flavor of her tanned skin.

Becca sighed, seductively. "Sounds like a recipe for more than dinner. But if you're cooking, count me in," she tittered.

The Eurus gently rode the gin clear waters having laid anchor off the reef on the lee side of the remote island. Sunset faded and the western sky grudgingly surrendered its display of brilliant pastels. Predictably, the blue-gray light of darkness cast itself slowly over the sea in its relentless chase of the fading sun.

Shadows danced in the warm glow of candlelight bathing the newlyweds in muted solitude as they dined. The white wine added immensely to the succulent flavors of the fresh fish and salsa, not to mention the mood. They shared laughter and hopes for the future while the latest track from Diana Krall oozed provocatively from concealed speakers. The world only waited for the handsome couple to make their mark.

She slipped her fingers from her husband's hand and emptied the remaining contents of the bottle into their glasses. The silky coolness of the chemise hugged her body closely, moving in perfect cadence with her taut form as she padded across the carpeting. Placing one foot on the stairs, Becca turned and threw a seductive glance over her shoulder. She let the thin garment slip away. Alex Ramsey smiled, knowing he had no alternative but to follow.

Becca's soft skin tingled at the change in temperature as she stepped into the warmth of the balmy night. The scent of the ocean filled her head while her eyes adjusted to the darkness. Above her, the nocturnal blanket gave way to a myriad of constellations in a display of cosmic beauty. In the distance, the faint rumble of breakers crashing onto the reef echoed in the night as her husband's strong arms encircled her.

Soon the only sound that either heard were the demulcent tones of their own lovemaking. Sensuously, their fingers touched the other's body. Exploring. Knowing. The caress of soft lips pressed into one another fueling the fires. Their passion consumed them. Becca moved skillfully above her husband and together they melted into love's ageless dance.

Alex softly mouthed her breasts eliciting a groan of heated pleasure as Becca's long hair fell across his face. His hands moved across her flat belly finding their way to her hips. Guiding her. A sheen of perspiration washed them in a testimony to flaming temptation as the couple's pace quickened under the watchful gaze of the tropical night.

Alex gazed hypnotically at his wife, drinking in the scene. Overcome with desirous need, Alex gave himself fully, filling her warmth. She tossed her head back and pressed into him, selfishly salving her own needs. Her lips parted. Becca called out his name in a breathy voice. She cried out for him again as her words cut into the night. Louder this time. Sucking in a deep breath, Becca became temptation's prey.

There was no world at this point. Only the two of them lost in a place where nothing mattered. Together they raced headlong, each wanting more yet hungry for that moment of delectable sweetness.

Suddenly, their ravenous ardor became overpowering, catapulting the young lovers over the edge.

Time held its breath and waited. Becca lay exhausted on top of him feeling the warm dampness of his skin. They kissed deeply, sharing the moment's joy. Soon they entwined themselves into each other's arms; speaking in hushed tones, keeping the world at bay, and reliving their spent pleasures. Eventually, their conversation languished and they succumbed to the night. The sound of Alex's steady breathing faded as Becca's eyes closed, captured in restful sleep.

She was unsure of what aroused her. Innately, she knew something had changed and it was puzzling. Becca slipped quietly away from Alex. The silhouette of her naked form spilled across the deck as she stood under the pale starlight. She stretched and rubbed the sleep from her eyes. The sound grew steadily in intensity, rising to a frantic crescendo. To her horror, Becca discovered the cause of her awakening.

The once calm waters now roiled around them, seemingly engulfing the couple in a boiling cauldron. Paralyzed from fear, Becca could only cry out for her husband. Adrenaline coursed through his body. Sleep quickly erased itself. Alex did not know the cause of his wife's alarm, but the urgency in her voice shot a chilling bolt along his spine.

Ragged senses, stripped raw and frayed, held him captive.

His heart pounded.

Alex's chest tightened.

The Eurus began to sink without warning. Quickly. Impetuously, the sea poured over the gunnels and across the deck. It surged recklessly through the open hatches into the cabins below. Within the hull, the rising waters invaded the electrical circuitry and blew the system. The interior of the Eurus was plunged into total darkness, signaling its death.

Their world spun at a dizzying speed. No time to call for help. Little time to think. If they stayed on deck, they would be sucked down into the depths as the boat sank. Becca had never experienced anything like this in all her years at sea. Nothing could have prepared her. She wanted to live. Now it seemed as if fate was going to play its hand in terrible fashion. Becca clung desperately to her husband.

There were no options left. Her scream was lost. The frightened couple launched themselves into the seething waters, swimming for their lives.

In a few moments it was over. The waters calmed. The stillness of the night returned, but no trace of the boat remained. She had joined the destiny of countless ships scattered across the oceans. Resting on her side, the once proud Eurus lay forever entombed within the confines of her watery grave.

Above the vast expanse of ocean, the stars could do little. In the distance, the island stood poised as a lone sentinel, witnessing, keeping its silent vigil.

Chapter Two

Seattle, Washington - Pacific Northwest

BRYSON MCGANN TUGGED AT THE ZIPPER of the heavy canvas duffel bag, closing it in one swift motion. The grating rasp echoed in the room. Just as he finished, the liquid crystal television screen, hanging on his bedroom wall, brought to life a news story the media could not let go.

The strange disappearance of the young couple remained unsolved for several weeks, and there were still no clues. Ordinarily, the story would have been long forgotten. However, both families of the missing newlyweds were prominent members of society, their names well accustomed to television viewers, political scenes, and the Hollywood crowd.

McGann found it peculiar that absolutely no trace of their existence had been found. His hazel eyes studied earnestly the CNN report; their faces, lifestyle, and the last photo of them taken in Hawaii, before leaving on their yacht to continue their honeymoon cruise. They seemed happy enough from the picture. His mind tumbled the possibilities and came up empty. He knew as much as anyone, and everyone had the same answer.

Nothing.

As the byline ended, another story sounded on about the upcoming G-8 conference being held in Davos. The report flashed images of the Swiss Alps. Snow-capped mountains, so picturesque they nearly seemed an illusion, filled the expanse of the screen, collaring McGann's attention. Sound bites and quick clips of world leaders scheduled to be in attendance appeared and disappeared from view. The English prime minister, Geoffrey Haines, dressed in a dark suit, was seen addressing a gathering in London. Curiously, he paused in mid-sentence and stared blankly ahead, his head twitching slightly. He promptly recovered and finished his speech. As quickly as it began, the report ended and the familiar face of Vernon Charles reappeared, announcing a commercial break.

Moving over to the dresser on the other side of the room, Bryson opened the passport, observing the face that mimicked the one gazing back silently from the mirror. A perfect match. The ever-present lopsided grin, resting below a straight nose, reflected back at him.

Ruggedly handsome, most women found him attractive and intelligent. McGann's features invited a familiarity that belied the resolve hidden beneath. Even more, it was his hazel eyes that drew one's attention: impenetrable, demanding, yet capable of emotion at the same time.

A light breeze drifted into the room parting the curtains. McGann stuffed the passport into his jacket pocket and ambled over to the window, peering out onto Lake Washington. A patchwork sky rode the lake's rippling waters. He closed the window and prepared to leave. Unexpectedly, the videophone erupted to life with the familiar features of Marion Turner filling the screen.

"Bryson," Sumner's assistant called out.

"Yeah," McGann answered, before Turner had the opportunity to say anything else.

Her southern accent flowed thickly, her lilt pouring from the speaker, "Bryson, Director Sumner would like to see you before you leave."

"Sure. Actually, I was headed in that direction. I have a few loose ends to tie up."

"I'll pass that along."

"Marion. One more thing. Heard from Joe?" McGann questioned.

"Assistant Projects Director Canton called a short time ago. It seems he's finishing with the project at L'Anse aux Meadows."

"Alright, I'll catch up with him at some point," McGann replied. "See you soon."

"Okay," she replied. Marion Turner's face faded from the screen.

Bryson McGann gave a voice command to turn off the television and the videophone. He turned, locking the door behind him and walked to his vehicle. The black Hummer's door closed with a thud and the engine roared to life. The massive truck, provided by NESSA, cruised along I-5 South, working its way through Seattle's heavy traffic.

The city's expansion had catapulted over the past decade and the burgeoning population taxed the abilities of the city to keep pace. A hub of business, Seattle was a gate to the Far East and a fast-paced corporate market for techno-junkies. Numerous firms called this town their home and it was filled with its share of well-to-do nouveau riche.

Fortunately, there were still many places that kept their charm, offering a peaceful setting for relaxation.

The faces were friendly.

The food was great.

But the weather…

Seattle's weather had returned to normal in the aftermath of the H.A.A.R.P. Project's demise, brought about by McGann and lifelong friend, Joe Canton. Cloudy skies and rain were the norm as systems blew in from across the Pacific. However, when the weather cooperated, nothing compared with the picture postcard image of Mt. Rainier rising up beyond Seattle's skyline. McGann enjoyed it. He planned on staying.

McGann snuck a quick glance over his shoulder at the Space Needle as he changed lanes and shot down the exit ramp heading for NESSA headquarters. Rising up forty-three stories, the massive, glass-encased structure was home to the National Earth Seas Science Agency where he had accepted a position after resigning from military service.

McGann wheeled the massive vehicle into his assigned spot and headed for the building. Ominously, the sudden threat of showers cast a gray pall to the skies above. McGann gave it a furtive glance and hurried inside. It was part of the package, a constant in Seattle life. He found his security clearance and flashed the ID at the guard seated behind the glass-encased counter. A scanner quickly provided confirmation of McGann's identity.

"How's it going today, Bart?" McGann questioned.

"Not so bad. How's yourself?" Bart Kline responded, his New Jersey accent coming through. Slightly graying hair and rugged features lent the security guard an air of authority.

"I'm heading upstairs to see the boss," McGann winked.

"Well, you just make sure you keep the General towing the line," the guard smiled.

"Right," McGann chuckled. "I'll see what I can do."

The building's designer had an eye for detail. The expansive lobby, bustling with activity, was filled with natural light from the glass roof forty-three stories above. Offices moved outward from the center like spokes on a wheel. This left the interior portion open and afforded a magnificent view from below. The edifice also housed numerous businesses and legal firms so the place was always a center of activity.

McGann made his way across the polished marble floor of the vast atrium toward the bank of elevators. Within moments, he stepped out onto the thirty-ninth floor, heading to his office. No sooner than he sat down the video phone came to life.

"Yes, Marion," he answered, searching through the bottom drawer of his desk.

"How did you know it was me?" Sumner's secretary asked, feigning surprise.

"One thing I know, Marion, not much misses your eyes."

"You're just too smart for your own good, Bryson McGann."

"I suppose he's ready? I'll be right up." McGann said. His finger stroked the touch controls, and Marion Turner's face evaporated from the darkening screen.

Pale blue eyes, peered hawk-like over the rims of her reading glasses when McGann entered the spacious lobby of Sumner's outer office. Her salt and pepper hair was pulled back tightly into a bun. Turner's burgundy business suit carried a well-known designer label. Marion Turner expected everyone to be as impeccably dressed as she. It was a trait that carried over from her days as Sumner's assistant in the military. No one was above her scrutiny. Many were intimidated by her attitude, but McGann found it amusing.

Without a glance, her finger flew to the panel on her desk, pressing the appropriate button.

"Mr. McGann is here."

"Okay. Send him in."

McGann turned the handle of the mahogany door to Randall Sumner's enclave and walked in. Diffused lighting fell from hidden recesses in the ceiling and spilled onto Sumner's desk. The former general mouthed the stem of his pipe and exhaled a puff of blue smoke into the air. An ionizing filtration system instantly whisked away the odor and smoke as Sumner stood and extended his hand.

"How are you, sir?" McGann asked, feeling the strength in the director's grip. Sumner demanded a punishing regimen of physical activity for himself. Lean and fit, his physique rivaled someone much younger than his fifty-nine years.

"I'm well. Good to see you, Bryson," Sumner effused, smiling at the younger man. "Please, have a seat."

He had taken over the NESSA organization nearly nine years ago, after its first director left it in shambles in just two short years. Retiring with two stars on his shoulder had taught him a lot about fighting for the things you believe in, and how to wage war in the political game. Sumner had numerous friends in Washington and more than enough enemies. Yet his flinty determination had brought the agency on a course that finally won approval with the country and the president. Bryson McGann and Joe Canton's successful escapades a few short months before in the Canadian Arctic only enhanced the National Earth Seas Science Agency's position, after the duo defeated Fletcher Durnulqc, and brought an end to the H.A.A.R.P. project's terror.

Without wasting time on any formalities, Sumner questioned, "Are you packed?"

McGann nodded.

"Good." Sumner paused, drawing on his ever-present pipe. "You don't know, but..." the director continued between puffs, "Kate Harper will be accompanying you to Frankfurt for the Euro Ecology Summit. Noel Johnson is wrapping up final details for the Pacific conference."

"Oh?" McGann raised a brow, masking his uncertainty in response to the unforeseen change in plans.

"Hawaii," Sumner stated in a flat, matter of fact tone. NESSA's leader got up from his desk and switched on the holographic screen. A syllabus was projected into the middle of the room, detailing an outline for the upcoming event. "You will have the pleasure of attending the Geo Conference after you return from Germany." The director handed McGann a folder containing all the required information.

Bryson McGann opened the folder and quickly scanned its contents, making mental notes as he went along. Sumner watched intently for a reaction. He lifted the Micro-Sun, a knurled-edged glass piece, just above the pipe bowl as the embers inside began to die. The golden reflective surface of the device instantly rekindled the tobacco as he exhaled a cloud of smoke. "Continental shifts. Active volcanic regions throughout the Pacific rim. Sounds like fun topics," McGann added wryly, his familiar lop-sided grin curling a corner of his mouth.

"Any questions?" Sumner paused briefly, tossing a glance at the view outside his office window. "No? Excellent," the former general sounded. "By the way, after the European conference, you will be escorting a passenger back here, and then on to NESSA's Pacific headquarters."

McGann accepted the dossier detailing the assignment. A puzzled look came over his face as he read the name. "Dr. Torfhildur Haroldson." Quizzically, he asked, "Who is this?"

Before McGann could ask another question, Sumner interjected. "She's a renowned volcanologist who will be lecturing at the conference. And you will be her escort to see her safely there."

Images of a plump grandmother squeezed into an apron a size too small came to mind. Quickly, he scanned the credentials. They looked good. Well educated. Numerous academic accolades. Numerous published articles.

No pictures.

No age.

Bad sign.

He chewed on his reply and decided against it. "Great," McGann added, as an afterthought.

"Problem?"

McGann scratched at the back of his neck before replying, "No, sir." His face tightened into a painful wince.

"Good. You'll stop in Amsterdam and meet her at the Krasnapolsky Hotel. Everything's covered. All the information is in your packet."

Before the director could continue, McGann asked, "How will I know what she..."

Sumner interjected, holding up his hand before he could finish the question. "You won't. She'll know who you are. And as I stated, your itinerary calls for a stop here in Seattle. I would like to meet her." Sumner clenched the stem of the pipe between his teeth, readjusting himself in his chair. "I think the three of us should have dinner at that place you and Joe like so much. Martin's, is it?"

"That should be a pleasant distraction," McGann mumbled, as he closed the folder on Ms. Haroldson. "I'm sure this will be an interesting assignment," he added reluctantly.

Randall Sumner remained silent, letting the quiet hang precipitously before continuing. "I'll ask Marion to make reservations for us."

The phone rang, interrupting their conversation, and Sumner answered. He replied in clipped responses, never wasting words or his time. The director brought the black stem of the pipe to his lips and gnawed the end while his fingers played over the smooth finish of the highly-polished, burled wood.

McGann got up and moved to the window to take in the view of the Seattle streets below. Cloudy skies prevailed today, and in the distance Mt. Rainier observed those who lived under the volcano's watchful gaze. A great city of diversity and culture had spread eastward past the deep-green waters of Puget Sound. Metropolitan, but it was a city that hummed to a different chord than most. Overcrowded streets and unpredictable weather were the norm. Still, the spirit of the city could be found in its people. The richness and flavor that were Seattle had become a part of him, and he enjoyed calling it home.

Bryson McGann's mind wandered and he thought back to the first time he and Randall Sumner met. From the very first, they had hit it off, each man well aware of the other's accomplishments. A mutual respect and friendship had developed. Sumner was always there with an approving smile or pat on the back. Yet, McGann knew Randall Sumner could play hardball with the best. He had been at it for a long time and his talents spoke well to his winnings. His losses were few and the former general liked it that way.

McGann turned to see Sumner scribble a quick note and sneak a glance at his calendar. "Thursday would be fine. One o'clock. Good. I look forward to it." The director disconnected the line. He rarely said goodbye. Barely taking a breath, Sumner added, "Don't know if you are aware of this. I'll get you up to speed. Joe has left Newfoundland, and on to another quick assignment. From there, he heads out to the southwestern Pacific on that joint Australian project."

"No, I didn't know that," McGann replied, shifting uneasily. He retrieved the file of papers on Dr. Haroldson and stuffed them into his case.

Wizened from years of dealing with men, the crow's feet at the corners of his steely-gray eyes crinkled hesitantly. Sumner sat back in the thickly padded leather chair and folded his hands behind his head, entwining his fingers around his slightly graying hair. He knew McGann. His normally impenetrable hazel eyes wore a mask of oppressive weight. Almost reading McGann's thoughts, the director finally spoke, breaking the stale silence between them. "May I hazard a guess and say that you're not exactly thrilled about your assignment?"

McGann thought carefully about his reply. "Actually, being a desk-jockey has its downsides," his voice trailing.

Sumner inhaled sharply, "This being one of them?"

Cocking his head and a grin slicing his face, "With a name like Torfhildur, how good can it be?" McGann mused.

Both men chuckled before the director spoke. "Accepting the promotion to Assistant Project Director has its benefits. It has drawbacks too, Bryson," Sumner added, blowing out a plume of smoke. The director placed his arms on the sides of his chair and leaned back before continuing, "I know you miss the field assignments. Once this is complete, I have something in mind that may be more to your liking."

McGann perked, "You've piqued my curiosity. I'll look forward to it."

Both men knew the conversation had ended. Sumner studied the man as he left the office. Bryson McGann was a man of incredible determination. His mettle had been tested and he had risen more than once to the occasion. Intelligent. Ruggedly handsome in appearance. His ability to command came naturally and was easily accepted. McGann's eye for problem solving was an intuitive part of his being, one that flowed as naturally as the blowing wind. Easy going and fueled with a will beyond measure when needed, the man did not believe in failure. It just never occurred. Sumner admired the younger man, thinking back to someone not unlike McGann a number of years ago. A smile etched his face as he tapped out the used tobacco from his pipe.

McGann allowed himself one more glance of the Seattle skyline, walking across the NESSA director's office. Gray skies encompassed his mood. His day had just gone from bad to worse as the latch to Sumner's office closed behind him.

Chapter Three

Namibia - Southwest African Coast

AN IRREMISSIBLE SUN BORE DOWN with relentless intent along the sands of the Namibian coast. The oppressive heat was merely an annoyance for Peter Oduru. It was only the prelude of things to come.

All of Oduru's family lived hundreds of miles to the north along the defiant Skeleton Coast. The area, infamous for its treacherous shoals and impenetrable fog, was the final resting place of countless shipwrecks. Rusted hulls lay impassively entwined in their death throes. The once proud, ocean going vessels, bore silent witness to their destiny while the action of wind and waves ate cancerously away at the doomed ships.

This area of the Namibian coast is deeply affected by the Benguela current, one of two major currents that move like 'swift rivers' through the ocean along the southwestern coast of Africa. Almost at a moment's notice, the current's frigid waters can cause calm seas to rise up into angry waves, or create thick fog banks that quickly enshroud the coastlines' rocky shoals. It was these same currents that made passage for Portuguese sailors so difficult on their journeys to India hundreds of years before.

Peter Oduru yearned to provide more for his wife and infant child. Thoughts of working in a hotel or answering repeated questions by tourists about the mysteries of the dangerous coast held no appeal. Opportunities to earn a decent wage were rare. When the chance to work for an internationally known diamond company came along, Oduru jumped at the offer, unhesitatingly making his decision. That had been over three years ago.

Peter Oduru was intelligent. Bright. He possessed an innate ability to adapt to various situations, and his willingness to learn did not go unnoticed. The Namibian's efforts and determination eventually paid off. After eight months, they had sent him out to work on one of the company's ships, lying a few hundred yards off the coast. Each day brought with it the possibility of advancement. His dream of an education at the university continued to foster his desire to work harder than anyone else.

Each day Oduru struggled. Working the mining ship was the easy task. He oversaw the process of sweeping the seafloor. A twelve inch diameter rubber hose was dropped over the side to the ocean bottom. The vacuuming process swept up sand, gravel, and diamonds as the diver moved along the bottom. For every ton of sand brought up off the seafloor, only one diamond is usually found. The shoreline had increased dramatically over the years and huge mountains of sand continued to pile up. Unfortunately for Oduru, he was unable to tolerate the rise and fall of the ocean's swell. Simply, Peter Oduru suffered from the effects of seasickness. The company offered him a chance to work the mines on shore and he reluctantly accepted.

Peter Oduru's black skin glistened with a sheen of perspiration from the blazing tropical sun. He took one last look around and silently mumbled a prayer, before entering the mine shaft. He smiled and spoke briefly with the group of workers before climbing onto the small tram, whose rusty wheels protested with a high-pitched squeal.

Overhead in the confines of the tunnel was an occasional glaring bulb that provided a dim glow along the darkened corridor. There were one hundred and thirty-two lights. Peter Oduru struggled each day to focus on counting them in an effort to stave off his claustrophobia. The cool air inside this portion of the tunnel caused his skin to erupt into 'goose-flesh.' He greedily swallowed a large drink of water to quench the dryness forming in his throat, in preparation of things to come. Oduru closed his eyes and sucked in a deep breath. The desire to achieve his dream spurred him onward, and besides, it was better than the rocking of a ship's deck under his feet.

The tram stopped, and the men jumped off, crowding into the wire cage of the elevator. A whining electric motor came to life and the elevator shuddered as it began its descent clinging to the thick-banded steel cable. Eventually, the sounds of voices and machinery rose up from below. With an abrupt stop twenty-seven hundred feet below the surface, the cage door was thrown open. Oduru scanned his clipboard calling out assignments to the other twenty-three workers. Two men were missing today from work, so Oduru would have to labor in the sweltering depths of the mine.

Throughout the day the normal routine came and went. The pinging ring of picks and scraping shovels, as newly blasted sediment was loaded, echoed in the tunnels. Sweat had long soaked through his clothing as the end of the shift grew near. Oduru had been working alone in a remote, newly exposed vein. He had found one small diamond and was about to leave, when something glinted across the cavern, captured in the beam of his headlamp. Curious, Oduru toweled off the sweat pouring from his face and eagerly drained the last of his lukewarm water.

On hands and knees he crawled into the farthest corner and inquisitively scraped away the loose rock. He tossed aside his clipboard and his fingers scooped up the white stone imbedded in the black debris. From a distance, Oduru heard the call of several of his co-workers urging him to hurry. They were not eager to spend any needless time in the black depths of the mine. He almost answered and thought better of it. Oduru's excitement grew in anticipation.

How many millions of years of years had it taken for this piece of carbon material to form, he wondered. The thought quickly vanished. Clutched in his hand was a diamond of at least forty carats, a fortune by Namibian standards. He turned quickly searching to see if anyone had observed him.

No one was there.

His face spread into a wide smile as the thought of a promotion crossed his mind.

As Peter Oduru turned to leave, he picked up his clipboard. What lay underneath nearly stopped his heart. Instantly his mouth dried. Electric excitement coursed through his veins. Oduru gasped watching a droplet of his sweat splash onto the surface of the milky-white crystal. His chest threatened to explode from the heavy pounding inside. The Namibian's eyes widened in disbelief from the enormity of the gem. Lying intact in the black dust was a stone of unbelievable proportion. It spilled over the sides of both his palms. Oduru held the diamond gently as if it were his infant son.

The fervent cries of the others brought him back to the moment. Peter Oduru's life changed remarkably with this incredible find. His mind raced with anticipation, running at breakneck speed. Barely able to contain himself, the ride from the depths of the mine shaft seemingly took eons to reach the surface. The intense heat of the tropical sun enveloped him. Time compressed and his world narrowed at a dizzying speed. Chattering voices of his fellow workers sounded like they came from a distant place as Peter Oduru made his decision.

Oduru allowed the others to go ahead of him. The smell of the day's toil filled the tiny air conditioned room with a stale odor. Each worker was searched and marched through the low dose X-ray scanner. Across the world, millions in diamonds were stolen each year. Scanning technology proved helpful in stemming at least some proliferation of the outflow of illegal diamond smuggling.

"Okay, Oduru. You know the drill." The bored voice of Albert Reiner barked out through the speakers. Each day was the same for him, but they paid him well. The rare moment of excitement came when a new worker would be caught, foolishly attempting to walk away with his precious find, a practice highly frowned upon by the company. "Hurry up," he commanded.

"Wait a moment," Oduru offered, his pearl-white teeth flashing in an immense grin. "Come around here, please."

Reiner's eyes dilated, unsure if what he beheld was real. Tentatively, he took the gem from the black man's hands. It more than amply filled up his trembling palms. The security man's mouth dropped. His eyes left the stone as they scanned the face of Peter Oduru in disbelief. The man had been working with the company for eighteen years and had never dreamed of seeing anything like this. His mouth remained open but no words were able to come out.

The black man broke into heavy laughter, bringing to an end the iron-weighted stillness of the room. As if on cue, Reiner followed, the two men sharing the moment, amazed at what lay in front of them.

Finally, a phone call was made and company security unit arrived. A number of executives were called in to view the gem. Congratulations were tossed about. A talk of promotion and even a bonus for Peter Oduru was offered and quickly accepted. Oduru and the others were sworn to secrecy and he was then allowed to leave.

Three hours had passed since the end of his shift when Peter Oduru finally arrived home. Greeted by a visage that held the burden of an extremely worried wife, a tear fell from her eye. "I thought something may have happened to you. I was so scared," Sarah Oduru blurted out. Relief washed over her face at the sight of her husband and the warmth of his kiss. Holding their small child in her arms, Sarah Oduru's concerns soon vanished and gave way to utter astonishment. Could fortune have favored upon them so greatly? She cradled her baby closely and kissed her husband again.

Upon finishing his incredible tale, Oduru reached into his pocket and set the forty carat gem he found on the table before them. Peter Oduru knew that the needs of his family were no longer a concern.

☙ ❧

Secrecy was of prime importance. The immense stone had been placed in the company vault until the proper arrangements could be made. An elaborate plan of deception had been mapped out to prevent the possibility of the stone's theft. Thirteen days after being pirated from its resting place of eons, four armed guards were charged with the safe keeping of the Oduru diamond.

The corporate jet rose into the limitless, blue skies above the Namibian capital of Windhoek, leaving the African continent below. Few in the world were skilled or trusted enough to make the precise cuts that would release the riveting, fiery beauty in what would be the mirror-like surface of its many facets. The stone waited impatiently for Abram Mossel, who was just such a man.

Chapter Four
Belfast - Northern Ireland

SUNDAY INTRODUCED ITSELF with a cool, misty rain blowing in off the Irish sea. Traffic was sparse in the streets, unlike the usual cacophony from motorcades of busy residents during the week. A few buses with even fewer passengers skirted the catholic section of the city this Sabbath morning.

Belfast's troubled past went far back in history with the Norman occupation beginning in 1177. Throughout the centuries, Scots and Englishmen inhabited and controlled the Irish seaport. However, it was the cry for independence that brought about a strife that plagued its inhabitants during the twentieth century. Blood feuds between peoples worshiping the same God filled graveyards with a litany of men, women, and children slaughtered in the name of religious freedom and political righteousness.

The last several years had brought about some reconciliation as understanding grew. Lurking in the shadows, remained the vigilant, those who could not put away the sword, relishing any chance to protract their demented views.

The bus groaned and belched black smoke from its exhaust as it carried the lone passenger to his destination, several blocks from the lower end of Falls Road. Church bells pealed in the distance as the old man checked his watch.

He was late.

Late, by intent.

The bus came to a halt with a high-pitched squeal from the worn brakes, signaling its arrival at the prescribed destination. St. Peter's Cathedral was several blocks away. The old man preferred to walk. He turned up his collar to offer some protection from the rain and shook off the dampness. To anyone who did not know, his stooped posture lent an appearance of frailty to the man. His shuffling feet and the metallic click of his cane were the only sounds, except for an occasional passing vehicle.

Carefully, he inspected everything surrounding him as he ambled towards the church. Turning the corner onto Derby Street, his keen attentiveness captured them immediately. Without a doubt, he knew there were others that remained unseen. It did not matter. They paid the old man no attention.

His eyes lifted and took in the twin spires of St. Peter's. It struck him odd that it was almost as if two hands were reaching skyward toward heaven in a gesture of prayer, imploring divine intercession in the coming moments.

Philip Jameson sat impatiently in a far corner at the back of the nave. A member of the Sinn Fein's clandestine militant wing, the Provos, he was here to seek absolution for his sins against the British crown. There were relatively few people attending this mass and they were occupying the pews mostly in the front of the church. Father Howe's voice rose up with great clarity, filling the great hall and resonating throughout the building. High above, saints watched, pictures painted by artisans of amazing talent. Icons of the catholic religion adorned the walls and pillar supports throughout. Hovering above the altar a large crucifix bore the lifeless body of Jesus Christ, portraying the pardon for the sins of those staring back, and also for what was to occur.

Jameson's brooding eyes darted about quickly, searching constantly for the person he was to meet. The heel of his left foot tapped out an impatient rhythm. He had followed his instructions carefully, knowing better than not to comply. A growing sheen of perspiration etched his upper lip. Nervously, he scratched the back of his head, fingers parting thick, black hair. He was becoming irritable, and was quite certain that those waiting secretly outside the church were too.

A shadow moved soundlessly along the cold stone wall of the church's interior. The solemnity of God's house was not lost on the old man. He felt confined, and the weight of this place pressed in upon him, causing a dryness to form in his throat. It ate at him cancerously, clawing insidiously at his soul. Shrugging off the pious cloak anointing this holy ground, he quickly moved undetected along the pew and sat down next to Jameson.

Startled by the interloper to his plans, Jameson's eyes flared under bushy brows at the intrusion of the stranger. The Irishman's plans did not include an old man looking for company. His nicotine stained teeth revealed themselves as his lip curled into a feral sneer, warning the stranger. “Piss off, old man,” he said vehemently, spittle flying from his thick lips.

A bemused smile crossed the weathered face of the man seated next to Jameson. He simply stared back silently with unnerving dark eyes.

The Provo member was about to forcibly impose his will when the recognition set in. His eyes widened in disbelief. Jameson clenched his jaw, muscles tightening. His plan had not been going well and a new twist had just been added. “You’re late,” he whispered angrily, in a heavy Ulster accent.

“No. It seems as if I am right on time,” the old man’s reply hinting at more than its intended meaning. He eyed Jameson thoughtfully, relishing the man’s distress.

“You were to have been here twenty minutes ago,” he shot back, his voice primed, edgy.

Without pause the older man parried, “You have the information I requested?” His words, more a demand than a question.

The service continued on throughout their conversation. The smell of burning incense clung thickly in the air as the familiar words of the litany were chanted, until the organ erupted to life, filling the sanctuary with the music of a dirge bellowing from its pipes. Father Howe stood at the altar, letting his voice carry over the few parishioners.

Philip Jameson reached into the pocket of his coat grazing the thin wire beneath his shirt. He pulled out the piece of paper and handed it to the old man seated next to him.

Rapidly, Jameson’s companion scanned the sheet, quickly assimilating the information and memorizing it. “I’m sure you won’t mind if I take this with me. I’ll be certain to destroy it.” A wan smile spread slowly, but the gray eyes never betrayed his emotions. “Philip, you have never disappointed me,” he intoned.

The Irishman’s tension was evident as he silently hoped the elements of the local constabulary, MI 5, the British commandos, and anyone else associated with this event, would storm the portals of the church and he could be done with this saga.

MI 5 had caught him in the act of planting an explosive devise. The IRA member knew there was no love lost between the Brits and Sinn Fein's radical wing. They offered a bullet. Jameson offered something more. His prize was a temptation that would ensure the purchase of his freedom. At least that is what they told him. He did not trust them. But the thought of execution and floating in the Irish Sea as fish food, was not something he could endure. Being tied to their strings might also bring about his death if they *accidentally* let the information fall into the proper hands.

The Brits had accepted his plan on his terms. They knew nothing of the actual reason for the meeting. They did not care. The reward in the game of no rules offered much more to them than his attempt to chart the course.

Jameson's hands trembled slightly. It did not go unnoticed by the gray set of eyes purposefully focused on him. The Provo member's nerves were raw with anticipation. "How did you plan to steal?" he stammered.

"Philip," the old man squinted, and held up a hand to signal an end to the question. "Let me worry about the details, my friend." He sucked in a breath, troubled by the weight of God's thumb pressing in on him in this place. The old man pushed it aside, intent on his mission. Soon he would be leaving.

"Are we through?" the Irishman asked, interrupting the other man's thoughts.

"Yes. We are quite through," he replied, succinctly.

Jameson pressed his feet into the floor preparing to stand. He knew it would not be long now before the arrival of the commando team and he wished to be well away from the old man when they showed up in force.

"One more thing, Philip," he said, catching the Provo's attention.

Jameson turned at the calling of his name. He stared deeply into the set of fervid eyes. Sharp. Intense. They were not rheumy eyes dulled by age. A quick flick of the wrist released the spring. The thin, surgical blade shot out from under the old man's hand penetrating deeply between the fourth and fifth rib. Razor sharp steel easily dissected the chambers of the traitorous Jameson's heart. The reality of what occurred set in as he blinked several times. His jaw slackened and his mouth opened soundlessly, the only movements his body seemed capable of accomplishing. Disbelief etched itself upon the features of the old man's friend, while death came calling expeditiously.

The blade retracted quickly, spilling little blood, as it cleansed itself on the material of Jameson's coat. A small rivulet of crimson fluid stained the cotton fibers of the Irishman's chambray shirt, while his chest began to fill with the life giving fluid that had coursed through him.

The assassin watched impassively, no stranger to death's greeting. He gently grasped the dying man's shoulder, propping him to position so he would not slump in the pew. The IRA man had but seconds to live. His attempt to speak produced a gurgling sound from deep in his throat, but no words came out.

"Did you take me for a fool, Philip?" His words were spit out through tightened jaws. "It is such a pity." The old man moved closer. "Sleep well, my friend," he whispered.

Jameson's eyelids fluttered. Some part of his brain registered the words as his world slid down an inky tunnel devoid of life.

The old man moved swiftly, knowing time was a precious commodity. He could sense their arrival, seconds away. He moved though a side corridor of the church into a back hallway, closing out the music as the last strains of the hymn ended.

The front doors burst open and soldiers of the counter-espionage group, bristling with weapons drawn, rapidly filled the church. There were others in plainclothes who followed, joining in the melee.

The stunned parishioners of St Peter's Cathedral sat rigidly silent, processing the events unfolding before them. Father Howe's garments swirled about him as he angrily moved down the aisle, his voice rising up defiantly over the commotion. "How dare you come into God's house with your guns…"

His words were cut short by the presence of British major, Evan Wills, who looked to be chiseled from granite. Stern features with eyes that were no stranger to violence burned coldly at the priest. The British officer made it explicitly clear, in no uncertain terms, that the priest should keep his mouth shut. Wills barely finished when a cry rose up from the back of the church. The soldiers had found the lifeless form of Philip Jameson, staring blankly at the dead Christ, at the front of the church. Vacant eyes bore witness to the cost of the Provo's sacrifice.

"Major, have your men fan out through the building," one of the older, plain-clothed men in charge of the operation barked. He expected no reply, just action. Rodney Lynch's face grimaced as he cursed the missed opportunity to apprehend one of the world's most wanted individuals. A long term member of MI 5, Lynch had advised against playing Jameson's game. They would not listen. Now they had no idea what their adversary was going to do, or where he would go. A soldier came charging through the door that earlier concealed the trail of the old man. He held some rumpled clothing and the remnants of a latex mask.

Outside, a priest nodded in recognition as he walked toward two armed soldiers guarding the street behind the church. The silver crucifix dangled mockingly from his neck. The uniformed men's rudimentary inspection of the man set them at ease. "Just a minute, Father," a corporal called out.

"Is there a problem, boys?" the impostor answered, in a perfect Irish accent.

"Just following orders." The second soldier pointed the barrel of his weapon at the priest while the corporal did a quick search. They found nothing. "Okay, move along, Father." After that, they paid little attention to the man betraying the purport of the vestments and white collar he wore, allowing him safe passage. The priest slipped around the corner of a building. One of the world's most infamous criminals eluded capture once more.

Chapter Five
Looe Key - Florida Keys

A BRILLIANT SUN LENT ITS WARM RAYS to the assuasive, blue waters of the Gulf Stream. Flowing through the Florida Straits and up the eastern seaboard, this underwater river eventually made its way to the northern European continent. Far off the starboard beam, a freighter rode low in the water, its holds brimming with cargo bound for some unknown destination. Soon the ship passed from sight of the yacht's pilothouse, and faded into the distance. The boat's captain kept a constant vigil despite all the latest gear for preventing any intrusion into the boat's path, in the busy, tropical waters east of Looe Key.

This area of Florida had seen hundreds of years pass along with the memories of English, French, and Spanish seafarers in their quest for dominance. Long faded, the roar of cannonade echoed dimly from the depths, while the sea floor was littered with the decayed framework and ballast stones of wooden sailing vessels. Ghosts of ancient mariners had returned in the form of modern day pirates smuggling contraband bound for Miami's shores. The subculture of the drug trade flourished, filling the streets with white line fever. Today, there was no evidence of their existence, only pleasure craft and shrimpers plying the outer reaches beyond the marine sanctuary.

Josh Deavers had landed himself a cushy job. It was a simple case of being in the right place at the right time. A friend of a friend got him the interview. The terms were perfect, and he was in need of a boat to captain. He had no family and rarely drank, so being on constant call posed little problem, especially with the salary being offered. A glad-handed smile sealed the sweet deal, plus he got to pick the other crew members.

A voice came to life over the intercom, distracting him momentarily. "Josh, I'll be heading topside. Are the ladies up?"

"Yes, sir. On the fly bridge. Taking a tan, I believe." His eyes crisscrossed the waters out to the horizon from his view behind the raked windscreen of the yacht. "Anything else, sir?"

"No. Just planning to enjoy life on my new toy."

They had made a quick run from Miami to Key West, on the maiden voyage of the Ferretti 880, a yacht of impressive stature. Now, Duval Street was just last night's memory, as Mick Henke came topside. Ambling barefooted out onto the aft deck, the ocean's scent assaulted him. A jaunt over to the Bahamas and the shakedown cruise would be complete. Henke slipped on the dark glasses and surveyed his boat's wake.

Tan and trim at forty-five, his handsome looks and charisma had seemed to be a perfect fit throughout his life in the privileged circle of those he had grown up with along the Chesapeake shore. His father's advertising firm, Berthold Henke International, had assured the family a more than ample lifestyle. The elder Henke's mounting fortunes had seen to the opulent comforts befitting a family of its stature. Their estate had been paid for through investments and connections to the right people many years before his birth.

In spite of their wealth, Mick's parents were doting and his father had passed along his affinity for the sea to his three children. They had grown up on the water and all were avid sailors. One sister and one brother, each attorneys, now working long hours and billing phenomenal fees. Mick Henke had chosen another path. He had applied to numerous medical schools and decided on the University of Miami. The winters agreed with him, and he fell in love with the tropical, cosmopolitan flavor of the city. It would turn into a prosperous venture.

Dr. Mick Henke had built a reputation on his skill and confidence. There was not much he would not tackle, and even less that he did not succeed in doing. Plastic surgery became his passion. His skills were impeccable. He worked with a rapidity uncommon to his colleagues. When he began his practice, Henke was bold enough to ask for payment far and above the norm, and he got it. Women were attracted to him, and for those with the means, it mattered little the cost as long as he achieved their desired results. His patients suffered no disappointment.

Henke opened his practice just over a decade ago. One of his first patients was an Englishman, accompanied by an attractive, dark-haired woman named Monique. The patient needed a repair of a gunshot wound to his left ear. Henke was hesitant at first, since his plan was to do only cosmetic surgeries. But the monies offered were exorbitant. Monique had only two requirements of her friend's physician. The first was to accomplish the task and restore with little evidence what was missing. Secondly, discretion was paramount, even more than the expected stipulation. Henke happily complied. Besides, he was obligated to by the Hippocratic oath. Monique informed the doctor that as long these two demands were accomplished, his practice would flourish. Never one to pass up an opportunity concerning monetary matters, Henke agreed to the terms.

Within months, the promise he had been given rang true. Sheiks, sultans, political figures, the fabulously wealthy from various parts of the globe, and some of the Hollywood crowd came calling. Henke's practice skyrocketed, and now his world renowned reputation was sought by scores of people. His waiting list was months long, but it did not matter to those who wanted and could afford only the best.

The doctor shook away the thought. He was determined to enjoy this short respite from the rigors of his vocation. Henke sipped the Sapphire gin and fresh grapefruit juice. He swirled the salty, sweet mixture in his mouth, before swallowing it eagerly. Mick Henke glanced at the black dial of his Rolex. Eleven ten in the morning, decidedly a civilized time to drink, especially since he was on vacation. Distinguished lines creased the corners of his blue eyes, while a slick smile oozed across his face. He spun around and made his way topside.

The Ferretti, an Italian luxury yacht, cut through the gentle waves sending sheets of water spraying along its polished, white hull. Its engines turned quietly below decks with such precision, their workings were almost imperceptible. The boat's appeal was apparent from the heads that turned at the sight of its raked appearance. Every appointment was carefully considered, down to the smallest detail. Exquisite leathers, wood, plush carpeting, and electronic gadgetry, filled the interior. The suites were impressive. The main salon was breathtaking and the boat even came thoughtfully equipped with a hot tub on the flying bridge. It was a dream come true. Considering the cool four million Henke laid out in cash for the craft, it should be. Nothing, but the best money could buy, was good enough. For Dr. Mick Henke, it was just another in a long list of toys.

The craftsman of human sculpture catapulted up the steps to the flying bridge, the uppermost deck. The black lens of his Ray Bans reflected the image of two beautiful women languishing under the warm sun. One blonde. One redhead. His eyes devoured the luscious women. Their choice of limited apparel was clearly evident from purple and scarlet G-strings tossed on the deck by their feet. These two were classic examples of his handiwork. Augmented, lipoed, waxed, nipped and tucked in the right spots, the sight of their taut bellies and firm breasts brought other lascivious images to the good doctor's mind. Michelangelo would have been proud of Henke's skill.

His connections with the questionable side of life brought with it all its trappings. He had sealed a lucrative deal with a private firm whose ties to a Washington financial group were shrouded in a mire of complexities. They asked for, and his skilled hands created, a bevy of flawless beauties who were abundantly paid to be in the company of the world's elite. His vacation getaways always included the added benefit of one or two recipients, perfect examples of his talents. Free from the shackles of married life, Mick Henke was living large.

Henke had delighted in their salacious appetites well into the night. He felt himself stirring, but filed it for later. Mick Henke was intent on demanding all Ferretti claimed the boat could do. He called down to the pilot house and instructed Deavers to open her up. A deep growl eminated from the stern as the twin MTU 2000 CV motors went to work, and the eighty-eight foot vessel's bow rose up on plane. Within moments, the Ferretti leapt from eight knots to thirty, greedily drinking from the almost twenty-four hundred gallon fuel tank.

Henke glanced back at the two women. Their hair danced around beautiful, tanned faces, filled with scintillating smiles of matched sets of perfectly straight, white teeth. Mick Henke felt the wind pouring over him. The pressures of his job began to melt away like ice under the Florida sun. His second drink had not hurt in helping bolster that perception. The icy gin drink was working its magic. Henke laughed out loud as the wind rushed past. It was the perfect day and nothing could spoil that. He slugged down the remainder of the refreshing liquid.

Life was good.

The intercom cut loose with the voice of Captain Deavers. "Excuse me, Dr. Henke. Ah, there's a call for you."

Henke waved a hand at the faceless voice as if shooing a fly, disturbed at the intrusion. "Forget it," he snarled. "Probably some goddamn Palm Beach bimbo wanting her wrinkles fixed. She can get Restalyn from anybody in town. Tell her to fuck off. I'm on vacation," the doctor laughed. "Oh, one more thing, captain, do it politely." Henke's finger shot out and killed the intercom button, silencing the annoyance and evaporating back into vacation mode.

A moment later, the hesitant voice of Josh Deavers spewed like rancid milk on Dr. Mick Henke's day. "Sir. The lady's name is Solange. She said I would not have to repeat that."

"I'll take it in my cabin," Henke fumed. Veins stood out at the temples of his reddened face. "Goddamn bitch." He threw his glass onto the deck, shattering it into splinters. One small piece hit the blonde, nicking the smooth skin of her tanned calf. A rivulet of warm, red fluid weaved its way to her ankle. "Pack your bags, ladies. Trip's over." Puzzled, the women watched silently as their departing host stormed from the deck.

"I'm on vacation in the middle of the frikkin ocean," Henke growled.

"Mick," the voice cajoled, in a seductive Grecian accent. "I'm so sorry, dear. You should know the rules by now. Besides, with what you're being so handsomely paid, I should think a little moonlighting would be welcomed."

"My patients are booked up for eight months," he shot back.

"Not my problem, darling," the latitude of the woman's voice changed abruptly. "But, it will be yours if you don't comply with the agreement," the woman added, caustically. "Obligations are just that. You must decide what's most important. It would be a shame if the world no longer had the capable hands of Dr. Mick Henke." The connection closed with a hollow silence. The veiled threat was not lost on the surgeon.

Momentarily he wavered, risking caution. Then the impact of her words struck him full force. Reality set in with a tenacious resolve. Henke knew his vacation had just ended. He was on a tight string. There were only two choices. One, he did not prefer to consider.

Chapter Six
Rutland, Vermont - New England

"MCGANN." BRYSON MCGANN RESPONDED into the onboard phone he had just cradled between his ear and left shoulder. His hands were occupied with reports for the upcoming meeting in Frankfurt. NESSA and other like organizations around the globe were gathering for a conference to discuss global environmental problems facing the planet and its inhabitants.

"Bry. T.C.," McGann's long time friend replied.

"Enjoy the Newfoundland climate?" McGann chuckled. T.C.'s friend stared out the window gazing at the rapidly disappearing eastern U.S. coastline from thirty-eight thousand feet. Shadows from the patchwork of clouds played on the distant white caps of the Atlantic far below, as McGann relaxed in the leather seat.

"The weather, forget it. We did get some great work done on a small excavation project."

"I thought L'Anse Aux Meadows was tapped out," McGann interrupted.

"So did everyone else. However, this latest find left behind by settlers from Greenland is impressive. Some newly unearthed runes hint of a lost colony of Vikings."

"Hmm." McGann responded. "Interesting."

Canton paused momentarily, letting the information sink in. "That's why Sumner asked me to stop in Vermont before I headed back to Seattle."

"I heard you were heading south," McGann interjected.

"Right. I am. I just called Red O'Brien, and told him I'd meet him in Darwin in a few days. We're supposed to head down there together on a joint venture with the Australian Geological Survey Institute. AGSI wants some assistance with their Project T."

"Seems we're regular globetrotters these days, T.C." McGann shot back. Memories of times spent in various parts of the world, courtesy of the military, flashed images of the big man at McGann. Affable and honest, Joe 'T.C.' Canton, NESSA Assistant Projects Director, was more brother than anything else. The two family's histories went back to the late eighteen fifties when Duncan McGann saved Black Elk from certain death. Their forefathers joined into a business venture that turned golden, and the close ties of the Scotsman and Cheyenne Indian had formed an iron bond that remained over the years. The two men thought of themselves as brothers although there was no direct relation.

"I'm out of the loop on the Southwestern Pacific. What's Project T?" Canton's friend asked. "But first, where and what are you doing in Vermont?"

"I'm staying at a place called Baker's Bed and Breakfast. Great view of Killington. Too bad it's not ski season, little brother." Canton paused, gazing out the second floor window at the distant sun-bathed slopes radiating in the hues of autumn's coat. "Seems a guy named Ed Brutsch came across an ancient sea cave that became exposed after a mild earthquake. He was grouse hunting on some property he bought about a month ago."

"I remember reading about a sizeable earthquake that took place several years ago not too far from there." McGann paused momentarily, letting the dials spin until they clicked in. "The epicenter was around Plattsburg, on the western shore of Lake Champlain. Isn't there a fault line that runs along the New York and Vermont border?" McGann queried.

"Yup, right on the money, Bry." Canton continued, "Apparently, a small hole opened up in the ground near Lake Bomoseen, so Brutsch decided to do some excavating. I guess he realized he needed some help, and through a friend in Nashville, Tennessee, got hold of Sumner. Since I was in the area…" Canton's voice trailed off letting the suspense build.

"Alright. You got me. What was so important?" McGann asked, setting down the papers on the leather seat next to him.

"Apparently, this fellow claims to have found a Viking ship in this ancient sea cave."

McGann was astonished. "Now that's incredible." He quickly opened his laptop and keyed in some data. The microelectronics came to life, displaying a topographic map of the area. McGann eyed the screen curiously before continuing. "So what do you think, T.C.?"

Canton paused to sip from the steaming coffee he held in his hand. "It's an interesting story. I've briefly looked at some satellite images.

There's some interesting topography around the southern shoreline of Lake Champlain and the Bomoseen areas."

McGann gazed at the computer screen once more before setting it aside. "Have you talked with this Brutsch fellow?"

"Briefly. From our phone conversation, he seems like a reasonable guy. I'm meeting him today."

McGann heard the lilt of an English accent calling up from the landing, asking Canton how he liked his eggs.

"Over easy, Steve," Canton responded to the proprietor, before continuing. "Here's the strange part. The tale gets twisted, Bry. The local rag ran a brief article about the discovery, and the few artifacts Brutsch found. WVNY out of Burlington did two spots on it. The story never got any national play. Probably because of the Taiwan situation. Seems that's all you hear about these days. The uncanny part is, he was paid a visit by a dark-haired woman who claimed to be from the Smithsonian, in D.C. He noticed after she left, the artifacts he'd brought back from the site were missing."

"What was that?" McGann interrupted.

"A large copper ingot about the size of your hand, a leather pouch, and some unusual red beads."

McGann scratched the back of his head, letting it spin for the moment. "Hmm. It's a shame they were taken, but they certainly aren't needed to prove the Vikings existence."

"That's what's so puzzling," Canton infused.

"If this is real, T.C.," McGann paused, "It seems like a rather inconsequential piece of antiquity to steal. Any ideas on the woman?"

"A dead end," Canton remarked. Leaving the room, the big man headed down a wooden staircase for the morning's breakfast.

"Another of life's mysteries waiting to be unraveled, T.C." McGann mulled it over silently before putting it to rest, and then continued. "So what's the story with Project T?"

"A joint venture with the Aussie's national agency responsible for geological sciences. They do a number of things for environmental improvement, as well as exploration on and off shore for minerals, monitoring geomagnetic disturbances, ocean drilling. I think you get the picture," Canton continued.

"Sort of a sister organization to NESSA," McGann interjected.

"Exactly. We've been asked to help in an ocean study aiding the Indonesian government regarding tsunami wave formation in the Indian Ocean and its effects on western Australia and the eastern most islands of Indonesia."

"Nothing like a live aboard in the middle of the sparkling Pacific. Just think of it as a south seas cruise, T.C."

"Your idea of humor leaves much to the imagination, little brother," Canton remarked, dryly.

"It seems your Cheyenne heritage has captured your sense of humor, big brother." McGann interjected, wistfully.

"Somehow, Red O'Brien is not my idea of the optimal cruise ship partner."

McGann laughed. Thoughts of the ruddy-skinned, ex-navy man chomping on a weathered cigar did not invoke images of a perfect tan line in a low cut bikini. "It'll be an adventure. Sounds like an interesting project, especially after the devastation four years ago. There'd been talk for a long time about a system of buoys for tsunami detection prior to that event."

"A lot of lives were lost before the world took notice," Canton replied solemnly. "Hopefully, our efforts will help focus attention and bring about some needed change."

"At least you can work on your tan, T.C."

"Right."

"Anyway," McGann asked, "How's Ashlyn doing? Between the two of you traveling so much, I haven't had time to catch up."

Canton and Dr. Ashlyn Sanders met while working on the Billings project NESSA continued to be involved in. The two had an instant attraction and through a strange set of circumstances, Canton discovered she worked for the NSA. "Ashlyn's in Ft. Meade. She needed some time to get up to speed on paperwork and some inter-agency work. She thought this would be the perfect opportunity since I was headed south. I'm dropping in to see her before flying back to the west coast."

"The three of us need to get together for another dinner at Martin's when we get back to Seattle."

"That's a deal," McGann's friend replied.

"I got to go. Say hi to Ashlyn. Keep me posted on the Vermont chronicle. I'll catch up with you after I'm finished in Frankfurt," McGann stated.

"Sounds good, Bry."

The connection died and McGann tucked the phone back into its cradle. He looked over to see Kate Harper brushing away a loose strand of hair from her face. She was one of the "Four Horsemen," as McGann referred to them. Harper was the lone female among the Projects Directors at the Seattle agency. Papers were strewn about the seat next to her. Harper was totally engrossed in preparing for her portion of the presentation she would be giving at the conference in Germany.

McGann's attention turned to a replay of the conversation he had with Canton. The peculiar nature of the dark-haired woman's arrival and subsequent theft of seemingly innocuous artifacts, struck him as odd. The possibilities were too numerous to consider. In a far corner of his mind, his instincts flared, indicating there was more to the story than petty theft. Someone had gone to a lot of trouble for such seemingly invaluable items, at least from a monetary standpoint. The question of who the mystery woman was and her intent plagued him until he let it slip into the crevices of his mind.

Chapter Seven
Sibenik, Croatia - Adriatic Coast

RUMPLED, WHITE SHEETS GATHERED LOOSELY around the naked form of the beautiful woman, as one breast peeked out from under the covers. Brunette hair lay strewn across the pillow, as if tossed about by unseen winds. Several strands lay across her face provoking thoughts of a child-like innocence. The rhythm of her breathing was regular. Her chest rose and fell deeply in silent sleep. He had not awakened her.

Sunlight sparkled on the calm, blue waters of the Adriatic Sea off the Dalmatian Coast. Pushing open the windows, scented breezes rose up to greet him. The man stood at the window of the bedroom, and let his eyes keenly survey the surrounding hills. The coolness of the morning air tingled on his unclothed skin. He let his gaze follow the winding dirt road, the only entrance from the road below. It gave no indication of activity. A good sign.

He had chosen this house, in part, due to its vantage along the coastal mountains. Thick stone walls rose up from the sea cliff, providing ample protection from the outside world. From a distance, the two hundred year old baronial estate conjured up a charming impression, attesting to the languid lifestyle of its well-to-do owner. The stone tower which housed the sleeping quarters afforded an impressive view of his property. More importantly, it provided ample opportunity, in addition to the high-tech electronics, to detect intruders brazen enough to enter the grounds. Monies made by his vocation offered him the ability to make the diminutive appearing manor into a fortress - a cache of arms, secret passages, and even a small helicopter were stored, and always fueled. He left nothing to chance, calculating every move of his day. In his profession there was no other viable choice.

Gregor Duvonich, as he was known to the people of Sibenik, a few kilometers to the north, had become an auteur in the movie business. That was the ruse he had perpetrated upon those of the medieval aged town. He had used so many names over the years. Stephan Kholos reflected on the ploy used to assure his safety. A smile crept into the corners of his mouth, pondering the gullibility of his neighbors. Tell them you are famous, and they will do anything for you. It also lent credence and gave explanation to his frequent travels, journeys in which the images he produced were grim reminders of his stock in trade, far from the cry of big screen theatrics.

Without warning, hands encircled his neck. His eyes flared. He did not move. Kholos felt the softness of her small, firm breasts press into his back. Her scent swirled around him in an unseen mist. The woman stood on tiptoes letting her tongue flick excitedly along the base of his neck and muscular shoulders.

"You think I did not hear you, Sahtay?" Stephan Kholos asked, still traveling the countryside with steely, gray eyes.

"How can you be so absorbed in your thoughts and know I was there? I didn't make a sound," the sultry voice whispered into his ear.

"I am always aware of everything around me." Kholos spun around and pressed his lips into the softness of her mouth. Memories of last night's ravenous flames evoked a chuckle from deep in his throat. He let a hand slide down and grasp the roundness of her buttock. His other hand moved to the crease of her neck, pressing her closer.

"Now you laugh at me?" the woman pouted, pulling away.

He gazed upon her flawless olive-bronze skin, an indication of her Grecian and Egyptian descent. Full lips, sensuous and skilled, masked her white teeth. Her hair spilled abundantly over her shoulders. Svelte and beautiful, her body exuded sensuality with all her mannerisms.

"Was there not enough of me last night for you, Stephan?" she asked, coyly. Kholos' paramour slipped from his grasp, seductively beckoning him to the bed.

The phone's unanticipated ringing disturbed their libidinous plans.

The muscles of Kholos' forearm rippled as he gripped the receiver. The female voice did not wait for him to answer. "You have not responded to my calls," the voice spit out. "You are with someone?" the voice, filled with contempt, demanded.

"Your intuitiveness surprises even me," Kholos stated flatly. He sat down on the bed and let his fingers explore soft skin. "The answer to your question, is yes. But, Solange, it was as if I were with you," he added, mockingly.

A silence hung thickly before she continued. "Your contact is in Amsterdam and waiting for your arrival. Everything is in place. Are you ready?" the angered voice demanded.

"You need ask?" he shot back, invectively. "Do not question me." Jaw muscles undulated beneath his skin, finally fading as his anger washed ashore like the waves below.

Changing the subject, the female voice continued. "It seems that your friend has stirred the interest of some people in the United States. Apparently, they are investigating."

"How touching," Kholos laughed. "Let them. I really have no concern for this," the man paused, inhaling a deep breath. "It matters little," he scoffed. "They'll never find the culprit who absconded with such inconsequential items."

Her skilled hands worked the tightening sinews at the base of his neck. The long, dark brown tendrils of her hair slid down his muscular back and along the angry scar across his left shoulder. Her finger traced the ridge of raised flesh, envisioning the pain that went along with its history. She had heard him say it was courtesy of an encounter in the Columbian jungle. "I will be heading to Amsterdam soon. When my contact informs me of its arrival, I'll leave." Kholos forced himself to inhale slowly, deeply, letting the tension settle.

"And whose identity will you be assuming this time?" the voice inquired through the phone's speaker. "The priestly garb you chose does not fit you well. I think the collar would be a little tight," the woman's voice mocked, implying much more with her comment.

Kholos offered nothing.

"I have my own circle of friends, Stephan. It seems our worlds are uniquely intertwined. Perhaps we have some of the same acquaintances. How about your financial plan? Are your assets in place? There are those with interests beyond our own who wish to see a successful venture," the woman's voice hinted. "Failure is not an option."

"Who are you to question my abilities?" Kholos flared again.

"Tell your friend we should meet in Cairo," the woman cut in. "She knows the place." The connection ended abruptly as the sound of the woman's voice vanished.

Kholos felt himself finally relaxing as his shoulders loosened. He reflected on the first meeting with the woman. He had been hired by a wealthy Greek banker, Dimitri Pendopolous. Kholos possessed abilities that were well touted in the shadowy circles on the back side of the law. A dispute needed mending, and Stephan Kohlos was the person with the skills to make the problem go away. She had been there, silent, during his conversations with Pendopolous. Her eyes had spoken volumes. Instantly, he had been attracted. Their lustful trysts continued for some time. There was no love between them. They were two serpents entwined in a venomous dance, each taking from the other with little but momentary gratification as a placard to their true intentions.

Stephan Kholos let it melt from his thoughts. The soft kiss turned his attention away from the previous conversation. Quickly, his mind filled with other things as the morning sunlight poured eagerly through the open tower window.

Chapter Eight

Pennsylvania Avenue - Washington, D.C.

THE BLACK LIMOUSINE MOVED QUICKLY through rain lacquered streets of the nation's capital. Benjamin Wolcott glanced up briefly from the stack of papers strewn about on the thickly padded, black leather seat. Oddly, he took notice of the watery, silver droplets, a reminder of the cold, misty drizzle, clinging defiantly in the form of miniature orbs to the wool nap of his black overcoat. The D.C. streets were playing host to a mournful and dreary autumn morning.

Annoyed by the chatter of the wiper blades, Wolcott responded curtly to the cell phone's interruption. His day had hardly begun and already he had dealt with a dozen calls. The conversation was short. The president's advisor snapped the phone shut, irritated, tossing a handful of papers onto the seat.

Passing through the checkpoint at the White House security gate, the chauffeured vehicle pulled up to the entrance as Wolcott ran a hand through his tousled blond hair. It was a natural fit for the ex-army officer, now presidential advisor. The limo eased to a halt and Wolcott jumped out. Two armed marines inspected the familiar face and fervidly snapped to attention.

President Richard Simon peered reflectively out the window onto the mansion's lawn, as rivulets of water meandered down the bullet-proof glass. He had been working since five-thirty, and at six, he had been handed "The Blue Thing," a quick two page *down and dirty* printed on blue paper, highlighting the world situation. Each day there was a modicum of routine, but each day also held promise of events outside his immediate control. Now an hour and a half after embarking on his slated tasks, Simon needed a quick break.

He and his team would be leaving later in the day. The president's agenda was brimming. Just into his second term, things had slowly begun to improve. Simon had been handed a full plate of problems from the last eight years of the previous administration's ungifted talent for decision making. Simon felt, at times, he was digging out from a deep hole. Trade imbalances, environmental concerns, financial, domestic, and a host of other issues, marred the beginning months of his second term. This did not even take into account the global implications and entanglements brought about by the cowboy-like attitude of the former president. Repeating the same mistakes under the guise of "what was good for us was good for the world," would have bode poorly for the world economic status.

Now with the G-8 conference in Davos looming, he had a thin line to walk. Simon's decisions were perplexing, and the weight of their ramifications bore heavily upon his shoulders. Each tentative step he took threatened to crack the veneer of thin ice on the steps to economic and political recovery. Not only the country, but every other country was looking to the U.S. for answers. Perhaps the world would remain still, at least for the moment. That is what he hoped. The chief of state did not relish any intrusions on the day's agenda.

Idly, his mind wandered across his life, and the events leading to the presidency. The pressures were at times almost intolerable, even though the thrill and challenge of caring for the world's bastion of democracy continued to drive him forward.

Simon's eyes caught the reflection of himself, peering from the glass in front of him. Now ten months into his second term, the evidence of the position's enormity had started taking its toll. His skin sagged slightly and his eyes betrayed the fatigue lurking behind them. Small crevasses in his skin, a testimony to the burdens demanded of him, attested to the pressures of his job.

"Mr. President," his secretary's voice erupted from the speaker, disrupting his thoughts.

Before he could respond, the familiar face of Benjamin Wolcott shot through the door. "Good morning, Mr. President."

Without turning from the window, Simon waved a hand, acknowledging his long-time friend and advisor. "Yes, Liz."

"Senator Ramsey is here, sir."

"Thank you. Send him in, please."

Simon cocked his wrist and glanced at the time. A small chuckle popped out from his throat, along with a fading grin. The president turned toward his friend. "Ramsey is the most punctual man I've ever met," the president threw out at Wolcott. "If only the rest of society functioned on his timetable."

"In a perfect world," Wolcott responded wryly, a smile creasing his face.

The chiseled features of Jason Ramsey moved out from behind the office door after the latch gave way. "Good morning, Mr. President," the senator's resonant voice sounded.

Simon moved out around the lustrous mahogany desk and clasped the firm grip of the long time senator. Ramsey turned, nodded, and added, "Good to see you, Ben."

Wolcott's eyes brightened, "Senator, good morning."

With the pleasantries over, Ramsey succinctly moved into his intended conversation. "I know you're extremely busy, Mr. President, so I won't keep you long. How may I be of help, sir?"

President Richard Simon held up his hand stopping the man standing in front of him. "Jason, have a seat. Before we get to the agenda, I know this must be painful." The president paused, unsure of exactly the words. His own painful memories boiled up at the remembrance of his wife's battle with the cancerous illness. "Is there any news about Alex and Becca?" he continued. The believability of his tone spliced through his words. "I'm sorry. I've not had the opportunity to ask recently."

Sucking in a ponderous breath, the senator shook his head slightly as the words spewed dryly from his throat in a raspy reply. "No. Olivia and I wish to thank you once more for all that you placed at our disposal in the efforts to find them." The gray-haired senator closed his eyes and painfully swallowed the acidic lump forming in his throat. The air in the Oval Office hung heavy with despair, as Wolcott watched the two long time friends battle desperately with their thoughts.

Simon nodded quiescently. He laid a knowing hand upon his friend's shoulder, not wishing to interrupt the grieving father.

"Olivia is taking this rather badly." Ramsey blew out a long breath. "Honestly, the only thing that helps keep my sanity is working." The senator chewed solicitously upon his lower lip, letting his eyes come to rest on the folded hands in his lap before continuing. "We've hired a private agency to look into the matter of their disappearance. Foul play has pretty much been ruled out after this many weeks. So far, nothing's come to light. No requests for ransom. We can only surmise they've been lost. It's the not knowing that's difficult."

"Jason, since my wife died several years ago, I've come to realize there are no words," Simon's voice trailed off.

Benjamin Wolcott added, "Please convey my deepest concerns to Olivia, Jason."

The presidential advisor always made it a point to address everyone by their official title except in the most private of conversations. Wolcott felt the pangs of the somber moment.

Senator Ramsey nodded, smiling wanly. "Gentlemen, shall we begin the business we were scheduled to do?"

Simon took his seat behind the desk and removed a stack of papers from a drawer.

"It seems as if we have some tough choices to make on economic policy in the coming months. As head of the budget committee, I need your advice and support on the next step."

Twenty minutes later, the meeting was over and the president moved along with his schedule. The afternoon would come too quickly. Simon was determined to have his desk cleared by the time Marine One landed on the White House lawn for the trip to Andrews Air Force Base, early in the evening. There would be more than a token press corps on the presidential jet to Switzerland, but Simon hoped for some much needed rest.

Chapter Nine
USS John C. Stennis - Southwestern Pacific

STEAM POURED FROM THE FLAT SURFACE of the expansive metal decking in expectation of what was to come. Below decks, the *great beast* waited impatiently for its command to come to life. The thick, steel cable was strung taut like the drawn string of a bow. The catapult was primed, as the pilot, twenty-eight year old Lieutenant Ron Wood, call sign "Black Dog," awaited a go from the flight deck officer, Lieutenant Junior Grade, Kendall Stevens.

Each pilot carried a nickname that he was known by in the fighter wing. Wood's name came about as a result of his younger years. Hailing from Cape Cod, Massachusetts, Lt. Commander Wood had spent a lot of time at the Black Dog, on Martha's Vineyard.

Its owner, a friend of Wood's father, and former F-86 Air Force fighter pilot, gave up flying for the sea many years before. Little did he know that his dream of becoming a ship's captain plying the waters of coastal New England in the Shenandoah, with his black Labrador retriever, would lead him onto a venture extremely different than that of sitting in the cramped confines of a fighter cockpit. The compass of his life's course sailed a reach, into uncharted territory. A quest for life on the Vineyard took root, and developed into a world famous restaurant and pub.

The tales Wood heard growing up kindled the fires of his imagination, and the dream of flying fighter aircraft had taken off. From that point on, there was no doubt that Ron Wood would do everything possible to land himself a position behind the stick.

Wood adjusted the webbing on his orange life vest and gripped the control stick a little tighter. Quickly glancing down at the array of glowing multi-hued navigational and computer equipment within the cockpit, the pilot looked out through the windscreen into the skies ahead. He flipped down the darkened visor of his helmet and gave a thumbs up as a voice rang in his headset.

"Black Dog, you are cleared for takeoff," the flight controller's voice sounded.

Wood pushed himself back into his seat, prepared for the weight of rapid acceleration. "Roger that," the lieutenant responded. Endless hours in the cockpit had never lessened the adrenaline rush of take off from the deck. Being catapulted from zero to over one hundred and fifty miles per hour in just a few seconds was a *balls out and belly to the wall ride,* Wood always said.

The pilot glanced out below the plane at Lieutenant J. G. Kendall Stevens, and tossed out a friendly smile. She was the flight control officer on duty. They had spoken in the officer's mess a number of times. The young naval officer was attractive, and her deep brown eyes had captured his attention immediately. He quickly wondered what led her to take on the periculous assignment. The flight deck was a busy place when sorties were scrambled, offering its own set of potential hazards. Every person showed up to play the game to its fullest. If not, one wrong move meant lives could be lost. Wood sensed, in the short time he had known her, a tenacity that signaled she could hold her own. He had inquired about her, discovering that besides her good looks, Stevens was highly intelligent and a capable decision maker.

The pilot snapped a sharp salute at the flight control officer. He quickly let his idle thoughts drift away and focused on the task at hand. Stevens knelt down on one knee. The officer's arm snapped out, pointing toward the end of the deck.

The engines of the sleek, gray twin-tailed craft roared to life in an increasing crescendo as Wood eased his foot from the brake. The catapult officer pressed the release button and the sequence of launch events took shape. The steam-driven steel cable, attached to a dolly on the nose wheel, sprang to life, propelling the jet aircraft across the flight deck. It was all automatic for Wood. His hands worked the controls expertly, bringing the aircraft up after its initial dip off the end of the carrier. Twin trails of orange fire followed the quickly disappearing craft into the distance of the late afternoon skies. Kendall's wishes for a safe flight were drowned out by the din of the Stennis' routine.

Wood's F/A 18E Hornet was a single seat jet fighter designed specifically for use on aircraft carriers. The Marines and Navy both used the craft, capable of speeds in excess of Mach 1.8 above fifty thousand feet. This impressive aircraft, with a wingspan of thirty-seven feet and an overall length of fifty-six, was attractive as she was capable. Driven by twin seventeen-thousand pound thrust General

Electric Turbofans, its performance attributes allowed it to be used successfully in the role of fleet protection and ground based attacks.

Wood settled back in his seat as his aerodyne streaked skyward, climbing to altitude and moving in along side the others in his fighter group. Their mission today was a routine patrol, and to rack up some flying time. Sunlight filled the cramped cockpit as Wood piloted his fighter jet above the blue Pacific waters thousands of feet below.

Captain Harold Culpepper watched the last fighter take off from his position on the bridge, high above the flight deck. Satisfied, he turned and called out a course change as a series of 'aye-ayes' were voiced around the massive control center of CVN-74. The John C. Stennis was a Nimitz class carrier, powered by a nuclear reactor that could send the over one thousand foot vessel through the world's oceans at speeds over thirty knots.

The skipper's eyes missed nothing. CVN-74's captain was a stickler for detail, and a man of quick decision making talents who was seldom wrong. Twenty-three years of his adult life had been given in service to his country. He was sustaining the long heritage of seamen who were in his family line. Tall and lean, with bushy eyebrows and a slightly off set jaw, Culpepper did not portray a Hollywood stereotype of a naval captain. From a distance, he appeared gangly, with arms slightly too long for his body, and his gait held a peculiar oddity when he walked. The navy man was, in no sense of the word, handsome.

However, naval command at CINCPAC could care less what he looked like. Intelligent, sharp, inherently attuned to command, were but a few of the words listed in his 201 file. There were few questions he could not answer when it came to commanding one of the world's greatest naval vessels. He was considered to be at the top of his field. A promotion to admiral lay in the offing in the near future.

None of that mattered to Culpepper. He would take the reassignment when it came and let the memories of the sea continue to wash through his veins. The nuclear powered ship had been his home for the last four years. It was as much a part of him as he was an extension of it. A marvel of modern engineering, someone had told him. Four screws over sixty-six thousand pounds each could propel ninety-seven thousand tons of steel, aircraft, and the Navy's finest at over thirty knots. One day he would have to give up command of this vessel of which he had grown so fond. Serving his country committed him to following orders. It was all part of the duty.

"Captain," Commander Sam Carr said, handing a folded memo over to the captain.

Culpepper rapidly digested the information he had been handed. An eyebrow arched in response. "Thanks, Sam. I'll be in my quarters." Culpepper turned and left the sunlit expanse of the Pacific behind him.

Carr allowed the captain time to leave and then turned his attention to managing the needs of CVN-74.

Kendall Stevens left the flight deck. The heat of the Pacific sun had taken its toll over the course of her shift. Dry-mouthed and tired, she was on the way back to her quarters for a much needed shower and some chow.

Hot racking was a term used by sailors on Navy subs when they referred to sleeping. One man left a bunk and another crawled in at the end of his shift. She was happy that conditions on a carrier were less restrictive. Although, with nearly six thousand people aboard, finding time to be alone to think, or with someone you like was not easy to come by.

Stevens finished in the mess and later went topside for a breath of fresh air. It was one of those moments where the flight deck was still. The young lieutenant wondered what life was like at thirty-eight thousand feet flying through crepuscular skies. Stevens let her mind roll over past conversations she had with Ron Wood. She liked him. He seemed like a good guy. Single. Not too much bravado for a sky jockey, she mused. Perhaps when they made port again, she would invite him to dinner. Why not. The worst he could do was say no. It was hard to imagine he would pass up a nice meal and a bottle of wine.

Kendall Stevens smiled as soft ocean breezes washed over her. Extinguished by the advent of the coming night, a fading sunset cast its diminutive shadows across the deck of CVN-74.

Chapter Ten
Amsterdam - Netherlands

THE WOMAN'S EYES STRAFED the darkened street, passing by each brick facade along the banks of the canal. The dank mustiness of the dirty waters assaulted her nostrils, its dampness invading her skin. She chose to ignore it. Amsterdam traced its heritage back to the twelfth century, but she could have cared less about its history. Her thoughts were focused entirely on the mission in front of her. Nearly invisible, garbed in the black, one-piece outfit, the soon to be unwelcome guest needed no one else. Only when it was done would she signal the vehicle to enable her retreat.

Two hours until daylight. The perfect time, the woman reflected, allowing herself a thought about the slack-jawed, snoring old man she would be meeting shortly. The intruder knew everything about her target. She had studied his dossier until able to recite its contents verbatim, and recall which page it was printed on. Her photographic memory was a tool she enjoyed and employed skillfully in her line of work. One look at the material and floor plan of the home was all that had been needed. There was the issue of the security system. However, she had never met a problem money could not solve.

The woman adjusted the dark balaclava covering her attractive face, momentarily exposing a small tattoo of a star cluster and the ancient, mythical Scylla. She tucked away a few strands of long brown hair up under the hood. Retrieving the night vision thermal optics from an inner chest pocket, she slipped them over her head, adjusting the head strap. They were not much larger than the framework of ordinary eyeglasses. Technology's innovation allowed them to weigh mere ounces. Pressing a small button on the frame above the right lens, the night world instantly came alive in an eerie glow.

In the left hip pocket of her garment, she carried a small folding butterfly knife with a razor sharp four inch blade; in her right, a set of professional lock picks. Under her right arm, a silenced Walther PPK nestled securely in a black nylon holster, along with two extra magazines. These last two were merely precautionary items. Her work demanded she be skilled with both weapons. She needed nothing more to accomplish the task ahead.

One last glance in both directions and she let her strong legs launch herself effortlessly across the street. With just a few strides, she was in place. The crepe soles of her shoes invited silence. The stealthy attacker stopped to listen, cautiously absorbing the slightest noises in the early morning as she stood in the shadows of the old home. A small wooden gate separated the two buildings, the only deterrent denying the assailant access to the home's inner courtyard. A quick spray of silicone lubricant to the entrance's rusty hinges assured their cooperation in her covert activity.

"I'm preparing to go in. Once I have secured our guest, I'll call," her voice whispered into the thin, wire microphone sewn into the mask next to her chin.

"Understood." The man's answer was clipped. His eastern European accent hinted to his Slavic origins. There was no other response.

Security cameras swept the area in a synchronized pattern. Precision was key to entering the old home undetected. Twelve seconds from the time she entered the gate was her allowance before visual detection betrayed her presence. Poor design accounted for a gap in the period in which the cameras overlapped their scanned zones. Her timing needed to be exact. No detail was too small for consideration. The rehearsals at a mock up facility would help insure her success. Still, the advent of the unexpected always lingered in the shadows during an actual mission. The unpredictable became the accountable in bringing it down to the wire. Failure did not hold an appeal she cared to sample, and in this assignment, there was little room for extravagancy.

Moving swiftly, her wraith-like form penetrated the courtyard, bounding up the cold, brick steps. The intruder expediently worked the lock on the old wooden door. Inserting the steel picks, her fingers expertly manipulated the tumblers with practiced finesse. She sucked in a deep breath and turned the knob. The door opened quietly, and the old home's invader was standing in the kitchen in under ten seconds. Closing it behind her, she knew she was safe. There had been no time for the hidden cameras to capture her image and trigger an alarm.

She hurried over to a false wall panel and swung the door back. Mentally, the infiltrator ticked off the seconds before this alarm came to life. The plastic box housing the security device glowed dimly with a green light in the darkness. Her fingers tapped in the memorized code, silencing the alarm. Next, she deactivated a string of motion detectors scattered throughout the house with seconds to spare, before it unleashed its signal. The sound of her own breathing seemingly invaded the quietude, while she strained to listen for any signs of discovery.

Antiques bathed in an eerie pall sat everywhere upon expensive hand woven Persian rugs. Painted faces stared in haunting silence from within their frameworks; a testimony to the old man's love of the masters. She proceeded cautiously, moving in the darkness toward her goal. In total silence, her shadowy form moved up the staircase with the agility of a cat. From above, the stertorious respirations of the old man's breathing filtered from behind his bedroom door, as she drew near.

Confident, she switched to the glasses' thermal imaging mode. A small but powerful computer chip continually sent signals detailing areas of heat and cold. It could outline a body easily in vivid detail. When the optics were in the thermal imaging mode, they emitted no tell tale greenish glow as customary with even her own night vision device. Though the actual image appeared in the plastic lens, the display harbored images in three dimensional detail, adjusting for distances and always focused. It was ideal for the assignment. Once she had the target in hand, the need for stealth would then decrease dramatically.

Pushing open the heavy wooden door to the oversized master suite, her silhouette skirted the distance to the somnolent form in the expansive bedroom. In one quick motion she pulled the Walther from its resting spot. The woman vaulted agilely onto the bed, straddling the old man's chest, while pinning his arms to the bed with her knees. With her right hand, she yanked down the infrared vision device. Almost simultaneously, her hand shot out covering the old man's nose and mouth, while the cold steel barrel of the pistol gouged a deep, painful crater into the target's forehead.

Awakened abruptly, and unable to breathe, panic coursed through Abram Mossel's veins. The whites of his eyes encircled pupils dilated with fear. The veil of sleep was shattered, and his mind could not comprehend what was taking place. At first he thought he was having a terrible nightmare until the gravity of the situation set in. Mossel struggled vainly as his sympathetic nervous system kicked into overdrive, sending his heart racing. His pounding chest ached with a threatening explosion. The inner workings of his brain signaled the adrenal glands to activate, sending adrenaline abundantly through his body. A fire raged as his lungs attempted to pump much needed air to his oxygen starved body. Every effort to remove his attacker was failing. His lower arms and legs flailed wildly. His eyes began to water furiously. Blinking rapidly, his attempts to flush the tears were futile. His protestations were but muted sound in the darkened room. The stark realization of his impending death was settling in on him. Mossel's attempts to extricate himself from his attacker was becoming less forceful. His body demanded oxygen and found none. An inky blackness hovered at the edge of his tunneling vision in this all too real nightmare.

The woman felt the slick spittle soak through the palm of her gloved hand. The sinews of her arms were constricted bands, clamping down hard upon the old man's face. She was taking him to the brink, relishing the moment. Sensing it would not be much longer, the black, clad intruder pressed her face next to his ear. The old man felt her hot breath as his consciousness faded. "I am God. I decide if you live or die."

Mossel's panic had demanded all his body could provide. He began to sink rapidly, hoping for death to end his incredible suffering.

"If you emit one word," the woman's voice continued, sounding as if it came from a great distance, "you will be dead before you can blink your eyes." The woman's face contorted into a vengeful smirk. "Do you understand? Do you understand?" she demanded, her words protracted, driving home the point of the last sentence.

The old man managed to understand as his fog clouded mind closed in around him. He felt his life forces waning. Abram Mossel was barely able to move. It seemed as if a thousand years had passed during his struggle of futility. Mossel began to slip into a long, dark tunnel, resigned to his fate. Relief would come very soon, and there would be no further need for worry.

Somehow his oxygen starved brain recognized that the hand was no longer clamped upon his mouth. Automatically, his brain caused the bellow of his diaphragm to begin working, greedily sucking in life saving air. It took some time for his ragged breathing to return to normal. Finally, Mossel's heart slowed its rapid pace, the furious pounding in his chest subsiding. The raging fires were quelled. His brain began to register the moment again. He was aware of his surroundings and the weight of the woman upon his chest. Between the man's legs, warm fluid soaked into his soiled pajamas and bedding. His eyes were still filled with the gravest concern, but he dare not speak.

"Get dressed," the woman commanded. "You know I can kill you at will?" the woman queried, not really seeking an answer.

Trembling fingers fumbled in the darkness with the buttons of his shirt. He hurriedly pushed his feet into his Italian leather shoes. "What have I done? What do you want with me?" Mossel cried out.

She tossed him a jacket. "Downstairs," she ordered.

The man nodded in response to his attacker. Together, they hurried out the back door of the home. The woman whispered into the microphone. "Come quickly. I have everything." Her words were chosen with care on the slim chance that someone could possibly be listening in on her frequency. If so, they would have no idea of what the conversation was about. She turned off the outside security cameras and together, they stepped out into the pre-dawn darkness.

Within seconds the Lexus 430 careened around the street corner, tires screeching as the heavy vehicle came to an abrupt halt. The back door was thrown open and the woman roughly shoved her captive inside. They would be safe within minutes, well hidden before daylight.

His eyes watched passively as they traversed the darkened streets of the city where Abram Mossel had spent his life. He was unsure of their destination. The old man's brain had barely registered the needle's pinprick moments before. The medicine's magic was bringing relief from the virulent predicament now attached to Mossel's life. A murky peace seeped into his being. There was silence. No one in the car spoke. He barely noticed the jabbing pain of the cold steel pistol barrel pressing into his ribs. Mossel's world began to spin. His vision narrowed, tunneling. He felt himself sinking into an inky void. What little sounds he heard became distorted. From a foggy crevice, the penetrating chill of the malignant trauma of the woman's claim of being God poured over him. Certainly, not the God Abram Mossel knew.

Chapter Eleven
AGSI - Darwin, Australia

THE DRIVER EASED THE VAN up to the security gate of the Darwin docks. A steel mesh of intertwined wire posed a formidable barrier for anyone attempting to make an unauthorized entry into the area. The uniformed guard scrutinized the American's papers, and cast a discerning glance at the vehicle's passenger before waving the van through. Traveling around the docks to the harbor master's office posed little problem for the driver, and offered Red O'Brien a brief tour. Numerous cruise liners and merchant vessels were in port, including several tugs and smaller cargo container ships. He had been around the world numerous times, courtesy of the U.S. Navy, and there were not many major ports that he had not dropped an anchor in. The ruddy face of the stocky, red-haired Irishman peered out from inside the vehicle. To Red O'Brien, ports were all the same. The sounds of machinery, the smell of diesel fuel, grease, and salt air made for an interesting mix. Braking to a halt, the van pulled up outside the harbor master's office. O'Brien thanked the driver and stepped inside to fill out paperwork that would allow him to hop a flight to the Australian Geologic Survey Institute's research vessel, the Narissa.

Flying was not a pastime to the NESSA Assistant Director of Offshore Operations. Rather, it was a required obligation on occasion. He was more at ease on the water. O'Brien felt more relaxed with his feet planted on the rolling deck of a ship, than strapped into an uncomfortable seat, winging his way through the skies.

Red O'Brien hated to admit it, but the view was impressive from the left seat of the Sikorsky S-76 helicopter. Outside the glass encased cockpit, a world of cloudless blue skies and endless blue waters of the Timor Sea raced by twelve hundred feet below.

O'Brien was fascinated despite his anxieties, and hopeful of the pilot's talents. He knew flying a helicopter offered more difficulties than imaginable. It wasn't much different than being a drummer, except people's lives were dependent upon the pilot *maintaining the beat*.

Busby's legs straddled the cyclic, gripped in his right hand. It allowed him to control the angle of the main rotor. If the helicopter needed to turn right, a gentle push in that direction would tilt the blades to the right, and send the Sikorsky S-76 in that direction.

Resting in the Aussie pilot's left hand, a tubular device jutted out of the cockpit's floor, similar to a vehicle's parking brake. O'Brien knew its purpose was much more valuable. Augmenting the pitch of the main rotor constituted pulling up on the collective. This increased torque and supplied lift. It also provided the aircraft with increased speed and maneuverability. Conversely, lowering the pitch dictated a decrease in speed necessary for descent and landing the aircraft. As if this was not enough to occupy the pilot's time, O'Brien noticed both of Busby's feet participated in helping support control of the helicopter. Two pedals were responsible for maintaining stability of the tail rotor. Without this assistance, the body of the aircraft would spin wildly out of control, underneath the main rotor. The thought was not one O'Brien allowed himself to linger upon.

A mechanical sounding voice came through on the headset O'Brien was wearing. "Should be out to the ship in another ten minutes or so."

"Sounds great," the thick, gravelly Boston accent returned with a fraudulent smile.

"Not much for flying, are you, mate?" the sandy-haired pilot, John Busby, replied, tossing a grin at his passenger.

"Not really. Riding inside the shell of a reinforced beer can has never been my idea of a good time. Give me a steel deck to plant myself on, any day." O'Brien remarked with a reticent chuckle. He watched the sea pass swiftly below the aircraft and in the distance, a more comfortable apparition took shape. The Narissa rode calmly at anchor, waiting for the arrival of one of the two guests from NESSA.

"She's only two years old," the pilot's voice crackled over the intercom. "Not much she can't take from the sea. Least that's what they tell me," Busby added.

O'Brien threw a glance at his pilot. "That's what they said about the Titanic, too." Both men laughed in response. "She looks pretty sound."

The helicopter circled the two hundred and twenty-five foot ship. She was painted in the AGSI colors of deep blue with two yellow stripes encircling the hull below the gunnels. On the bow, the agency's emblem poised itself beneath the hawser, offering silent tribute to the Australian sister agency of NESSA. The Narissa's high foredeck and superstructure, with clean raking lines back to the stern, presented a sleek appearance.

Rising up out of aft section, an A-frame crane capable of moving submersible vehicles and other experimental equipment, pointed skyward. Strapped to its carriage, one of NESSA's latest toys sat below the crane. On loan to AGSI for this assignment, the deep diving vessel SEATAC-1 waited to explore the ocean's depths.

Below decks, the four massive diesel engines generated enough power to achieve a top speed of eighteen knots. After the once around, Busby touched down on the raised heliport amidships.

"You sticking around, John?" O'Brien inquired, climbing out of his seat harness and exhaling a long breath. He ran a hand along the back of his neck, willing the tense muscles to relax.

"Sorry, mate. They keep me pretty busy. Just dropping off a few things, and I'm heading back to Darwin. When's your friend supposed to make it in?"

"Soon."

"I guess I'll be stopping in again. Might see you then, mate." Busby's hand shot out and pumped the Irishman's hand several times. "No worries."

O'Brien reached into his pocket, pulling out a leather case. "Thanks for the ride. Here you go." The pilot reached out, accepting the offering. "It's a Cohiba Triangulo. Dominican. Finest cigar made. I don't give a damn what the Cubans say."

John Busby gave a thumbs up. O'Brien closed the door of the cockpit, ducking his head, moving quickly out from under the verticillating rotors. Busby wasted no time revving the engines to a plangent decibel. The heavy *whump* of the rotor's blades sliced the air, lifting the helicopter off the deck. Soon, the sound of the aircraft's rotors faded into the distance.

Two members of Project T walked out to greet the NESSA employee. O'Brien sized up the men making their way in his direction, and lit up the end of the dark brown Cohiba. A fiery-orange glow spewed from the end of wrapped tobacco, forming puffs of gray smoke that were carried away in the tropical breeze.

The two men smiled, and Captain Ryan Wyborn began the introductions. He stood a head taller than O'Brien. His leathery, tanned skin attested to life on the world's oceans. A salt and pepper mustache rode above his smiling, toothy grin. "Pleasure to meet you, Mr. O'Brien."

"Red, works for me."

"Name's Skiddy Pete, mate," the second man said. A small, thin, wiry man with a grip like a vice, clamped down on O'Brien's hand. Dark lens hid his smiling eyes from the afternoon's sunlight. Both men wore standard ship's attire, khaki pants and tee shirts emblazoned with the AGSI emblem. The Irishman got a good feel, and took an instant liking to the two Aussies.

"Sweet Mary, mother of Jesus. What the hell kind of name is Skiddy Pete?" the red-haired Irishman asked, with a face-filling grin.

"Earned that one. Nearly cost me my life. My real name is Pete Burbridge,"

"Don't believe half of what Skiddy tells you and you'll be better off," Wyborn chided. "I'll let you in on the real skinny. Wouldn't happen to have an extra one of those stogies, would you?"

"Are you a fan?" O'Brien questioned, raising an eyebrow.

"Absolutely, mate. They say the Dominicans make a good cigar."

"No. They make the best," O'Brien responded. Offering one to each of them, the men walked on down to the main deck of the Narissa for a tour of AGSI's newest research vessel.

"Skiddy got his name years ago when he was a young Turk. He'd been sailing a couple of years as a member of a science team doing geological studies of the seafloor in the Marianas. They got all wrapped up in a bugger of a cyclone and Skiddy was helping out on the bridge."

O'Brien's mind shot through a series of memories of his days upon the water. He was intrigued. "Now, don't you know, Skiddy, you're to leave the sailing to us old salts," the Irishman admonished in a humorous way, with his gravelly Boston brogue.

"You never will let me live this down, will you?" Pete asked, feigning indignity.

"So the story goes," the captain continued, "there was a bit of a problem with a tie down on some of Mr. Burbridge's scientific equipment. It came loose and was making a hell of a racket on deck. So our valiant Skiddy decides to take it upon himself to fix it. Don't know what the hell he was thinking. But before anyone noticed what was happening, Skiddy pulls on a slicker and slips out of the bridge before anyone can stop the bloke."

The trio were becoming fast friends as they stopped on the port bow to enjoy the view and fine smokes. Soft breezes and warm sun spilled across the deck, while O'Brien simultaneously eyed the Narissa. Spotless. No rust. These boys were adept at taking care of their ship. O'Brien admired their hard work, while sneaking a quick glance at the smaller man standing next to him. Wyborn continued the tale, and he let himself slip back into the conversation.

"As you probably can guess from looking at the size of old Skiddy, he can hardly stand up in a light breeze. So, you can only imagine what happened next. Our friend here tied off on a lifeline and somehow managed to almost get to his precious cargo when a large wave washed the decks, and Skiddy, too." Wyborn incited laughter and grins from the other two men. Creases wrinkled at the corners of his eyes, as the captain was barely able to control himself.

"Okay. Just finish the blooming tale and be done with it," the Aussie scientist interrupted.

"Go on," O'Brien, said through teeth clamped tightly around his cigar. "I can't wait to hear how this ends."

"The storm's furious. Raging." Wyland's Australian accent intoned, setting the stage for the finale. "The seas are riled and the wind's howling," the captain said, spewing out his embellishment. "Next thing you know this wave has got Mr. Burbridge, and he's skidding across the deck. Suddenly, his life line gets caught. Snaps right in two. No one can believe the bad luck he's having. And to make matters worse, poor old Skiddy just about went through the scuppers ending up in the drink." The three men laughed, each well aware of the sea's nature and the possibilities of what could have happened.

"Ah, bugger off," Skiddy Pete chuckled, letting the laughter die down. "Here's the rest of the story. What he didn't tell you mate, is that he's the bloke who came out and saved my bloody arse. If it had been me, I'd of left him for fish food."

The story had been a great ice breaker. Red O'Brien felt right at home amongst his new found cohorts. He was anxious to have Canton arrive and proceed with the latest task earmarked for the NESSA team. In the meantime, he would get to know the ship and enjoy the hospitality of his new found friends.

The three men ambled around Narissa's deck. O'Brien was enjoying the tales. Twenty-seven years in the service had fueled the fires of the ex-navy man's memory. The Irishman had his own stories to share. The warm air felt much better than the Pacific breezes blowing in over Puget Sound back in Seattle. Red O'Brien was beginning to enjoy NESSA's latest assignment, despite the trauma of having to climb aboard the helicopter and endure a flight out to the ship.

The men finally settled in on the bridge. Wyborn took O'Brien over to the chart table and showed him the course he had mapped out for the first leg of their journey. Once Canton was aboard, the Narissa would sail. Red O'Brien was looking forward to this job and being back out on the ocean. Clear skies and calm seas were forecast. A perfect sail. How could it get any better?

Chapter Twelve
Air Force One - Atlantic Ocean

"I'LL TAKE THAT REPORT, CAPTAIN," Benjamin Wolcott stated, in a matter of fact monotone. The Air Force officer responsible for its delivery handed it obediently to the West Point graduate. Years of military life equipped him with decisive abilities. Service alongside the chief executive had taught him invaluable lessons.

"Yes, sir," the Air Force captain replied.

"The president should be rising soon," he remarked, after rapidly eyeing the first two pages of the report. "If there's something that requires his immediate attention, I'll wake him." The officer waited for Wolcott to finish scanning the sheets. Within moments, he turned to the last page. "Thank you, captain," the presidential advisor added, without lifting his eyes from the paper.

Turning sharply, the Air Force officer walked away, leaving the president's advisor contemplating the six page report in more detail. The golden glow of morning's light spilled across the pages Benjamin Wolcott held in his hands. All in all, the world seemed at ease. Still, there was nothing positive to report on the Taiwanese problem that continued to rear its oppressive head. The economic blight in Europe was deteriorating into a mire of unforeseen consequences. Wolcott reflected. It almost seemed as if subversive plans to undermine the solvency of the Economic Union were being shaped by hidden agendas. It troubled him that a series of sequential events had occurred, bringing further turmoil into the world economy.

The president's advisor sat down and leaned deeply into the plush leather seat, loosening his tie. He had been awake since five o'clock Zurich time. Wolcott had caught up on writing several reports, and was perusing a stack of papers that required his scrutiny. The former military man possessed the ability to process and memorize a written page moments after reading it. Since his childhood, this talent had served him well. With the imperative demands of his job, spare moments were a precious commodity, and his unique talent, a remarkable asset.

Wolcott set aside the report, scouring the agenda for the economic conference. He had meticulously researched any and all information on the world leaders who would be in attendance. A quick smile flashed across his face and quickly disintegrated. An advantage in the game of world politics was never a bad thing.

The G-8 economic conference in Davos, Switzerland, held some very interesting possibilities for the president. Successful implementation of the president's financial strategies would buoy the dilemma facing the world. Still, there happened to be a line of hard edged dissent by some influential icons. Benjamin Wolcott was glad he was not the one responsible for jockeying the positions associated with the current state of affairs.

President Richard Simon awakened, rubbing a hand across his face, struggling to arouse himself from a deep sleep. Focusing in on his watch through bleary eyes, he realized he had captured over seven hours of much needed rest. He felt refreshed. Padding across the carpeted floor, the president shuffled quietly across the private suite, entering the bathroom. The shower's invigorating hot water erased the remains of clouded sleep. He whisked the razor around his face, erasing any traces of his growing stubble. Simon ran through a mental checklist of important details he had to key in on for his presentation. Convincing the world's *politicos* would not be an easy task, and he was counting heavily on Britain and Japan's assistance. Some other EU members in attendance were wary of U.S. intentions. They had become reticent in their outlook of the former administration's policies, which placed further demands on Simon's abilities to coalesce this group of world leaders into a unified force.

The intercom blared with the news that Air Force One was beginning its initial approach to Flughafen Zurich. The Swiss airport would be the gateway of the presidential entourage for the Davos conference. Richard Simon knew that the international press corps would ride this story hard for the next week or two, and then be forgotten as other momentary newsworthy events vied for public attention. However, the decisions reached by these eight world leaders would have much longer lasting implications.

Air Force One banked into a left turn. The familiar markings of this plane had been known the world over since the Kennedy administration, almost fifty years before. Bold, blue letters emblazoned on its fuselage spelled out United States of America. The well-known aircraft had stood as a symbol of democracy wherever it traveled around the globe. The expanse of runway 10 rose up quickly to greet the descending airplane, filling the cockpit windows of the 747-200B. The president's aircraft touched down softly, leaving puffs of bluish smoke trailing from the tires after hitting the runway.

The colonel piloting Air Force One followed the air traffic controller's direction to a secluded section of Zurich's terminal. The cold morning air bristled with security. Already stationed along the cordoned off area, U.S. Secret Service agents aggressively scanned their surroundings. Details had long been planned, and strategies envisioned in the case of any problems. Computer scenarios had spilled out numerous possibilities, and contingencies were in place in the event of the unthinkable.

Swiss military personnel, and the *Kantonpolizei,* members of the regional police force, hovered anxiously around the tarmac where the president's plane would park. Dignitaries of state were being afforded the highest security possible as they entered the country. Snipers discreetly placed on rooftops were concealed from public view. Tensions ran high throughout the cadre of leaders responsible for the detail. No one wanted problems. More than just careers were at stake. An attempted assassination on Swiss territory would undermine the long held theory of neutrality of the Swiss state, at least that was the common belief. Within the terminal and inner corridors of the Zurich airport, the *Stadtpolizei,* in their familiar bluish-gray uniforms, carefully eyed the flow of people awaiting arrivals and departures in the recently expanded complex.

"Ben. What's the latest? Get me up to speed," Richard Simon said, as he closed the door to his private suite behind him. Impeccably outfitted in a dark, blue suit, crisply starched, white button down, and red tie; the freshly shaven president looked ready for the world's press corps he would briefly address, after departing the plane. He took a seat as an Air Force steward offered the two men coffee.

"Actually," Wolcott spit out, "the political arena granted you a reprieve. Little has changed since we left D.C. There's a communiqué that just arrived from Senator Ramsey." The morning's light highlighted the boyish grin spreading across Wolcott's face.

Simon reached out and optimistically inspected the text. Drawing in a long breath, the president gave the paper a second look through.

His fingers traced a path across his cheek and settled around his chin, a habit of many years. Simon contemplated the message.

His advisor sat in silence. He allowed the nation's leader time to assimilate the profound significance of the message's implication. This man he had known for over ten years was not given to bouts of profound elation, and the president's response was much as he anticipated.

"Damn good job. I don't know how Ramsey managed to convince Senator Childers, but this gives us a narrow margin. I think we might be able to push this through the House and Senate." A wry smile stretched over the president's face as he shook his head still in disbelief over what he had just read.

Wolcott added, "It's about time we pass some measures of meaningful change for middle class citizens."

"Send along my congratulations. It's a great way to start the day."

"I'll take care of it, sir." Wolcott reached into his attaché and pulled out a copy of the day's itinerary. "I've spoken with Agent Reynolds. We are good to go. He's been in contact with Commander Reiner of the *Kantonpolizei*, Mr. President."

" Problems?" Simon asked, arching an eyebrow in response.

"No, sir," Wolcott replied, tightening the knot of his tie. "Everything's locked down and ready." He quickly stuffed the remainder of the papers scattered around him on the leather seat back into his case. The twin locks closed with a smart snap. "Anything else, sir?"

Simon sipped the remainder of the coffee and placed the mug on the table next to him. "No, Ben. I think that's it. Let's just hope the conference goes as well as this morning's news."

Wolcott nodded in response, "Let's pray that it does."

Agent Stan Reynolds' impressive stature filled the space in front of the chief executive as he moved along the open aisle. The agent was a walking example of 'brick and mortar,' with a pair of eyes that Simon thought could burn holes through steel. This man was all business. Reynolds had already informed the other team members that *Boxer* would be enroute shortly. A code name was given to the president as a way to clearly define who he was, especially in the event of an emergency. The Secret Service had dubbed the president with the title of *Boxer* after his favorite pastime.

Reynolds' recent assignment as the main man responsible for President Richard Simon's protection had come after fifteen years in the Secret Service. His exemplary commitment over the years added impressive weight to his resume, effectively aiding in his promotion. Though it had only been six weeks since the man he replaced had been killed in an inexplicable automobile accident, Reynolds felt at ease in his leadership role. Nothing would stop the agent from carrying out the duties his allegiance swore him to uphold. Exacting performance was the creed Agent Stan Reynolds required of himself for every task. He meant to see that this detail was no exception.

Wolcott rose from the supple leather, contemplating the latest addition to the president's team. The former military man ran through a snapshot mental checklist of the man's attributes. The stony face standing before him was impenetrable, devoid of emotion. Wolcott knew the man's mind was spinning the tumblers of possible scenarios even before the group deplaned.

Reynolds was a likeable enough fellow, at least to the other team members and they seemed comfortable enough with him. That was a required trait for all leaders. His dossier indicated that the agent was capable of appropriate decision making in crisis situation testing. He possessed adaptive instincts required of exigent assignments. Simply put, Reynolds passed the litmus test with flying colors. Reynolds' extremely high scores on the Agency's tests affirmed the validity of that point.

The presidential advisor had spoken to other agents assigned to the president's detail, and they too expressed confidence in their new leader. Wolcott had no doubt the man could perfunctorily perform whatever the situation deemed necessary. Trial by fire was a scenario Wolcott had faced himself in his own military life. He knew, as well as any other, the rigors of stress. The ability to detach oneself from lethal surroundings as bullets streaked by, and think clearly, was often the only life saver. Wolcott's assessment passed muster, and he felt confident in knowing that Agent Stan Reynolds would perform as he had been specifically instructed. Still, something about Reynolds rankled him.

Simon savored the last swallow of coffee and placed the mug on the table beside him. He raked his teeth across his lower lip, rubbing his chin. "Oh, Ben."

"Yes, sir," Wolcott replied, instantly.

"Get in touch with Admiral Sizemore. Set up a meeting upon our return. I want to know the latest on military presence in the Western Pacific. Should a crisis develop in the Taiwanese situation, I need to know how long it would take to deploy the appropriate firepower. Also, I want all the latest intel updates." President Richard Simon stood and brushed a hand through his graying hair. He glanced out the window onto the tarmac where a podium was surrounded by TV cameras and microphones. Security details hovered about, mouthing clipped statements into microphones as wary eyes surveyed the crowd. Simon took in a deep breath and shook off the slight twinge of nervousness. He turned from the window and smiled, "Shall we go meet the press, gentlemen?"

Chapter Thirteen
Frankfurt - Germany

BROODING SKIES HOVERING above the Frankfurt skyline threatened to turn the morning into a wet and miserable day. Bryson McGann had concluded his work at the Euro Ecology Summit. Kate Harper was remaining behind to wrap up the final details, before continuing on to the next several stops throughout the continent. NESSA's goal was to enhance its position with like agencies, and offer its assistance to fledgling operations in several other countries.

Frankfurt's Rhein-Mein airport bristled with activity; taxis, trains, buses, and private vehicles moved in and around the aerodrome. A major European aviation gateway, the terminal heralded passengers arriving and departing to and from destinations throughout the world. The continuous, deafening roar of jet engines attested to the activity taking place at the German air hub, keeping air traffic controllers well occupied. Thankfully, McGann did not have to suffer through the long lines of impatient travelers inside the terminus.

Parked on the south side of the airport at a private hangar in the General Aviation Terminal, the Gulfstream G550 with it's upturned wingtips, awaited Captain John Beech's and his co-pilot, Pat Evans' inspection. The duo did a once-around the sleek NESSA aircraft. Their pre-flight ritual always followed the same routine, and each man insisted on the need for two sets of eyes for the visual. Problems prevented on the ground translated into safe flights, which suited both pilots well. Satisfied, the men climbed the steps and entered the ultra high-tech cabin, waiting for their passenger to arrive.

McGann's hazel eyes took in the skies above as he stepped out of the Steigenberger hotel's transport vehicle. Something had been nagging at him. It left him with an unsettled feeling. McGann had learned to listen to that inner voice, but the root of its cause remained a mystery. Grabbing his bags, he zipped up his leather jacket in defense against the harsh temperature. His brown hair ruffled at the wind's calling as he strode across the tarmac. Moving around the front of the aircraft, McGann caught a wave from Evans behind the windscreen of the jet's cockpit. Bryson McGann tossed a retreating smile in the man's direction. The twin turbofan engines came to life in a rapidly whining, high-pitched noise, signaling the trio's imminent departure.

A black Mercedes passed through the gate and moved out into the private section of the airport. The driver accelerated, bringing the powerful engine to life as it bolted across the tarmac. Upon reaching the NESSA aircraft, the Mercedes screeched to a halt. Barely stopping, the driver threw open the door and called out, waving frantically. "*Herr* McGann."

McGann paused. Curious, he headed back down the steps in compliance with the man's wishes. Tall and thin, with glasses perched atop a beak-like nose, the driver walked hurriedly in McGann's direction.

"*Guten Tag,*" he began, wishing Bryson McGann a good day. "I am Joseph Edel," the tenor-pitched voice spewed out in heavily accented English. "The concierge received this just after you left this morning. I'm happy that I've not arrived too late." The hotel's employee held a package with the familiar blue and orange markings of a company who delivered on a world wide basis. Edel kept a tight grip on the box, feeling further explanation was needed. "It arrived by courier and is from the U.S." Performing in the perfunctory German manner, the young man spit out exactly what he had been instructed. "It's from a company in Colorado," the last word enunciated with difficulty. Suddenly unable to remember the name of the sender, the slightly embarrassed Edel's cheeks flushed momentarily. He turned the box around. "International Mining Technologies," he said, slurring the final word in his thickly, accented English.

McGann held out a hand. In the background, the engines revved, making the conversation more difficult. "*Danke,*" McGann tossed back, smiling at the young man.

Relieved that he had performed satisfactorily, Edel shot back with a regained confidence, "*Bitte, Herr McGann. Ich wuensche Ihnen eine gute Fahrt.*" McGann nodded in recognition, understanding perfectly the man's wishes for a safe journey. Without another word, the hotel employee turned and hurriedly retreated to the Mercedes. Engaging the seat belt and placing the automobile in gear, the young man spun the wheel of the hotel's expensive sedan, leaving the NESSA aircraft behind him.

"Hey, Bryson, what you got?" Beech asked, as McGann came aboard.

"Well, the good news is, it's not ticking," McGann volleyed, his familiar lopsided grin curling. "I guess I'll find out."

The radio crackled to life into the headset of the pilots, instructing them on runway clearance and the initial flight sequence. Hints of aviation fuel wafted into the cabin as the stairs folded automatically, and the door closed. Unlocking the brakes and checking their instrumentation, the aircraft taxied to the runway.

Cinched into his seat, McGann settled comfortably, letting his thoughts drift as the jet powered into the ashen skies. McGann threw a cursory glance out the window, watching Schwanheim, a suburb of Frankfurt, pass underneath the plane. Below, the Main River meandered quietly through the city, splitting it in half. The reaching spires of the downtown section of this German city reflected an almost Manhattan-like appearance. Since the post war days of World War Two, Frankfurt had grown into a city of diverse culture, becoming a premier financial center, home of the powerful European bank.

Unfortunately, the bombings of the Second World War had destroyed much of the old city of Frankfurt. The beautiful structures of traditional theme were mostly gone, although those remaining had become revered icons of previous days and simpler times, before the strife of war had brought about their destruction.

The onboard phone rang in front of Bryson McGann. Inquisitively, he picked it up. "McGann," he offered to the unknown party on the other end of the connection.

"Bryson."

McGann instantly recognized the voice of his father. "Did my package arrive in time?" McGann pictured the image of his father, Walter. Graying hair and slate-blue eyes, sharp and discerning. Intuitive and competent, the elder McGann had led IMT into a thriving business while at the helm of the international company.

"Hey, Dad," McGann answered. "It arrived just before we took off. I was getting ready to open it." McGann's hands tore open the package, revealing a set of gold dual scan nano discs encased in a small plastic container. There were six in all.

"Okay, I'm stumped," McGann said, cocking his head. "Hold on. Let me put you on the speaker." He touched a control button on the armrest next to him, adjusting the volume as his father continued the conversation.

"I finally got all the McGann family journals placed on disc. I know it's something you've been after for some time. The original handwritten accounts are in the family vault, but I think you'll recognize the voice of the individual reading the text. He owed me a favor."

"That's great," Bryson returned, sincerely. "Thanks. It'll give me something to investigate on the short hop to Amsterdam."

"By the way, I spoke with Randall Sumner yesterday. Things are going well on the undersea mining project at Billings. Actually, they're ahead of schedule."

"Good."

"Randall said he sent you packing on an all expense paid trip to Europe."

"Director Sumner has an eloquent sense of verbiage." The two men laughed, sharing the moment. "I am merely a humble servant," Bryson McGann quipped. "Did he tell you I'm escorting a Dr. Torfhildur Haroldson back to Seattle, and then on to Hawaii, for a sunny respite in the islands?"

Walter McGann remarked, "Do I detect a note of cynicism?"

"Well, Dad, duty calls. Perhaps Haroldson will be able to keep herself occupied without needing my services too often."

"It's all part of the package, son."

"Suppose it could be worse," Bryson McGann answered, glancing out on the landscape below.

"Can you hold just a second?" There was a brief silence before Walter McGann's voice came through the line. "Look, I've got another call coming in. Call me when you get back. I've got to come up to Seattle in a couple of weeks. We'll plan on getting together. Dinner?"

"Sounds like a deal. By the way, Dad, thanks again. I'm looking forward to hearing the audios."

"My pleasure. Take care. Love you, son."

"Me too, Dad."

McGann cradled the phone and opened the small case holding the metallic gold dual-scan nano discs. Picking up the first one, he felt the cool, smooth surface of the gleaming disc between his fingers. It caught the overhead lighting, and winked a momentary, starlight reflection of light back at him. Thanks to recent developments in the way information was processed and aligned for storage, these small discs were capable of holding vast amounts of data. Pressing the eject button on the console in front of him, the tray slid out soundlessly, anticipating its role in revealing the contents imbedded on the disc. McGann offered a voice command as the disc entered the machine. He pulled apart the headphones and seated them comfortably.

Passing through the brief intro, the booming bass voice of the well known black actor came to life reading the McGann manuscript. This living history instantly drew him into the past generations. A momentary glimpse into the life of Duncan McGann.

How could I have known four days ago that as dawn's light revealed slate gray skies clinging desperately to the rocky, granite faces looming over the landscape, fate would change life so desperately. It is with me now. I can still hear the whistling air of the brutish north wind blowing snow into swirling mists all around us. Black Elk and I left behind what had months ago been lush meadows, filled with the vibrant colors of wildflowers. Now, covered with winter's cloak, the trails lay hidden beneath a blanket of white. Our journey had encompassed several days of travel, from Denver up to Longmont. Now, in the early morning of November twenty-ninth, eighteen sixty-four, we were almost to the Cheyenne encampment. It is only at this time, that I realize the events of the past two years have been the catalyst for the incident of this day.

There were several recent accounts cited in the newspaper, detailing the war's progress these past few weeks. Thankfully, the Colorado territory had been spared the terrible carnage of the campaigns in the east. There had only been some minor incursions, until 1862, when Confederate General Henry Silbey's Texas force was soundly defeated at Glorietta Pass. The Union soldiers, along with members of the Colorado regiment, brought an end to the Texan's desire to move with will into the territory. Those unfortunate souls who died that day left behind little memory of themselves, as their blood seeped into the thirsty soil. All the while, men still perish in the bloody conflict choking the nation, while brothers fight and die, each believing they are taking arms for their version of a just and noble cause.

Silbey's resounding defeat added great credence to the Colorado governor, John Evans, and his abilities as a leader. I regarded him to be a fair and honest individual, having come to know him. Still, growing consternation between Evans and Chivington continued. It also fueled the animosity of the man responsible for the confederate Texan's defeat. The same John Chivington, whose unit distinguished itself in the Glorietta Pass battle, sought command of a regiment for the sole purpose, in his own words, to teach the Indians a lesson. His seething hatred for them was well known and applauded by many in the territory. Colonel Chivington had pressed many times for the permission to accomplish his heinous plan. He had been refused by Evans. Chivington was a man I despised, arrogant and assuming. I have no use for men of his caliber.

With the worries of civil unrest stifled, the only looming problem of the day were the Indian tribes. Autumn's passing brought a new season to the rugged peaks of the Rockies, and many bitter hearts were as cold as the coming snow. Black Kettle and the Cheyenne were entrenched upon their reservation and, for the most part, living peaceably. Unfortunately, Chivington manipulated matters to suit his own purposes, when Governor Evans left on a trip to Washington, D.C.

I wrapped myself tighter in the thick buffalo coat in an attempt to stave off the early morning cold that day. From under the beaver hat, my eyes scouted the horizon, a habit from years of exploring. Black Elk rode beside me, encased in the great bear's fur he had long ago killed, grateful for the warmth the beast provided. There was an uncertainty to the day. The feeling that something was wrong haunted me as Black Elk and I rode in silence to the Cheyenne camp at Sand Creek.

My memories caught up with me that early morning. It hardly seems six years had passed since our lives converged in a struggle where I saved Black Elk from certain death, and nearly lost my own. I have kept the gold nugget I found there at Dry Creek. That piece of metal has led us on an incredible journey, and spelled the path our lives would take. Our venture in the Colorado mining industry continues to flourish. We have many friends in Denver, but because Black Elk is Cheyenne, we are not without enemies in the wild Colorado territory. Envy and hate are words that fall easily from the tongues of numerous individuals.

In the distance a rifle shot spilt the air, ripping apart the morning stillness. Suddenly a volley of shots, followed by a cacophony of rifle and pistol reports erupted. We acted together, each spurring our mounts in the direction of the Cheyenne village. Pulling up on a rise, we were afforded a view of the devastation occurring below. Men in blue Union uniforms were engaged in an attack on the hapless village. The gruesome slaughter took on a surreal appearance as men, women, and children were butchered. Mounted troopers brandishing swords, wheeled into the unorganized group cutting down anyone in their paths. The savagery of their actions defied description.

Without thinking, Black Elk cried out and dug his heels into his horse's flank. The animal bolted, taking off at breakneck speed, careening into the melee. I had no choice but to follow my friend, knowing what needed doing.

Closing the distance behind Black Elk, I saw his hand fill with a pistol. The barrel erupted as he charged up behind a mounted trooper, pulling the trigger and taking off the back of the man's head. Another soldier shot and narrowly missed the Cheyenne. He, too, was not spared Black Elk's fury. In the distance, Black Elk saw his sister, Evening Star, running wildly with her firstborn held tightly in her arms. His horse charged as he fired another shot, missing the soldier chasing down the young woman.

At this point, there was no recourse except action. I came to the realization that no one would be willing to spare me because I decided to involve myself in someone else's affairs. An astonished soldier looked up at me when I came riding in, unsure of my intent for being involved in the bloodthirsty hostilities. The trooper hesitated an instant too long and missed with his shot. I charged by at a full gallop, kicking the man's head with the heel of my boot, sending him reeling backwards.

Gunpowder hovered like a thick fog throughout the camp as lives were taken, mostly on the unsuspecting. I had hoped the recognition of a white man in the melee, by those perpetrating this offense, would force them to cease their actions. It instead had the opposite effect. I became a target. The colonel wanted no witnesses to his regiment's atrocities, certainly not one who knew the governor. Our eyes met across the battlefield. His attempt to fire at me was blocked by an attacking Cheyenne warrior. It was then I lost sight of him, concerned by the events around me.

A young soldier fired at nearly point blank range, but his shaking hands caused him to miss. I gripped the horse tightly with my legs and loosed the reins. Pulling out my twin Navy Colt pistols, I turned and fired in one swift motion, dispatching this closest threat. From the corner of my eye, I spotted another invader raising his sword above the head of a screaming child. I acted quickly, shooting him through the heart without remorse.

I was sickened as I rode around the side of a lodging to find a soldier pulling his sword from the body of an old man. Listless eyes stared skyward from the cold ground at their assailant. Taken by surprise, he must have thought I was a part of his murderous band. His flushed cheeks wore a grotesque mask of satisfaction, his smiling face filled with missing teeth, peered up at me. He stepped closer to say something I could not distinguish above the clamor of battle. I watched the trooper mouth the words, 'damn bastards.' I raised both Colts ending any further comments with point blank shots to the head, spraying the ground with the blood of the dead man. The reports of weapons continued and the frigid morning was alive with the screams of those dying, and the angry sound of bullets ripping through the air.

In the distance, I somehow spied Black Elk in the frenzy. There was no turning back for the man whose people were being butchered. A kneeling soldier had taken careful aim and fired his Sharp's carbine directly at the Cheyenne. The bullet tore through his coat and exited, leaving a great hole in the fur. Inexplicably, the soldiers face filled with fear at the knowledge he had misjudged his shot. Black Elk threw his leg over the side of his horse and jumped off, landing on his feet on a dead run, directly at the soldier. The man's eyes widened in terror, knowing his attempt to reload was a futile effort. He stood in a feeble attempt to defend himself. The Cheyenne's knife hissed in the deadly air raking the man's throat. Black Elk did not even glance back as the man fell to the ground.

Black Elk's sister cried out for him. The Indian spun, drawing up his pistol, but it was too late. The sergeant, who had been chasing Evening Star, ran up behind her pulling the trigger as the heavy pistol bucked in his hand. Black Elk let out a scream of defiance. Firing without aiming, his first shot missed, but his second shot found its mark, dropping the man to his knees. Hate flowed from Black Elk like a raging river as he unleashed it upon the wounded sergeant. The Cheyenne's eyes were black coals alive with burning fury. He pulled the soldier to his feet by the hair of his head and sank the blade of his knife to its hilt into the soldier's stomach. With all his strength, he pulled the blade upward lifting the man off his feet. A quick death ensued. The Cheyenne let the body crumple to the ground, lifeless.

My heart sank, knowing that soldier's bullet had cored through Evening Star, taking her life and the baby she held tightly to her chest. Her body fell heavily, the ground around her stained with innocent blood. Black Elk helplessly sunk to his knees beside her, anguish etching his features. I hurried to Black Elk's side. Kneeling sorrowfully in the midst of the murderous inferno, the Cheyenne was oblivious to the threats raging all around him. I struggled to pull my friend to his feet. The agonizing rictus of grief encompassing Black Elk's face, imperceptibly yielded to the reality of the situation. Somehow, my words managed to convince him there was nothing further either of us could do for Evening Star and her child. If we stayed, we also would become Chivington's victims. Our only hope lay in fleeing along with those fortunate enough to miss death's greeting in the Colorado countryside.

The once peaceful village at Sand Creek had been turned into a savage battleground. Winter's albescent covering had been scarred with the crimson stain of death, and the undistinguished banner of inglorious murder, set forever upon the souls of those responsible for the massacre.

Duncan McGann - December 2nd, 1864

Bryson McGann was riveted at the tale told by his forefather. There was more to this particular entry, but it would have to wait. The entire nano disc encompassed many other sagas from his family history as he left the Sand Creek massacre behind. Until now, McGann had not noticed the descent. He felt the gentle pressure building in his ears. He looked out the window onto the Dutch countryside. Amsterdam's Schiphol Airport came into view as the jet casually turned to a new heading, continuing its descent. The pilots busied themselves with landing preparation. Tuned into the tower's radio frequency, they followed instructions, aligning the aircraft with runway 36 Right, as they prepared to land. From underneath the plane's belly, Bryson McGann felt and heard the mechanical sound of the hydraulics lowering the wheels into a locked position. Brisk winds buffeted the Gulfstream 550 as the runway drew closer. It rocked gently, but under the skilled hands of its pilots, touched down easily with a burst of smoke from the spinning tires. Within moments, the reverse thrusters were engaged, forcing the plane to decelerate. The aircraft quickly moved off the runway, while Evans pushed the radio button to select the proper ground control frequency. A voice broadcasting on one eighteen point nine five directed them to General Aviation East. This was the area in which all the business and private jets were allowed to park.

Beech rolled the Gulfstream up to the front of a hangar temporarily assigned to NESSA aircraft. The pitch of the twin engine's whine quieted as they shut down. From the cockpit, the clicking sound of toggles turning off instrumentation under the pilots direction, snapped in the small confines.

McGann grabbed his jacket. "We're a little early, guys," he stated to the two pilots. "Dr. Haroldson won't be through with the conference," McGann twisted his wrist, checking the time on his Breitling Colt Super Ocean, "for another hour or so," he finished.

"No problem, Mac," Evans tossed back. "It'll give us some time to gas up."

"Besides," Beech cut in, "I have to file a final flight plan with the tower. Also, we had a warning light flash on during the flight over. Probably nothing, but we'll check it out. Don't worry, we'll have everything tidied up by the time you get back with Frau Haroldson." The two men chuckled in unison. Even McGann smiled briefly. An electric motor signaled the opening of the fuselage door, inviting a chilling blast of cold air into the cabin. Automatically, the steps from the aircraft unfolded. Outside, the limousine waited to carry McGann to pick up NESSA's guest.

A hint of sunlight momentarily drilled through the dull, gray skies above. Thoughts of the German's wishes for a safe journey returned and taunted Bryson McGann. He had not been able to shake whatever was boiling up and troubling him. McGann finally zipped up the leather jacket and exited the plane, still haunted by the nagging feeling.

Chapter Fourteen
Schiphol Airport - Amsterdam

THE MAN KNOWN AS GREGOR DUVONICH evaporated shortly after leaving the rail station in Sibenik. His deceptive journey carried him through a number of European cities, before arriving at his final destination. Budapest, Venice, Gdansk, Stockholm, Hamburg, and finally, Amsterdam. Six cities in as many countries. Stephan Kholos had established routes all across the European continent. His notoriety never allowed him to travel anyway other than a circuitous and cautious route. Each city brought on a subtle change of character; a change in gait, a new hair color, a different face staring back from the passport at the customs agents in each terminal. Business, pleasure, sightseeing - names he casually pitched about to cloak the intent of his travels - satisfying the often bored inspectors.

Amsterdam, he knew from experience, posed the least problem of being recognized by members of international law enforcement. Despite this, Kholos never permitted an over exuberant confidence that would allow him to drop his guard. Still, he felt somewhat more relaxed whenever he paid a visit to the old city.

Memories of that cold winter night returned. It had been the starting point of his string of illicit deeds eighteen years before. The lessons he learned from that assignment honed the legend of his talent, pitching him deeper into a world of subterfuge.

General Eric DeVries, in charge of Dutch NATO forces, had left The Hague after a grueling day of meetings. Now just past ten o'clock, snow had begun blowing as the officer's car exited the parking lot. Thankfully, most of the city's traffic was not about the streets at this late hour.

The general's bodyguard, Hendrik Smit, mentally noted the slowly approaching headlights in the rearview mirror of the Mercedes. It took several minutes for the automobile to pass. Cautiously, Smit regarded the blue BMW and its two occupants as they gazed at the passengers in the Mercedes. The other automobile gradually increased the distance between them, allowing DeVries' driver to relax. Abruptly, the red glow of brake lights cut a swath into the night. The driver of the BMW spun the wheel hard, braking, and downshifting, and expertly reversed direction.

Smit had little time to react as the other automobile slammed head on into the front of the Mercedes. Momentarily shaken and realizing the danger facing the two military men, the officer's bodyguard shoved the gear lever into park. In the back seat, DeVries pulled a pistol from his briefcase, jacking the slide and chambering a round. Nothing about this perpetrated event came close to being termed an accident. DeVries' military experience had taught him enough lessons to understand the deadly nature of this intimate encounter.

The Mercedes grill works had been crushed, only one headlight functioned in the veil of steam spewing from the damaged radiator. This vapor added an unearthly touch to the scenario taking shape. Twisted metal lay upon the roadway as men scrambled for their footing on the slick pavement.

Kholos remembered the stop action drama playing out before him in a slow motion sequence of events. In the pitched gun battle that ensued, the sound of shots firing was dampened, seemingly from a distant place. The general's bodyguard fired first. Kholos' driver returned fire. Even though the men were within a few feet of each other, several bullets were dispatched before the first found its mark. Kholos turned his head at the sound of his driver's anguish, a bullet catching him in the right shoulder, a second grazing his right flank. Smit had found his target. His adversary triggered another shot, causing the NATO driver's feet to slip out from under him, pitching him to the cold street. A well aimed bullet to the throat took his life instantly, blowing out the base of his skull. The gory residue of what was once his life spattered on the ground and onto the general's woolen uniform as he exited the vehicle.

Kholos now raised his Heckler and Koch pistol, aiming at his intended adversary. The weapon bucked twice in his hands. The concussive force from the nine millimeter rounds blew in a warm wind around his face. His aim was true. The copper tipped, hollow point slugs struck their mark. The Dutch general was thrown heavily against the automobile, blood flowing freely from two ragged wounds in his chest. Somehow DeVries' hand held steady as he loosed a shot, striking Kholos' driver in the forehead. The man's body made a sickening sound falling heavily onto the pavement.

Kholos moved hastily around his open door. His foot slipped, but he quickly regained his balance. He remembered now the icy windows splashed with crimson, and a streak of his target's blood, where the general had slid, along the door panel. The Dutch army officer's eyes fluttered, blinking away the falling snow, bewilderment masking his features. Kholos hovered over his opponent, an arrant smirk filling his face. With each labored breath, the two wounds bubbled from the bloody air leaking from the officer's chest. Death eagerly anticipated another visitant into the realm of its lurid arena.

Kholos unremorsefully regarded the ebbing life of Eric DeVries, struggling vainly in attempt to raise his pistol in a gesture of defiance against his assassin. Kholos kicked the Dutch officer's pistol from his hand. At that moment, the recognition of defeat settled upon the pallid face of the NATO commander. Without another thought, Stephan Kholos emptied the remainder of the pistol's magazine into the man at his feet. Dispassionately, Kholos watched each projectile destroy flesh and bone, the dead man's body recoiling under the impact of every bullet. Ejected casings somersaulted in the air, pinging as they came in contact with the cold pavement. Cordite and blood mingled together in a strange scent, quickly carried away on the frigid winds.

Tales of his skills spread quickly throughout the shadowy corners of the world. Instantly, "The Greek" was in demand. Kholos continued to expand his horizons, linking into smuggling, drugs, and terrorist groups. The success of his accomplishments over the years were ones he profited from; not only in experience, but in secretive wealth stashed in numerous accounts around the globe.

Kholos planned every task with the steely sharpness predicated by a military mission. He analyzed each job upon completion; picking it apart, separating the minutia, reevaluating it, exploring the possibilities, and all the while, perfecting his talent. In his business, ignoring such things came with a morbid price tag attached.

Stephan Kholos became an enigma. Hushed tones were often used in conjunction with his name, revered and feared by those of dubious character. He had become the scourge of international law enforcement, and tops on the list of the world's most wanted criminals after his second successful political assassination.

All those times wreaking havoc upon the unsuspecting were preparation for what was to come. "The Greek" had never taken on simultaneous assignments in the past, but he was intrigued by the challenge.

Readily accepting.

His gift to the world was at hand. He had chosen living on the razor's edge and acknowledged its consequences. Stephan Kholos had built a reputation as a complicated and dangerous individual, yet he remained, always, the merchant of death.

No one from Sibenik, whose lives interconnected in the same circles as Gregor Duvonich, would have recognized the individual stepping out onto the sidewalk at Amsterdam's airport. Long hair fell out from under the black ball cap ensconced with a logo of the Dutch soccer team above the brim. A worn leather jacket draped his shoulders and slightly frayed jeans covered the tops of his leather boots. He looked much younger than his age, and fit in well with the thirty-something tourists crisscrossing the continent. Wary eyes cautiously surveyed his surroundings. Crushing the butt of the cigarette onto the sidewalk below his feet, Stephan Kholos exhaled a plume of white smoke.

The taxi had dropped Stephan Kholos off two blocks from Kazerne Straat. He ambled along, unnoticed by the locals and tourists who passed him by. He pretended to check out his location on a map, the wind rustling the paper as he unfolded it. Kholos knew precisely where he was. Assuring himself that he had not been followed, he walked the remaining distance to the dingy houseboat on Singelgracht Canal. Its polluted waters and mawkish scent hinted to the effluence dumped daily into the canals by those who lived on them. The boat had been in his possession for some time, evidenced by its faded and chipped paint. Kholos purposefully let the exterior appear weather beaten and well worn. He wanted no uninvited guests gawking at a luxurious boat that, in reality, had served as a safe house for many years.

Kholos stepped down onto the wooden deck and walked to the cabin, quickly eyeing the canal and street one more time. His fingers inserted a key, unlocking the door. Upon entering the darkened cabin, the snapping sound of the pistol's hammer drawing back rang in his ear. Hard steel pressed into the flesh of his neck.

"Very good. Even I was not expecting such a welcome."

"We've been expecting you," the woman's voice, holding the pistol, shot back.

"Now that I am here," Kholos never finished his sentence. In a blur of motion, he wheeled around and slid his hand on top of the pistol, bringing it to rest between the slide and hammer, pulling with a downward motion. He followed through with his other hand underneath the slender wrist, bending it to an acute angle.

"Stephan. Stop," the woman yelped.

The woman released her grip on the weapon. Kholos removed it from her hand, a smile spreading across his face. Pushing on the safety, he handed the gun back to its owner. "Sabrah, you've become remarkably better, but don't think I have lost my skills."

The dark-haired woman fell into his arms and kissed him fully. After a moment, they parted. "I have tea," she stated, arching an eyebrow as she glanced in his direction. She poured herself a cup of the steaming liquid, awaiting his reply.

"Yes."

"Everything's in place just as you planned. All the details have been rechecked to your exacting specification, Stephan."

His eyes rose from the rim of the cup to the slender figure sitting down across from him at the old wooden table. "There must be no mistakes." He pulled the remaining Dunhill from its pack and lit the English cigarette. "When it comes to a mission, I'm not foolish enough to think there cannot be problems."

"Stephan. I know you worry, but how can we fail?"

The woman's unfaltering desire to succeed had always held an alluring appeal for him. Yet Kholos knew well the dangers involved with that kind of thinking. "Overconfidence. Your zeal for a perfect mission without considering the unknown will get you killed, my darling." The air in the small cabin quickly grew stale from the burning cigarette. "I've changed the plan. Once we have what we came for, only you and I will be leaving with our guest," his tone flat, implying nothing more.

Her eyes widened in surprise to the news. "What brought this about?" she questioned, uncertainty filling her voice.

"Caution."

"And the others?" she responded, hesitantly.

Stephan Kholos set the half empty mug of tea upon the battered table. His eyes searched the face of the woman seated next to him. Her olive-bronze skin glowed radiantly in the dim light. Long brown hair hung around her shoulders, lighter highlights glinting under the bare bulb hanging over the couple. Sabrah's lithe features belied the fit and well-toned body underneath. He reflected upon the softness of her skin and the warmth of her breath. His mind wandered to their passions and quickly slipped away, regaining its focus. Her charming smile could disarm almost anyone. Yet Kholos knew well the capabilities Sabrah possessed. Under the veneer of a beautiful woman lay a heart, chilling as glacial ice.

"The Romanians are of no concern, they're fodder. Their accounts will be paid as promised. If they're caught by Amsterdam's *politie,* they can tell them very little. They only know what they need to know. Besides, they're all mercenaries, no better. None of them are unfamiliar with the various law enforcement agencies throughout Europe."

"Stephan Kholos, you're a hard man," the brown haired woman infused into the conversation, a laugh erupting from within. "And what's our plan of escape? You have given me the appointment of scripting your play, but I don't know the ending." Her eyes narrowed, staring deeply into the man of many talents. She sipped at the hot tea, tentatively swallowing the dark liquid. Letting the silence hang before she continued, Sabrah informed him of her own changes. "You have no reason to know this, but one of the men you hired is sitting in jail."

A look of consternation grew into an angry cloud upon "The Greek's" face. Eyes flared. "*Vastardos*." Without warning, his meaty fist smashed down upon the table, threatening to topple his mug, startling the woman. "What happened?" he snarled in a menacing growl, filling the cabin.

Stephan Kholos' anger demanded an answer. Sabrah eyed her companion, cautiously selecting her words. "Apparently, from what little I can gather, he couldn't hold his liquor. A problem with some other fool over a whore. He couldn't keep his dick in his pants. So, now we're a man short." The woman got up to pour herself another mug of tea, her chair scraping on the wooden floor. The sound knifed into Kholos, irritating him further. "Don't worry, Stephan, I have our answer."

"And what precisely is that?" he thundered.

A disarming smile shot out at him. "I'll take his place. It won't be a problem. I just won't be riding in the auto with you and our old friend."

Kholos considered her words carefully. He mulled the options, stirring the cauldron of possibilities and could come up with nothing. "The Greek" was left with no other option. His jaw tightened, exhaling through clenched teeth. He pressed the replay button of their conversation, and realized she had led him into a corner without the chance of any other possibilities. He knew if she had brought this up at the beginning of their meeting, he would have attempted to find a solution. Kholos loathed problems which caused him to disrupt the plans of his mission. However, at this point, there were no other choices. Sabrah knew the plans as well as he. "Very well," Kholos finished with a knowing nod of his head. "And what of the old man? Anything I should know of him?"

"Not really. He should be awake by now. I've told him to expect a trip with his new acquaintances," she chuckled, eyes gleaming. "I believe he realizes that any attempt to escape will be dealt with severely. I've made that explicitly clear to him on several occasions. I could be wrong, but I don't believe he will be any trouble."

"His tools?" Kholos interrupted.

"I took them the night I broke into his house."

She was good. Kholos admired her skill and professionalism. He was glad that he was not working against this woman. She possessed the ability to be a tenacious adversary. The unnerving image of a black widow spider came to mind. Deadly. In a word, the adjective that best described his accomplice.

"He's in the other room. Shackled," tossing her head in that direction.

"I want him healthy for the work he must do. Reflexes sharp. After that," his voice trailed.

"Mossel certainly has no possibility of dying from starvation," Sabrah replied. "I'm glad we are about to embark on our mission. I'm tired of feeding the old Jew."

Reaching into his jacket, Stephan Kholos pulled the red box from his pocket, ripping away the cellophane from the package. The gold letters emblazoned upon the container denoted the coveted Dunhill's.

The man from Sibenik thumbed the lighter drawing the flame to the tobacco and quickly exhaled the smoke. Kholos rose from the table. "I'll go and introduce myself to our new traveling companion."

Kholos' fiery gaze etched itself in the woman's mind. Sabrah was eager to proceed with the first part of his plan. The beautiful woman knew he was a master tactician, and not one to be crossed. She had heard of the results from that mistake. The Irishman's death had not been pleasant, although, she had to admit, the traitorous fool had it coming. As he walked passed, he stopped to kiss the woman. Faintly, the tobacco's stale taste passed between them. Fingers slid along her cheek, to her breast, feeling its roundness. He quickly stepped away, "Call the others. It is time."

Chapter Fifteen
Grand Krasnapolsky Hotel - Amsterdam

BRYSON MCGANN'S HOUR HAD LAPSED, sitting in the midst of a traffic tie up due to a careless Dutch driver. Several automobiles were tangled in a web of useless parts and broken glass on A 10, a major highway leading into the city. It only added to his downward spiraling mood. His attempts to contact the concierge at the hotel resulted in a dismal and perplexing dead end. Finally, traffic began to move and McGann checked his watch. If he was lucky, he would only be forty-five minutes late. Weaving through traffic as safely as possible, the taxi drew close to its destination. McGann was treated to a view of the impressive Koninklijk Paleis, the Dutch royal palace, and the rising obelisk of the National Monument. Wheeling around Dam Square, the driver pulled up in front of the well known edifice of the five star hotel.

McGann raced into the lobby of the Krasnapolsky, the sound of his footsteps pounding upon the tiled, marbled flooring. Behind an ornate wooden counter, several members of the hotel's staff smiled at his approach. McGann hurriedly asked directions to the conference room. Setting off across the vestibule, he hoped Dr. Haroldson would still be there. To his dismay, the room was unattended except for the hotel's cleaning crew.

"Excuse me," McGann asked, returning to the reservation desk.

The man replied with a thick accent pasted over his English, "Ah, you are back. May I help you?"

"Could you please ring Dr. Haroldson's room?" McGann locked on to the gold colored name pin above the upper left pocket of the man's blazer.

"Your name please, sir. And the room number?"

"McGann. I'm afraid I don't have that, Herr Meijer. Dr. Haroldson was one of the members attending the conference."

"If you will give me a moment, sir," the annoyed face returned.

Across the lobby, the woman took in the person of Bryson McGann. She eyed him carefully before making her way toward him. Outwardly, she found him attractive. Casually dressed. Tall, much to her liking in men. It was obvious that McGann kept himself in peak physical condition. The woman knew from the information she had received about him, he had an impressive history with many accomplishments in the military and his private life. McGann had packed a lot into his thirty-some years. While he waited for the Krasnapolsky's worker's reply, his eyes shifted, gathering in the activity surrounding him. Travelers moved in and out. Bellmen tugged at carts containing the luggage of those passing through the Dutch hostel. The woman sensed that very little passed by this man. She could tell he had an acute awareness of his environment, although his affect displayed an overall easygoing attitude.

"Herr McGann, I am afraid there's no answer. My records indicate Dr. Haroldson checked out fifteen minutes ago."

"Did she leave a message for me?" McGann was already spinning the wheels in hopes of finding the whereabouts of the good doctor. His mind raced on to the next option in locating the lady he was assigned to bring back to the States.

"Unfortunately, no," Meijer said, apologetically. "I'm sorry."

"Damn," McGann muttered under his breath.

"Is there anything else I may assist you with?"

"No, but thanks. Wait. What about a phone number, any luck with that?" McGann asked, hoping to find some way of contacting the woman. "She has to be somewhere."

The unexpected hand upon his arm vied for McGann's attention. He spun and stepped back, focusing in on the person standing next to him. Bryson McGann took in the gracile woman who seemed molded into the black leather outfit and boots. Her thick, platinum-blonde hair, layered into a punked out shag, fell to just above her shoulders, providing an enclave for inviting china blue eyes. Only a couple of inches shorter than McGann, she peered back at him and lent an appealing smile. When she spoke, her voice was soft, holding a sensuality all its own. "I'm Tori," she stated, offering her hand and a smile.

Hesitantly, McGann replied. "Who exactly are you?" he asked, baffled. The oddity of his day seemed to continue with the appearance of this stranger standing next to him.

"I'm Tori Haroldson," a slight frown of uncertainty knitting her brow line.

McGann's mouth opened. "I'm sorry, but I…" his words were cut off before he could finish.

"You are Bryson McGann?" her questioning, gouging at him.

"Yes."

"You are here to pick up Dr. Torfhildur Haroldson. Right?"

"Yeah," McGann shot back, intrigued and alerted by her knowledge of his assignment from NESSA's director.

"You're late and I've had a bad morning," her words now resonating with irritation. "I also have another stop to make before we leave."

"Whoa. You're Dr. Haroldson?" McGann queried. He shook his head, still unsure of the situation.

"Dah. Who else would I be? Didn't Randall tell you anything?"

Bryson McGann's mouth curled into a lop-sided grin as laughter erupted. "I can't believe this. You know Randall Sumner?"

"And what exactly is it you can't believe, Mr. McGann?" Tori Haroldson drew her hands up on her hips, legs spreading into a gunfighter's stance. Annoyance filled her voice. "For your information, I don't relish the thought of being laughed at by you or anyone else." Her tongue cut sharply, biting with an edgy caliber. Clearly, Tori Haroldson was not amused. Her flinty glare bore into him. "I've a suggestion for you. Let's go. I don't plan on missing my appointment, Mr. Bryson McGann. And, by the way, in response to your first question," she snapped, "I've known Randall Sumner since I was a child. He and my father are best of friends."

"You're Dr. Sigurd Haroldson's daughter?"

The woman turned, not bothering to answer his question. McGann had little choice but to follow. He scratched the back of his neck, realizing now why there had been nothing to indicate Haroldson's age, or a picture of the volcanologist. Director of NESSA, Randall Sumner, had pulled off the ruse and duped McGann. He could only imagine the Director grinning at McGann's thoughts of a matronly Dr. Haroldson. Those images could not be further from the truth. Tori Haroldson was, as he had to admit, inimitably attractive with a spitfire attitude. Hopefully, she would allow him to explain the predicament he had been placed in, or the trip home was going to be a long and lonely flight.

Haroldson was standing beside a limo as the driver placed her bags in the rear of the vehicle. She tossed a look over her shoulder, eyeing him impatiently. The blonde cocked her head in his direction, a signal that perhaps he should be moving more quickly. Complying to her wishes at this point would certainly be to his benefit. He jumped into the back seat as she spoke in fluent Dutch, informing the driver of their destination. When she finished, she turned toward McGann waiting for him to offer a challenge.

Haroldson sat silently, turned slightly away from him. He tucked into his memory a quick flash of the woman's profile. Tori Haroldson's skin was smooth, pale, attributing to her Icelandic heritage. The blonde's face was filled with a matched set of high cheekbones and a soft jaw line. Full red lips were tight with irritation that had not quelled. McGann allowed himself to settle in and relax. He realized that fighting the current was not the thing to do. For the moment, he was just along for the ride. Glancing out the window of the taxi, Bryson McGann carefully considered his words as they traveled along Vijzelstraat on their way to an art dealer's shop in the museum district of Amsterdam.

☙ ❧

The group had traveled by automobile from Antwerp. Belgium's second largest city was the world's hub of the diamond business, and precisely why Amsterdam had been chosen for the final destination of the Namibian gem.

The diamond factory charged with the stone's care was taking no chances. Its employees in the nondescript blue Mercedes adhered to the speed limit, carrying the four armed passengers and their precious cargo, to the agreed upon destination. The journey had taken the men on a secretive route that would soon end at a well known address on Paulus Pottersraat, in Amsterdam's museum district.

This particular firm of note had a significant history in the gemstone business. In eighteen fifty-two, they were charged by Prince Albert of England to again polish the surface of the famous one hundred and nine carat Koh-I-Noor diamond. This magnificent stone was part of England's crown jewels. Their diligence had renewed the illustrious beauty of the blue-white gem, returning life, under their skilled care, to its gleaming facets.

The Oduru diamond rested quietly in its familiar padded surroundings. Only after relinquishing the contents of the magnetically locked, heavily padded, titanium case would the cartel's four employees relax. The stone, which had been dug from the depths of a mine along the Namibian coast, longed for the intimate caress of the stonecutter's percipient hands. Once sculpted and polished to meticulous specifications, the massive diamond would be revealed to the world, capturing its astonishment. However, nothing had prepared the gem for what lay ahead.

Chapter Sixteen
Museum District - Amsterdam

THE MOTORCADE MOVED QUICKLY through the streets bordering the numerous canals in the enchanting Dutch city. Four pairs of white motorcycles, lights flashing, adorned with the blue and orange striping of the *politie,* moved in tandem, each pair roaring ahead to block off a street, leapfrogging the others. The four sets of imposters, clad in uniforms denoting their authority, moved expediently, halting traffic at various intersections. All of them were in constant radio contact with a surveillance vehicle tightly bound to the rear of the blue Mercedes carrying Peter Oduru's jewel. Every move came under intense scrutiny of the chase vehicle. Each turn was relayed via a scrambled signal to those following the course of "The Greek's" ingenious scheme. The four men charged with the safekeeping of the world's largest diamond were unaware of their fateful meeting with the holder of destiny's winning hand.

Kholos' fingers flew across the keys, the mini computer's navigation program selecting the streets swiftly, precisely. He was setting up a meet with those who carried his invaluable reward. Together, they would join their lives for only the briefest period. His calculations were quickly proving true. It would be a matter of moments before the accident occurred. In the end, there could be only one outcome. That result would be much to the liking of "The Greek."

The large diesel delivery truck, boldly adorned with a fictitious company painted on its side walls, moved under the guidance of Kholos' direction. It twisted and turned around the corners of the narrow streets according to his bidding, spewing black smoke from the tailpipe, as the driver shifted through the gears. The two men inside knew their assignment. There were no questions.

Sabrah turned her head, looking through the visor at Radi Corcesceau working the gearbox of the 1150 RT, BMW motorcycle. The last minute change of plans had left the Romanian unsettled. He had protested slightly, appeasing his own mind, but knew no other choice existed except to go through with the operation. Corcesceau did not place great credence in the mysterious woman. He seldom trusted anyone to whom he contracted his skills. Dealing with anyone but an inner circle of associates, brought with it the possibility of dire consequences; even then, uncertainty always loomed.

His was a game of perceptions. If they liked his resume and the others who worked with him, business could be done. Avoiding a bullet in the back when the mission was completed was a necessity. And always, there was the issue of reimbursement to consider - wired money sent from some distant place where bankers turned their heads so long as their reputable institution continued to acquire wealth - a sizeable down payment was always a requirement. Only once had payment in full not occurred. Corcesceau responded with a payment of his own, a nine millimeter slug sealing the deal.

The man and woman rode the heavy motorcycles through the streets, openly displaying their flashing lights, a call for everyone to move aside. Vehicles as well as pedestrians were compliant, quickly clearing streets and intersections so as not to interfere with police proceedings. She allowed herself a brief smile of self satisfaction at duping the populace in the old city's streets.

The voice in her headset crackled. "Ready?" Kholos asked from the rear seat of the black Lexus 430 sedan.

"Yes. We're moving up to block off the next intersection now."

"Sabrah, the truck is in position."

"Don't worry, Stephan. You won't be disappointed. I'll see to that by this evening. Interested?" his accomplice asked, suggestively.

"Stay focused," Kholos demanded. "Celebrate later."

Her headset emptied itself of the voice spilling out of it, replaced by the growl of the bike's four stroke, 2 cylinder boxer engine. Her hands, encased in black leather gloves, worked the throttle and depressed the clutch expertly, kicking the vehicle through its gears on a long stretch of pavement. Her partner followed suit, racing past a team already in place blocking an intersection, rapidly shaving the distance to the next street corner.

☙ ❧

McGann's attempt to mollify the renowned scientist was having little effect breaking through the crustiness of her temperament. Haroldson's silence intrigued him. Somehow, feelings had been hurt and he was the cause. It perplexed and annoyed him at the same time.

He wondered how he was responsible for committing an act of which he had been completely unaware. Their cab turned, leaving Bolstraat behind, moving into the sparse traffic on Baerlestraat. McGann caught a glimpse in the rearview mirror of flashing blue lights in a rapidly approaching motorcade. The taxi driver slowed and moved to the side, permitting the *official* entourage to pass. The NESSA employee's curiosity became aroused. Two police officers had slowed their bikes and prepared to stop, not allowing traffic through the next intersection. Unfortunately, the taxi driver was trailing too closely behind and had maneuvered around them. There was no time to stop.

Corcesceau's bike ran through a slick spot on the road causing him to swerve, nearly crashing the motorbike. He downshifted, eased back on the throttle, struggling to keep the bike upright. Sabrah's eyes riveted themselves in her rearview mirror. She watched Corcesceau's dilemma playing out, unaware of what caused his near mishap. Realizing he managed to regain control, her gaze shifted forward, alarmed that the cab had slipped through the checkpoint. The operation, so cautiously planned, now ventured into the unknown. Kholos' words of overconfidence rang in her ears. She hoped the haunting conversation would not prove true.

Wrenching back on the throttle, the front wheel of the motorcycle lifted from the ground momentarily and settled back upon the Amsterdam street. Her partner attempted to catch up but was still lagging behind. Sabrah called out into the microphone. "Stephan." Those were her last words before the mayhem started.

Bryson McGann leaned forward in his seat, instincts flaring, taking in the events unfolding before him. Instantly, the world outside the vehicle's windows changed before his eyes. McGann unconsciously processed each bit of information, becoming acutely aware of what was about to happen. Tori Haroldson turned her head at the unexpected sound. Before he could speak, her words were cut short by the lethal drama, as the cab driver slammed on his brakes.

Two blue-uniformed, mounted police officers happened into the intersection at precisely the wrong moment. Roaring into the cross streets, two of "The Greek's" cutthroats drove the heavy vehicle with deliberate design, crashing into the rear of the blue Mercedes. The back end of the sedan fishtailed wildly, sending the car careening into an oncoming van. The sounds of squealing tires and crashing metal momentarily petrified the two officers and pedestrians lining the streets, as waves of shock washed over them.

From the cab of the truck, a gunman jumped from the passenger's seat onto the pavement. His Russian made Bizon submachine gun sprayed a volley of nine millimeter rounds into the framework of the German car. The Romanian hit man's finger tightened once again on the trigger, quickly depleting the extended magazine. Forty rounds flew from the hot barrel taking lives indiscriminately, and creating havoc in the streets.

A man in the rear of the Mercedes died instantly amidst a hail of bullets and broken glass, while another guard was wounded. The remaining two men scurried out of the Mercedes and returned fire, sending lethal projectiles sailing through the cold air of Amsterdam's streets.

One of the mounted policeman attempted to call for assistance. Before he could act, his horse took a round in the right shoulder, splintering bone. Both animal and rider dropped to the pavement. The *politie's* leg snapped under the weight of his fallen horse. The panicked animal's frantic movements elicited agonizing cries of pain from both man and horse.

Momentarily, the second policeman was distracted by the screams and blood from his fallen comrade. His face clouded in uncertainty. The chilling clarity of the dilemma came to life when he fixed his gaze on the truck's other armed occupant. The officer yanked his weapon from its holster, snapping his arm into position to return fire. The swarthy features of the assailant came into focus along the pistol barrel. Unfortunately, the policeman's initial hesitant response became a costly mistake. The second Romanian's handgun erupted twice. Two gaping holes in the officer's chest were a solemn testimony to his assassin's accurate aim. The *politie* fell to the cold pavement,staring skyward with vacant eyes.

McGann reached out for Tori Haroldson, pulling her to the floor of the taxi, just as the windshield erupted into a spider web that formed from the onslaught of bullets. McGann knew instinctively there was no hope for the driver. The man's body slumped over the wheel as the vehicle drifted, rolling slowly. Its right front tire impacted the curb abruptly, bringing the taxi to a jarring halt.

"Out, now," McGann commanded, shouting at the woman to get her attention. He kicked open the door, and together they scrambled to the rear of the vehicle.

"What's happening?" Haroldson screamed above the cacophony.

A counterfeit police motorcycle quickly closed the distance between them, while the officer riding the bike unleashed a string of bullets, scarring the trunk just above their heads. Behind her, another bike was quickly approaching, its screaming engine echoing off the old brick buildings. McGann looked up to see a wounded man step around the taxi, pointing a gun at the couple. Realizing they were no threat, he stumbled forward and aimed at the approaching officer. He pulled the trigger. His shot went wide but the other man's bullet struck home, dropping the cartel employee.

Without hesitation, McGann leaped forward in one fluid motion, retrieving the dead man's pistol, rolling into a prone firing position. Both McGann's hands wrapped around the checkered grips with practiced ease. He unleashed two quick shots, spilling the rider. Radi Corcesceau's lifeless body slid across the slick pavement along with his motorcycle, sending up a shower of sparks and broken plastic.

Haroldson jumped up, eyes widening, witnessing the horror of the event. "Are you crazy?" the doctor's voice shouted from behind him. "You just shot a policeman." Littered upon the surrounding sidewalks were the bodies of the wounded and dead. McGann moved quickly beside her, pulling the doctor back to the relative safety of the rear of the taxi.

"If you don't keep your head down, you'll be next." McGann peered out from under the automobile. The two remaining cartel employees continued firing. Suddenly, one of the two drivers of the truck dropped heavily to the ground, unmoving. Without warning, the black Lexus that passed the taxi McGann and Haroldson were riding in, slid into the intersection, tires squealing in protest. The passenger in the rear seat opened fire, instantly killing one of the Oduru diamond's protectors. Several motorcycles, engines screaming like angry bees, also joined in the frenzy. The last cartel employee had only moments to live.

Bryson McGann made his decision. "Stay here and keep your head down." He took off, firing his pistol on the run. After three shots, the other member of the truck driving team fell dead. McGann whirled at the sound behind him, his finger taking up the slack in the trigger. "What the hell are you doing? I told you to sit still."

"I'm not staying there by myself," she cried out defiantly. "As far as I'm concerned, I'm a witness. It doesn't look like these people want any. So, I'm sticking with you." Haroldson's face was a portrait of fierce determination. She was not giving ground, and McGann had no time to argue.

"Keep your head down, damn it. And don't get your ass shot. You move when I tell you to." His hazel-green eyes bore into her with riveting intensity. He did not need to say anymore. "Let's go."

The duo raced to the rear of the smashed delivery truck. The dead driver's Bizon offered greater fire power than the spent pistol. McGann scooped up the submachine gun, and detached the empty magazine. He patted down the dead man, finding a spare sixty-four round magazine, and inserting it. Pulling back the bolt, the Russian weapon was made ready for its grim assignment. Taking a quick glance around the front of the truck, McGann saw two approaching motorcycles. He stepped out of the cover and held down the trigger. Both riders went down, of no more concern.

Stephan Kholos had killed one of the two remaining men guarding the diamond. The one cartel employee who was left, was now out of his direct line of fire. Kholos held his position, waiting patiently for the man to make a fatal mistake.

The noise of gunfire drew his attention. Someone was firing from behind the truck just as Sabrah roared past on her motorbike. Bullets sailed harmlessly around the woman as she sped past the Mercedes. He watched her fire, and strike the remaining guard. Kholos knew this was his opportunity. He ran from the cover of the Lexus to the cartel's vehicle. A heavily padded case lay on the floor. "I've got it," he shouted into the thin microphone next to his chin. "Everybody out. Now."

McGann rushed out onto the street to fire at the man carrying the heavy case. In the distance, the sounds of police sirens filled the air. The noise of gunfire withered, becoming sporadic. Suddenly, two more motor bikes came roaring through the intersection, providing protection for the diamond thief's escape. McGann aimed carefully at the imposters, letting loose with several controlled bursts.

Stephan Kholos ran back to the Lexus, thankful for the distraction. Instinctively, he turned at the sound of automatic fire, knowing it must have been the person by the truck. He jumped into the back of his vehicle as the Romanian driver placed the gear in drive and spun the wheel. The eight cylinders of the sedan's powerful engine roared to life, its tires screeching on the pavement.

McGann's aim was accurate. Almost simultaneously, the two motorcycle assailants fell from their bikes, their bodies cart-wheeling across the street. There was no need to worry about them trading shots. McGann's weapon locked open, signifying an empty magazine. The buzzing sound of the lone motorbike's revving engine caught his attention. The rider held a pistol out at McGann, pumping the trigger, sending a string of lethal projectiles heading in his direction. McGann had no time to reload as chunks of pavement flew up around him under his assassin's fire.

Haroldson's blue eyes dilated at the bloodbath taking place, chest pounding from the effects of her own adrenaline. A bullet sailed past, dangerously close, slamming into the metal framework of the truck behind her. Only sight and sound seemed real, and that had become a blur of motion and a distant ripping sound of automatic fire and sporadic pistol shots. She had seen McGann drop the two riders and another firing in his direction. Haroldson's eyes went from the rider to the pistol. She reacted without thinking, her own words sounding as if they came from a deep abyss. Tori Haroldson dropped to the ground and picked up the weapon at her feet. "McGann," she yelled.

Bryson McGann caught the weapon Haroldson tossed in his direction. He did a shoulder roll, coming up into a one knee kneeling stance. He had moved just in time. The motorcycle's rider had found her mark, unleashing the remaining bullets that would have ended his life.

Sabrah dropped her now empty pistol and concentrated on escaping. Her hands and feet worked the controls. The BMW motorcycle did not hesitate, responding to her needs. Kholos voice filled her earpiece. "Meet me," his only words. She began her response when her cry returned into Kholos' headset.

McGann's arms came up, extending out into a two-handed grip on the pistol. He tracked his adversary and unleashed three rounds. The first missed its target, the next two struck perfectly. Shredding from the blast of the slug, the rear tire of the motorcycle lost its grip causing the bike to fishtail. Sabrah's attempt to regain control failed when the second bullet struck her right thigh.

Stephan Kholos turned automatically at the sound of Sabrah's pained voice, contempt filling his face. McGann moved out quickly from the side of the truck only to see the Lexus speeding away. Hate filled eyes returned his stare through the rear glass of the heavy sedan. Bryson McGann let the image of the man burn into his memory. The vehicle rocketed down the roadway, leaving behind the grisly scene, and left McGann no chance for a shot at stopping whoever had propagated this well executed event.

Turning his attention to the motorcycle rider, NESSA's employee walked cautiously toward the fallen accomplice, pistol at the ready. He noticed the person was still alive. She held one hand tightly to her thigh to staunch the bleeding from the bullet that furrowed through skin. Although it was a painful wound, she would survive. McGann dropped to his knees, pressing the warm barrel of the pistol into the chest of the downed rider.

Through the darkened visor of the helmet, Sabrah suspiciously eyed his approach. Her leg ached from the wound. However, when the man shoved the pistol roughly into her chest, the focus of her pain abruptly quelled, waiting for the bullet that would end her life. Sabrah dare not move. Neither the man or the woman looked like police, not that it mattered. Obviously, he had no compunction about killing.

"What the hell was that all about?" Tori Haroldson cried out, physically shaken from the event. She took in the scene of the carnage littering Baerlestraat, now filled with the blood of mostly innocent victims. The cries of a half dozen wounded survivors replaced the sound of bullets. In all, eighteen unwary victims had met their fate. The dead were scattered about, some laying with limbs bent at awkward angles. People were beginning to help the survivors. "Who in God's name were those people?" Her eyes betrayed the gripping anguish tearing at her gut.

The sound of the sirens grew closer. McGann patted the woman down, removing a folding knife from her pocket. Undoing the chin strap, he pulled the helmet off the pseudo officer's head, revealing a beautiful woman with long dark hair. On the olive-bronze skin of her neck was a small tattoo of a star cluster and the ancient, mythical

Scylla. McGann was perplexed by the situation. The last thing he expected was a woman, and a deadly one at that. McGann unleashed a withering stare. "I'm not particularly fond of people shooting at me."

Sabrah's eyes spoke defiantly, hatred spilling out in a thick ooze with her vexatious curse. "*Pigene esting Colassy.*"

"*Issos essy na dihnes tan dromo?*" Bryson McGann fired back in Greek, surprising the murderess. The grim meaning of his words, that of attaining her place in hell long before him, were not lost upon the woman. Without looking up, McGann replied to Tori Haroldson's question, "I don't have a clue who these people are." He slowly turned his head toward her, before finishing his remark, "But, I do plan on finding out."

She let the silence hang between them. Nervously, the woman licked her lips. Her body trembled from the after effects of adrenaline and the gruesome scenario that had played out before her eyes. The doctor reflected on how badly her day had started, and how much worse it could have been. A slight mist crept into the corners of her eyes. Her mouth and throat were dry, imparting a raspy hoarseness to her voice, making it difficult to speak. She finally pushed out the words. "Well, Mr. Bryson McGann, perhaps we should start our day over," a fragile smile etching itself briefly upon her face.

"I could think of a few ways to make it more pleasant," McGann returned.

"Me too," she added, attempting to further defuse the situation.

"Oh, Dr. Haroldson?"

"Yeah."

"I think you can forget about that appointment today," McGann added, wryly. She noticed his eyes had softened and a smile crept into the corners of his mouth. Tori Haroldson's gaze lingered, realizing there was more to Bryson McGann than what was indicated in the bio she had received.

Much more.

Chapter Seventeen
Cairo - Egypt

THE GREAT RIVER HAD SEEN ITS SHARE of civilization over the millennia. Flowing out from one of its remotest headstreams, thousands of miles from the sea in Burundi, the great waterway traveled northward from this central African country. The people living along its banks had depended upon the Nile for transportation, food, and a host of other things vital to their existence for eons.

The woman discarded the colorful brochure she had picked up off the back seat of the cab without finishing it, disinterested. Her intentions for arriving in Cairo were far from learning a lesson about its history or tourist industry. Her mother had been born in the city. She was well aware of its trappings.

Barely an hour had passed since the ink had dried upon her passport. Sahtay impatiently traversed the dust-clogged streets of the ancient city in the back seat of a grimy cab. Her driver offered explanations for their delay as they made their way through the crowds jamming the streets. She replied coldly in Arabic that she was not a tourist and did not need his commentary. His forehead wrinkled into a frown, and his black mustache hovered over pursed lips. Muttering quietly, the taxi driver lit a cigarette, the smell of its harsh tobacco drifting back toward her. Outside her window, Cairo's populace gave no notice to the traveler.

Resting beside the wooden dock, the *felucca* gently rode the dirty waters of the Nile. A familiar site along the river, these small wooden boats, rigged with a triangular sail, were readily available for hire. Tourists could take day trips or pay for passages of several days. However, this was not the case with this boat as it strained its moorings. Its pilot waited nervously for his second passenger to arrive. The first one had raised hackles of alarm until the vacant stare of the Sphinx, printed upon the wad of one hundred pound Egyptian notes she stuffed into his hand, had changed his mind. He was a businessman after all, and Shaban Azmy was in the business of making money. If she wanted to pay above and beyond the customary fee, he would not argue. Azmy was also smart enough to keep his mouth shut.

A swirling cloud of dust enveloped the taxi as the cab's tires ground against the loose gravel, coming to a halt at the prescribed destination along the river. The woman offered money for her fare. The image of smoke curling from the cigarette bouncing up and down between the driver's lips, filled the rear view mirror. Speaking in rapid Arabic, he intimated her payment was much less than customary. His hand shot up and the thumb and forefinger of his right hand formed an inverted 'V,' which he placed over the left index finger. He demanded more. What he got in return sent a cold chill shooting along his spine.

Sahtay crumpled the bills in her fist, stuffing them back into her bag, finding no humor in his Arabian gesture of lewd sexual practices. She smiled serenely and in a voice just above a whisper, spoke quickly to the driver in a menacing fashion. It caught him completely off guard. His eyes grew wide in response to her words. No woman dare speak to an Arabic man this way. He turned in his seat to face his passenger. The driver unexpectedly felt the razor sharpness of the steel blade tucked neatly under his chin. His mouth fell open silently. The man's eyes stared into hers, mirrors reflected the frightened features of his own face. Slicing off his testicles and stuffing them into his mouth now seemed a real possibility. Sweat gathered across his brow, trickling into the corner of his left eye. He barely noticed the sting, rapidly blinking it away. Her smile evaporated as she cocked her head, waiting for his response. The woman's inimical expression never wavered until fear completely enveloped him. The taxi driver croaked out a hoarse reply, defeated, and the blade disappeared. No further words were needed. Sahtay closed the taxi's door. The vehicle quickly disappeared, leaving behind a choking cloud of brown dust.

Without looking back, she walked across the plank onto the wooden boat. Taking his cue, Azmy instructed the young apprentice to loosen the ropes. Ezmat Taiwab scampered onto the dock, releasing the boat's moorings and hurried across the plank onto the deck. The felucca moved out into the main current of the Nile.

Fortunately, the weather at this time of year was relatively cool by Egyptian standards. An urging breeze pushed the boat along against the current. Shaban Azmy's calloused hands worked the tiller sending the boat into deeper waters, as the wind rippled through his galabiyya.

Although the long cotton garment offered protection from the effects of the harsh sun, still his skin was tanned a leathery brown from years working his trade.

Once into the mainstream of the river, the pilot called out to his young apprentice to steer the boat. Shaban poured himself a cup of the hot *karkaday,* allowing the soothing taste of the milky hibiscus tea to relax him. He lit a cigarette, inquisitively watching the two women, wondering what their conversation was about and making sure Ezmat operated the tiller skillfully.

Solange poured two cups of the strong Egyptian tea, handing one to her companion. "Did you know there's been a problem?" Solange uttered, barely above a whisper.

Sahtay turned her head, letting her eyes settle on the olive-skinned woman seated next to her near the bow of the felucca, before replying. "What is the nature of this dilemma?"

"Amsterdam has created problems for us."

Sahtay sighed, "Mossel?"

"Far from that," Solange offered. "Stephan has assured me that our friend will be arriving with the complete package. That's the good news."

"So what can be so bad?" Sahtay asked, uncertainty lingering in the undercurrent of her words. "Stephan's plans for escorting our guests to join us are still…"

Anger boiling at the reminder of the disruption of their plotted scheme, Solange sliced a hand through the air, stopping the woman in mid sentence. "I warned him. He never listens. Last minute changes."

Sahtay countered, her eyes narrowing into a mask of concern, "What exactly are you talking about?"

"Problems with the team. One of the players couldn't keep his pants on. He ended up in a jail cell because of some *mouni*."

"Has he divulged any information?" she spit back, captured and concerned by the mounting drama.

"Not as far as we can tell," Solange returned. She cast her eyes up and down the river, watching the sunlight ripple upon the wind-stirred waters. "At least, not yet. However…" her voice trailed. The boat's sail ruffled and snapped. Ezmat quickly corrected their course, the sail billowing once again. This brought a smile to the pilot's features. "Once the pieces of the puzzle are put together, who knows." She continued, “Worse matters are at hand. Sabrah is under constant guard in a Dutch hospital.”

Sahtay attempted to shift into a more comfortable position, feeling the sinews of her shoulders begin to tighten. Agitation crept into the corners of her mind as the possible scenarios played out before her. “How?”

“Kholos said Sabrah insisted on substituting for the Romanian. There was no other choice. She knew the plans as well as anyone. Circumstances dictated a change of script, and fate added an uninvited guest who decided to play hero. The latest news reports state that an American, someone named McGann, working for NESSA, intervened.” Her slender fingers spread and turned palms up in a gesture of contempt for the man she did not know.

“I have heard of that agency,” the olive-skinned woman, seated beside Solange, interjected.

“It doesn’t matter,” she said flatly, turning her head to meet the dark eyes boring into her. “He killed Corcesceau and several others. Kholos told me that Sabrah was attempting to get away when he shot her, too.”

“Exploration and science are a far cry from the lethal skills this man has added to his list of talents. And what of Sabrah?”

“For now, nothing. She will not talk. I have intentionally kept certain information from her,” Solange answered, brushing aside her long dark hair to reveal the tattoo on her neck. “Unfortunately, nothing can be done for her now.”

“We must plan carefully for her escape. Thankfully, the Germans or Italians don’t have her.” Sahtay sipped at the milky tea provided by their host. “So who’ll be escorting Mossel?” she questioned.

“Stephan’s driver. They’re already aboard the chartered plane. He was Corcesceau’s second in command. When he arrives with the old man, he will be disposed of quickly. Stephan has no further use for him. Besides, that’s one less mouth to be concerned with, even though he knows little else.”

Sahtay nodded in agreement before continuing.

“Do you believe Kholos is prepared to carry out the rest of our plans?” Solange asked pointedly. Her voice harbored a tense quality, hoping their plot was not unraveling before them.

Solange's counterpart flashed a soothing smile. "You don't need to worry about that. Everything will continue on schedule."

"You have Stephan's assurances, no doubt," a hint of skepticism tracing her voice.

"His record is flawless," Sahtay offered, encouragingly. "Even you must admit that."

"Yes, that is true, although, there's a first time for everything." Her lips parted, revealing white teeth surrounded by a grimace of uncertainty. Solange let the words slide slowly. "Let's focus on the next part of our plan. We can do nothing for him at this point. He has his people in place." The dark-haired woman's own words placated the undercurrent of her concern, providing a salve for a festering sore. "If all goes well, we'll be together soon." Solange's mood lightened, allowing a wisp of a smile. "Let's enjoy what is left of the trip. Our plane departs this evening. For now, let's just savor the moment together."

"And them?" Sahtay asked, with a slight tilt of her head sent in the direction of the felucca's stern.

"They are of no matter." Solange set her empty cup on the table between them, wiping her lips with the linen napkin. "I have paid Azmy handsomely for his efforts, and he also knows of my demands for discretion. Besides, killing them would only bring about unneeded troubles."

Shaban Azmy scratched at the gray mustache resting upon his sun-creased face. His apprentice had learned his skills well. The young boy was no expert, but his hands could hold a steady course. Under Azmy's tutelage, his apprentice would learn much about the way of Egypt's Nile.

Over the course of time, Shaban knew that the mighty river had seen its share of mystery and intriguing events. It occurred to him that the meeting of these two women did not happen by mere circumstance. There was an aura of foreboding in their whispered conversations. The pilot neither cared or needed to know its context.

Mindful of his place, Azmy muttered a silent prayer to Allah. His petition of fortune was meant to be far more than the generous fee he had been paid. The river pilot preferred on this night to sleep well in his home, rather than being found sleeping eternally in one of Cairo's darkened alleys.

Shaban Azmy let the thoughts of these calculating strangers pass away on the balmy breezes playing over the ancient river's waters.

Chapter Eighteen
Politie Headquarters - Amsterdam

MARION TURNER TAPPED HER PENCIL in a thrumming drumbeat upon the desk. Her irritation at being kept on hold for such a prolonged time was bubbling to the surface. Turner was iron and steel when it came to the business that fell into her realm of control at NESSA. Working for Randall Sumner had taught her many lessons over the years, and her knockout punch style at getting things done was well known at the Seattle organization. She was not a woman who waited patiently when it came to official business.

Finally, a face appeared on the video screen of her phone. The police officer apologized for the delay and proceeded to give excuses why Comissaris Jochem van Woort was not available.

"Perhaps I did not make myself clear, officer Peterson. You are holding in custody one of our employees. You may also be interested in knowing that Director Randall Sumner is a personal friend of Commissioner van Woort. When the commissioner eventually receives this message, and he will…" Turner paused briefly, tapping the pencil in a pronounced cadence. Sumner's assistant sighed heavily and then continued, "I'll be delighted to mention your name. I'm sure the commissioner will enjoy speaking with you regarding your inability to provide assistance to one of his dearest friends." Turner adjusted her glasses, sending a burning stare into the face on the screen in front of her.

"Madame, if you'll give me a moment, I will try again." The policeman's voice indicated he understood perfectly the nature of the meaning of her intimation.

Turner knew she had captured his attention, so she yanked hard to set the hook, just to insure he would return. "I don't expect to be kept waiting like before." Her clipped statement did not offer any indications that she expected a reply, only action.

Within less than a minute, another face appeared upon her screen. A man nearly Sumner's age, cherubic looking with coarse white hair and stern eyes, greeted her. "I am Comissaris van Woort. I'm not accustomed to having my meetings interrupted. However, when officer Peterson said you worked for Randall Sumner, I acquiesced. What may I do for you, Ms. Turner?"

Turner was unfazed by his brusque response. She picked up where she left off with the other policeman. "Due to the events in Amsterdam earlier today, Assistant Projects Director, Bryson McGann, and Dr. Torfhildur Haroldson, were taken into custody." Turner spit out her words in a rapid-fire southern accent. "Obviously, there has been some unfortunate misunderstanding. Director Sumner wishes to speak with you about the event and secure their release. You'll wait one moment while I put Director Sumner on the phone." Without giving him the opportunity to respond, Marion Turner placed the high-ranking official on hold. The Dutch police officer mused to himself that if he had half of his force with as much *chutzpah* as Sumner's personal assistant, they could accomplish much more.

"Yes, Marion," Sumner responded to Turner's voice pouring through the intercom. Turner informed NESSA's top official of the incoming call which he readily accepted. Sumner punched a control and a three dimensional holographic image of his friend appeared in the middle of his office. "Jochem, good to talk with you. It's been a while. I'm sorry to call and disturb you."

The police commissioner cut him off. "It is no bother. Nice speaking with you, old friend, although the circumstances are, shall we say, perplexing." A brief smile curled across his wide mouth.

"Then you're familiar with the events of today," Sumner questioned.

"Quite."

In typical Sumner fashion, mincing little when it came to words, he asked, "What can I do to clear this up? Obviously, Bryson McGann and Dr. Haroldson were not the perpetrators of this heinous debacle that occurred. By the way, I'm terribly sorry for the loss of innocent life. My condolences."

"Thank you, Randall. I had to tell one of the officer's wives about his murder. I have never relished that task."

"An unfortunate aspect of the business, I'm afraid." Sumner stuffed the pipe into the leather pouch of tobacco, pushing just the right amount into the bowl, carefully tamping the contents. The lighter flared in his hand. A puff of smoke filled the air momentarily.

"I see you haven't given up on your bad habit," van Woort chuckled.

"Everyone needs at least one vice," a brief grin came and went in response to his friend's chiding. "Now about McGann?"

"I've been dealing personally with the matter, Randall. Actually, he and Dr. Haroldson are here in my office as we speak. I've shared a couple of stories with them about our younger years when we were assigned to NATO." The commissioner erupted into laughter brought about by some pleasant memories.

"I can only imagine," the NESSA chief replied. Sumner got up from his desk. Outside on the streets below, Seattle rode the wave of daily life. For the moment, that was all forgotten as the Director focused on the holographic image of his friend.

"Randall," the Dutch police officer's tone reverted back into a more official structure. "Ordinarily, the fact that Mr. McGann took it upon himself to get involved with a matter of this importance could have serious implications. I'm also reminded that his actions saved the lives of a number of bystanders, and allowed us to apprehend a prisoner. She is out…"

"She?" Sumner questioned, drawing on the stem of his pipe.

"Yes, a woman. We don't know who she is at this point," a weighty sigh spilled out behind his words. "We're waiting on replies to our international inquiries. So far…" his words trailed into a brief pause. Sumner let the air hang, not wanting to interrupt at this point. "She's in surgery at the moment, having some of Mr. McGann's handiwork undone. I'm told she'll live. The wound was not life threatening. Once she is no longer sedated, we will find some answers." The Dutch police commissioner left little doubt that it would be accomplished.

Sumner fingered the polished briarwood bowl of his pipe, exhaling a thick plume of smoke. "Thank you very much, Jochem. I am deeply appreciative of all you've done." The director glanced out the window of his office as sunlight appeared from behind a cloud and filled his enclave. The view of Mt. Rainier was spectacular. Its snow capped peak covered the long extinct volcano, miles to the southeast of the West Coast city. Diverting his attention back to the image of the Dutch police official, the former general continued. "Is there anything else I can do? If there are any international laws that…"

A thin smile evaporated quickly upon the face of the policeman. Waving a hand to signify the dilemma had reached its end, van Woort interrupted his long time friend. "We're prepared to let Mr. McGann and Dr. Haroldson leave. Any final paperwork or details at this point can be handled by fax. We have both of their sworn testimonies, so I suspect there's little else we need at this point. Would you care to speak with Mr. McGann?"

"Certainly."

"Good. I shall leave you alone with Mr. McGann and Dr. Haroldson. I look forward to your next visit, Randall."

"Until then, Jochem," Sumner watched as the Dutchman left the room and the familiar face of Bryson McGann appeared along with Haroldson. "Tori. It's been far too long, and you're as beautiful as ever. I hadn't thought our meeting would be under these circumstances."

"It's great to see you, Randall," the doctor tossed out. "Believe me, after today, I'm just thankful to be alive." Haroldson had recovered from the shock of the gun battle, but Sumner could tell by her strained features that its effects would be far reaching. Death at the hands of violence never faded easily from one's memory. The ghosts of friends from his own military days haunted his past. Sumner pushed it back down into a deep recess, allowing her to continue.

"I," Tori stammered. She threw her head back and peered directly into the face of NESSA's director. "I want you to know, if it wasn't for Mr. McGann, I probably wouldn't be talking with you."

Sumner nodded his head in silence, raising the knurled, glass disc above the pipe bowl, rekindling its contents. Sumner had watched this woman grow from a child into a well-respected professional, and her pain cut to the very core. A mist grew at the corners of her blue eyes. "Fortunately, you're safe. I hope you can put this behind you."

McGann interjected, "Director."

Sumner remarked, "It seems you have tied the cat's tails together again, Bryson. You have an uncanny ability to find yourself involved in impossible situations. You either have nine lives, or the gods smile favorably on you." NESSA's director returned to his desk and sat down. "Bryson, thank you. If something had happened to Tori…"

"I appreciate that, but no thanks needed." McGann's lopsided grin appeared, wryly adding, "I'm just glad to be walking in my own skin."

Tori Haroldson had to admit she was impressed with the man standing before her. Their initial meeting had come apart at the seams. In retrospect, she realized McGann was completely unaware of who she was. His responses had been genuine, given the circumstances. She had put him on a defensive track, irritable now with herself for her own lack of patience. She rubbed her thumb and forefinger together, a nervous habit acquired from childhood.

There seemed to be two Bryson McGann's. One who had been capable of killing, automated and accurate. No thought, just action as demanded by the circumstances laid out before him. A man who was no stranger to situations like the one they faced together this morning. Death had played its hand and McGann rose up to meet the challenge. His actions were instinctual as much as they were initiated by training. Tori Haroldson believed that Bryson McGann acted not only out of the need to protect themselves, but also, out of the responsibility to respond because of his ability to do so. She realized that anything else would have been far less than his being demanded.

Tori Haroldson also sensed there was another side to this man standing before her. She had seen it in his eyes after the day's events had played out. Something burned deeply within him that led McGann to walk a line of deep conviction in doing what he believed was right. Although she had known him briefly, she considered herself a good read of character. He was a man of honest intent. He lived his life fully. Bryson McGann was a man capable of great passion. Haroldson's thoughts melted at the return of Sumner's voice.

"Jochem will send me a full report. I am anxious to see what the official spin on this matter is."

"Whoever perpetrated this crime had it well planned. They were after something of great value and nothing or no one was going to deter them from accomplishing their mission," McGann injected. "I have my own ideas. Commissioner van Woort was very tight lipped about the entire event. He seemed rather edgy."

"Understandably so," Sumner responded.

"To a certain extent, I agree. However, I got a sense he knew more than he was telling, and I don't think the media will have the answer anytime soon, if I'm correct."

Sumner slipped his hand around the pipe and placed it on the ashtray upon his desk. His forefinger sawed back and forth along the edge of his lower lip. "What exactly do you mean?"

"From what I witnessed today, the official spin, and what I can garner from the limited news reports," McGann paused. His brow furrowed contemplating his choice of words before he continued. "Somebody wants this shut down for whatever reason. Why, I don't know. I'm curious, but I think we should wait to finish this conversation until we return."

"Agreed." Sumner shot back.

A faint knock sounded on the door behind McGann and Haroldson as a uniformed officer entered, informing them he would be taking them to the airport. He closed the door behind himself after telling them he would be right outside.

"I guess that's our invitation to leave," McGann said. "Miss Haroldson, after you."

"Dinner at Martin's," Sumner added, watching the images fade as the hologram disappeared. Escaping the world's craziness was becoming problematic even for ordinary citizens. The one debt everyone eventually pays took without discrimination in Amsterdam's streets. Hapless souls in the right place at the wrong time paid the price; only to be transformed into earthen covered memories stained with tears.

NESSA's director wondered what McGann knew of the situation. What had been so important that had cost the lives of innocent people? His friend in Amsterdam had not been extravagant with details. Under the situation, Sumner thought that perhaps he might not be either. It was not a matter of trust, and he did not take it personally. As a former military commander, he knew there were times when discussion was not an option. The director rubbed his fingers along the curve of his chin. Perhaps time would be the telling factor to the mystery of mayhem that occurred in the Dutch streets. At this point there was nothing left to be done. The former general mentally filed the matter, knowing that McGann's gut instincts were seldom wrong.

Chapter Nineteen

Narissa - Timor Sea

JOE CANTON STEPPED OUT from the glass encased cockpit of the Sikorsky S-76 onto the painted white metal decking of the Narissa's helipad. The chopper's pilot, John Busby, shut down the engines as the waning octaves of the turbines signaled an end to their task. Canton tucked his head in response to the whooshing sound of the slowing rotors revolving above him. He peered out across the deck through the polarized lenses, searching for a familiar face. Canton heard the laughter before he saw the man behind him. He turned, knowing the familiar face of Red O'Brien would be standing there with a cigar stuffed into the corner of his mouth. Canton wondered sometimes if the Irishman had been born with one.

"Hey, Joe. How the hell are you?"

A smile flashed a set of white teeth at the Irishman. "Pretty good, Red. It looks like you've taken well to your new digs." Canton nodded in the direction of the smaller man standing next to him. "Whose your friend?"

"You sure are a big bloke," the man offered, extending his hand. Well tanned and clad in shorts and a T shirt, the smaller man continued, "Skiddy Pete's the name, mate. Welcome aboard."

"Joe Canton. Pleasure to meet you." The big man cocked his head with a puzzled look pointed in Red O'Brien's direction.

"Know what you're thinking, Joe. Odd name. You're right. It's a story for later."

"Well, I can't wait to hear it."

Busby walked out from behind the other side of the helicopter painted with the AGSI's colors. "Hey, mate. Forgot your bag."

"Thanks," Canton responded, relieving the pilot of the weighty case.

"Joe. Let's head up to the bridge and I'll introduce you to Ryan Wyborn. He's the captain of this old rust bucket."

"I'd say this old rust bucket is in pretty good shape, Red," Canton remarked.

"She's a fine lady. We've been through a couple of good goes together. Still got all her parts," Skiddy Pete mused.

Canton quickly warmed to the man's affable style and could see why O'Brien had taken a liking to the Australian. The big man gave the Narissa a celeritous once over, and quickly realized that the AGSI boys were all no nonsense when it came to maintaining their equipment. Canton surmised that the Narissa was a relatively new vessel. She was spotless, nothing loose or out of place lay about the decks. NESSA's assistant projects director was impressed by the well seasoned crew and their dedication to their floating home.

From the stern, the deep rumbling of powerful diesels erupted, signaling the engines coming to life. The metallic clanking of the anchor's heavy metal chain being hauled into place at the bow of the ship drifted back towards him. Within moments, the research vessel set sail. Imperceptibly at first, the Narissa moved forward, quickly picking up speed while her bow parted the clear blue water, sending sheets of white spray along her sides.

From the azure sky above, tropical heat blazed upon the aqua blue waters of the Timor Sea. The scenario was picturesque. Canton turned for one last glance before entering the wheelhouse. Cool air greeted the trio upon entering the confines of the air conditioned space. Wyborn lifted his head from the chart table, offering a smile to the newest member of Narissa's crew.

Handshakes and introductions, followed by conversation, ensued. Histories were passed as the men got to know each other. The mix was good and Canton felt at ease with the Aussies.

"Jeff, would you mind taking Mr. Canton's bag to his quarters?" Wyborn asked one of the on duty crew manning the bridge.

"That's Joe." Canton tossed in.

"Okay, Joe it is."

"Be happy to, Captain," the crewman replied.

"We'll get you situated a bit later, Joe," the Australian captain's accent poured out. Wyborn checked his watch and cast a long glance ahead of the ship. The outside world was a mix of sky and sea, blended into an indiscernible point, on that fictitious spot known as the horizon. "If you don't mind, I'd like to go over a few things about the journey. That fit in your pocket okay?"

Canton nodded in reply. "The devil's in the details, as they say."

"Anybody hungry?" Skiddy Pete questioned. "We can talk over lunch."

"You don't have to ask me twice," Red O'Brien tossed back.

The ever-smiling, sandy-haired helicopter pilot shot through the door, and tossed down his flight bag in the corner. "Hey, Cap. What time you serving lunch on this old tub?"

"Strange thing about Busby," the captain joked. "The bloke's got a nose like a shark. If there's food, he'll find it, alright. Well, Buz. We've just about wrapped up the grand tour. I guess now is as good a time as any."

"So, let's go. I might grow a wrinkle standing here much longer."

On their way to the mess, they passed a large room brimming with electronics. "Mind if I take a look?" Canton ventured.

"Be my guest," Wyborn replied.

Canton ambled over to the bank of hardware, impressed by what he saw. "Looks like you've got some top of the line items. Underwater acoustic positioning and side scanning sonar?"

"Sure enough, mate," Skiddy Pete replied. "Comes standard with long and short baseline."

"We also have a multi-beam echo-sounder, latest GPS equipment, and sat com. If you need to make a call, feel free," the captain added.

"Pete, you sound like you're trying to sell a car," the cigar chomping Irishman chimed in, his comment invoking smiles amongst the group.

Self sufficient, the Narissa's hi-tech capabilities were completely capable of providing everything the survey group would need for Project T. The arrays and output circuitries were laid out in a bank of faceplates, teaming with dials and switches. Adorning the electronic marvels were sets of multicolored blinking lights. Numerous three dimensional video screens waited to be called upon to produce the images needed for the deep sea exploration. Humming in barely audible tones, the electronics exuded an intrinsic scent and a slight warmth, oblivious to Canton's scrutiny. "You even have over the horizon radar? Impressive."

"There's a relay from the bridge's unit. This boat's loaded with all the latest computerized navigational gadgetry imaginable." Skiddy Pete remarked, his facing beaming like a proud father of a newborn baby boy.

"It's amazing how you can use atmospheric reflection and refraction to widen the range capability of radar beyond your line of sight," Canton remarked.

Pete cackled, "Sure enough, mate. OTH is the crackers."

O'Brien raised an eyebrow and readjusted the well-worn cigar. "OTH, A or B?"

"B. I'm rather partial to the back scatter system. It has some obvious advantages," the captain interjected. "Old Pete worked pretty hard to get us all this mechanical wizardry."

"Must've told some pretty good lies to get that kind of money," Red cut in, eliciting laughter from the group.

"Couldn't of done without him though," Wyborn replied. "It's great stuff. But still, there's nothing like your own eyes and ears when you're out on the briny. Eh, mate?" Wyborn led the way with Canton and O'Brien close on his heels. The other two Aussies followed suit, expectantly waiting to see what the ship's galley master would serve up.

The calamari had been excellent. Lightly breaded and crisply fried, possessing a tenderness that attested to its recent departure from the blue realm, it paired well with the light salad of mixed greens and raspberry vinaigrette dressing. Cold and refreshing pineapple sorbet proved to be the perfect accompaniment to the chef's midday repast.

Two carafes of freshly ground, rich, dark coffee followed, while the men continued their conversations about their assignment.

"As everyone's aware of, the Pacific has no buoy system for tsunami detection in this part of the world," Skiddy Pete stated.

"It certainly would've been helpful in December of '04," O'Brien winced. The painful memories of the staggering loss of life returned as Canton replied. "The undersea earthquake in the Indian Ocean sparked a tsunami of incredible proportion. The loss of life was staggering. Red and I went in with a team from NESSA to the hardest hit areas along the Sumatran coast."

"Had there been a warning system in place, it may not have helped many of those people in that area." Busby offered.

"That's mostly true," Canton returned.

"Yeah, but if a system had been in place, countless others around the Indian Ocean danger zone would still be alive," Pete added.

"True," the chopper pilot added. "A lot more blokes in Sri Lanka would be alive today, that's for sure."

"There were no means to relay information about the seismic event and potential devastation half a world away in a timely fashion. It was too late for most, when it was finally understood what was going on," Joe Canton responded.

"Precisely why we're here and prepared to undertake this venture with NESSA," the ship's captain cut in. Pressing a button on the control panel of his chair, Wyborn darkened the lights at the other end of the room. A map of the southwestern Pacific appeared before the men. Their present location was marked by a flashing green marker off the northern coast of Australia. The captain worked the display, enlarging a section of the area they were sailing in. "Joe, would you do the honors?"

"By all means," he returned, his palm turning upward toward the ship's officer.

Canton touched the controls and expertly maneuvered to exactly the place on the map the Narissa would be sailing. Quickly tapping a few buttons on his own control panel, Canton highlighted an area of the Pacific, then enlarged it. "This, gentlemen, is the area where we'll be doing some investigation." A detailed version of the previous map burst forth onto the screen. Dotted with hundreds of islands, the eastern edge of Indonesia was on display before them. "The Narissa will sail past the Lesser Sunda islands and into the Banda Sea. As I'm sure everyone knows, this area is within the ring of fire and is host to numerous underwater quakes and volcanic events."

O'Brien asked the obvious question on each person's mind. "Ryan, how fast will this old bucket go? And when do you figure we'll arrive?"

"With the current speeds and predicted weather conditions, we should arrive in less than two days."

The men continued to discuss the joint venture and deliberate on the plans for when they arrived at their destination. Several hours passed as the team of men worked out details for the survey. Finally, the decision was made for a well deserved break. There would be plenty of time for further discussion in the ensuing days.

The men gathered their belongings and went topside, greeted by a fiery, golden orb. Since the beginning, a brilliant tropical sun had ridden the skies above this aqua marine world below. Its duty now, keeping a quiescent vigil over the research vessel, Narissa.

Chapter Twenty
Sula Kai - Banda Sea, Indonesia

IT WAS AS IF THE GEM had been placed carefully by hand upon the azure waters of the Banda Sea. A tropical paradise with lush vegetation and a ring of sandy, white beaches encompassed the remote island. Off shore, an ancient coral reef rose up nearly to the surface, surrounding the island, except for the cut that allowed access to the ocean depths beyond. At the change of tides, this channel harbored pelagic fish from the deeper ocean waters. These creatures, intent on feeding on the smaller reef dwellers, had practiced this cycle of events over countless eons. Nature had played its hand well at Sula Kai. For most, it would be a destination longed for only in dreams. However, this private island possessed its own secrets that were hidden to the outside world, and they were meant to stay that way.

The events of underwater life were far from the mind of the man sitting under the bank of bright, circular lights. The room's temperature was cold. It was the way he liked it when he was enmeshed in his life's calling. Behind the mask, practiced eyes carefully guided the skilled hands through their work. Besides, he had little choice. The woman's subtle, but uncompromising threats, haunted his memory.

Seated across from him, the face of an Asian woman stared back from behind her own mask, watching the craftsman at work. A nurse with convoluted connections to the darker side of life, it was not by coincidence she was chosen for this assignment. Noi Lin's resume had spoken well for itself. She jumped at the offer, tired of barely making ends meet and little respect. Lin knew better than to ask many questions. After her brief interview, there had been no need for a reminder. Her hiring incentive had proven quite lucrative. Once finished, retirement would come. At forty-one, it was not a bad deal.

Lin and the other team members involved in this complicated surgical procedure did their jobs well and that was enough. Noi Lin's capability of anticipating Henke's needs attested to her talents, deftly passing off instruments, rarely speaking. That was also the way he liked it. The surgeon had no use for idle chatter when so much was demanded.

In the background, the muted tones of his assistants were drowned out by the ardent vocals, stinging riffs, and pulsing bass beats, all kept together by the band's drummer, pumping from the surround sound speakers. The only time Henke listened to edgy hard rock was in the surgical suite. It grated irritatingly on everyone, but he found it relaxing when facing the arduous strains of a complicated surgery. The doctor raised his eyes briefly, indicating a needed adjustment to the overhead light. Noi Lin complied, reaching upward, moving the large round light into place, illuminating his operative field.

He sat back in the chair, paused, and concentrated his focus through the powerful magnifying loops attached to his glasses. Meticulously pondering the nuances he must achieve for perfection, Dr. Mick Henke continued on. Several more hours would pass before he completed work on his patient. What started with an unwilling cadaver and a patient of similar bone structure to his replacement, had morphed into an exact replica of a current political leader, but only after all the blood vessels, major nerves, and skin were reattached.

Dr. Mick Henke had no love of politics or its leaders. To him they were all the same: dealmakers, seeing to their own needs for the good of the party. Self-ascribed heroes for the cause, rallying around the flag of their own country, bent on agendas prescribed by their own dictum, or worse. He swallowed the bitter flavor and refocused on his work.

Henke wondered at Solange's ability to scour the globe for candidates. An immense data bank had to be at her beckoned call. He could not fathom the woman's ability to gather such a vast amount of information. Henke believed she had to have connections with some very important people, ones he had no desire of knowing their names.

The doctor exhaled in a long sigh and adjusted his neck, snapping the bones into alignment and relaxing the taut muscles. Facial transplants had been the thing of myth until just a few years before. The Miami surgeon has spent countless hours investigating, studying, and practicing computer generated images, virtual patients, until satisfied with his own skills. The surgical procedure performed on the first candidate had gone as expected. The next three progressed satisfactorily, and this man's new face was coming together quite well. The doctor knew it would be weeks before the final healing occurred and his patient could pass for the selected world leader he would replace.

In a few days the impostor would be spirited off to another location for intensive training; vocal, nuances of character, and recuperation. It would be some time before he was released to tackle his assignment. Time was something his employer had aplenty.

Mick Henke raised a hand and simultaneously it was filled with the needed suture. The fine blue synthetic thread would stitch together the remaining section of skin into the hairline behind the ear. Within a brief period, the scars would vanish except under the most careful inspection. Lin wiped away a rivulet of blood while the curved needle cored a path through the patient's dermal layer. In a blur of practiced motion, the plastic surgeon tied an incredibly fine knot and laid the needle holder down on the drape covering the patient's body. Lin quietly gathered all the instruments while a count of each and everything was made. She left nothing to chance.

Henke knew it was a waste of time, having mentally accounted for every piece of equipment, sponge, and suture used. He stood and carefully tugged at his right sleeve, removing it and the glove in one swift motion. The rest of the blue protective garment followed and was tossed aside. Reaching up, he removed the loops and admired his handiwork. There was no evidence of bleeding under the skin and blood return in the facial skin seemed appropriate. Confident, Henke left the suite without a word. He knew what lay ahead. After this many hours he needed three things; a piss, food, and a couple of drinks.

Mick Henke poured his third Tanqueray and tonic. Free from the surgical garb, the light breezes of the early evening cooled his skin under the silk shirt and pants. Overhead, the revolving paddles of the fan circulated the warm breeze flowing in from the ocean. Seated under the shaded deck of the compound's magnificent house, Henke swirled the refreshing liquid and ice, sipping eagerly. The alcohol's soothing effects were taking hold, allowing the stress of surgery to wane like the fading colors of a tropical sunset.

Peering from behind the dark, polarized lenses of his glasses, the doctor gazed inquisitively at the tanned figure below. She idly walked the beach below the cliff, gazing out towards the crashing surf at the reef's edge in the distance. He picked up the compact binoculars and quickly adjusted the focus. A smile filled his face. Everything in perfect proportion.

"Like what you see?" the familiar voice called out from behind him, interrupting his lurid thoughts.

Henke sat the glasses down, turning his head to the woman taking a seat next to him. "As a matter of fact, she is quite lovely," the surgeon said, raising his glass towards his host.

"Don't even think about it. She's off limits," Solange returned caustically.

"Never hurts to dream."

"How did everything go?" she asked, changing the course of their conversation.

"There should be no problems. If all is well by tomorrow, the chip can be safely implanted in a couple of days. It'll be relatively easy compared to the surgery."

"Come," Solange invited, offering her hand. "Walk with me." The beautiful woman's demeanor turned to another tangent. Henke realized how dangerous this woman was, and yet, something about her stirred him. Their chemistry blended in a swirl of spiraling passions. She felt it, too. There would be time later, but only if she chose to do so.

"You know how important this project is to me," she intoned demurely.

"It's obvious by the money you pay me," he said, toying with the beads of water condensing on his glass.

"Are you not curious?"

Mick Henke paused, weighing the possible responses, choosing his words wisely. "Look, let's get something straight. I'm happy to take your money."

The couple walked together through the well tended tropical grounds. Lush vegetation and a dazzling array of floral colors accentuated a landscape seemingly painted with the skill of a master artisan. Sweet scents hung heavily in the air. Henke examined the woman next to him, her olive-bronze skin flawless, radiant. "I've surmised much more since my services were originally requested in this venture. To put it simply, I know when to keep my mouth shut."

The woman smiled coyly. She noticed a sheen of perspiration on his forehead which she knew was due less to the tropical climate than to the white-hot topic they were discussing. Her lips parted, preparing to speak.

Henke stopped her from continuing, holding up a hand. "Let me finish," the doctor commanded, the effects of the alcohol loosening his tongue.

"Fine," her eyes flashed in momentary defiance.

"I've done exactly as you ask. I'll continue to do so. Once all this is complete, I'm troubled by the fact that I'll be no further use to you." Henke's brow knit together, concern filling his face. "You're a woman of reckoning, Solange." The physician tossed back the remaining gin. "I'm sure your conscience would suffer little despair if I suddenly turned up missing. However, I am not without a few face cards of my own. I have, shall we say, respected friends in some very important places."

In a mocking tone, Solange returned the serve that placed a streaking shot into center court, "Are you threatening me?" Her head snapped in his direction, sunlight playing over the strands of dark hair moving in cadence with her body. "You should be very careful," her tone flat, devoid of any emotion.

Her sudden change in attitude ate cancerously into his very core. An electric chill raced along his spine. Holding the upper hand by a thin margin, he pressed ahead. "If I should suddenly vanish, there would be repercussions." Henke let the silence hang between them.

Solange contemplated her options. "Mick," the beautiful woman stopped, turning her head and peering directly into his eyes. "I appreciate your loyalty. You don't have to worry about your future health. I can assure you of that."

Henke took little comfort in the words spoken to mollify his concerns She was a skilled craftsman in the art of deception. Either way the script read, he walked a fine steel edge. Should the need arise, there would be time at some future point to make good on his own plan, at least he hoped.

Solange slid her fingers along his cheek, tracing a line past his chin and trailing to his chest. She moved closer. Purposefully, she slid her body in close to him, letting her lips brush sensuously against his. Her face pressed closely to his ear, whispering words that chilled him. "The world travels in small circles, Dr. Henke. You may be surprised to find that we know many of the same people," intimating much from her statement. Solange pulled away as Henke peered into the deep well of her black orbs. Her stare filled a void of vacant emotions, the eyes of a predator, he reflected. His attention was suddenly drawn to her left eye. Oculus sinister, the medical terminology, flashed through his mind. There was an almost imperceptible difference between the two. He wondered why he had never noticed it until now. Henke dismissed it, more concerned at his attempt to read the woman's true intentions.

Solange's final sentence bit in callously. "Now, Mick," her words ignited with malicious overtones of indignation, "Don't ever threaten me again."

Chapter Twenty-One
Davos - Switzerland

ECONOMICS WAS THE FUEL that stoked the burning fires of the eight world leaders' conversations. Simon had a few allies - a couple on the fence, and one or two so disenchanted with his predecessor - they were very troublesome in their dealings with him. His feelings of irony were not unfounded when the smiling group gathered for the obligatory photos that would be promulgated by the media.

Their forecast of world trade and future economic indicators hung heavily over all the group. Decisions of past conferences made in the closed meetings had long been a thing of speculation, with theories of global conspiracy. Words spoken by a United States president almost twenty years before in a telling speech directed at the American public, alluding to a new world order, had raised concerns for more than a few individuals. The words had taken on a meaning of complicity and deleterious intent. Now, whenever a conference of world leaders occurred directing a course of action, those scandalous ideas rose to the surface.

Simon's goal was to change the heart and minds of his own citizenry, and that of the world. The demands were heavy to repair the damage. Long discussions with Benjamin Wolcott, numerous other top advisors in government, and the private sector had supported his own beliefs that change of a positive nature could occur. This monumental meeting would mark the start of a long distance race designed to turn the tables and provide some sensibility to the problems at hand.

Davos had sparkled under sunny skies until the predicted weather front moved across the Swiss Alps, delivering a heavy layer of clouds and threatening rain. The wind's teeth bared themselves in the cold breezes, kidnapping the mountain retreat, not unlike the egos, tempers, and bravados that flared at times into raging maelstroms. Those accords which invoked thoughts of collaboration among delegates and those that pointedly caused an unwillingness to change direction, were the lynchpins of Simon's potential success. Richard Simon juggled an almost insurmountable agenda, somehow managing to wade through the jumbled confusion, directing the talks into line with what he felt would be beneficial to his colleagues.

He was 'step by step' winning a newfound respect, not only for himself, but for his country also. Elevating the status of America in the eyes of the world was the challenge of his office. If successful, he would be heralded in the history books. If he failed, the president preferred not to think about that.

After a long day of wrangling, Richard Simon was exhausted. He had just sat down when a knock sounded on the door of his suite. It opened, and Benjamin Wolcott entered along with Stan Reynolds, and two other Secret Service agents. "I'm sorry to bother you, sir. I just received a request from French president, Henri Becque. He's asking to speak with you privately. He indicated he fully realizes the imposition, but asked me to tell you it's urgent." Wolcott finished his remarks, folding his hands in front of him.

"Is that all he said? Nothing else? The man practically chewed my ass off over the last two days and now he wants to meet privately for an urgent matter. What the hell's so important?" Simon spit out, irritation filling the tenor of his voice. The president fumed at the intrusion. "Tell that son of a…"

"Sir," his long time friend cut in. "Perhaps acquiescing to his request may enhance your chance to convince him to saddle up to your ideas and offer his support," Wolcott tossed out. "Discretion is the better part of valor."

"Shit. Save the words, Ben. When and where?"

"Now." Wolcott replied tentatively, wincing at his own words.

"Just the two of us?" the president returned, casting a glance from under a narrowed brow.

"Yes, sir. That's what he asked."

Richard Simon took a moment before making his decision. "Alright, let me change my clothes. I don't think a coat and tie will do with the weather today." After entering the bedroom of his suite, Wolcott left the president in the company of the three agents.

"Higgins. Williams," the AIC barked. "Why don't you two take a break," Reynolds told the two other agents. "It's been a long couple of days and you both look like you could use a rest."

"Ah, sir," Higgins shot back. "That goes against standard procedures." The other agent nodded in agreement.

"Look, guys," Reynolds continued, "Any other place in the world and I'd say you're absolutely right. This place is tight in the ass when it comes to security. Besides, I'm the AIC, and if the boss tells you take five, you got to do it, right? As the agent in charge, I accept all responsibility. Anyway, I'm sure Frenchy will have a detail of his own. Go on. You've earned it."

The two agents assigned to *Boxer* looked at one another, waiting for the other to accept the offer. Finally, Williams answered for the duo, "Alright boss. It's your call."

Reynolds patted both men on the back as they left the suite. "You're officially off duty," the agent grinned, calling out behind them. "Have a drink and relax. I'll see you both tomorrow. Don't worry, I'll fill Johnson in at the change of shift." The AIC watched the men disappear and turned back to wait for the commander in chief.

"All set Mr. Reynolds?" Simon asked, now dressed appropriately for the inclement weather. Simon took a quick inventory, "Where are the other two?"

"Well, sir, I relieved them. They've put in a lot of hours, and I felt they could use the rest. Besides, Mr. President, with security as uncompromising as it is around here, I didn't feel there would be a need for them." The AIC waited for the president's response.

Simon digested the information and ascertained the accuracy of what his bodyguard was saying. It made sense. "Good enough." Simon cocked his wrist noting the time. His aptitude for delicacy on important issues was wearing thin with the French president. Hopefully, Becque's attitude would change over the course of the next hour. "Ready when you are, Mr. Reynolds."

Stan Reynolds let the president walk by, quietly closing the door, tagging closely on the heels of Richard Simon. Reynolds spoke into the lapel microphone. "Boxer is mobile." In the secret service command center, someone was supposed to have heard.

Chapter Twenty-Two
G-8 - Conference Leaders

THERE HAD BEEN SEVERAL PLANS for the direction in which the complicated scheme could come to life. The one that would play its hand had been the most acceptable. Its nascency evolved many months before in an exiguous cabal of individuals, bent on their own desires. All the requirements set in motion were unknown but to only one person. Sworn to secrecy, conspiring together, all knew only what was needed to insure success and preempt failure in the event of disclosure.

The low cloud cover above the mountains was perfect, the faint mist even better. Few people would stray outside, preferring instead the warmth and comfort the resort offered. Detailed planning had seen to it that all the needed material had long been cached along the isolated trail the two men would walk. He could monitor their conversations at all times from the hidden microphone one of them wore. Defying the odds, the eminent success of his contriving would herald him as a genius, at least in the felonious shadows of the world.

Stephan Kholos squinted behind the green shade of the helmet's faceplate as bright sunlight bit into the cockpit of the fiberglass glider. Launching the vehicle from a secluded slope miles away, Kholos expertly piloted the engineless craft and allowed the thermals to lift him high above the cloud layer. He directed his eyes to the altimeter and noted his height above the mountains below. Twenty-three thousand feet above the Swiss countryside offered plenty of distance between the mountains and the fragile craft. The specially designed suit provided adequate insulation to prevent him from freezing to death at this altitude. A lone green cylinder tucked in under his seat provided the needed oxygen to keep him and his passenger alive.

Kholos loosened his grip on the stick, wiggling his gloved fingers in an effort to increase circulation. Piloting a sailplane was a complicated task that demanded his utmost attention. Numerous factors played together to insure that the wind reliant sailplane remained aloft. Just turning, required tight control over the ailerons and rudder to maintain the exact course. Loss of air speed, factor in pitch and yaw, drag coefficients, and unpredictable winds, the entire mix required a rigid mental alertness to remain airborne.

Strapped securely to his left wrist, the GPS device signaled the precise locatiòn below. "The Greek" disconnected his hose from the life giving oxygen tank, reattaching it to the small canister secured to the rigging of the equipment harness. The man seated behind him mimicked his every action. What came next was a bold move. Working both feet and hands simultaneously, Kholos rolled the glider into an upside down position as if preparing for an aerobatic stunt.

The gleaming sunlight now poured down on the belly of the sailplane. He held a steady course, checked the GPS once again to ensure the coordinates were appropriate, and his left hand pulled hard on the orange handle below the instrument panel.

The maneuver had to be executed with distinct precision. Kholos had dwelled on the edge for most of his adult life, and although his plans were always carefully contrived, he craved the adrenaline rush in the midst of hazardous situations. He would get his fill within moments.

Kholos again pulled hard on the release handle. The canopy clung tenaciously to its hinge on the fuselage. The wind rocked the aircraft violently. Kholos had not anticipated the Plexiglass covering to remain attached. In doing so, it caught the brunt of the wind like a large gloved hand, making piloting the engineless craft nearly impossible. Finally, a loud exploding sound filled his ears, letting Kholos know the canopy shattered, fragmenting into minute pieces.

The mastermind had planned that at the same time the canopy was jettisoned, the two men would undo their seat harnesses, and launch themselves out and away from the unmanned glider. What Kholos failed to notice, after connecting the air hose to his personal oxygen tank, was a large D ring on the webbing of his harness unexpectedly caught on a seat hook designed to hold a small gear bag in place.

At the sound of "The Greek's" command, he and his passenger released the buckles of harness restraining them, and pushed hard against the floor of the craft, fully expecting to be instantly suspended in freefall. In actuality, Kholos was caught in an entanglement, hanging upside down in the glider, pounded by the force of unrelenting winds. It hammered into his body with a concussive force that jolted his very being. He had not accounted for this unexpected event, but willed himself to remain calm in spite of the treacherous situation.

His right hand groped at the harness as he hung suspended below the cockpit. Amazingly, he managed to find the cause of his problem. There was little time to determine if what he did next would provide a solution. Kholos could not take much more pounding from the winds that beat him against the sailplane.

It was now or never. His body was already aching and the aircraft had nosed down, gaining speed. He fought with all his strength, fingers fighting to grip the handle of the knife encased in its sheath on the chest harness. Finally, he pulled it free, and made several quick attempts to cut the nylon webbing holding the ring. On his fourth try, Kholos was successful. His body rocketed away from the glider as he spun in a dizzying tumble at a phenomenal speed.

Kholos realized he had to quickly regain control as he plummeted wildly towards the ground below. He dropped over two thousand feet before managing to flatten out his body into controlled freefall. Adrenaline jolted through him in an electrifying dance, bringing a clarity to his thoughts. Staring hard at the GPS, he slowed his breathing and adjusted his direction, tucking arms and legs close to his side. "The Greek" maneuvered purposefully into a heads down vertical position, accelerating rapidly.

His eyes searched desperately for the other man who was falling through the skies somewhere below him. A voice called out in the headset of his helmet. Kholos looked to his right and saw its origin. He had to make every effort to get as close as possible before the man entered the cloud bank. Kholos kept falling knowing precious time was ticking away as the ground raced up to meet him. Now only seconds behind, he carefully tracked the figure below him, evaporating into the thick, gray wall below.

Kholos spread his arms and legs, slowing his descent, and once more checking the instrument strapped to his wrist. His course was directly on target. Satisfied, he pressed a button that released the wings of his specially designed suit. A framework of rigid struts snapped open on both arms and legs, locking into place as Kevlar wings unfurled. These wings slowed his fall even more and provided greater maneuverability. It also let him come much closer to the ground before releasing the small para-wing that would soon open from the pack on his back.

Stephan Kholos substituted the sunlit world above for one layered in thick clouds hovering above the resort at Davos. He glued his eyes to the GPS screen overlapping a real time digital image of the ground below. Without this, the possibility of disorientation loomed menacingly in the encircling, gray veil. The last thing he needed now was a mistake. He had come too far to lose his life, or foul his plans because of one stupid mistake.

Kholos tracked the beacon below, confident it was the proper time. He pulled the cord, and the para-wing unfurled above his head. Kholos pushed his legs out in front of him into a seated position. The wings attached to his suit also helped slow his speed as he steered a course that would take him to the destiny fate had prescribed.

The two leaders walked in the misty rain. Becque offered apologies, indicating that his thinking had been skewed and he wished to make amends. Richard Simon was usually a good reader of people's intent. He had to be in his role. After twenty minutes of the French president's explanations, followed by promises of his support, Simon became less skeptical of his colleague in the political arena.

There was some satisfaction in knowing that he had another supporter, or at least, the promise of one. It would lend a stronger credence to his agenda. Hopefully, it would sway others onto the same line of reasoning, so that the ultimate outcome of this gathering of influential men would bring much needed changes. Richard Simon felt life was improving rapidly. All the sleepless nights and tiring hours spent nurturing his country's needs would prove worthy of his sacrifice.

Stan Reynolds walked at a discreet distance out of earshot of the two men. Becque's words informed Simon that he regarded the need for personal bodyguards as inconsequential for their meeting. Besides, he mentioned, one Secret Service agent should be adequate to provide for their needs on the secure slopes of Davos. The AIC spoke softly into the small microphone he had removed from his pocket after the three men began their hike along the trail. Any other day he would have enjoyed the scenery, but Reynolds' attention was entirely focused on his assignment. The government agent scrutinized both men, stepping up his tempo, moving definitively within a few paces of the two presidents. The trio stopped near the edge of an overlook, gazing into the valley far below.

"Spectacular, is it not?" Becque questioned, turning with a smile toward Simon.

"It's a remarkable view, probably more so, under fairer circumstances." The United States president returned, directing a purposeful stare into the eyes of the man standing next to him.

The subtlety of his language did not go unnoticed by the Frenchman. "I believe there's more meaning to your words than just idle talk of the weather."

"You're very discerning, Mr. Becque."

"Henri. Please. That is the way of friends. No?" The French president cajoled, in his typical charming demeanor. "The world's stability is dependent upon many factors. Some are beyond our control, some are not. It is our duty to do what's best for our own country and its people."

"That is true. However, Henri, the world today has expanded into an up to the minute, moment by moment, cavalcade of changing scenarios. More than ever, there's a greater meaning, and an exponential reaction to the domino effect." Becque nodded silently, in full agreement with his counterpart's assessment. "Globalization has forced everyone into positions whose dynamics evolve on a daily basis."

Reynolds heard the voice in his ear bud. It would be only a matter of moments before he was required to perform his next act in the well scripted performance playing out on the picturesque Swiss slopes. The AIC slipped a hand into the jacket pocket and retrieved the pen-like device. A simple twist of the pen's barrel activated the mechanism. His thumb rested on the release button. He waited anxiously, oblivious to the chilling wind.

Scanning the skies and locating the other man, Kholos estimated they would land probably less than fifty yards apart. He focused in on the individuals below, spotting the intended target easily. It would be only moments before his feet touched the ground. Once he set foot on the rocky path, the rest of the plan would be undertaken.

Kholos pulled hard on the right hand riser, circling, and bringing himself into alignment with his objective. He prepared himself for a soft touchdown and landed a few feet behind Agent Reynolds. Instantly releasing the harness buckle, the straps parted, and the small canopy of the para-wing fell limply on the trail.

Struck by the sound, both men turned, looking past the Secret Service agent. Henri Becque's face held little emotion, knowing what would come next. Simon's mouth opened in disbelief at the intrusion of the interloper and another black clad figure running towards him. His brain had not yet processed the possibility of deception. Out of the corner of his eye, he noticed Becque gave no indication of surprise. Shock held him in check momentarily. Surprised that Reynolds was moving in his direction, the president was unaware of the aerosol mist swirling in front of his face until it was too late. Reynolds kept the button depressed longer than necessary to compensate for the wind. It was enough.

Upon coming to grips with the ploy, Simon struggled briefly with Reynolds in a vain act to get away. The powerful man was more than a match for Simon. Within moments, the president felt the muscles in his arms and legs weaken into a rubbery gel, his vision danced in a surreal blurring of images. The president lost control, and his legs buckled beneath him. He attempted to speak but no words sounded.

The last memory Richard Simon had was of the men gathered around him. Two he knew - Becque, and his own traitorous bodyguard. The other he could not recall any recognition as to his identity. Soon, a fourth man appeared, bringing an unnerving level of uncertainty. Simon did not know if it was the effect of the drugs clouding his mind, or if he was hallucinating. Prior to lapsing into unconsciousness, he struggled to focus on the image of the fourth face hovering over him. The final team member to join his assailants sent a compelling chill of dread cascading over his being. There could be no doubt to this person's identity. The haunting features were a mirror image of a face he recognized all too well. Richard Simon unwillingly slipped into a pitch-black void. His last thought was that the face he was staring into was his own.

The three men worked quickly. They stripped the president of his clothing while the impostor changed into his garb. Kholos moved to a concealed spot, removing the large package hidden from view. He moved with practiced ease. The parts locked into place easily and very soon the framework came together. Next came the material which stretched out and attached at specific points. Wire struts followed, for stabilization. Finally, the black webbing of the harness was attached.

Richard Simon was bound, just in case by some chance he should awaken. They placed his limp body in a black nylon bag which hung from heavy straps below the rigid framework. Kholos climbed into his harness, adjusting it to fit precisely, and gave a once over to the rigging.

"Everything in order?" Becque called out, his words provoking a splenetic assault from "The Greek's" dark eyes.

Reynolds was becoming greatly concerned, thinking he and the president had been gone too long already. "Hurry it up, damn it," his irritation exacerbating into a burning edginess.

Kholos flashed him a menacing glance that would have sent most people into a cringing retreat. Reynolds shook it off, unfazed. He was not bothered by the man's reputation. Any other time, he would have gladly placed a bullet between the eyes of Stephan Kholos, but today they were playing for the same stakes.

The sound of snapping metal filled the air as Kholos finished attaching himself to the frame. "I'm ready." He placed the helmet back on his head, sliding the visor into place. Together the men lifted the metal framework. Simon's dead weight added greatly to their task. "Move," Kholos shouted as the four men began to run down the embankment toward the cliff's edge. Picking up speed, Kholos felt the wind's effect. At the last moment, he shouted, "Now."

The others released their grip on the cold metal, skidding to a halt. Stephan Kholos raced headlong over the precipice, leaping out into space. Becque, Reynolds, and the new president watched the man from Sibenik fall from sight. Suddenly, the air currents filled the material of the parasail, providing lift, stabilizing the flying wing. Stephan Kholos and the unconscious body of Richard Simon glided across the tenebrous, brooding skies. Only three witnesses remained behind, unseen except by the shadow filled mountains in the waning light. They watched the duplicity unfold, their silence assured.

Flying over the Alps was a scenic exploit for which most would pay handsomely. The beauty and grandeur of the magnificent peaks were rivaled by few places in the world. The sense of freedom derived from gliding soundlessly around the peaks and over the valley below was one of those once in a lifetime encounters. None of that mattered to Stephan Kholos. Given a choice, it was an undertaking Richard Simon wished he would never have experienced.

Chapter Twenty-Three
Chesapeake Bay - Virginia

A STIFF BREEZE BROUGHT TO LIFE a moderate chop over the dark waters of the expansive estuary. Sunlight filtered down, only emerging when the wall of gray clouds permitted. Small whitecaps protruded from the wave tops, disappearing only to be born again in an endless dance. The vast waterway was dotted with a small armada of expectant fishermen, their boats, bobbing like corks on this late autumn day. Blues, as the locals referred to them, were running hard, and eager sportsmen worked feverishly, pulling in their allotted catch.

From the fly bridge of the twin engine diesel Bertram, Martin Boggs brought the motor to an idle and came down to the bow, dropping the anchor. He called back up to the older man to kill the engines. The deep, gurgling rumble and white vapors of the exhaust faded, carried away across the windswept bay. Together, they made their way to the stern. The men took their seats. Boggs rigged the fishing equipment, eventually casting lines into a curving arch across the water, letting the weighted line sink into the depths. To the casual observer, the old friends were making a day of it. Spending time whiling away the hours, committed to proffering their share of the bay's inhabitants.

Unexpectedly, Boggs already had a fish bending the heavy pole and challenging the tensile strength of the monofilament. Within several minutes he landed a large blue. From under the long-billed cap, the slightly pudgy face with narrow set eyes took in a view of the surroundings. He landed the fish with a display of false interest, tossing it into the bait box. Boggs broke out into an Eastern shore accent, "Some day, huh?"

"Truly is," Foster Hughes replied, wind ruffling the dark green nylon of the windbreaker covering his upper torso. Hughes was in his late sixties, a few wisps of white hair topped his scalp. He was well tanned for someone who spent so much time devoted to the inner workings of the capital's daily challenges. "I love the sea, Martin. It's my place of rest. I do some of my best thinking out here," he shared, cautiously scanning the waters encircling them. Hughes was fifteen years older than the man seated next to him at the stern of the luxury fishing boat. His face wore the crinkled skin of a heavy smoker and intermittently his cough interrupted his raspy speech. "It looks like we picked the right day, my friend."

Boggs' pole bent again, and he began the process of hauling his catch aboard. "Not having much luck, eh, Foster," the barrel-chested man laughed.

"Fuck you," the Supreme Court Justice replied, with a slick grin. Both men laughed in response. Through a Virginia accent, Foster continued their conversation. "Speaking of luck, I heard from our friend."

Hughes' words seemed to elicit a slight agitation in Martin Boggs. The CEO of the Carlton Trust turned in all directions, peering at every boat short of the horizon. "When?"

"You look pretty tense, Martin. Relax. You act like you're walking barefooted on glass. I can assure you, no one's listening. There is not a boat close enough to hear anything we say, even with the clandestine community's high-tech stuff." Foster Hughes pulled the cigarette from its pack and lit the end, deeply sucking in the smoke before exhaling. He raised a nicotine stained finger in the direction of his fishing partner. "No one followed me to the marina. You?" the Justice asked, elevating an untrimmed, bushy eyebrow.

"No, I don't think so."

"You don't think? My boy, you better do better than that," Foster Hughes responded. "This isn't a sandlot game."

Boggs cut in, "Okay. I got it. I'm a little edgy today." He reached up and readjusted his cap, pulling down the visor low across his forehead. "No one followed me. Okay? No one," he said, some confidence returning as he tossed a glance at the older man.

"Good. I understand Red 7 arrived safely, and is enjoying the hospitality."

Boggs' tension seemed to fade at the news, the financial group's leader brimming with satisfaction. "That's partly the reason we're here. However, you hadn't given me the chance to tell you. It seems as if everything is progressing accordingly. Within the next few months, the others will take their respective places. Once that happens, the operation will set in motion a chain of events that will forever change the world."

"Exactly." Foster Hughes pulled a long drag on the cigarette, causing the end to grow in a fiery red ember. With nothing left but the filter, Hughes flicked the butt into the water, sitting silently for some time before he began again. "I'm going to tell you something, Martin. Only a handful of people know this." Hughes eyes narrowed, crinkling around their edges. "The events of one particular day set the stage for a scenario similar to what's occurring now. The players and circumstances were different, but the game was the same."

The Carlton Trust director listened intently, puzzled, unsure of what was to follow.

"It was a fateful day in late November forty-six years ago. Hell, you were probably still shitting your pants back then," Hughes chuckled in a wheezy tone.

The implication struck Boggs full force. He quickly realized the issues the two men were here to discuss had been a table top item for longer than he had imagined.

The older man continued, "A week later, an airliner, Trans-Canada flight 831, crashed at Dorval Airport."

Boggs had not heard of the name of the airfield the court justice poured out, indicated by the puzzled mask washing across his face.

"It's in Montreal. Trudeau International now," he answered, seemingly reading the CEO's thoughts. "Used to be Dorval, before those Frenchies in Quebec decided to change it."

"What the hell took place?" Uncertainty crept into the pitch of Martin Boggs' voice. The CEO placed his rod in the holder on the transom, preferring to fully focus his attention on the conversation.

"Hamilton Page, a friend of my father's, was on that flight." Foster Hughes sat back in the seat, feeling the warmth of a brief period of sunlight. "He was the catalyst. Everything collapsed with his death." Hughes eyes glazed with the memory. "There was talk. Lots of it. Several important figures got scared. Gutless fucks, now that I think of it." Hughes expelled a thick, rumbling cough from his chest, courtesy of the cigarettes he was a slave to. "Fortunately, they were never heard from again. Everything snowballed and a lot of people got cold feet. Then the news of a suicide hit the papers. A prominent D.C. attorney decided he'd take a swim in the Potomac. He was another major player. Affluent. Well connected. Everybody had their own speculations as to how and why." A sour expression erupted across the wrinkled skin of Foster Hughes' face. "After that, not much mattered. The whole thing went to shit."

"Won't happen," Boggs shot back, confidently. "The roots have taken hold."

"Nothing is impossible, Martin. Need I remind you of that? You think you got where you are simply by your business skills and financial investments? Sure, and your cronies did their homework since you created the company. Slick, too. Right in the heart of D.C., on Pennsylvania Avenue. Under their very noses." Hughes coughed, spitting a thick wad of tan mucus over the side. "That was a smart move. Sure, it's true you've helped maneuver and manipulate the proper people to accomplish your purposes, and well, I might add. But, don't ever think it was all your doing. If it hadn't been you, there were others. Remember, overconfidence is a troubling aspect of success, my friend. One that can crumble like a dry turd, and very quickly. Remember that," the older man cautioned.

Boggs digested the words. "Since you are baring your soul, what sparked your interest in all of this?" he questioned.

"In fishing?"

"You know damn well what I mean, Foster."

The justice's features clouded into a serious expression. "My father was in the Senate at the time. I'd graduated from college that summer and was enrolled at Georgetown. Law department." The justice's memory catapulted him back in time. "It was a late September afternoon. Crisp, falling leaves, blue skies. Looked like a damn postcard. My father arrived home early and told me we needed to talk. He swore me to secrecy, asked me to help carry on the dream. Laid it all out. Goals. Directives. Everything." He paused, his eyes replaying memories as if he were watching a movie. "My old man had no use for their bleeding heart agendas and the changes that were happening in the country, hell, in the world for that matter. I bought in to the idea. It all sounded so good back then. The right thing to do. Still is," he paused, regurgitating the bitterness of failed events. "Then two months later, well, we covered that already."

Both remained silent for a prolonged time. The men considered the choices that had been made, and things that could not be undone. It was all the more reason to continue on the course they were charting. "Drink?" Boggs asked, shaking his head.

"Hell, I could use one."

"Usual?"

Hughes nodded, affirming his answer.

Martin Boggs returned with two glasses. The men touched rims in a toast, sending a splash of bourbon onto the boat's deck. The first swallow bit hard and sent a fire into the CEO's belly that quickly softened. Another swallow and the mellow flavor of the aged bourbon followed through.

"How about the woman? Everything proceeding as planned?" Hughes questioned, licking a drop from his lips.

"She's doing well. Enough information's been provided to satisfy her needs. Besides, what she doesn't know about all the events going on around her will cause her no concern."

Hughes stopped, pausing to light another cigarette. "Being played is a game that requires a skillful strategist to pull the strings. Frankly, her own agenda snuggles in very closely to the ideas we have. On a much smaller scale, of course. Actually, she has saved us a lot of work."

A large cruiser motored past within fifty yards of the anchored boat. Several people onboard waved at the two men idly fishing, totally unaware of who they were or the conversation. Both Hughes and Foster went through the motions, as if enjoying their outing, returning the wave. Once assured that the passing boat had been no threat, they picked up their talks.

"What about your guy? Compliant? I sure as hell don't trust him."

"Foster. You wouldn't trust your own damn mother. Look. Forget about him. He's okay as long as his bank account continues to grow," Boggs replied.

"Reckless is my take," the older man mentioned in a sour tone.

The Carlton Trust's leader winced at the acrimonious gouge, "I suppose in his line of work a certain amount of risk taking is acceptable. It's also that risk taking that keeps him sharp, honed. With all that's going on, a man of his talents is greatly appreciated. Besides, Foster, even you have to admit, he's the best."

"I'll give the bastard his due. That job he pulled off last year in Chechnya certainly caught the world's attention."

"And it saved me, no, us a lot of problems. Men like him are needed, at least temporarily. Once we have accomplished our purposes, I'm sure the world will not weep at his passing." Boggs raised his glass in a mock toast.

Hughes' thoughts were interrupted by the tugging of his line and his pole bending nearly in two. "Shit," he groaned.

"I guess that fish has no idea of who he caught," Boggs erupted into a deep belly laugh that irritated his partner. "Hope he doesn't pull you in."

"I don't have time for this crap," the nation's top judge spit out in an irascible manner.

"You're the one who likes the water. Helps you think, didn't you say?" mocking the older man.

"I like the water. Sailing or boating. Whatever else the fuck you want to call it, but I hate fishing."

"It's no wonder you've survived this long inside the Beltway. You've got to be one of the orneriest old son of a bitches I've ever met."

"You're about as much help as a boil on my ass, Martin. Take this pole before I throw it over the side."

"Not even curious, Foster?" Boggs laughed.

"Hell, no," he spit back, shoving the pole at Boggs.

The CEO took the fishing pole and cranked the reel, playing the line with just the right amount of tension. The fish struggled, running with the monofilament, fighting, and eventually being pulled back to the boat.

Boggs' affluence had allowed him to practice his hobby around the globe. He was considered an expert fisherman. The Carlton Trust's leader had even been featured in a sport fisherman magazine a couple years back. The photos were shot in some exotic location. Cool shades, a smiling face, and a deep tan and blue skies, all enhanced by digital imagery. Great advertising for the boat builder, a majority interest of which Boggs' firm owned. Trouble was, most people who turned pages from cover to cover could never even hope of traveling to such a destination. The printed visions left the readers with only their dreams.

Ten minutes passed and the line slackened. The creature tired. The reel had recaptured most of its contents, when the big fish came up from the depths at the transom. "One last chance. Sure you're not curious, Foster?"

A fresh drink filled the hand of Chief Justice, Foster Hughes. He walked nonchalantly to his chair, waving a hand, accentuating his disinterest in anything to do with the hooked prize. Martin Boggs lifted the rod tip high in the air as the creature broke the surface, water splashing into a white froth at the boat's stern. Boggs looked at the animal. It was about three and a half feet long, but its exposed teeth were just as sharp and white as one twice its size. Martin Boggs placed the rod in the holder, and leaned over the stern. "An appropriate catch, Foster. It fits your style." A white toothed smile of his own slipped across his face, mimicking the captured animal.

Reaching into his pants pocket, he removed and snapped open the razor sharp blade. Its steel glinted, winking a reflection of pale sunlight overhead. In one swift motion, Boggs cut the line, allowing the creature a reprieve and another chance at life. He shook his head, "A damn shark."

Chapter Twenty-Four
Seattle - Washington

BRYSON MCGANN HAD RESTED WELL on the long flight back from Amsterdam. He needed it. Sitting with his eyes closed, he relived the events. Faced with little choice in the matter, the NESSA employee acted out of need to save lives, especially that of Dr. Haroldson and himself. He had gone over the details countless times - stopping, evaluating, all the while estimating in his own mind the reasons for the offense perpetrated in Amsterdam's streets. Several possibilities rose to the surface from McGann's subconscious, presenting images which he had mentally noted during the gun battle. His memory replayed the gruesome scenes, vividly etching an even clearer snapshot of the events.

Fortunately, his accurate assessment of the situation turned out to be correct. Still, one item from that day remained elusive. The set of glowering eyes staring into him from the back of the luxury sedan was troubling. He made it part of his plan to closely follow the unfolding events related to the case in the Dutch city. A call to Ashlyn Sanders at some point might prove beneficial, too. Having an 'inside connection' at NSA could prove quite valuable. The fact she was T.C.'s fiancé did not hurt either. McGann made a mental note to call her in the next several days from Hawaii.

What he had learned from the official circles bothered him. Sumner's friend in the *politie* had not been very forthcoming with information. The commissioner had been decidedly cagey answering their questions, a tribute to his years in police service, or was there something more? McGann suspected the latter. Obviously, whatever had been stolen was of great importance. Anything someone was willing to kill or be killed for held a more than paltry value to its thief. McGann had his own ideas, but decided to keep them tucked in his vest for the moment.

"Bryson?" He felt the fingers lightly brush his left shoulder. She stood there quietly as he contemplated his next move. Feigning sleep would only prolong the inevitable. McGann heard her turn, and walk back down the aisle to her seat. "Dr. Haroldson." He straightened himself in the plush leather seat the designers of the Gulfstream had so aptly thought of, when laying out plans for the aircraft. The volcanologist appeared in front of him. Smiling. A nice change, he mused.

"Got a minute?" she asked.

"I'm a captive audience," the reply came. Her first reaction was to bristle at his remark, and then she realized it was only McGann's sense of humor. Traveling through the skies at thirty thousand feet did not leave much opportunity for him to have any other choice. Tori Haroldson thought carefully before she spoke. "From the outset, we started off on the wrong foot."

McGann stared into her china blue eyes. There was a depth to them that spoke more than words ever could. "I," she paused, "I'd like to call a truce." She sat down across from him, adding quickly, "I also want to apologize for my behavior in Amsterdam."

McGann remained silent, observing her behavior as the woman spoke. Haroldson rubbed her thumb and forefinger together quickly, a nervous habit McGann surmised.

She had a faint scar, barely discernable at the corner of her right eyebrow that had gone unnoticed. Now for the first time, McGann realized just how beautiful this woman was. Up until now, there had been little opportunity to pay much attention.

McGann inhaled deeply, "Shall I run up the white flag?" A lopsided curl grew from the corner of his mouth.

"Perhaps you could present me with your sword, Mr. McGann. A sure sign of capitulation," she mused.

"Surrender is not something I believe in, Doctor Haroldson. However, I will make an exception in this case." McGann reached out, offering his hand.

Tori Haroldson's gaze fell to the outstretched open hand. Her right arm reached out in response. Her hand clasped around his, sealing the treaty with a handshake. She held on slightly longer than needed, but was not embarrassed by doing so. "Oh. One more thing. I haven't thanked you for saving my life. If it weren't for you, I would probably be dead. I'm grateful."

"Tori, if it wasn't for me, you might not have had the experience. Ironic, isn't it?"

"I hadn't thought of it that way." The intercom came to life with the voice of co-pilot, Pat Evans, informing them of their imminent landing.

McGann cut in after the pilot's voice faded, "You're welcome."

She smiled. "I'm glad that wasn't too painful," she added, strapping herself in the seat next to him. They continued their conversation while the Gulfstream made its final approach to Sea-Tac International Airport, tucked in between the cities of Seattle and Tacoma.

The aircraft came to a halt after it taxied to a NESSA hangar. Inside the cockpit, the pilots went through their routine of shutting down the plane's engines. A list of other necessary procedures needed checking off before they finished their job.

"Looks like we've arrived," McGann tossed out. "There should be a vehicle here to pick us up," he added, looking out the cabin window.

The outer door opened and the stairs descended. They grabbed their bags. Tori Haroldson turned and thanked both pilots before leaving the airplane. "Well, Bryson. Randall will be happy to know that we're on speaking terms," her eyes lighting with the words, before she walked down the steps to the tarmac.

"Don't suppose it would sit too well with him if I wasn't conversing with his best friend's daughter. And considering the three of us are having dinner this evening, it would ruin a truly pleasurable dining experience. Since I've been assigned to escort you to Hawaii, the gentlemanly thing to do is to put on a good face and do my best," McGann quipped.

"It'd be a very miserable experience for you, if things didn't improve between us," she responded, her eyes smiling.

"After you." McGann gestured with a wave of his hand toward the door. He thought about her last remark, and then mumbled quietly, "It would indeed."

Martin's was a Seattle hotspot. Its menu was unrivaled by anything in the Pacific northwest. Chef Martin's ability to fuse numerous cuisines with succulent flavors using only the finest ingredients, drew faithful patrons back time and time again. McGann and Canton were two who personally knew the Chef, and delighted in his presentations, even more so in eating them. Martin's reputation had grown amazingly after only three years. Featured in magazine articles, newsprint, and television, the restaurant had skyrocketed in its run to the top, earning a five star award several months before.

McGann entered, nodding a hello at the maitre de, picking his way through the crowds. He paused several times, stopping to talk with a few friends. Numerous women allowed themselves more than a cursory glance at the handsomely dressed figure, clad in a beige silk turtleneck and tailored woolen sports coat. McGann finally arrived at the table where Sumner and Sigurd Haroldson's daughter were engaged in conversation.

"Bryson. Good to have you back," the NESSA director said. He stood, patting McGann's shoulder in a warm manner.

"Nice to be back, sir." McGann eyed the blonde woman momentarily, appreciating her taste in clothing. "Good evening, Tori."

Haroldson returned the salutation as the trio settled in at the candlelit table, continuing their conversation. "I took the liberty of ordering. Red or white?" the NESSA director offered.

"White. I'm trying a new seafood dish Martin has come up with," McGann replied. Bryson McGann swirled the contents, evaluating the liquid's golden color and clarity. Satisfied, he briefly inhaled the bouquet and let the tasting do the rest. "Excellent Viognier. Mendicino?"

Sumner twirled the bottle, casting a glance at the label. The vintner's placard confirmed McGann's appraisal of the bottle's contents. "Impressive."

"I didn't know you were an aficionado," Tori stated.

"I paid the waiter," McGann said, insincerely. The trio laughed. Sumner realized the younger man's humor often caught many off guard. He was also well aware of the falsity of McGann's statement. Their waiter appeared, offering suggestions as he worked his way through the special appetizers and dishes prepared for the evening.

"I would suggest leaving room for dessert," McGann spoke up. "The house specialty is not something you want to miss."

The group ordered their meals and moved through a series of tales of Sumner's history with Tori's father. McGann refilled their glasses while the stories continued. Sumner was a natural when working a crowd, and time easily slipped away. The conversation halted and all eyes focused on the entrees when they arrived.

Sumner had chosen a grilled filet with porcini mushrooms and potato galette. A smile of anticipation filled his face when the dish was placed before him. NESSA's guest lecturer's tastes were far from the sea, with her decision to try the quail, stuffed with roasted nectarines and lentils, and presented with a red wine pancetta vinaigrette. The aromas tempted each of their palates. McGann's grilled sea bass marinated in a white wine, lemon butter and cumin sauce, was served with seasoned grilled vegetables. He let the succulent aroma envelop him, as the meal was placed on the fine white linen tablecloth. McGann knew the Zinfandel Sumner had chosen would pair well with each of his companion's choices. They dug in, enraptured with the nuances created by the master chef. Not surprisingly to McGann, the meal matched his expectations.

"There is an old Polish proverb," McGann offered, as the trio delighted in the flavors of Martin's creation. "Fish, to taste right, must swim three times: in water, in butter, and in wine. I'd say Martin has outdone himself again."

Haroldson dabbed at the corner of her mouth with the crisp linen napkin. Smiling, she raised her glass. "To friends, and friends who are chefs." Their glasses touched in salute. The group worked through the meal, enjoying the food as much as the companionship. With the dessert ordered, they engaged the topic of the upcoming Hawaiian conference.

"As I'm sure you know from the syllabus, Tori, there will be scientists from all around the Pacific rim," Director Sumner advised.

"I saw that Dr. Takaniki will be there. I'm impressed. He's a bit of a recluse, and usually doesn't attend, let alone speak at many of these affairs. You must have some incredibly persuasive powers."

"He's worked with Noel Johnson before. A night of sake and sushi and the two have been best of friends since."

"I heard about that after I started working here," McGann interjected. "I think we'll leave that for another time." The two NESSA men laughed, leaving a quizzical look on the attractive woman's face.

"I spoke with Noel today. He's looking forward to meeting you and discussing your recent article on volcanic activity in Iceland," Sumner remarked.

"I'm anxious to meet him," Haroldson responded. "All in all, it should be an enlightening seminar."

"One of the things that will be a topic of discussion is that of an early warning system for tsunami events within the ring of fire," McGann cut in.

"There's an established system already operating in the Atlantic, and also up and down the west coast," Sumner added. "Hopefully, one that will never be needed."

"As a matter of fact," McGann continued, "T.C.'s involved with AGSI in a joint venture between the Australian group and NESSA. It's been long in coming, but once in place, it could potentially save the lives of untold numbers of people."

The waiter arrived at the table preparing the finishing touch to an exquisite meal. After melting the butter and brown sugar, he placed the bananas into the caramelized mixture and gently heated them to perfection. A sprinkle of cinnamon fell atop the warm fruit, and some banana liqueur. Finally, rum was added, and with a slight tilt of the pan, the vapors ignited. The blue flame quickly died and the dessert was spooned over dishes of creamy vanilla ice cream, much to everyone's delight. The scent of rich, dark coffee accented the splendid dessert, as their cups were filled with the steaming brew.

Sumner eyed it enviously. "I can't say this is on my usual diet. But, it looks far too good to pass up."

"Everyone has to treat themselves once in awhile," McGann added.

Tori Haroldson simply scooped out a portion and ate it. "Excellent. I'd have to say, probably, the best Bananas Foster I've ever eaten."

"Without a doubt," McGann replied, catching Tori's eye. She returned the gaze, smiling. He was intrigued by the woman seated next to him. Not only attractive, he sensed an inner quality that he found highly appealing.

The group continued their discussion. Scientific matters, more tales from Sumner's past, and some interesting stories of Haroldson's adventures pursuing her quest of studying volcanic activity. The night moved along far too rapidly, as pale moonlight invaded the window where they overlooked Puget Sound. McGann always enjoyed the view and the Sound's activities that were a part of Seattle's lifeblood.

"I can honestly say that was one of the best meals I've eaten in some time," NESSA's director expressed, enthusiastically.

"Absolutely incredible." Sumner quickly reverted back into his perfunctory mode, addressing McGann. "What time will you both be leaving tomorrow?" he questioned, raising an eyebrow.

"I spoke with Beech on the way here tonight. He wants to get an early start. We should be airborne by eight."

"Weather?" Sumner asked.

"Fine. Clear skies for the next several days across the islands," McGann responded.

"Great," Haroldson interrupted, "I can work on my tan."

"I thought you were supposed to be working," the director scolded, mockingly.

"A girl has to have some fun. Although, since I'm in the company of Mr. McGann, there's no telling what might happen. It can't all be dangerous stuff though, can it?" Tori asked, flashing a smile.

Together, the group left the five star restaurant while the valet retrieved Sumner's car. "I'll drop you off, Tori. Then I'm headed back to the office to pick up something I forgot." The car pulled up next to them, and Sumner opened the door to the silver BMW. Haroldson slid into the fine leather seat.

"I'll see you in the morning, Tori. Around seven?" McGann asked.

"Sounds good."

"Good night, Bryson," the director added.

The car's engine came to life, fading as it disappeared around a corner. Bryon McGann reflected upon the evening and realized that Tori Haroldson was crawling under his skin. He turned up a corner of his mouth. "Not such a bad idea," he mused. McGann drove off with a number of things on his mind.

Chapter Twenty-Five
CVN-74 - Southwestern Pacific

A SQUALL LINE RAKED THE VAST DECK of the John C. Stennis with stiff winds, bringing sheets of rain, pounding in an unrehearsed rhythm onto the metal tarmac. Twin rows of glowing beacons, along with a sequence of blinking lights running up the middle, indicated landing access for the inbound aircraft on the slick flight deck.

Lt. J. G. Kendall Stevens hated duty in weather like this. Somehow, the downpour had invaded her yellow uniform, sending rivulets of water cascading along her spine. There was little she could do about the discomfort. It was not just the misery of being wet and clammy, but these conditions made working even more perilous. No matter the time of day, if you were not on full alert, the hazards could ensnare a person in its grip. At best, a minor injury; above that, the stakes were raised tremendously. Stevens had been told that working on a carrier deck with all the powerful aircraft was the most dangerous job in the world.

Stevens had learned how much truth there was in that statement. In similar conditions just a month and a half ago, a sailor had been blown overboard. They scrambled the search and rescue team, but unfortunately, only a body was recovered. The lieutenant was sure that the letter to the young man's parents was not one the captain wanted to write. Kendall Stevens made certain she was 'in the moment' each time she stepped out on the deck to do the job. A body bag and a letter home was not how she wished to end up.

A flash of lightning streaked across the darkened, cloud-filled sky, followed soon by a rumbling thunderclap, reverberating with a deep bass tone. Its echo rode across the ocean. Briefly, the world lit up in a display that appeared surreal. She saw the images of two of the carrier group's escort ships, the Howard and the Ford, in the distance off the starboard beam. Just as quickly, they evaporated back into the sombrous night. It only added to the sensation of being a spectator on an elaborate Hollywood movie set.

In addition to returning F-18's *putting down*, the next sorties were engaged in takeoff activities. Between the voices in her headset, the roar of jet engines, and the catapult, the cacophony could get overwhelming. Stevens never would have guessed five years ago, as she graduated from college, that she would find herself on the rolling deck of a carrier at 0200 hours, *directing traffic*, as she liked to call it.

Jet aircraft were in a continuous cycle of either taking off or landing. The carrier's crew worked diligently, as if they were in a full tactical situation. In the darkness, extra care was imperative, making the operations slightly longer. Captain Culpepper decided that it would be the perfect time for training. The Lieutenant knew that the skipper had no intention of endangering anyone's life. Conditions were miserable, but not so unsafe as to abort the exercise. She also knew that war was not fought only under sunny skies or moonlit nights. Training was just that. The better the training, the better the individual. Nothing could take its place. Ultimately, it was that very thing that saved lives.

Stevens made the appropriate checks. "Roger that, Cowboy," using the pilot's call sign. "You are a go." She dropped to one knee and with a quick wave of her arm, signaled to the waiting pilot, he was cleared for take off. Orange flame spit from the tail of the craft in a thunderous roar, as it rocketed a short distance before lifting off the deck into the rainy skies. Simultaneously, another Hornet was landing.

Kendall Stevens admired the ability of the 'AB' in the control tower seven stories above the ship's deck. The Air Boss directed a well-choreographed ballet from his perch in the 'Pri-Fly.' Inside the Stennis' tower, the primary flight control team kept a diligent watch over everything regarding plane movements on the deck. The 'AB' had a demanding job with tremendous responsibility. Room for error was not an option.

Nothing escaped his attention, keeping in constant radio contact with all personnel involved with flight procedures. His headset buzzed with operations on the busy deck below.

Through the cockpit of his Hornet, Lt. Commander Ron Wood, spied the darkened silhouette of the carrier. Black Dog glanced at the instrument panel. Direction was dead on. Quickly checking the altimeter, Wood watched the numbers melt away. Flaps down. In the nearing distance, he could see the *meatball* aboard the ship. Winds buffeted his aircraft, causing him to dip below the acceptable level for a *hard down* onto the flight deck. A red light appeared through his windscreen. Wood had been through this routine hundreds of times. Still, he knew each time could be different. In conditions such as he was facing, the need for all his attention was imperative.

Over the radio, he heard the voice of the air traffic controller. "Black Dog. Be advised. Wind speed across the deck is at two-two miles per hour."

"Copy that." Wood raised the nose of the plane. The lights emitted from the Fresnel lens of the *meatball* glowed evenly with the horizontal green bar. Trying to keep aligned in the middle of a storm, with a pitching deck rising and falling constantly, was not an easy task. The last pilot got a wave off and had to circle around to try again.

Wood's airspeed was down to one hundred and fifty-one miles per hour when his wheels slammed the deck. The impact always came with a resounding jolt that shuddered throughout the Hornet's airframe. Immediately, he pushed the throttles to full, in case the plane *boltered.* It had been some time since his tail hook missed an arresting cable. However, with the engines revved to full, he could take off safely should the need arise. He did not plan for that to happen now. The hook caught on the second wire, and the force of rapid deceleration pushed him tightly into the back of his seat. Burning up three hundred and fifty feet of carrier deck, the F-18 came to a halt when Wood killed the throttle.

Kendall Stevens wiped the rain from her eyes, catching a glimpse of Wood's safe return. A team quickly swarmed around his F-18, performing their assignments with practiced ease. They quickly removed the aircraft from the path of the final incoming Hornet. She knew the next thing awaiting Black Dog and his wing, was a debriefing and mission evaluation. It would be a little while longer before she was able to get inside. She could not get off the deck soon enough. A hot shower and dry towel were tops on the list.

The debrief went as usual. The simulated mission had been picked apart, discussed, evaluated, and in Navy terms, shot up the ass. Every pilot offered input and finally at 0330, it was time for some sleep. Wood was beat. It had been a long day and even longer night.

"Hey, Ron," Lieutenant Casey Slater called out.

"What's up?" he asked, rubbing the stiff muscles of his neck.

"Can't believe I missed the hard down," Slater remarked.

"Happens. Don't beat yourself up. Look, weather conditions sucked, and the deck was bouncing like a rubber ball. I came in low myself and almost had to abort."

"Yeah, but you know how tight-assed the old man gets about wave offs."

Wood smiled, "As they say, any landing is a good one."

"Just as long as you walk away from it," Slater remarked, dryly.

"Forget it," Wood replied, his hand waving off the comment. "I'm sure the AB would rather have your skinny ass sitting down here with your twenty-four million dollar airplane safely secured on deck, than fishing you out of the drink. Uncle Sam doesn't like his toys ending up in Davy Jones' locker," the Lt. Commander smiled. "Get some rest. It won't be that long before we'll be back in the saddle."

"Alright. Up for a cup of coffee?"

"Thanks, I'll pass on this go round. Besides, I got to go topside for a minute. I'll catch you later." Wood left the briefing room and made his way through the ship's corridors. Navy gray. Could there be a more dismal color? Ron Wood turned a corner and ran headlong into Kendall Stevens, nearly knocking the woman off her feet. Instinctively, his hands reached out, grabbing her by the arms, keeping the young officer from falling on the deck.

Stevens quickly regained her composure. "Excuse me, sir. I didn't see you," she stammered.

"No excuses necessary. I should apologize. I ran into you. I'm sorry," came Wood's reply.

Lt. Commander Ron Wood stepped back, only now realizing that the woman was drenched. Her brown hair hung in limp strands around her slender face. It caught him off guard, but in the times he had spoken with her before, it had not registered how pretty she was. Kind of that girl next door look. He had enjoyed their talks and felt some attraction, but his duties aboard ship kept him well occupied. Black Dog suddenly found it difficult to speak.

She was soaking wet. Her hand nervously pushed back a wet strand of hair over her right ear. She felt her mouth become dry. Stevens looked down and saw a small puddle forming below her feet, letting her thoughts run wild. *I finally have a few moments alone with him, and I look like crap. No make up. I'm dripping wet in a soggy uniform. Great. What's he thinking? He's just standing there with nothing to say.* It was hardly the scenario she had envisioned. "Oh, what the hell," Stevens spit out. "It can't get any worse than it already is, unless of course you say no."

Wood's features twisted into a look of puzzlement.

"Sir, would you like to have dinner with me when we make port again? Just yes or no will do."

The pilot blinked in amazement. "Ah, that would be great. Yeah, great."

"Okay. It's a date."

"Look, I'm headed topside, but I'll see you later. We can talk some more."

"Good," Kendall nodded her head. Lt. J. G. Stevens watched the officer disappear into the corridor and around another corner. Kendall knelt down into a stance with one leg forward and her knees bent. Her fists balled and her arms flew forward, striking an imaginary target. She quickly looked around to see if anyone had seen her, slightly embarrassed by her response. Her faced filled into a beaming smile. That had been easier than she ever imagined. She did not even feel the cold of her wet uniform sticking to her skin as she made her way back to her quarters.

Chapter Twenty-Six

Narissa - Banda Sea

BLUE SEAS ROLLED GENTLY beneath the hull of the Australian research vessel. Narissa had followed Wyborn's charted course, eventually passing through the southwestern edge of the Banda Sea. Aboard the ship, a flurry of activity centered itself near the stern of the vessel. Numerous members of the research team picked apart the pre-dive checklist, ensuring all systems were go for NESSA's submersible vehicle. Each minute detail became a matter of scrutiny, while SEATAC - 1 waited impatiently for its test dive into the depths of the nearly fathomless ocean below.

Red O'Brien and Joe Canton had spent much of the last two days in preparation for this initial dive. There were two undersea plateaus beneath the water where SEATAC-1 would roam. The first would be in relatively shallow waters, a little over thirty-nine hundred feet below. Canton and O'Brien would pilot the vehicle running through a series of tests and checkouts. Their next descent was scheduled to proceed to much deeper depths, and include a member of the Australian team. Together they would scout the ocean floor nearly six thousand feet below the surface, placing the first set of underwater recording instruments for tsunami detection.

"Hey mates," Skiddy Pete called out. "Skipper wants to know when you'll be ready?"

The cigar moved from one corner of O'Brien's mouth to the other before the gravelly Boston accent spit out the reply. "Well, Skiddy, Joe and I just put the finishing touches on this baby, and we're ready to climb aboard. So tell the good captain, we're golden."

"Red, you going to stand around all day talking, or are you going to help me get this thing in the water," the big man joked.

"Guess that's my cue, Skiddy. Hold on, Joe, before you mess around and break something in Sumner's new toy." O'Brien turned and climbed the steel ladder to enter the submersible vehicle's hatch that Canton had already squeezed through. Once on top, the Irishman disappeared inside the vessel.

O'Brien dogged down the hatch, while Canton ran through a checklist of details and performed a communications check. O'Brien sat down and buckled himself into his seat. In front of the two men, a panel of multi-colored video screens lit up, displaying a host of technical information. Inside the totally windowless hull, the two men continued their work.

Joe Canton activated the armrest control. Two panels, covering the large screen in the front of the submersible, parted. Next, he tapped several other buttons, and the outside world invaded SEATAC-1. Sunlight poured into the interior of the titanium hulled vessel. Cameras mounted on the vessel's exterior brought to life real time digital images with amazing resolution and clarity.

"Gives a whole new meaning to being in the belly of a whale," Canton remarked.

"How's that?" Red shot back.

"This thing looks like some giant bug with those two big mechanical arms sticking out in front."

"Guess you could say that. Hell of an expensive one," O'Brien laughed.

Skiddy Pete eyed the vehicle one last time, checking that all the cables were attached properly. Satisfied, the Aussie moved around to the front of the submersible. "Looks good, mates." Pete's voice sounded over the intercom, giving the men inside a thumbs up through the vehicle's viewing screen. Reflexively, O'Brien returned the gesture while the two NESSA men waited for the crane to lift them out over the water.

Neither Canton or O'Brien heard the groaning strain of the heavy motor. Each felt the vibrations of the powerful winch as it tightened the cables. "A" frame hydraulic arms lifted SEATAC-1 from its docking cradle. The mechanism moved the submersible vessel out over the stern, setting SEATAC-1 gently on the crystalline blue sea. In the relatively calm waters, the maneuver was accomplished with little difficulty. More cable unwound from the winch, allowing the craft to float away from the stern of the Australian research vessel.

From their vantage point inside the submersible, two worlds appeared outside. Through the eye of the camera lens, the audio visual equipment brought into focus heaven's creation above the ocean, and the near limitless blue depths below. It was as if the two men were gazing through a clear glass eye at the front of the submersible. So exacting was the equipment's abilities, water seemingly dripped over the surface of a convex bubble at the front of the miniature submarine. Even the illusion of sunlight streaming into the interior of the titanium hull appeared realistic.

A team of support divers surrounded SEATAC -1, each running through a checklist of details. Well trained, they searched for any apparent malfunctions before detaching the steel cable, keeping the sub tethered to the Narissa. The dive master swam in front of the view port. A trail of exhaled bubbles rhythmically flowed from his regulator, ascending to the surface with each breath. He patted the top of his head, signaling everything was okay, which coincided with his words pouring out of the intercom. He quickly disappeared from the view port, as he swam back to the exploration vessel.

State of the art, surround sound speakers, erupted with the voice of Skiddy Pete. "Looks like a go, mates. Don't mess around and bugger that beauty up. Remember, I get to take the next ride with you boys. We've got some real work to do then."

"Alright, Skiddy," Canton returned. "Just sit tight and we'll be back in no time."

Both Canton and O'Brien occupied themselves with their predescent checklists and once satisfied, engaged the motors and trim angle of the dive planes, rapidly descending into the underwater realm far below the Narissa.

Canton manned the joystick control and O'Brien monitored their equipment. A bank of dials, colored lights, and communications gear was housed on the wall to their right. In front of the duo, liquid crystal screen monitors offered up readings on everything from water temperature and currents, to battery life powering SEATAC-1. The onboard computers were not only capable of producing enhanced three dimensional views, but also had the ability to convert infrared thermal imaging into life like images onto the screen. That would come in handy for them, as they explored the thermal vents, negating the possible blinding effects of bright spotlights on creatures living in total darkness.

Sunlight soon faded as the ocean's depths swallowed them. Canton tested the maneuverability of the submersible, satisfied by the sub's quick response. Red O'Brien shuffled through a procedural list of tasks, required by NESSA's technology director, Dr. Gerald Pierson. GPS coordinates were locked into the computer, providing a constant course for the two men. At thirty-nine hundred feet, a larger area of the continental shelf flattened into a vast expanse, before falling away to even great depths.

"You know, Red. These waters were teaming with convoys and submarines sixty-five years ago, during the battles in the Pacific. The Banda Sea saw its share of war, up close and personal," Canton remarked.

O'Brien looked up from his current task of plotting site coordinates for the location of undersea equipment for the tsunami warning system. "Yeah, can't say I'd relish being stuck in one of those old boats with some 'gung ho' ship's captain up above dropping depth charges on my head."

"Not a pleasant way to go," Canton returned idly.

"Hey, Joe," The thick Bostonian accent spit out. "Considering we're nearly three fourths of a mile under water, do you think we can change the subject?"

Canton laughed as the vessel's speakers filled with Skiddy Pete's Australian accent. "Hey mates, not having too much trouble down there, are you? Everything topside looks good. Whoever put that blooming tub together must have known what they were doing."

"This old tub," O'Brien shot back, shifting the stump of the cigar in the corner of his mouth, "will run rings around anything anybody's got, anywhere. You can take that to the bank."

"All the readouts are right on the money," Canton interrupted. "Actually, the sea floor terrain looks even more suitable than we expected. If the second plateau looks this good, it'll be a great place to set up shop for Project T."

"I'll let the skipper know. He'll be happy to hear that. Listen, you two blokes keep me advised if anything unusual pops up."

"Roger that." Canton returned.

"It should take us about an hour or so to get back to the Narissa," O'Brien said. "We've covered a lot of ground over the last three."

"See you topside. I'll see if Cookie can get you boys a bite of food once you're back aboard."

"Deal me in, Skiddy," O'Brien shot back, the intercom returning to silence.

Canton typed in a command on the virtual keyboard in front of his seat and the panel's screens in front of the two men instantly filled with reams of information. Joe Canton tore through the data, checking and rechecking as quickly as he could process the information. “Red,” the big man remarked. “Looks like the inputs are all working properly. The computers are uploading some great data.”

From the wall next to the men, the electrical machinery winked with colored lights, indicating that everything was running smoothly. O’Brien scanned the equipment. “Everything’s damn near perfect, Joe. I’d say we’re ready to take passengers aboard for the next ride. Old Skiddy will be like a kid in a candy shop once he climbs inside this boat.”

“I’m sure he will,” Canton smiled. The computer logged in the heading back to the Narissa. After a thorough going over and a good night’s sleep, the NESSA employees and their AGSI guest would submerge again to the deeper waters where the thermal vents were located. All in all, the first portion of Project T was progressing very smoothly. Joe Canton meant to see it stayed that way.

Chapter Twenty-Seven
Big Island - Hawaii

BRYSON MCGANN LOOKED ACROSS THE AISLE, silently watching Tori Haroldson, a woman intently focused on her work. The dinner in Seattle had greatly helped to improve their relationship. However, the long flight had left her free of distractions and preoccupied with her presentation for the Geo Conference. Neat stacks of papers lay in piles on the leather couch. A number of reference books were on the floor at her feet. Haroldson's eyes fixed themselves on her laptop screen, rechecking the slide presentation she would give to some of the world's top scientists. She had barely noticed the landing as the Gulfstream slowed on the tarmac at Kona International Airport.

The Big Island was home to NESSA's Pacific research complex, where leading experts were gathering for the conference. The agency's tropical headquarters was located on the leeward side of the biggest island in the Hawaiian chain. Tucked into one hundred and sixty-two acres of lush foliage, a portion of the site's pristine grounds were open to the public when not in use for meetings. NESSA's island home had been a gift in perpetuity from the MacMichael Foundation. Their only stipulation: ensure that all buildings fit into the island motif, and no buildings could be over three stories tall. Sumner had been eager to oblige. The results were fantastic. The working station looked every bit the part of a resort, yet the ongoing scientific research within the compound raised the bar around the world in geological and ocean studies.

The realization the aircraft had finally rolled to a halt settled in over Tori Haroldson. She shut down the computer, looking up to see McGann's lopsided grin.

"Paradise," he remarked.

"I've always wanted to come to Hawaii. I've traveled to so many places around the world to study volcanoes. I just can't believe I haven't been here before," Haroldson said, reflectively.

"Well, I have a surprise for you," McGann tossed back.

Tori Haroldson arched an eyebrow, curious. "Okay, I'm biting. What is it?"

"I'm afraid you'll just have to wait until tomorrow."

Wearing a mock frown, the volcanologist replied, "That's not very nice, Bryson McGann. Don't you know that you never offer a lady anything, and then not tell her what it is? You sure know how to hurt a girl," Haroldson offered through a broad smile. "Waiting is not a favorite pastime of mine."

"I'm intimately familiar with that," McGann returned, both of them breaking into brief laughter. "In the meantime, gather up your things and we'll head over to the Hualalai compound."

"The what?"

"We just call it the 'H.' It's the place you'll call home for the next week."

Looming to a height of over eight thousand feet, NESSA's spot in paradise was nestled into the shadows of Hualalai. This ancient mountain comprised of volcanic rock provided a magnificent backdrop to the manicured surroundings. "It's one of the most scenic spots on the island."

John Beech opened the door to the cabin. "Enjoy the ride? No better pilot on any airline," the captain said, with a wink.

Pat Evans followed closely in step behind Beech. "I personally wouldn't believe a word of it," the co-pilot mused. "It's just a good thing I was here. He slept all the way over."

"I'd say we were lucky to survive the landing, let alone the flight across the Pacific," McGann chided, joining in the humor.

Haroldson was a quick study, adding her take on the play. "The three of you together worry me. I think I'll fly coach on the way back." Her remark sparked laughter from the group.

"Are you two riding with us to the 'H'?" McGann asked, as the laughter faded. Evans replied,"Nope. John and I have a few things to take care of with the plane."

"I guess I have my orders," Beech shot back.

"After you, Tori. We'll see you two there," McGann said, turning to leave.

"Thanks, guys," Tori tossed back over her shoulder as she made her way down the steps of the plane.

"Always a pleasure for a beautiful woman," Beech added. The two pilots watched them leave the aircraft and make their way to the waiting NESSA vehicle.

"So what do you think, John?" Evans asked, inquisitively.

"About what?" the pilot returned, scratching his head.

"Are you blind? McGann. What else? If I didn't know better, I'd say he's got himself hooked pretty good."

"You think?" Beech responded, turning to face his friend.

"Sure do."

"Well Patrick, my boy, I could think of a lot worse things than being caught on a line with Dr. Haroldson reeling me in." The two men set about their work as McGann and Haroldson drove away.

McGann decided on the more scenic route to the lesser used entrance of the research center. Within minutes, they had left the coast behind and were climbing the winding road to the compound. At one point, McGann eased to a halt to take in the view of the ocean, sandwiched in between a break in the dense green foliage lining the road.

Tori Haroldson fixed her eyes on the scene of turquoise blue water and green vegetation framing the setting. She threw a quick glance back at McGann. "It looks so much like a painting, it's almost hard to imagine it's real."

After a moment, the car continued along the road. "We're almost there," McGann said, wheeling the vehicle through a large gate. Since the conference was being held on the grounds, the couple had to pass through a rigid security checkpoint. McGann presented their ID's to the guard, and after careful inspection, were waved on through.

"I'm stunned. I've seen pictures, but I had no idea how beautiful this really is," the doctor exclaimed.

"It is, but just wait."

"Part of my surprise?"

Smiling, McGann simply nodded. Following the directional indicators on the pavement, McGann drove only a short distance before the vehicle descended down into an underground facility. "A neat thing about this place is that you won't see many cars or trucks on the grounds. There are several centralized parking areas for employees. From there you can take a shuttle to your destination. We have our own subway system." He pulled the car into the assigned parking spot, and killed the engine. "We'll get our things. I'll take you to your room, and then I'll introduce you to Noel Johnson. I know he's anxious to meet you."

"Good. I've been looking forward to finally meeting him."

"Just so you know, all the rooms are adjoining suites that can be opened up or separated for more privacy. Director Sumner wants me to keep a close eye on you."

Puzzled, Haroldson turned to look at McGann as they walked through the hallway. "I'm not sure I understand what you mean."

"As I said, he wants me to keep a close eye on you."

"Why? What could possibly happen here?"

They climbed aboard a tram and took a seat, while McGann filled Tori in on the history of the complex. Within a couple of minutes, they stopped at their destination, where they moved into a lavishly furnished lobby. After scanning their ID badges, they walked down a thickly carpeted corridor. McGann stopped in front of a set of double doors and waved his ID across a hidden scanner. The doors opened to a magnificent suite, luxuriously furnished with a spectacular view of the Pacific from the spacious balcony. In the distance, the vast sea stretched out a into an almost limitless expanse.

"Wow. It just keeps getting better," Tori exclaimed.

"It's an incredible view from up here. You're staying in the premier suite. Sumner wanted you to have the royal treatment. "

"Sunsets must be over the top. I'll have to thank Randall in person."

They set their belongings down and walked out onto the balcony. McGann spoke a command and brought to life a voice from the computerized controls. "Welcome. How may I be of assistance, Dr. Haroldson and Mr. McGann?"

Haroldson's mouth opened in surprise. "It's the brainchild of Dr. Gerlad Piersen, the gadget wiz at NESSA. Actually, it's a prototype for an automated system to be used in some future development projects. He thought this would be a good place to try it out."

Tori Haroldson shook her head in approval. "That's pretty cool. I like it."

"Thought you might. Doors," McGann commanded. "It takes a bit of getting used to, but then," McGann let his voice trail off as the glass doors to the balcony parted, and a light breeze filtered in from across the slopes. Skirting the coastline to the south, a wall of clouds released a passing shower, bathing the landscape in the ever-present rain that kept the islands so picturesque. A rainbow formed and proudly displayed its colorful bouquet as a gift for the island's newest visitor.

"Did you have that planned, too?" the doctor asked as she stood next to McGann at the railing of the balcony.

"That would have been a nice touch on my part. I'll have to speak to Piersen and see if he can work something out." The couple shared a laugh, and the conversation languished for a moment.

Finally, Tori Haroldson turned to McGann. "What exactly did you mean when you said Randall wanted you to keep an eye on me?"

"Amsterdam."

"Oh?"

I spoke with him in Seattle. He feels as I do about the situation."

"And that is?" she asked.

McGann readjusted himself and turned, staring silently into the china blue eyes of Tori Haroldson.

"You mean it's not over?"

"Tori. Randall was able to get some more information about what happened. Whoever was responsible for that debacle got away with the Oduru diamond. It was reputed to be the largest ever discovered. A security detail was transporting the stone there to be cut and polished." McGann's eyes hardened at the memory. "Do you remember the man who was shot after we got out of the cab?"

"The one who came up behind us?"

"Exactly."

"Yes, I thought for a moment he was going to kill us." The painful remembrance licked at the edges of a still raw wound as the image of the dead man floated to the surface of her memory. The indelible scenes held Tori in its grip until McGann's words interrupted her thoughts.

"I noticed an ID on the man's belt when the wind blew his jacket open."

"What does that have to do with me? Us?"

"Probably nothing, possibly everything. I'm not exactly sure. I need to do some investigating. You and I witnessed something that went, at the very least, not according to plan. That makes us potential targets. I'd say the chances are pretty slim, but Sumner would rather error on the side of caution. I have to agree."

"So now you're my personal bodyguard?" Haroldson asked, a hint of the unknown tracing her voice. The woman's eyes bore intently into Bryson McGann's, searching for any clue that he knew more than to what he was alluding.

McGann paused, choosing his words carefully before speaking. "Sounds like it, doesn't it? Look, as I said, it's probably nothing. The conference starts the day after tomorrow. There're no planned changes for your schedule. Hopefully, that gives you some reassurance. Other than that, I don't know what to say, Tori." McGann centered his gaze upon her face. He sensed her uneasiness with their conversation, but still, she needed to know the truth.

She sucked in a breath and sighed deeply. McGann noticed her thumb and forefinger rubbing together. "Okay. Life goes on," Haroldson smiled.

"There're no certainties in life, Tori. Best you can do is plan for the worst and hope for the best."

"That's rather simplistic, isn't it?"

"Yeah, but I find it fits most situations. Paradise, remember?" McGann tossed out. "Put all this on the back burner and leave it there. Let's go and I'll introduce you to Noel Johnson."

Haroldson and McGann left the room and walked around the grounds. McGann hoped their conversation would not ruin Tori's stay in Hawaii. He pointed out a number of important buildings as they made their way to the research center where Johnson was waiting. Tori Haroldson felt the tensions ease and let herself relax as she took in the lush setting.

McGann interrupted her thoughts. "This isn't all for show. Everything here is part of a working lab, with studies continually conducted on plant life, weather effects, and all the boring stuff scientists like to do," McGann chuckled.

"Sounds like some planning went into this place."

"Since the foundation provided the land for NESSA's use and offered some financial assistance, it left open a lot of opportunity to take on some ideas that were on the wish list." They turned the corner along the path and arrived at the research center.

Following the introductions, Haroldson and Johnson became engaged in a ranging conversation regarding seismic activity and volcanic relationships. McGann had liked Johnson from the first time they met, shortly after his arrival at NESSA. He was the picture of the absent-minded professor, wrinkled lab coat and ruffled hair, but that belied the man's intelligence. He was one of the world's leading authorities in his field. Between his work for NESSA, and as one of what McGann termed, the 'Four Horsemen,' he and the other three assistant directors helped Sumner steer the science agency on a steady course.

McGann excused himself, allowing Noel Johnson to show Dr. Haroldson some of the work he was involved in, and discuss the upcoming conference. McGann left the building and made his way back to the suite. Events of the last several days had left him behind in almost endless paperwork. Tomorrow would provide a pleasant distraction for Tori Haroldson. He would not mind either. The strain of the last few days had brought on a needed break from reality. Doing so in the company of Dr. Haroldson was an added benefit.

McGann fully digested the caution in Sumner's words. Whoever the mastermind behind the diamond's theft was, McGann knew that he was no stranger to trouble, and certainly harbored no compunction when it came to killing. From experience, Bryson McGann knew that men like that seldom rested when their plans were disrupted. The image from the back of the Lexus sedan still tugged at him, especially since the police were unable to identify the mysterious figure.

Chapter Twenty-Eight

Surgical Suite - Sula Kai

STAINLESS STEEL EQUIPMENT GLISTENED under the overhead lighting in the sterilized operating suite. Meticulous attention had been paid to everything involving the upcoming event, under the exacting specifications of Dr. Mick Henke. A stickler for the finest detail, the doctor scrutinized preparation for the surgical procedure from his vantage point behind the glass panel. Filling the console before him were numerous dials and controls for the laser devise. Above the specialized mechanical table that the patient was to be placed on, a thin, folded arm waited to be put to use. A miniscule clamp at the end of the arm would hold the implant. Monitors provided three dimensional imagery of the operating field throughout the entire surgery, as well as simultaneous observation of the patient. Henke looked up, nodding as he watched Noi Lin push the button, activating the specially designed air flow unit. He had insisted upon this feature. Filtering the air within the room for brain surgery was not a necessity, but he had no desire to take any chances.

Henke had performed the procedure before. The other candidates were already performing their assignments with a flawless perfection. Still, Mick Henke was nervous. This was more than the old adage of, *'see one, do one, teach one,'* from the days of his medical training. The implications of bad results would lead to more than the death of the patient.

The person being prepared for the day's procedure had been the accomplishment of a prolonged and tedious selective process. A data bank had found three suitable candidates. None of the men had family, an absolute prerequisite. Each had been carefully studied before being approached by Solange's representative. Under the guise of important work for world security, and the offer of handsome payment, the initial interviews were conducted with the insistence of total secrecy. The dark-haired female agent stressed that paramount, above all else, this was a necessity. While it offered a thin veil of disguise for the actual purpose of the mission, it was enough to catch the undivided attention of the individuals. The alluring face leading them on this journey was also an enticing distraction that captured each man's fascination.

The men were suddenly whisked into a world of secrecy where hushed conversations and glances over the shoulder were norm. All were naive as to the nature of the elaborate plan. No time was allowed for them to think. None of the men understood the complexity of the ruse being laid upon them, and the changes occurring in their lives.

In every case the drama was different. In essence, there were staged events that added mystery and hints of danger. Well thought out and planned with straight lined precision, the scenarios jacked up the importance for the need of their involvement in the particular situations. Their world, as they knew it, no longer existed. They were pawns to be used for other's covert agendas, all the while believing in flag waving patriotism and the lure of a small fortune. These candidates, one American, would assume the role of a very important person in world government, namely, German Chancellor, Kurt Huber.

The second of the three men *chosen* for this assignment had misgivings. He began to question certain aspects of what was going on around him. He had kept silent, telling no one. During his final meet with the female agent who offered him a chance to do a great service for his country, the chancellor's replacement decided to decline the offer. It was a costly mistake. Quite easily and without the slightest hesitation, the woman dispatched a bullet to the back of his head, and the man simply became another in a long list of people who mysteriously ceased to be.

When he did not show up at his workplace, police were notified. Since he had no family to put pressure on the local police agency, or get the FBI involved in a missing persons case, he quietly faded from most people's memory. Even the few close to him at work chalked up his disappearance to that of another missing person: someone whose face showed up on the back of those annoying postcard advertisements. Delivered to countless homes around the country, the cards were considered a nuisance by most, something to be tossed in the trash without so much as a second glance. The person who might have become the replacement for Chancellor Huber vanished, forgotten, with few to mourn his passing.

The other two men jumped at the chance to climb aboard. Each of them had their particular reasons. They had resigned from their jobs, eagerly expecting an adventure of unprecedented nature. After arriving at the compound, the final interviews and aptitude testing were completed. Both were suitable, but the third of the chosen three men had scored slightly higher in the process. He had won the game. The loser was just that. Nature ensured his silence. His body had been dumped out beyond the reef at the changing of the tides, offering the pelagic predators a tempting morsel. The life that was his, simply, ceased to be.

Mick Henke could have cared less who had been the chosen ersatz. It did not matter. He was here to perform, nothing else. Anything other than that would not sit well with Solange. He had spent part of the night studying and reviewing the computer simulations until he felt completely confident. There would be no consents offering up the countless possibilities of what might go wrong. The imposter had done well with his facial transplant. Except for the bruising and swelling which would soon fade, the patient offered no sequelae from the surgeon's knife. Henke's skills had carefully crafted a direct copy of the world's influential and well known figure.

The man posing as the future German leader was strapped onto the surgical table. An intravenous line was placed, and medications given by the anesthetist. The patient was intubated, and connected to the mechanical ventilator. The introduction of numerous medications and inhalation agents assured the fact the patient would remain motionless, unfeeling. Satisfied the man was completely unresponsive, the anesthetist gave the go ahead to raise the table into a sitting position, placing a steel halo over the man's head. Screws were tightened into place, keeping the skull in the precise location needed during the entire procedure. Once the operation had been accomplished, there would be little evidence, and within two weeks, any traces of Henke's work would be virtually nonexistent.

Noi Lin and the crew of the surgical team scurried about the room, placing the finishing touches on all the necessities. Carefully, the nurse rechecked every detail. Satisfied, Lin's voice called out that they were ready. She and the other two surgical assistants, along with the anesthetist, placed dark plastic colored lenses over their eyes to prevent any possible damage from the laser device. Henke's fingers wrapped confidently around the control, positioning the laser according to computer guidelines. Once through the outer surface of the skin and creating a hole in the skull, he could complete the operation in the brain itself.

Henke turned at the sound of the door to the paneled room opening. “Damn it, Solange. What do you want?” Distractions were something he never relished when he was concentrating on his work, this one even less.

Smiling, the attractive woman replied, “That’s not a very friendly gesture after last night’s well spent time. I would have thought maybe at least a thank you would be in order.”

The physician sat back in his chair rubbing a hand across his face, while the surgical team grew impatient wondering what the delay was all about. They could see the couple in the room, but Henke had cut the audio connection. Solange’s eyes peered at the doctor without emotion. “If you want me to do this, you either leave or don’t say a word until I’m finished. In here, I’m the boss, end of story. If you can’t accept that, get someone else,” Henke spit out angrily.

“Sometimes you are far too serious for your own good, Mick.”

“If something happens, it’s my ass on the line. I really don’t care to end up like this guy’s twin. Being a fucking happy meal for a shark isn’t my idea for the ending of a perfect day.”

High pitched laughter erupted from the woman standing next to him. Her hands reached out and rubbed his shoulders. “Mick, so tense. You should learn to relax,” she interjected in a mocking tone. “I think I’ll stay and watch the great Mick Henke perform.”

The surgeon blew out a forceful breath, attempting to ignore her presence. “What is it with you and all of this? Are you so bent on revenge for who or what you believe was responsible for your father’s death that you’ll do anything to bring about your agenda?”

“My father’s death was no accident, unlike all the trumped up news events.” A red polished nail snapped up in his direction, the finger pointing at him like a compass needle. “I swore that I would make those people responsible pay for their actions,” Solange said invectively through clenched jaws. The muscles on her face quivered slightly. Her eyes flared in wrathful indignation. “Proceed,” she commanded venomously, ending their conversation. Henke closed his eyes, willing himself to relax. Finally satisfied, he opened them after a prolonged period and his hands began their task.

Inside the surgical suite, a mechanical arm straightened, and with an electrical whirring sound, moved into position. Henke threw a quick glance at the computer guidance data screen, satisfied with the positioning. The doctor flipped a toggle switch, activating the laser. A buzzing sound like that of a small insect filled the room. Suddenly, an intense pinpoint blue beam shot out from the laser, onto the exact location on the man's head. Careful to make certain all things were in order, Henke checked one more time. Turning the dial to the prescribed setting, the laser intensified, as the insect-like sound inside the operating room grew in pitch.

The blue beam advanced through the skin into the bony material of the cranium. Any traces of smoke and the easily recognizable smell of burning tissue were instantly erased by the air flow unit. Within a matter of seconds, the intense beam passed through bone, penetrating the cerebral cortex. It did its work efficiently and bloodlessly, cauterizing at the same time it cored a hole into the patient's head.

The computer operated flawlessly, only allowing the laser to penetrate to the specified depth. Minimal damage was done to the brain itself, and it would regenerate within a brief period of time. Henke maneuvered the stainless steel arm, placing a miniscule conduit into the man's brain tissue. The doctor's eyes flashed across the control panel, quickly rechecking the computer calibration. Everything was set for the placement of the neural chip.

Henke stopped and keyed in another command, bringing to life a three dimensional image of the man's head. Sticking up from inside the brain, the conduit was waiting to accept the chip. Solange sat rigidly silent, impressed with Henke's abilities. His success was essential for the covert program to be completed. Her eyes widened as the doctor moved the stainless steel arm into place. He averted his gaze and scanned the monitor to insure proper alignment of the equipment prior to the implantation.

Noi Lin stopped, casting a glance at the monitor's screen. A quick check of the patient's vital signs was simply an automatic response from years of working in an operating room. All the usual were being recorded; blood pressure, pulse, temperature, and in addition, an end tidal carbon dioxide monitor flashed its numbers across the screen. Nervously, she licked her lips behind the paper mask. All seemed well. Hopefully, it would stay that way.

With the arm in the proper position, a tiny steel rod descended with a staccato-like clicking sound. It passed easily into the tubing, stopping at the precise depth. Henke tapped a button on the command console. The end of the rod opened, revealing a small basket at its tip. This basket opened and immediately, a neural chip fell into place and attached itself to the brain tissue. It was as much living tissue as it was a computerized silicon chip. Over the next two weeks, this incredible technology would weave a fine thread of tendrils into place, permanently preventing any movement of the chip. No matter what actions the new president would do, the chip would be unaffected.

"Perfect, Mick. Incredibly done. Perhaps an article in a medical journal would be in order. Too bad the world would frown on your accomplishment," Solange intoned. "Join me later." Solange sauntered from the room, satisfied that plans were progressing appropriately.

Henke let the tension ease that had been building on his shoulders. He knew her words were more command than request. The doctor often wondered sometimes how he had gotten into such a setup. Henke let the thoughts slip away, leaving the command console to scrub in, with the intention of erasing any evidence the skull had been penetrated. His years of surgical skills would be put to good use with the short procedure. The anxiety had left him craving something alcoholic. The physician checked the clock on the wall in the operating room. Two fifty three p.m. It seemed like a reasonable hour to have a drink. However, it would have to wait at least another thirty minutes. His work was not quite finished.

Mick Henke slipped his arms into the sleeves of the bluish-gray paper gown. With Noi Lin's assistance, his hands worked their way into the sterile gloves. Henke walked to the table where the man assuming the chancellor's role was being prepared. His practiced eyes surveyed the anesthetized patient. Wasting little time, he took on the task of the repair. Whatever troubling experience Henke had with Solange moments ago quickly ebbed as he became absorbed in his work. Once the operation was completed, he would allow himself to relax. Then he could get that much needed drink.

Chapter Twenty-Nine
Princeville - Kauai

PRINCEVILLE RESTED QUIETLY on the northern shore of the Hawaiian chain's most undeveloped, and arguably, the most beautiful island. A tropical paradise, inhabited by only fifty-five thousand residents, awaited those who dared leave behind the more notable and familiar hot spots. This ideal setting was a place where little attention was paid to its visitors. It was a place that suited Stephan Kholos perfectly.

Early morning rain had left the air fresh and filled with a gentle trade wind flowing over the coast. Now at midday, a warm sun rode high in the azure sky, peering down on the sandy beach below. The man was just another tourist. Clad in a blue Hawaiian print shirt and straw hat, he strolled the beach, ever mindful of his surroundings. Behind the dark lenses of expensive sunglasses, his eyes took in everything around him. Kholos let nothing escape, quickly processing whatever his eyesight captured. Doing so could be the mistake that might cost him his freedom or his life.

A child ran past, squealing with delight while his mother hurried to catch up with her young son. Kholos stopped mid-stride. The tourist responded with a smile that was false in its pretense, and evoked a brief wave of caution from the child's mother. Her concern quickly faded with another strident squeal, and she became immediately distracted by her child's playful attitude.

"The Greek" continued ambling through the stretch of sandy beach, eventually reaching a point where no one was in earshot. He tapped out a Dunhill and lit the end of the cigarette, blowing out a cloud of smoke. His finger hit the speed dial button for the number programmed into the phone's memory. He waited. "The Greek's" phone connection automatically routed itself through three different numbers in various locations around the globe. Simultaneously, his voice was scrambled, making anything he said nearly unintelligible to even the most sophisticated electronic surveillance gear. It took some time, but once connected, the delay in conversation was no different than making a local call.

"Where are you?"

"Are you secure?" Kholos answered tersely.

"Of course," Martin Boggs returned, irritation hinging in his voice. Carlton's head man sat behind the wheel of the black Bentley automobile, driving through D.C.'s congested traffic. Windshield wipers slapped away the raindrops performing a perfectly timed cadence. "I just left the office."

Kholos remained silent. He paced off a few more steps and moved into the shade of a palm. A light gust of wind blowing in across the water rustled the fronds above his head.

"Look, I've tried contacting you," Boggs continued, attempting to mask the agitation. In the background he could hear the sound of waves breaking along the shore. "Where are you?"

"Kauai."

"Damn it, Kholos. What are you doing there? You're supposed to be..."

He cut Boggs off before he could finish the statement. "I'm attending to some unfinished business. It has to do with my vacation to Amsterdam."

"You got what she asked for. Leave it alone, whatever it is."

The accented voice filled the speaker phone in Boggs' luxury vehicle. The words he heard caused him to suck in a deep breath, the meaning behind them leaving little room for doubt. Fear pedaling was something he knew the assassin could easily back up with action. There was nothing to assume differently in the financial firm leader's mind. A chilling cold flowed like running water, racing along his spine.

"Never tell me how to do my work." The corner of Kholos' left eye twitched behind his glasses. Anger flamed through his body, leaving behind smoldering embers of indignation. "Let me tell you, Martin, I enjoy our relationship. Money is good." The tourist paused briefly, surveying the beach, greedily drawing in the tobacco's warm smoke before continuing. "I accomplish whatever you want done. But, I am not on your clock. Remember that. I do the work when I say. Not you. I can do more to harm you from where I am, than if I was standing in front of you with a pistol pressed against your head. Never forget this, my friend."

Boggs glanced in the outside mirror before switching lanes. He knew full well of Kholos' talents, and the outcome of a visit from the man. Martin Boggs was irate, but the last thing he wanted to do was piss off the man who would be responsible for making the elaborate scheme come together. Beads of sweat gathered on his forehead. There was nothing to say about it at this point. Boggs knew once everything was set in motion, it would be time to bid farewell to Stephan Kholos, Greogor Duvonich, or any other in the list of names his false passports carried. "Okay. Sure. Whatever you say."

"Good. I'm glad we understand each other."

"So what's this left over business that's so urgent, if I may ask?"

Kholos left the shade of the palm. "The Greek" never allowed himself to remain motionless in the open for too long. Old habits die hard, and he meant to see that his cautionary approach to life kept him breathing for a long time. Kholos felt certain no one was following him. He had not told anyone of his destination, not even Sahtay, the last time they spoke. Still, the discovery of his true identity would be a prize for any law enforcement agency. He knew he was at the top of their lists, in demand around the world. Kholos wanted to insure his visit to paradise remained just that. "I have to meet a couple tomorrow. One is a man I met a long time ago. I owe him a special favor," Kholos added, cryptically.

"When are you going …" Boggs' words were cut short. He had been distracted by an attractive woman passing him in the next lane. The CEO looked up in time to avoid becoming the third vehicle tangled with the back of a delivery truck His foot tramped the brake. The Bentley's tires screamed under protest, causing the rear end to slide on the slick pavement. Boggs worked the wheel easing out of the skid and guiding the vehicle back on course. The capable brakes brought the vehicle quickly to a halt. The last thing he needed was to be stuck in the midst of a traffic jam. Unfortunately, he had no other option. The thick congestion of D.C.'s notorious streets combined with the mishap would cause him to be late for his upcoming meeting. *What the hell. Let them wait a little longer. I'm the one controlling their money.*

"You ask a lot of questions. I think we're finished."

"Hold on, Kholos. Don't hang up on me." Boggs demanded, his palm pounding the wheel in frustration.

"Time is up." "The Greek" cut the connection, putting an end to the Carlton leader's questioning. Kholos reversed directions, immediately eyeing everything in site, searching for potential obstructions to his plans. As he suspected, there were none. The blue-shirted *haole* walked at a leisurely pace, portraying the image of the quintessential tourist. Kholos' mind had already focused on his next destination, the marina.

The smell of salt and diesel fumes wafted in the air around him. Millions of dollars lay collectively anchored to their moorings. The chugging sound of a large inboard leaving the harbor caught his attention. Several young women were sipping drinks on the fantail, while loud music spilled from the deck of a fifty foot Bertram. He smiled to himself. It always amazed him how insulated most of the world was to their surroundings. It was far better for him that it remained precisely that way.

Kholos walked along the wooden planking until he reached the slip where the sixty foot, dual-hulled powerboat was docked. He had hoped for something less notable. Still, he realized the craft would be better than the Coast Guard searching for someone piloting a stolen boat. The vessel possessed elegant lines and a paint job that turned heads wherever she motored. He knew the motor craft was capable of fifty-five knots with her unconventional engines. Two turbines greedily sucked in water and powerful pumps ejected it in twin streams with great force. It was more than adequate to do the job Stephan Kholos had in mind. His eye caught the name painted above the transom. *Makana*. Solange had told him one time it was the native term for gift. It would be the perfect gift for what "The Greek" had in mind.

His money had paid well to find the man and woman's destination. A smile touched the corner of his mouth, as laughter erupted from deep within. Kholos lifted the straw hat, wiping away the perspiration inching down his temples from his bald scalp. Stephan Kholos was determined this would be their last interference in any of his future plans.

Chapter Thirty
Davos - Switzerland

STAN REYNOLDS FELT MORE THAN EVER the strain of the duplicitous game he had involved himself in. Upon entering the Secret Service, the agent had sworn an oath to uphold the law, and to protect the president of the United States of America. In doing so, he would put his own life at risk, if need be, to save the commander in chief from harm. Every agent was well acquainted with the fact that this possibility was an event that could occur anywhere and at anytime.

Preparedness came with the cost of hours of relentless training and personal sacrifice. Agents could be called on at a moment's notice around the clock. For those who were married and had families, the grueling demands of the job and frequent travel made life difficult. The uncertainties were just the hazards each agent faced. Sometimes marriages fell apart due to the demands of the potentially lethal vocation.

Forty-two and unmarried, the AIC liked it that way. There was no one he had to answer to, except the agency. The former ex-marine had no attachments and did not want any. He was not Hollywood handsome, but not unattractive. Tall, with dark eyes, was a recipe enabling him to fulfill his needs with one night stands. There were enough willing to spend the night after a few drinks, particularly after learning of his intriguing occupation. It was a part of his realm that he kept well hidden. The less the agency intruded into his personal life, the better he liked it.

An uncomplicated lifestyle also provided him the ability to carry out his agenda more easily. There had been numerous late night meetings with various individuals, whose ideals met with his own. Reynolds harbored resentment for what he believed was a stranglehold on the nation: liberal agendas that had turned the country in the wrong direction. The bitterness of dissatisfaction had rumbled around inside him for years, looking for the perfect outlet. Through circumstance and a friend, Reynolds was casually introduced to a few of the players. They checked him out thoroughly, waiting and watching until fully confident of his allegiance.

Once they decided to deal him in, they made it implicitly clear that deviating from their standards would cost him his life. They suggested a possible accident or much worse. It was a consequence Stan Reynolds was willing to accept, in a game beyond anything the world's political arena had witnessed. He decided the uncertainties were no worse than that required by the demands of his gold shield.

The AIC tossed aside the latest report from D.C., satisfied that there would be nothing but the routine of the last several days. The agent picked up the Sig Sauer pistol off the table in front of him, and slipped it into the leather shoulder holster. A slightly oversized jacket hid the pistol's details from view. Reynolds never went anywhere without a back up. Five hot-loaded bullets rested in the cylinder of the small Smith and Wesson thirty-eight caliber he strapped onto his right ankle. His days in the marines had taught him to plan ahead and never be over confident. Arrogance was a killer he never shook hands with, under any circumstance.

The Secret Service agent opened the door to his room and stared into the face of Benjamin Wolcott. Reynolds disliked the presidential advisor and did little to hide the fact. Although technically not his superior, Wolcott was, after all, Simon's right hand man. There was a tension between the two that dug deep. However, Reynolds knew his limits. The agent had no other choice.

"Agent Reynolds. Good timing," Wolcott mused.

"I was just headed out to make the rounds," Reynolds replied, dispassionately.

Wolcott had realized since their initial meeting, there was a deep chasm that separated the two men. That trail of tension had continued to the present, but Wolcott decided to let it pass. He realized Reynolds could be intimidating due to his stature and position, however, the president's advisor was unfazed by the government agent. "Anything new from D.C.?" he questioned.

"No, sir. Everything points to things being right on track."

"Let's take a walk, Stan." Wolcott commanded, leaving the Secret Service agent no choice but to comply with his wishes.

Reynolds fixed his gaze on Wolcott. His eyes searched for a hint of potential problems, any indication of the impossible being discovered. Together the men left the building, stepping out into the cool mountain air. When they were out of earshot, Wolcott continued,

"The president is finishing up in a meeting, so we have a few minutes. We need to talk."

Reynolds tossed around a few possibilities as to what the other man would say. He remained unflinching in his attitude. Calm. "About what, Mr. Wolcott?" he shot back acerbically, stopping to turn and face the president's advisor.

"I think we need to clear the air." Remaining silent, he let Wolcott continue. "To be truthful, I didn't want you on this assignment. I asked for someone else. However, that didn't happen. Some things are out of my control. Look, if you don't like me, fine. I can live with that. Trust me, I'm not losing any sleep over it."

The ex-marine bristled, taking on a defensive posture. "Is this off the record, sir?" he asked indignantly.

"Suits me," Wolcott replied. The muscle along his jaw line twitched slightly as he held himself in check, eyes boring into the man of equal height.

"Frankly, I don't give a shit about you. You aren't my concern. What I have to do far exceeds any expectations you may have. You want to make me happy? Stay out of my way and let me do my job. If there's anything work related, we'll talk. Other than that, piss off. I've nothing to say to you," the agent spit back.

Wolcott forced a half grin. "Everyone said you were a pain in the ass to work with. Looks like they're right."

"You have any other revelations, Wolcott?" the AIC snarled.

"Just remember, my word carries a lot of weight with the right people. I have a little more pull in the D.C. circles than you. The ins and outs of how things work are more complex than you might imagine." The presidential aide let the words sink in, while his features grew sharp with contempt. "Be careful whose toes you step on, Reynolds."

"Are you resorting to threats?" Reynolds laughed. "If you are, I'm not fazed. You're nothing but a load of copper-bottomed bullshit."

Wolcott cocked his head, carefully selecting his words before he spoke. "Reynolds, everyone has their place. In the scheme of things, you and I matter very little. We're both dispensable. Simple fact." He sucked in a deep breath and stopped, turning to smile at the intruders of their discussion. Two German female attendees walked by, arms filled with papers and pocketbooks. Wolcott had met one of them previously, and nodded in recognition. Allowing them to move past, he waited until he felt it safe to renew his conversation. "We both have a job to do if we're going to pull this off. I don't need you crawling up my ass. Understand?"

"I get the message quite clearly," the AIC responded, fire burning in his dark eyes.

"Hopefully, you do." The intonation in Wolcott's voice resonated in Reynolds' ears. As affable as most seemed to think the president's advisor, Reynolds saw a deeper and more menacing side to the man. The thing that gnawed at him the most was Wolcott's supercilious demeanor. It was a side he did not like, and something over which he had no control.

"You have anything else worthwhile to say?" the agent questioned. A voice burst through the miniature receiver in the agent's right ear. He held up a finger at Wolcott indicating a need for his silence. Wolcott complied, irritated with the interruption. He shifted his gaze to his watch, checking the time. "You're right," the AIC responded. "Doesn't sound like much. I'll be there shortly," he replied, speaking into the lapel microphone. Reynolds pressed a control button to close out their conversation. "So that's it? Pep talk over?"

"I'd say it is," Wolcott returned with a honed edge to his words.

Stan Reynolds turned to leave, spinning on his heel. Before he could take a step, he felt a hand knotting his sleeve. The agent snapped his head in Wolcott's direction, remaining silent.

"One more thing," he paused, letting the air grow colder between them before he spoke. "Keep this in mind. We're all here for the good of the country. That's the ultimate concern. I don't believe I'll have to remind you of that again." Wolcott loosed the AIC's arm, staring coldly at him.

Reynolds slashed a hand along his sleeve straightening the material. A conversation came to life again in his ear. "I'm on my way," he shot back gruffly.

Benjamin Wolcott watched the agent walk off to whatever duty was calling him to service. He willed himself to remain calm, slowing the pace of his breathing. Reynolds would have to go. After this conference was over, the president's advisor and friend of many years would see to it. Anything less would be unacceptable. He turned and moved along the sidewalk, following the flock of reporters heading to the building where meetings were letting out for the day.

A BBC journalist noticed him and asked if he would mind answering a couple of questions. Smiling, he agreed. A barrage of other reporters came up with a laundry list of items after Wolcott's response to the initial questioning. His clock was ticking, but a few minutes remained before meeting with the president. He answered another string of queries, passing on a few. Microphones and television cameras had become a way of life, just part of the daily process. Everything that was said went out on a live feed to some news service somewhere. Those who were savvy in the political world had learned to choose their words carefully. Once spoken, there was no chance of retrieval, just like water spilled in the dirt.

"Ladies and gentlemen, please," he said, holding up a hand. "No more questions." Wolcott excused himself, marching off into a guarded entrance. Thankfully, the news hounds could not follow him on this route. Wolcott knew reporters were a necessary evil. They were ticks, clinging tenaciously to their victims; sucking information like blood and digesting whatever they were fed. Then they put their own spin to the wheel. They force fed the public, shoving their ideas down the world's throat. He shrugged off the thought and let the annoyance fade. Everyone had a job to do.

Richard Simon, at least the person who looked like him, had just shaken hands with the German Chancellor, when Woloctt caught his attention. Smiles were handed out all around as everyone seemed enamored by Simon's abilities to bring about some ideas for real and palpable changes to the economic issues facing the world.

It was a challenge few men wanted to tackle, and even fewer were prepared to do. Simon seemed to be rising to the occasion in spite of the stressful demands. Playing the role effectively, the president was slowly winning them over. He spoke very pointedly on issues of great interest - trade embargos, tariffs, the fate of underdeveloped countries facing overwhelming financial burdens, disease, terrorism - no card was left unturned. President Richard Simon's continued mantra of environmental concern, while at the same time, embracing the needs of big business, caught the world's attention. Simon was playing his role effectively, and precisely in the planned direction.

His skills were sealing the promises of his political colleagues. This president was making a difference and restoring the world's faith in a country whose principals were founded on the issues which he spoke about. The nation's chief executive seemed to be living up to the promises made during the campaign of his second term.

Before Wolcott could speak with his boss, the group of dignitaries were whisked outside for the obligatory photo op. They shared a few comments on the progression of the economic summit with the press. Wolcott followed, standing off to the side, listening to the words each voiced into the myriad of media microphones.

When it came to Simon's moment, he moved fluidly into a conversation that was on target, nailing down the issues, and one that offered more than hollow words on world concerns. Suddenly, Simon paused, staring ahead blankly for a brief moment. The press waited politely for him to continue. He quickly picked up where he left off, pressing ahead with his off the cuff speech.

Benjamin Wolcott stared inquisitively, unsure of what made the president pause in mid-stride. It seemed odd, and about the time he was ready to move to his assistance, the president began again. Maybe he just lost his train of thought. Perhaps he was overly tired. Wolcott knew the demands of the position, and the toll it collected on the individuals who governed from the Oval Office. He would speak candidly to Simon about it later when privacy permitted.

The players were wrapping up when a cold breeze pushed against the back of Benjamion Wolcott's neck. He tugged at his collar, hoping to keep out the invader. It had been a long day and it was far from over. The presidential advisor dismissed the chill along his spine as simply the wind.

Chapter Thirty-One
Nepali Coast - Kauai

EIGHT HUNDRED FEET BELOW THE HELICOPTER, the azure water of the Pacific rolled gently under a yellow sun filled sky. Far past the starboard window of the craft, the silhouette of an island took shape in the distance. Tori Haroldson sat transfixed by the exquisite grandeur of the place many called paradise. Each time her eyes captured something incredible, along came a replacement, even more spectacular.

The microphone attached to her headset created a tinny aspect to her voice. "Great view from up here."

"It's pretty impressive," McGann agreed. He glanced down at the instrument panel, checking the GPS coordinates. He had flown here enough to know his way, but NESSA regulations required the instrument's engagement. "Tori, that's Molokai."

"Didn't it used to be a leper colony?"

McGann pushed back the dark lenses on his face. "Sure was. And since I'm your official tour guide, I can pretty much tell you anything you want to know about the islands."

"Well, Mr. McGann, I'm impressed," Haroldson said.

"Just don't ask too many questions," McGann chuckled. A bright smile lit up Haroldson's face. She found herself enjoying the banter. "Actually, Molokai has that reputation. In the mid-eighteen hundreds, the native Hawaiians contracted the disease from Chinese laborers brought to the island. Since it was highly contagious, they were quarantined on Kalaupapa peninsula. It's a magnificent place."

Before McGann could finish, Tori cut in, "Actually, I know a thing or two about that."

McGann nodded, "Fill me in."

"About a million and a half years ago, three volcanoes formed the island. Eons later, after continued pounding from the ocean, a large slab of the island fell into the sea. That's rather simplistic, but you get the idea."

"That must have created one heck of a tsunami."

"I'm sure it did. Probably much larger than the mega tsunami of Latuia Bay, Alaska in nineteen fifty-eight. That one produced a wave around four to five hundred feet high. It's been estimated that ninety million tons of rock broke off the mountain, sliding into the sea. "

McGann collected his thoughts. "I remember reading something about a father and son. Ulrich was their last name." McGann turned his attention to the dials on the instrument panel and quickly checked the surrounding air space before continuing. "That must have made a memorable fishing trip. Must've been pretty frightening riding the crest of a wave out to sea at twice the height as we're flying now."

"It's remarkable they survived," Tori remarked.

"Anyway, what was left on Molakai after the event is what we see today. A peninsula surrounded on three sides by enormous cliffs."

"Exactly why the unfortunate souls who contracted leprosy were abandoned there. If it hadn't been for Father Damien…" McGann added.

"Who's that, Bryson?" Tori interrupted, inquisitively.

"He was a Belgian priest who arrived in eighteen-seventy three. He offered more than salvation for those poor folks. He gave them a bit of life, even though he himself became a leper. Sixteen years later, he died."

"The ultimate sacrifice," Tori said quietly, watching as the island disappeared from view.

The chopper's rotors revolved in a faint circuitous outline above the cockpit as they flew on toward their destination. After a few minutes, McGann sliced into the silence. "Okay. Let's brighten up the day. We're not too far from our destination. Care to guess?" McGann asked.

Tori turned the cap and took a long drink of the bottled water. "Well, we're heading northwest, and the last island was Oahu. That only leaves Kauai. Right?"

"Exactly," McGann responded.

"So what's there?"

"The surprise I told you about."

A few more minutes flying and McGann brought the helicopter in low over Kipu Kai beach. The rocky outcropping was accessible only from the water along the southern coast of the northernmost island in the chain. Overhead, the rotors continued their steady drumming. The expanse under the belly of the aircraft had changed, from blue water to one of unparalleled proportions. McGann hugged the terrain where he could, giving Tori a thrilling ride across the island. All around, steep mountain peaks formed by millennia of volcanic activity, knifed skyward to towering heights.

He glanced across at his flying partner who drank in the beautiful, nearly surreal images. McGann worked the controls, sending the helicopter to an altitude that would allow them to cross the slopes in the nearing distance. Once he worked the ridge, the chopper angled into a steep descent, rocketing down into the verdant Honopu valley. Lush greenery covered the steep walls of the volcanic cliffs.

"Wow. I can't believe what I'm seeing." Haroldson threw a quick smile in McGann's direction, not wanting to miss any of the spectacular view. "It looks like a stage set in a movie," Tori exclaimed, the excitement of her voice ringing in McGann's headset.

"It has been on a number of occasions." McGann skillfully sent the aircraft flying out of the valley and racing towards the vast stretch of the Pacific Ocean. "Now for the surprise. Close your eyes, Tori. Don't open them until I tell you."

"Your wish is my command," she responded, curious as to what lay in store.

Several hundred yards from shore, the aircraft slowed. Expertly working the controls, Bryson McGann brought the craft to a hover and turned back towards the island. "You can open your eyes now."

Tori Haroldson's eyes dilated in response at the sight looming before her. Her mouth formed into a silent circle of astonishment. She was unable to speak. McGann turned towards her, smiling, remembering the first time he been afforded the pleasure of this spectacular vista.

A seamless sky separated itself from the blue seas by rocky slabs of emerald mountains, rising up thousands of feet from the ocean. Covered in beautiful hues of lush greenery, the vegetation seemingly had been placed by careful brushstrokes of a talented painter. Of all the places McGann had traveled throughout the world, this remained his favorite.

A juxtaposition of incredible dimension.

Nature reveling in her finery.

Wisps of white clouds encircled the peaks all along the coast, adding to the flavor of the tropical setting. In his headset, he heard Haroldson's breathing. She slowly turned her head, looking in his direction. "That is one of, no, that is the most beautiful sight I've ever seen. It's truly indescribable."

"It still gives me a thrill. See that strip of beach down there?" McGann asked, pointing toward the shoreline. "That's where we're setting down."

The helicopter landed softly. The blades of the rotor eventually slowed, as the engine's high pitched whine evaporated. McGann unbuckled himself from the harness and pushed open the cockpit door. He walked around the front of the chopper as Haroldson followed his lead. McGann slid back the door along the side to reveal two plastic cases a number of feet in length.

"Tori, can you give me a hand?"

"Awfully large picnic baskets," she joked.

"Better than that. Kayaks. Conditions are perfect. You'll be up close and personal with the Nepali coast. Guess I should've asked if you've ever done this before."

"I haven't," Tori returned. "I'm game for anything."

"Don't worry, you'll catch on. Can you hand me that bag?"

Flat seas made for the ideal adventure. They set out from the beach, paddling away from the island. Haroldson was a quick study. Sun glistened on the slight sheen building along her shoulders. McGann was happy to see she was enjoying herself. He could not help but noticing how nicely she filled out the bikini she wore. They turned and headed in a westerly direction, vanishing around a point, leaving the beach where the helicopter waited for their return.

☙ ❧

Princeville evaporated in the distance. Powerful jets launched twin streams of water shooting from the stern, propelling the twin hulled boat over the relatively calm seas. Racing the wind, sprays of water flew out from both sides of the bow, occasionally splashing onto Stephan Kholos' bare shoulders. He stood at the wheel, powerful legs planted on the deck, while firm hands gripped the gleaming metal, making certain the boat remained on course. "The Greek" did not need a map to locate his destination. He had only one intent in mind. NESSA's Bryson McGann and the blonde bitch would pay dearly for their intrusion into his plans. No one crossed him, and lived long to tell about it. Plus, he owed the NESSA employee a debt from long ago.

Rounding a headland, Kholos slowed the boat. The spectacular backdrop of the famed coastline was of no concern. What he captured through the binoculars brought a wicked smile to his face. The digital rangefinder's readout, superimposed on the image, gave an exact distance to his target. Gunning the engine, Solange's sleek boat leapt to top speed in mere seconds. He barely noticed the feel of the water passing beneath the hull. The pulsing rhythm of the motor played a sweet song in the background, as "The Greek's" mind envisioned the finality of his plan.

He maneuvered the boat in close to shore, tossing out the anchor. Kholos jumped over the side into the knee deep water. On his back, a dry bag held the implements of his trade. Wading onto the beach, Kholos eagerly set about his work. He knew there were a couple of options. He mulled them again, momentarily. The second one would be more spectacular, even he had to admit. Watching the helicopter disintegrate at a couple thousand feet in the air would provide quite a show. Kholos' decision rested on the practical. He would relish their deaths up close, sticking to his first plan.

"The Greek" had learned years ago that killing was a business. One to be done swiftly. Needlessly wasting time at the scene might invoke questions, and quite possibly, get him identified by anyone that might happen to sail past. Complications were not an option he wished to deal with. The pleasure would come in knowing success.

Kholos cautiously eyed his surroundings, a reflexive predatory instinct, sharpened through years of experience. Determined strides measured his pace, as he hurried towards the helicopter. He silently studied NESSA's emblem painted on the side of the aircraft, running his fingers across its warm aluminum skin. An almost three dimensional likeness of the earth, filled with crisscrossed latitudinal and longitudinal lines, with the words of the organization painted in gold letters inside a black ring, stoked his ire.

Ever mindful, Kholos cast an eye over his shoulder, assuring his dirty deeds went unnoticed. He dropped the bag onto the sand, and removed the *plastique*. "The Greek's" meaty fingers worked the explosive charge like dough. Kholos pushed the material directly into the middle of the NESSA emblem. A thin trace of satisfaction appeared and quickly erased itself from his face. Knowing hands inserted a small radio controlled device into the center of the charge. Satisfied his task was near completion, he gathered his belongings and returned to the boat.

Growling engines came to life at his command, quickly propelling him to a safe distance several hundred yards from shore. The boat slowed and its pilot turned the wheel. The sleek boat rocked gently on the nearly calm sea. Several seabirds left no trace of their passing, as their dark shadows sailed across its deck. The assassin wasted no time flipping the switch on the hand held device. A blinking red light flashed when he triggered its mechanism. The beautiful peacefulness of this tropical paradise was shattered by the concussive force of the explosive event. It took a moment before the thundering sound reached him, confirming what his eyes had just witnessed.

The helicopter erupted into a ball of orange-yellow flames, ravaging the solitude of the isolated beach, as it blew apart from the explosion. Pieces of the aluminum skin were sent flying in all directions. Sections of the rotors whizzed through the air, deadly scythes waiting to rip apart anything in their paths. Flames rolled skyward, followed by boiling plumes of thick, black smoke from the furious intensity of the burning fuel. The last remnants of the disintegrated aircraft fell from the sky, scattering themselves across the golden-brown sands of the deserted beach. Eventually, even the concussive rumbling faded away into stillness.

Kholos smiled with grim satisfaction at his handiwork. Now, McGann and the woman had no way of leaving Kauai. Not only did it seal their fate, it also stuck a thorn into the side of the internationally known science organization. Anything associated with McGann deserved no less, he thought to himself. Beads of sweat dripped from his bare scalp. Kholos flicked at one to keep it from falling into his eye. He powered up the boat. The sleek hull raced headlong, running the coastline at a fevered pitch. "The Greek's" jaw clenched into a tight grimace. His words were lost in the wind. "Now its your turn, Mr. McGann."

Chapter Thirty-Two
Sula Kai - Banda Sea

PALE VIRIDESCENT LIGHT FROM THE LASER bathed the gem in a surreal hue as it sat atop the pedestal that had become its resting place. The only sound in the darkened room was the faint hum of the scanning device, moving continuously around the milky colored stone. To someone untrained in gemology, the object would be nothing more than a curiosity; something, after a second thought, to be disregarded as of little value. That had not been the case to Peter Oduru when he dug it from the earth of a Namibian mine.

Now was not the case either to the trained eye of the old man seated in front of the flat panel monitor. Skilled in the art of gem cutting, Abram Mossel diligently studied the multitude of views revealed on the screen. He had learned to trust his instincts over the years, as well as his skilled hands. Mossel had cut some of the world's larger gem stones, and before retirement, was a handsomely paid cutter in great demand.

Mossel stared in disbelief at the three dimensional computer driven images, detailing the exact location of where the stone should be cut. He had held the stone himself. He felt its weight. Carefully his practiced eye had inspected it, over and over again. The old man held no doubt regarding his judgment on where to make the cuts so the stone would be unflawed. Now the computer in front of him derided his decision, causing ambiguity to swirl around him in an unseen mist.

The Jewish diamond cutter from Amsterdam trembled with uncertainty. His family's talents were second nature to the old man, passed down from generation to generation. It was in his blood. Never before had skepticism ever hovered in the shadows of his mind. The veritable fortune this gem offered was unlike anything known to exist. Abram Mossel knew if his cut was incorrect, the stone's value would diminish immeasurably. He debated the choices. Following instinct could either bring to life a stone of flawless beauty, or shatter the Oduru diamond into pieces. Mossel struggled, evaluating his choices. He felt the tension rolling into a knot, causing his heart to race.

Solange burst into the room seeking a reason as to what was taking the old man so long. Her anger was readily apparent by the expressive mask she wore. "What's the problem?" Solange demanded. Rippling beneath the surface, a cauldron of hatred seethed at a constant simmer.

"I'm uncertain," Mossel stammered, his Dutch accent heavily salting his words.

"Over what?" the wrathful woman shot back.

"My dilemma is this," Mossel uttered. "My years of experience tell me to do one thing. Your machine tells me something else," he finished, his hands splaying outward, shoulders arching.

"Old man, I brought you here to cut a stone. I didn't ask you for your opinion."

"You don't understand," he implored.

Solange unleashed a bruising backhand to the man's face. Her hand left a reddened imprint, testimony to her bristling rage. Mossel's head whipped to the side by the fury of her assault. Instantly, a trickle of blood escaped from the diamond cutter's mouth. He ran a dry tongue across the wound, tasting the metallic, coppery flavor of his own blood. Mossel was about to speak, eyes flaring with disdain. Realizing it would be a grave mistake, he corralled his contempt. He gingerly dabbed his mouth, erasing any traces of his blood. The Dutchman wished he could as easily remove the pain.

"It's you who doesn't understand. You were brought here for one purpose. You will accomplish that. If the computer's telling you something different than your instincts dictate, I don't care. Here you play by my rules. There're no other choices." Solange hovered above the man, silently daring him to say more.

Life drained from Mossel's brown eyes. The Dutchman knew he had no other options. Even through all this, his mind was contemplating the cut and polishing the stone. It was Abram Mossel's penchant. Turning his back to the woman, the diamond cutter capitulated to the brazen woman's demands. "I'll follow your directions. Please leave me. I need just a bit longer. I'll cut the Oduru diamond within the hour."

"See to it," Solange turned, "and one more thing, Abram Mossel. Get it right." She left, leaving the old man with his thoughts.

Mossel required complete solitude. No distractions. When he was at work, it swallowed him, demanding exigent standards. If the Oduru diamond was to come to life through his hands, there was only one opportunity. Anything less would be a failure of epic proportion.

Mossel had declined the use of a diamond saw. He preferred to cleave the stone by hand, an age old method that few had the capability to do anymore. Picking the object up from its pedestal, Mossel set the incredibly large stone on a scale to confirm an accurate determination of its weight. A digital read out indicated the Oduru diamond came to four thousand, one hundred and twenty-two metric carats. Mossel gasped. He had not suspected it to be quite that large. The Jew worked silently, gathering his tools.

Mossel shrugged, exhaling forcefully at the decision the computer made. A machine might be responsible for ruining his reputation. The impact of failure had never set in until now. If the diamond failed to meet expectations, he would not live long enough to worry about his reputation. His chances of surviving for longer than he was needed were, more than likely, nonexistent. The old man resigned himself to fate. If nothing else, the right cut might allow his name to live on a number of years to whomever owned the valuable gem. He mused at the thought, finally resigned to the idea it would be his final legacy to the world.

Mossel removed the stone from the scale. His hands felt stiff. Tension wrapped itself around his chest, gripping him tightly, constricting his breathing. Somehow the rough stone nearly slipped from his hands. Miraculously, he recaptured it before it hit the floor. Sucking in a few deep breaths and sounding like wheezing machinery, he forced himself to relax. The diamond cutter laid the gem gently onto a cradle that would hold it in place while he made his strike.

From his bag, he removed the old diamond knife, essentially a chisel, and a long heavily-weighted metal rod. They were a gift to his father and had been passed along to Mossel. These were also the same instruments that had brought to life the famous Cullinian diamond, set into the British crown jewels.

He could feel the anxiety gnawing. The old man's throat felt dry, raspy. One final time he inspected the computer's rendering of the stone and the precise location for the cut. The old man closed his eyes and mumbled a quick prayer. His heart raced with the decision. The choice had been made. He knew, from years in the trade, the two metals would sing when they came in contact with the other. The sound would gradually fade and for good or bad, the stone would be split.

Mossel held the diamond knife tightly in the sweaty palm of his gnarled fist. In his other hand, he lifted the metal rod. The old man hesitated only briefly. He made his decision. In a blurred motion, Abram Mossel brought the cold steel down swiftly on top of the knife. Mossel's eyes widened. His hands shook. He dropped the diamond cutting instruments and stepped away from the Oduru gemstone. "My God, what have I done?" he gasped.

Chapter Thirty-Three

Davos - Switzerland

RICHARD SIMON'S LOOK-A-LIKE had a trail of staffers asking questions and seeking directions on all the usual matters of daily affairs. One by one, they broke off to attend to their assignments. While the G-8 leaders were gathered to chart the world's future course, life continued for the citizens back home. Wolcott tagged along closely, watching the president. He thought the nation's leader seemed in rare form. Exceptional. Vibrant. Perhaps the commander in chief had needed some time away from the daily grind of being tied to the White House leash. Whatever, it appeared to be working.

The president's advisor was the last person remaining to share the hallway with him. "Ben. Get with Senator Ramsey and see what progress has been made on spearheading this economic package. Tell him it's imperative we have support from those sitting on the fence. We can't drop the ball on this."

"Yes, sir. I'll do that."

"Anything else from the home front since this morning?"

"Nothing. As they say, no news is good news," the advisor replied. Wolcott was the poster child for multi-tasking. He had a stack of papers tucked under one arm, while keying entries into his PDA, and simultaneously carrying on a conversation with the president. It was a credit to his talents.

The men stopped in front of a set of double steel, mahogany-veneered doors. Two armed sentries warily guarded the access leading into the security briefing room. All conversations in this room were considered off limits to the press, or any one else, for that matter. The room's four windows were especially designed to prevent lasers from overhearing matters of state secrecy. Thickly lined walls prevented any outside intrusive equipment from eavesdropping on world leaders' private conversations and secretive deals.

All electronic equipment, and the room itself, had been swept for eavesdropping devices and hidden micro lenses. Modern technology had provided miniature gadgetry with abundant ability. To all but the most sophisticated devices, much of this equipment was nearly undetectable. Once the room had been cleared, it was locked down tight. No one was allowed access. The sentries posted outside the room knew their orders. The gathering place for the world leaders was considered clean at the time of the meet. The security room was just that, secure.

Simon's hand turned the heavy brass latch, pushing the door ajar. Remarkably, the weight of the door rested upon specially designed hinges, allowing it to swing open effortlessly. Turning towards his friend of many years, he remarked, "Take some time off. You look like shit." Simon smirked, patting Wolcott on the shoulder and closing the door behind him. Wolcott's plans on attending this meeting with Simon were just cancelled when the door closed behind the president. He hadn't even had the chance to offer resistance to the presidential order.

Inside the lavishly appointed room, the glow of muted lighting lent a warmth to the atmosphere. Oil paintings clung to their holds on richly paneled walls. Surrounded by an ornately carved mantle of Georgian marble, yellow flames licked the air, dancing atop the glowing logs. Snapping and crackling, the wood brought to life tiny red embers that rose above the burning pyre, disappearing up the flue. The room was filled with a mix of a slightly woody scent and old leather from the volumes ensconced on the shelves lining the walls.

Simon's highly polished shoes squeaked in mild protest as his footfalls echoed off the lustrous hardwood flooring. Three men rose up to greet the newest member of the secretive enclave, smiles filling their faces. Hands were extended, clasped, and pumped in a gesture of friendliness, cementing a bond with implications of something more.

Comfortably dressed in a silk sports coat and expensive slacks, Henri Becque, the French president, offered Simon a drink, pouring his favorite single malt from a crystal decanter. Richard Simon liked his whiskey neat. Unfortunately, the president's impostor hated it, but there was nothing they had been able to do to change his taste buds. Besides, anything out of character would be a potential threat to the overall plan.

"Now that we are alone, how are you feeling, my friend?" the Frenchman asked, dark eyes warily raking the man fully a head taller than himself.

"Well, no problems that I'm aware of," Simon returned. His mannerisms were perfect, the overall effect would more than suffice to ensure their heinous deeds would come to fruition.

Italy's prime minister, Giovanni Bertoluzzo, peered from under bushy eyebrows down his prominently curved nose. The middle-aged dignitary had an owl-like appearance. Wrinkles formed from earlier in the day had erased much of the crisply starched cotton of his white shirt. He found the ruby colored wine's bouquet quite pleasing to his palate, as he tugged at the blue silk tie hung loosely around his neck. His focus did not center itself on formalities at this meeting. Pressing the glass to his lips, he quietly took stock of the man standing before him, searching out any detail that seemed out of place. Finding none, Bertoluzzo resigned himself to the capable talents of this man's *creator*.

The third man in the room, British Prime Minister, Geoffrey Haines, sat his scotch on the table beside him. Those who knew him found him stiff and formal, even when involved in casual events. His bowtie pressed tightly against his neck. The PM shot off a rapid fire string of sentences in a richly traditional, highbrow English accent. "Good to see that everything is up to par, Simon. Don't mind if I have a look, do you?" Haines stepped toward Simon, not expecting a response to what was, in essence, a demand. "It's just to make sure." The gray haired Englishman moved in behind Simon, taking his arm and guiding him to a chair. The offer left no other choice, but to sit. Becque positioned himself beside the two men and switched on the lamp. "You'll pardon me," Haines spit out unapologetically, "but some things are better not left to chance." The PM's fingers explored the top of Simon's head, parting the thick hair.

Bertoluzzo took in the reflection glinting off the lenses of Haines' eyeglasses. The mirror image displayed the top of Richard Simon's head, finally revealing what the world leaders were searching for. Almost indiscernible, the faint ridge where Henke repaired the skull, passed underneath Haines' finger tip. "Very good. Actually, quite remarkable," the PM beamed, slapping the man on his shoulder.

"Now that everything is in order," Bertoluzzo paused, capturing each man's attention. "A toast to the future." The four men raised their glasses, sealing a kinship unseen by the world before.

Becque cut in, "Gentlemen, the stage is set. It's time for the plans to be unleashed. We have waited many months for this moment. World markets are about to witness nothing they've ever seen before. European financial institutions will tumble. Solange will have her vindication."

"Yes, those she holds responsible for her father's death will lose millions in assets," the English PM offered. "All the while, she'll be playing into the greater plan. One that eventually will bring about…" the Englishman took a sip of his drink, letting its slow fire warm his belly before continuing, "control of certain commodities on the world market by our Washington friends."

The four conspirators moved to a table to sit and discuss the forthcoming events. Their planned reactions to the financial devastation that lay ahead for the European banking system, and other events that would surprise the world, had to be well choreographed.

People would look to these leaders for hope and direction in the coming days, and they would see to it that their plans moved along in the prescribed manner. All the while, the head of the Carlton Trust, Martin Boggs, would move matters along on a charted agenda. The escalation of this group's alliance with certain factions, that for years dreamed of the catastrophic financial implications, would all but see to the fact, that this time, no outside interferences would occur. Nothing or no one could deter them.

Richard Simon listened from a detached perspective. It seemed as if a part of him was viewing this drama from the fourth row in some theater. He scanned each face, peering at each imperfection, each wrinkle on the other men's skin. Faces cast from waxy molds gave off a near death look in the pale lighting of the dimly lit room. Simon heard each word, digesting it, and offering his own comments and ideas when needed.

Several hours passed. Bertoluzzo closed his eyes, the need for sleep impinging upon him as the meeting drew to a close. He rubbed at his reddened eyes. "Thankfully," he spit out in a thick, Etruscan accent, "we've agreed upon our plan of action."

The other three men nodded silently, lending their hand to the envisagement of their proposed scheming. All had bitten on the lure of money and power. All had been dissatisfied with life's dreary role. Now, they held tomorrow's destiny in their hands. Soon the world would be a far different place as it slid along the slippery path to a destination preordained by those whose plans had waited for just the right moment to come to life.

Richard Simon allowed himself a brief smile of satisfaction when the meeting finally ended. The realization that he would be shaping the world of tomorrow struck him like a slap in the face. Power was a position he envied long before the offer he had been given; one that had allowed him to rise above the other competitors for this job. He liked the idea, relishing it until the sounds of chairs scraping against the wooden floor pressed into his thoughts. He tossed the irritating intrusion aside.

The perfect ploy, Richard Simon thought. A wry smile grew slowly, creasing his face in strident features upon the leader of the free world. A bubble of laughter erupted from his throat. There was a connectivity between this coven of political leaders. He knew the men gathered around him held the same ideals. Why wouldn't they? Every man was growing the same implanted chip within their own brain.

Chapter Thirty-Four

Nepali Coast - Kauai

"I PROMISE YOU A MORE sumptuous repast this evening," McGann quipped.

"If that's your invitation to join you for dinner," she toyed, a façade of elation riding a close second to her words, "well, Mr. McGann, consider it a date."

Resting under the visor of his hat emblazoned with the Flying Tiger's crest, the reflective surface of Bryson McGann's polarized glasses held the sun at bay. He and Tori Haroldson rode beside each other on the calm, coastal waters of a slack tide. A slightly stiffening breeze played across the sea, as she rummaged in the dry bag tied to the hull of her kayak. The volcanologist came up with a bottle of water to help wash down a granola bar and quench her dry throat.

"Good. I know a great place. Actually, I made reservations." McGann paused, "Too presumptuous?"

"In your case, I'll make an exception." She smiled warmly, her eyes searching through the pale green sunglasses. Realizing she was staring, Tori quickly took a long pull from the water bottle. Inside, she was squirming. She felt giddy, but enjoyed the sensation. Tori Haroldson had not harbored any notions of this sort in a long while, and she liked the way it felt.

Unexpectedly, the bottle slipped from her grasp. McGann and Haroldson reached out to catch it as their hands tangled in a desperate attempt, hoping to keep the container from falling into the ocean. The simple act of touch, arcing with sensual excitement, spurred a wave of electrical energy that jolted through each of them. Embarrassed by the childish spell, yet captivated by its grasp, both felt the warm breath of the other as they drew close. Teetering on a precipice, the world was swept away. Their only thoughts were of drinking in the moment.

Bryson McGann let his right hand move along her cheek, fingers tracing the outline of her soft skin. She found herself plummeting into a fiery cauldron, as her eyes closed. Hesitantly, her lips brushed McGann's. Together, they became ransomed prisoners of the luscious temptation that craved much more.

The serene, tropical fabric was shattered by a pulse-ripping explosion precariously reverberating across the face of the shoreline's steep pinnacles. Their pleasurable moment was erased. Instantly alert, McGann searched the ocean for any indication of danger. He could find nothing to indicate they were in immediate peril. Yet, the fact that an explosion occurred, coupled with their inadvertent dance with death in Amsterdam, brought to life a very serious potential. The blue waters of the Pacific, seemingly immune to the trouble, took little notice of their predicament.

"What was that?" Tori cried out, confounded, a specter of uncertainty rising up in disquieting alarm.

"I'm not sure, but I have an idea," her companion returned, "and it isn't good." McGann surmised the situation, fully realizing the possibilities. His mouth tightened. "Tori, whatever happens, do exactly as I tell you." Bryson McGann's voice possessed a calmness, yet his words left no doubt to the meaning of his command. "No questions, okay?"

The beautiful woman sitting in the kayak next to McGann wore a mask of trepidation. The implications of what occurred brought back buried memories of the deadly gun battle. She had just begun to close the envelope on those painful visions, and now, a maelstrom of uncertainty encircled the volcanologist. Her pupils dilated. She felt a tightness of apprehension filling her chest. Tori fought the raspy dryness coming to life in her throat, swallowing hard against it. Silently, she nodded in recognition of McGann's directive.

Bryson McGann weighed the options before them. The steep, insurmountable cliffs above offered no protection, but were also an unlikely spot for anyone peering down on the couple through the powerful lens of a rifle scope. Staying put was not even worth consideration. No protection. Deeper water offered the same impracticality. Paddling back to the spot where they had landed might offer hope. At some point, someone would come looking, if they survived. It could also bring them face to face with the perpetrator of the explosion. McGann winced at the thought, certain of what awaited them on the once peaceful beach. "I've got a plan."

A ridge of concern grew between Haroldson's brow. She felt her pulse shift gears with the unknown.

"Look. We don't have a lot of choices. An attack could come from the air, but I suspect it'll be from a boat. Problem is, the tide's coming in. Wind's picking up. It'll get rough close to shore." Mc Gann stopped in mid-sentence, scanning the water before continuing. "We'll have to be out beyond the breakers. That leaves two choices. Try and go in the opposite direction and hope someone picks us up. However, that's doubtful. This part of the coast is pretty barren. Or, we can take the offensive. Not a real great choice either."

"Do you think…" She attempted to digest everything McGann said, while wrestling with the fear. "How about walking back?"

"We'd stand out like sitting ducks on the beach."

Tori brightened momentarily. "What about your satellite phone?" she asked, hopeful.

"Sorry. Forgot to bring it. It was in the helicopter." McGann replied, chewing at the corner of his lip.

"We can call when..." Haroldson stopped in mid-sentence, puzzlement replacing her soft features. "Was?"

"Tori, that explosion was the helicopter." McGann let it sink in. He realized she might have guessed that, but was unable to accept the fact without hearing it from him. He had seen similar things occur in combat. The sudden shock of being thrust into the unknown was a recipe that had devoured soldiers, particularly those whose fears overwhelmed them at critical junctures. An inability to comprehend impending danger was something that many times got people killed.

McGann quickly pulled the strings, closing the circle on their only choice. "Follow my lead. If you can't keep up, say so." He observed her carefully, confident in her abilities. McGann knew Haroldson possessed a strong will - she was a woman of great determination - when she put her mind to it. "Let's go."

The duo dug their paddles deeply into the clear blue waters, quickly gaining speed. She kept the pace, resolute in her actions. McGann's powerful shoulders worked in machine-like fashion, as they moved along without speaking, conserving their energy. The sound of their heavy breathing was swept away on the increasing breeze. In unison, they followed an outline of a small headland. Faced with no other choice, they pushed farther from land when the winds grew and the seas rose up. Being swept up by crashing breakers and tossed against the towering cliffs was not an option. Consigning themselves to fate, they continued the grueling pace.

From a distance the muffled sound of a boat's engine caught their attention. McGann spotted it, acutely aware of the impending danger. The sleek-hulled craft rode a course straight in their direction. Together, they bobbed on the swelling seas, concern etching McGann's face, while the boat rapidly closed the gap between them.

"Tori," McGann said calmly. He turned to look at her. "I don't think that boat's here to help."

"What?" Tori Haroldson licked the dryness from her lips. The hot sun was beginning to burn her shoulders, but she barely noticed. Her eyes took in the scene playing out like another bad Hollywood drama. It all seemed surreal. "Oh, God, no. Why…"

"Tori. Stop. You know the plan. It's our only chance." McGann added as an after thought, returning his attention on the speeding boat. His entire focus was on playing the angles, hoping their slim chance of surviving would become a reality.

Stephan Kholos bore down on the two kayaks with murderous vengeance. A meaty, left fist held the wheel in check, as he stood at the helm, confident in his objective. The other held the binoculars to his eyes, their image stabilization allowing his gaze to be riveted on his nearing target. At top speed, he knew Solange's boat would filet the kayaks, bringing a permanent end to McGann's meddling.

Revenge was a plate he relished, one he enjoyed serving cold and deadly. Instinctively, his hand relinquished its tight grasp, permitting a slight course adjustment. Within seconds he would be upon them, and then quickly carry out his escape. The blue-shirted tourist would disappear, forgotten, and few would notice. Solange's boat would burn to the waterline, leaving no trace of its pilot.

The two kayaks moved straight towards the oncoming vessel, offering a weak challenge against a much stronger opponent. Sweat inched out from under McGann's cap, trickling along his chin. Tori Haroldson was his responsibility. His idea of a fun filled jaunt had disintegrated into a life threatening tale. McGann had wasted little time parsing his decision. He only hoped their assailant would decide not to linger after completing his task. They were out of time. The boat was on them. "Now," McGann shouted.

In unison, both kayaks moved at an angle away from the deadly water craft. At the last moment, McGann looked up, catching a glimpse of the murderer in the boat's cockpit. A wicked grin filled the man's face, the same face McGann saw in the back seat of the Lexus sedan in Amsterdam. He reacted automatically, praying it would be enough.

Kholos heard and felt the kayaks strike the hull of his boat. The bow tore through them, sending shards of fiberglass in all directions. "The Greek" kept the boat's throttle pushed to the limits, holding the rpm's near the redline. Kholos threw a long, hard defiant stare into the wake of his boat. Pieces of debris floated on the surface. There were no signs of life. Confident his actions ended as planned, Kholos spun the wheel, turning the craft into the direction from which he had come. The craft's wake only briefly marked the man and woman's watery grave. Sated by the death of McGann and the blonde woman, "The Greek" was now able to fully concentrate on the next aspect of his elaborate scheme.

Chapter Thirty-Five

Nepali Coast - Pacific Ocean

RACING WITH THE WIND, Kholos never looked back again, assured of his success. Fragments of colored fiberglass, the remaining traces of McGann and Haroldson's kayaks, drifted apart on the current. Rolling waves of blue water washed over the spot, erasing any evidence of "The Greek's" heinous act. He had but one thought at the moment, as matters of great importance were at hand. It was time to disappear. Stephan Kholos had a flight to catch.

Sunlight poured through the blue water's fabric, bathing the undersea world with rippling, white light. A circling school of small, silver fish scattered at the instant the woman's head broke the surface. Greedily, she sucked in several lung-filling breaths of air. Finally satisfied, she kicked her legs and moved her arms in a figure eight fashion, easily treading water. She turned in the direction of the retreating boat, watching it grow smaller, as the distance between them increased. Tori Haroldson felt relieved, hedging on the bet her attacker would not return.

Haroldson replayed the events in her mind, each agonizing frame passing by in slow motion. McGann's words had been barely audible above the clamor of the oncoming boat's engines. The scientist barely caught a last glance of him before she intentionally rolled her kayak. She pushed away from the overturned boat, scissoring her legs in powerful downward thrusts, praying to avoid the brief agonizing pain of being sliced in two from the menacing boat's hull.

Only now did the realization strike her that she was fully alone. She floated over and into the troughs of the rolling waves. She spun in a circle, hoping to spot him. "McGann," she called out desperately. Tension gripped her, twisting her gut into a painful knot when no one replied to her cry. The shore waited several hundred yards away. Tori Haroldson had no choice but to swim, her life depended on it.

The blue depths sank limitlessly off the Nepali coast. From above, the surface beckoned. More than a competent swimmer, many hours spent in the water had allowed McGann to hold his breath for a prolonged period. He listened carefully, the sound of the engines fading. The ocean was a powerful transducer, allowing sounds to be heard for great distances. At the moment, there was little he could do for the woman. He swam slowly towards the surface, arms at his side, strong legs propelling him to life giving air.

Bryson McGann wiped away the salty water from his eyes, holding a hand above them to act as a shade. He scoured the water in all directions, searching for any signs of Tori Haroldson. Straining for any evidence of the woman each time he rose to the top of a wave, he finally spotted her as he floated down into another wave trough. She was headed towards shore, moving effortlessly through the sea.

McGann set out, his internal compass guiding him along an azimuth that would carry him to her. Until he closed the distance, it was pointless to attempt to call out.

He let his powerful muscles push him through the water. Several minutes later, he had nearly caught up with her.

Tori Haroldson stopped to let herself rest, floating on her back. She was a good swimmer, confident she would make it to shore, but it was a long swim. Her head suddenly snapped in the direction of the sound. She willed herself to remain calm, not letting her mind run wild with the possibilities. Surviving two attempts on her life by some lunatic was bad enough, but now, the thought of being an hors d'ouevre for some giant fish looking for an easy lunch, was not a palatable choice.

Finally settled with the fact nothing wanted to invite her to dinner, she turned once again in the direction of shore. Tori Haroldson gasped at the sight, frightened by what was looming in front of her.

Popping up out of the water with a lopsided grin affixed to his face, McGann said wryly, "Nice day for a swim."

"You scared the… Oh, God, I'm so glad… I called out… You didn't answer. I thought you were dead." Tori Haroldson shoveled out her words at a frantic pace. McGann moved in front of her, not letting the woman finish her sentence. Rivulets of water filled the hands cupping her face, peering into her soul through the depths of her eyes. Their lips pressed together hungrily, a multitude of emotions spilling out in their tender moment. She kissed him once more and then playfully slapped him on the shoulder. "Don't ever scare me like that again," Tori threatened.

"I never make a promise I can't keep," McGann shot back. A level of concern hovered at the edges of his voice. "This may not be over."

"So much for romance. Whoever that was must think we're dead, or he wouldn't have left. Right?"

"Tori, people like that never leave back doors open. He'll continue to search for any signs that we're alive. Count on it."

"Hanging around you is becoming a dangerous habit," Haroldson remarked.

"That's what I'm concerned about." He made one last attempt to make her see the potentially menacing future that lay ahead.

"Just shut up, Bryson McGann. Randall said you were to watch over me. You're my personal bodyguard," she said with authority. "So, that means just that. You're stuck with me. I'm not going anywhere."

Bryson McGann knew when he was beaten. He had no out. She placed a finger on his lips to silence him, then kissed him once more.

Early evening unveiled itself on the pastel palette of the western sky by the time the couple finally arrived at the beach where they began their journey. Their companion, a reddish-orange sun, hovered valiantly above the horizon's edge. Kholos' handiwork had scattered the useless pieces of the helicopter across a wide swath of once pristine sand, now bathed in the sunset's warm glow. McGann surveyed the area, quickly realizing nothing of value remained.

"Where do you think he is?" Haroldson asked, staring across the deep blue of the water, her back to McGann.

A darkened visage of her silhouette was outlined by the dying sun, as he turned in her direction. "If you're referring to our mutual friend, my answer would be long gone," McGann offered, tossing a piece of a shattered instrument back onto the beach. He wiped the sand from his hands, and walked up behind the blonde woman. He let his hands rest on the back of her neck, softly rubbing the tenseness buried there. "Where, is another question. I might have someone who can help us out with that. If anyone can come up with some answers to our mystery man, she can."

Tori closed her eyes for a moment, languishing in the feeling. "Who's she?"

"Joe's fiancé, Ashlyn Sanders. She works for the NSA."

Tori turned, cocking her head with an inquisitive look, "As in the spy agency?"

"None other."

"Mr. McGann, you continue to amaze me," Tori chuckled. "Now, amaze me some more. How do we get home? Any ideas on that? Swimming's definitely out of the question," she added, sliding her arms up around his neck.

McGann replied lightly, "Well, Ms. Haroldson, the thought of spending the night on a tropical beach with you isn't all that bad. In fact, it's quite appealing. However, I would say we'll be back in time for dinner, just a little later than I had originally planned."

"That would impress me. I'm getting pretty hungry. But I don't think even you can come up with a magic carpet." She stepped back, puzzled by his confidence in the midst of the seemingly impossible.

McGann tossed a glance at the hands on the face of his Breitling watch, a treasured gift from his grandfather. "If I had to guess," he paused, "I'd say in less than five minutes, we'll be out of here."

Tori Haroldson laughed. "You've got to be kidding. How do you plan on conjuring up that?"

"Always have a backup," McGann retorted. "There's a NESSA research vessel heading back to port from an expedition in the Aleutians. Currently, it should be about fifteen miles on the eastern side of Kauai. Not knowing what to expect, I told flight ops that if anything happened to the chopper's transponder signal, give it three hours, then send a helicopter from the ship to this location. They could organize a search party from there," McGann finished, arching an eyebrow. The barely audible sound grew increasingly louder, bringing with it the familiarity of thumping rotors, cutting the air in an endless circle.

Tori Haroldson shook her head in disbelief. "I can honestly say, I've never met anyone like you."

"Is that good or bad?" he asked.

"Is that good or bad," Haroldson parroted. "And what do you think?" the blonde finished with a smile.

"I'll take that as a compliment." McGann paused, relishing the moment, enjoying the comforting feel of Tori Haroldson's head nestled on his shoulder. "One thing you can't say," he spoke, barely above a whisper.

"What's that?" she asked, allowing the day's tension to melt away.

"It hasn't been exciting."

A balmy breeze wrapped around the marooned couple standing shoulder to shoulder, enveloping them in what would have been, under ordinary circumstances, a more romantic setting. The amber glow of the sun would soon quickly extinguish itself, sliding effortlessly into the deep blue Pacific waters. The cycle had remained unchanged since time's beginning.

Night's approach brought a serenity, returning a sense of majesty to the tropical land and volcanic peaks. Yet, this paradise was indifferent to their needs, it was incapable of anything else. It had no other choice. The island could only provide that which it had always offered. A place of remarkable beauty.

Nothing more.

Chapter Thirty-Six

AGSI Research Vessel - Banda Sea

CRADLED ON WATERS OF crystalline blue, the Narissa gently rocked in an endless dance above SEATAC -1, fifty-eight hundred feet below her keel. Onboard the ship, technicians monitored every aspect of the work the submersible vehicle was doing. With the first seismic buoy firmly placed upon the sea floor, Canton, O'Brien, and AGSI employee, Skiddy Pete, set about the task of 'planting' the next one.

A network of underwater buoys was being constructed to provide a safety net in the event of a potentially devastating tsunami, generated by another powerful undersea earthquake. This assignment was the forerunner of a very ambitious project involving numerous nations around the Pacific ring. A warning system that would provide real hope, for real people, in the event of an oncoming event.

NESSA engineers had designed this prototype, and Sumner had pushed to make it happen. A series of buoys were to be placed at various locations in the southwestern Pacific Ocean, above and below the surface. Each would transmit information to a centralized receiver. These would instantly relay the information to a satellite hundreds of miles above. From there, the orbiting watchdog would signal ground stations below. It was all to work in a span of less than three minutes from the actual event until land based stations received their alert. Working in a cooperative effort of nations, the project's goal was for completion within three years.

"Copy that, SEATAC-1," the tinny sounding Aussie accent spilling from the intercom, replied.

Red O'Brien shifted the stump of the Dominican to the opposite corner of his mouth. "We're a go down here. Let's get her done," the Irishman's gravelly voice stated.

Skiddy Pete laughed, "If I didn't know you better, I'd say you were one cocky bloke. You make it look too easy, Red."

Canton smiled, eyeing the controls, and interrupting Pete's speech. "Nothing that checking and rechecking things won't do for you."

The Aussie poured out in a mocking tone, "Wrapped a little tight, mate?"

O'Brien's feigned expression of a pout brought a round of laughter from the men, and a relief from the tense and tedious work they were accomplishing.

Through the computer driven images of the view port, a world of immense dimension continuously revealed itself. Glowing creatures, capable of bioluminescence, swam through the darkness around SEATAC-1. The three men were privy to sights unseen by most living on the surface world.

Straight ahead, an extraordinarily large thermal vent spewed fiery, hot magma. This opening in the earth's crust created a passage for the glowing red, liquid rock to escape. Almost immediately upon contact with the colder seawater, the magma turned black as clouds of steam shot out.

This steady outflow of molten rock not only released some pressure from far below the seafloor, it also brought with it abundant minerals. Throughout the area, long, tubular, red sponges thrived in the nutrient rich waters, along with a variety of sea life, large and small. It was a vision of science fiction, yet a real world unlike any other.

"I can't believe the size of this thermal. This is just incredible. Hey, Red, get some readings and video on this. I'm sure the boys topside will be interested."

"You got it, Joe," the Irishman replied, pressing an assortment of switches on the console in front of him.

"This is quite extraordinary. I've seen a lot of these over the years. Never anything like this. I can't wait to see your home movies, mates."

Canton remarked, "I'd say the site of the next buoy will be in a prime spot if this area ever decides to cause some problems."

A quarter of a mile past the vent, the NESSA employees brought the submersible to the prescribed spot for the next *planting*. Hovering just a few feet above the seafloor, the depth recorder marked them at fifty-nine hundred and thirteen feet. Sediment covered the bottom of this area in a blanket several feet thick. Eons of sea life had lived, died, and fell to their final resting spot, in a repetitive cycle.

Skiddy Pete eyed the view screen silently, watching one of the powerful mechanical arms of SEATAC-1 lift the buoy's anchor from its cradle on the submersible. Effortlessly, the four hundred pound weight settled with a feather touch on the seabed, barely disturbing the sediment.

Canton kept the vehicle hovering in the current. He preferred tending to the manual controls in situations like this, rather than let the onboard circuitry operate the underwater craft. Red O'Brien occupied himself working the joystick, attaching the transponder's cable to the heavy anchor. After a few minutes, the tether was given its freedom. The positive buoyancy in the mechanical equipment allowed it to float upward, extending to its full thirty feet. Instantly, the buoy began sending out readings of currents, temperatures, salinity, always prepared in the event of an undersea quake to signal a warning.

A call came over from the Narissa a short time later. The voice of Captain Wyborn followed next with congratulatory praise. "Just want to let you boys know, the relay signal functions appropriately. We have all the test data. Both buoys are now sending current readings from their locations."

Well below the Narissa, the three men inside SEATAC-1 smiled and shook hands, satisfied with their accomplishments. "Now that's a fine job, mates," the Aussie offered.

"It's all about keeping things simple, and in working order, Skiddy," O'Brien returned.

"How about we head back and call it a day, gentlemen?" Joe Canton broke in, turning in their direction. "I could use something to eat."

"I'd say, I've got a bit of an appetite myself," Pete remarked.

The journey back to the surface was uneventful, forty-five minutes slowly shaved away from the digital clock on the instrument console. This portion of the trip seemed endless, now that the excitement of completing their task had passed. More frequently, sea life passed by their digitalized view port. Drawing closer to the world above, the intense lighting from Narissa's decks began to filter down into the deep, blue depths. The world the trio left behind had been filled with sunlight. Darkness had now cast itself across the Banda Sea.

Thirty yards off the stern, a team of divers watched the submersible break the surface. The brightness from the ship's powerful lights flooded the interior, causing the trio to squint briefly, until their onscreen automated visual adjustments kicked in. Joe Canton looked up in time to notice the ship's helicopter lifting off the deck. It quickly disappeared into the darkness. The big man simultaneously eased the craft dead astern, aligning SEATAC-1 with the large hoist mounted there.

An image of a diver appeared on screen in front of the men. He signaled Canton to cut the electric motors. The dive master oversaw the process of directing the team of divers as they connected the steel cable to the submersible. Within moments, Narissa's large winch began the task of hauling SEATAC-1 back aboard the research vessel. Inside the submersible, the three men watched as the Narissa grew closer. The men relaxed while deck hands finalized preparations for the underwater craft to be hoisted aboard.

Unexpectedly, a gushing of bubbles rose up to the surface, engulfing the Narissa and SEATAC-1. It quickly turned into what appeared to be a boiling cauldron upon the waters of the Banda Sea. Everything stopped. Crew members peered warily over the sides of the ship at the frothing ocean all around them.

O'Brien eyed it all with curious fascination. "Sweet Mary, mother of Jesus. What the hell…?"

"Ever seen anything like this, Skiddy?" Canton cut in, anxiously.

"Not me, mate." the perplexed Aussie spit back.

"I'm getting a real bad feel about this." Canton's face grew into a mask of worrisome concern observing the unusual event. The only problem was, none of them had any idea of what was occurring outside the submersible.

Then without warning, the roiling sea grew in intensity. Inexplicably, the Narissa began to sink. In the blink of an eye, the ocean greedily washed over the open stern spreading out across the deck. A few of the men were knocked off their feet, swallowed up by the sea. Others were running up ladders, scurrying to the momentary safety of the upper deck.

"Narissa. This is SEATAC-1. What's going on?" Joe Canton's efforts to hail the ship were futile. It was all happening too fast. The imperiled crewmen aboard the research vessel had forgotten about the three men bobbing on the current astern. No one aboard the doomed vessel was thinking rationally. Their first concern was saving their own lives.

The black water rose insatiably to the upper decks as the ship sank deeper into the waves. The trio inside the undersea boat watched helplessly as they realized the fate of the Narissa's crew. Those left of the crew were huddled helplessly together on top of the wheelhouse. Suddenly, the lights of the upper deck exploded, pitching their world into darkness as the seawater swept over the halogen lighting. The men and women of the Narissa succumbed to a horrid fate, their cries for help unheeded. Swallowed by an unrelenting sea, the crew and vessel vanished, plummeting into the depths.

"Switch on the outside lights, Red." O'Brien reacted immediately. The insanity of this dire situation gripped them in tense silence. Each man sat alone with his thoughts, wondering about what they just witnessed, and the death of friends aboard the doomed ship.

Outside, one of the dive team desperately clung to the hull of SEATAC-1. "Damn. That's Nick Jones," Skiddy Pete called out. "Can't you boys do something to help him?" The other divers were gone. Seized by panic, they had attempted to return to the Narissa, and were sucked down as she plunged to the bottom.

It caught them all by surprise. The underwater craft was jerked violently downward into the darkness below the surface. If they had not been strapped into their seats, they would have been tossed wildly about the cabin. The image of horror on the hapless AGSI man's face knotted Canton's stomach. He watched helplessly, as the diver was ripped away from the hull of the craft.

The steel cable that had been ready to pull them back to the ship, was now dragging them towards the bottom. Increasing pressure from the surrounding water squeezed unmercifully on the research vessel's hull. Sounds of the dying Narissa echoed hauntingly through the hull of SEATAC-1.

Apprehension clawed at the three men, unwitting captives on a wild ride. Twisting and turning, the tethered submersible followed helplessly in the wake of the larger ship. A tool kit broke loose from its mounting, scattering contents through the interior of the sub. A large wrench whizzed past dangerously, nearly taking off Skiddy Pete's head.

Alarmingly, darkness swallowed the interior of the boat. The electrical system failed. For an agonizing moment, they were catapulted into a nigrescent void. Fortunately, the emergency lighting was immune to their troubles. It came to life bathing the cabin in an eerie orange glow. Canton looked up amazed. Somehow, the external cams were still functioning. Unfortunately, their only offering was a vision of a jet-black, liquid environment.

Inside the craft, Canton, O'Brien, and Skiddy Pete clung tenaciously to the hope that fate may redeem them from the inevitable. Each second that ticked off the clock was one survived, and possibly one closer to their last. The men whose world had come together for the purpose of saving lives, now unfolded into a perilous voyage of uncertainty, racing behind the doomed Narissa into the inky depths of the Banda Sea.

Chapter Thirty-Seven
NESSA Pacific Headquarters - Hawaii

IT WAS NOT EXACTLY THE EVENING McGann had envisioned. Dinner had been less than planned, no candles or wine atop white linen. Instead, sandwiches filled the void. Paired with a couple of chilled ales from the Kona brewery, it was the perfect compliment to help wash away some of the day's tension. Neither said much while they ate. They were mentally exhausted and numb from fatigue. Contemplating their trials, both Haroldson and McGann were more than thankful to be alive after cheating death.

A gentle offshore breeze filtered in across the balcony of their suite, rustling the fronds of the surrounding palms. McGann had left to shower, leaving Tori Haroldson alone with her thoughts. She needed a diversion. Eyeing McGann's headset, she pushed the earpieces in place, and pressed the play button on the nano-recorder. About the size of a silver dollar, the recorder operated with a dual scan nano-disc. One of the golden discs had the capacity to house massive amounts of information, and could play over an extended period. The ability to compress digital voice or music files into such a small format, offered hours of play time with the advent of the latest contrivance from the techno world.

Tori Haroldson recalled a conversation with McGann, regarding his eclectic musical tastes. She was puzzled at first. Expecting to hear some island flavored sounds inspired by the musician's past Key West life or other Caribbean adventures, maybe even some hot jazz tunes, but instead, the woman was perplexed by what she heard. Resonating in her ears, the booming bass voice of a famous black actor poured out at her. Unsure of what she was listening to at first, Tori remembered something McGann had briefly mentioned about an ancestor and a journal he had kept.

Inquisitive, the blond attuned herself to the story filling her ears. The tale of Sand Creek had been riveting, but what followed next drew her in even farther. She was enraptured by Duncan McGann's life story, and how events played out after the massacre. So enthralled with what she was hearing, Haroldson never noticed McGann step from the shadows on the balcony. Bryson McGann felt the gentle breeze blow through his purple silk Hawaiian shirt, as he stepped out on the balcony. A quick smile grew across his face while he observed the woman sitting under a pale moon looking down from the night sky.

McGann moved over to where she was, her back towards him, and let his hand rest lightly on her shoulder. Tori Haroldson jumped, turning her head in his direction, relieved it was him. "My God, you scared the crap out of me," she exclaimed, slowly taking in a deep breath to relax herself.

"History buff?" McGann asked, taking a seat.

She removed the headset. "I'm fascinated with your ancestor's story."

"From what I know, he was a pretty incredible fellow."

"I'd say some of it got passed on through the generations," her remark left him slightly embarrassed, and at a momentary loss for words.

McGann sat pensively for a moment before responding, "Where did you stop?"

"It's where the Colorado governor, John Evans, was in Washington, D.C. when Colonel Chivington attacked the village."

"Yeah. That's interesting and curious. There are numerous accounts of what actually happened, depending, of course, on who you want to believe. Napoleon said it best. *History is a set of lies agreed upon*. Basically, it boiled down to greed, hate, power, and egos," McGann remarked dryly. "Hmm, I guess some things never change."

Tori's face grew into a puzzled look. "What happened?"

"As governor, Evans was in charge of the state's Indian affairs. His duties included protecting the rights of the Indians, as well as the citizens of Colorado."

"That must have placed him in an awkward predicament," Tori questioned.

"Unfortunately, it did. Evans was also friends with Chivington." McGann paused, pulling his chair closer to her before continuing. "Chivington acted without specific orders, defiantly overstepping his bounds. However, the massacre at the Indian encampment helped serve the governor's purpose as well. It was well known that Evans had no love for the tribes living in the territory. Together each man's actions were instrumental in bringing about the eventual end of the Indian presence in Colorado."

"How could something like that occur? Didn't anyone find out?" Haroldson asked.

"Chivington had friends, and with the war back east still raging, a lot of what occurred took some time to come to the public's attention."

"So what did your grandfather do? Chivington couldn't have been very happy with Duncan and Black Elk," Haroldson returned, fully captivated by the tale of intrigue almost a hundred and forty-five years earlier.

"They knew Denver was not a possibility, so they headed for Pueblo, planning to stay with James McKenna, a friend who was also a Scotsman. Turns out, he was also in D.C. at the same time." McGann nodded, taking in a deep breath before moving along. "McKenna was a businessman, and a relative of a fellow by the name of Meredith."

"Okay. Another player in the mix. I'm in. Who was he?" Tori interrupted, arching an eyebrow in response.

"Former Secretary of the Treasury, before Lincoln came to office."

"Never hurts to have allies in the right places."

"In this case, absolutely. Duncan wired McKenna explaining the entire affair. The tale gets a little murky from here. I'm unsure of Meredith's connection to Chivington, but I do know there was no love lost between the two men. The colonel was looking to scrape the hide off my grandfather and Black Elk after Sand Creek. He didn't need or want them talking about his murderous deeds. So McKenna and Meredith went on the offensive, mounting a campaign of their own against the militia officer."

Tori Haroldson brushed back a strand of blonde hair from her face. She eyed McGann as he recounted the tale of his ancestor. The scientist wondered how two men could be so alike, separated by so many years. She decided an inherent link existed between them.

"Due to circumstances of the times, the best they could do was play to a stalemate. The Secretary of the Army forced Chivington to resign his commission. It proved to be a smart move, one that offered protection for the colonel. Since he was no longer in the militia,

Chivington could not be held accountable for his butchering of several hundred Cheyenne and Arapahoe. But, there's another curiosity that haunts this histrionic account."

"And just when I thought I knew the whole story," Tori replied, fascinated by the intriguing drama.

"Silas Soule was a former officer under Chivington's command. He became a key witness and outspoken critic of the colonel's actions. A few months after the militia's attack, he was murdered in Denver."

"How convenient," Tori remarked. "It's unbelievable that Chivington was never prosecuted for his crimes. So what about the governor?"

"He eventually resigned from office and moved back to Nebraska. Although he remained influential in Colorado history. But that's not all of the tale," McGann smiled.

"More?"

"Meredith was so impressed by Duncan's heroism, he sent McKenna back with a gift. That gift possesses as many secrets as do the entire affairs of the debacle at Sand Creek."

Tori Haroldson was mesmerized. Caught up in the turbulent tale, she was spellbound by McGann's account.

"In eighteen forty-nine, then Secretary of the Treasury, Meredith, called for a new coin to be minted. It was a Double Eagle twenty dollar gold piece. Only two proofs were struck. One is currently in the Smithsonian."

"And the other?" Haroldson asked.

"It's said that it was presented to Meredith as a gift and sold with his estate upon his death. That's not exactly how it happened. Meredith had a replica made. He realized the value of the coin. Whoever purchased the gold piece after he died received a very nice, but very real fake."

"Alright, I'm game. So what happened then?"

"James McKenna told my grandfather that Meredith was so inspired by his courage, that he wanted to give him a valuable gift for risking his own life, and offering help to the Cheyenne."

"The real coin?" Tori Haroldson's mouth fell open. Where is it?"

McGann looked out over the balcony across the NESSA compound. "That's a very good question. No one knows. It was stolen a few years later. It's surprising that after this many years, its whereabouts is still unknown."

The phone rang inside the suite and McGann moved to answer it. Pressing the button brought to life the beaming image of Ashlyn Sanders on the video screen. They had a brief conversation, and then McGann cut the connection.

Tori Haroldson walked inside just as the screen went blank. "Who was that?" she asked, feeling the exhaustion fed by the day's events.

"Ashlyn Sanders."

"Joe's fiancé?"

"She'll be by in the morning. I guess she's got some time off, and decided to head to Australia to see Joe."

"I can't wait to meet her," Tori replied, stifling a yawn.

"You look beat," McGann said.

"Actually, I am. I need some sleep." Tori looked up at him, "Thanks for saving me again. It's becoming a habit." Her arms encircled his neck as she kissed him softly. "Good night," she turned quietly, heading to her room.

McGann's eyes followed her until she slipped around the corner. He unbuttoned his shirt and fell back on the bed. Within moments, he was sleep's prisoner.

ᘓ ᘐ

The dank smell of the jungle returned: thick, humid air, oppressive, even in the midst of his restless sleep. McGann was transported back to a place that he had buried long ago in the crevices of his mind, along with soldiers of the special-ops team who had died.

Captains McGann and Canton, along with two eight man squads, were to rendezvous with a Columbian army unit, prior to the attack on a large processing plant deeply hidden in the jungle. The illicit operation was responsible for a large portion of the addictive white powder ending up on streets across the United States. More of an advisory role than military, the U.S. soldier's mission was to take down Julio Esperanza. It was rumored the infamous Columbian drug cartel leader would be making an appearance to complete a deal that could significantly enhance his illegal fortunes.

The elusive drug kingpin had agreed to a pact with a ruthless, middle European by the name of Michel Cervanofski. Esperanza was acutely aware of the man's alias. The drug merchant knew no one in the business used their real name. Passports were fraudulent, visas bought and paid, for allowing access under assumed names. It was the only way to travel in relative safety in the perilous circles their world revolved around. Esperanza himself possessed all the necessary paperwork to keep secret his identity, that being the nature of the game. Simply the way the chips were played, that is, if you lived long enough. In the end, it mattered little to the drug lord, just as long as the deal was sweet and the currency green.

The two squads had hiked about six *klicks* in from the drop zone. They found themselves dispersed on a hilltop overlooking the compound about a hundred yards from the rendezvous point. Through the optics of their night vision devices, the world was illuminated in an eerie, pale green shade. Each man sat stoically, alone with their thoughts, fully comprehending the serious nature of their business. Death's calling card might be laid in front of any one of them at any moment. The right bullet at the right time, and the dealer gets it all.

To make matters worse, their meeting with the Columbian military unit was thirty minutes behind schedule. The soldiers were to have been in place long before McGann and Canton's arrival. McGann still could not raise them on the radio. Caution flared at the discrepancy unfolding. "T.C." McGann whispered into the miniature microphone extending from his left ear to the corner of his mouth.

"Not looking too good, little brother," he responded, wiping away the sweat gathering on his face from the humid air. "If we wait much longer, we'll be hung out to dry when the sun comes up."

"If we don't go in, we'll miss an opportunity to take down Esperanza," McGann replied, constantly searching the landscape around him and his men.

"Roger that. So what's next?" Canton surveyed the area behind the group, looking for any signs of trouble while he waited for McGann's decision.

"I'll take Sergeant Barker. Wynn, Ellis, saddle up, you're with Sergeant Mason. Barker and I will cover the left. Mason, your team has the right. We'll move down the hill for a recon. Once we're in place, we'll make a decision."

"Sounds good."

"T.C., is Reynolds set up with the Barrett? If the shit goes down, I want him pumping some hot lead up their ass with the fifty."

"You're covered, Bry. He's got his eye in the scope. Locked and loaded."

"Good." Captain McGann spoke to both squads, "Let's cowboy up, gentlemen. You know the drill. By the numbers. I want everyone out in one piece. No mistakes." McGann and his team disappeared into the thick vegetation. The night time noises of the jungle's inhabitants accompanied them on their journey through the darkness. Whisper quiet, they moved soundlessly towards the compound. Something stirred his gut, more than the anticipation of a firefight. The whole situation had a bad feel. A dreadful cold raced through McGann, raising the hackles of his neck. Still, the special-ops group had a job to do and ultimately, it was his call.

From inside the compound, a tortuous scream pierced the darkness, sending a chilling message to all those in earshot. McGann now knew the fate of the Columbian army unit. He and the others tried to ignore it, knowing someone was paying a terrible price. Cautiously, they continued on their clandestine mission. The special-ops team was within twenty yards of the wall surrounding their objective when things went terribly wrong.

An innate alarm triggered, signaling his instincts to take over. McGann's eyes shot downward, catching a glimpse of the trip wire. His next footfall would have landed directly upon the lethal trap. His mouth went dry. "Everybody freeze. Tripwire," McGann whispered into the headset.

Another wrenching cry from within the compound pierced the night, lost in the sound of the explosion that followed closely on its heels. Off to McGann's right, a brilliant flash of light tore apart the darkness. The thunderous explosion erased any chance of a stealthy approach. For a brief moment, there was only a strange quiet while the rumble faded on the nocturnal stage.

McGann and the others fell to the ground. The night erupted into a deadly display of orange tracers, as all hell broke loose. Bullets sailed wildly through the air, angry hornets ripping pieces of bark from trees and tearing leaves from branches. Copper-jacketed slugs searched diligently for recipients of their deadly gift.

Sergeant Nick Mason's voice screamed through his captain's earpiece. He had taken a hit in the leg. Now, three members of McGann's squad were down. Ellis and Wynn had been torn apart by the initial explosion.

Out of the corner of his eye, McGann caught a glimpse of Sergeant Barker moving forward towards the compound wall. Both men faced the dilemma of firing on the run, and hopefully, not stumbling over another tripwire. McGann's options dwindled quickly. He knew if he remained in his current location, the *trafficantos* would zero in on his position. Staying put was not an option. There was no one else to provide close cover fire for Barker. His decision was automatic.

From their vantage point atop the ridge, Canton loosed deadly series of three round bursts into the camp. He had sent everyone besides Reynolds in a flanking maneuver off to McGann's right, hoping to take some heat off of them. Meanwhile, Reynolds took careful aim with the fifty caliber sniper rifle. The sniper fervently searched through the thermal imaging scope for targets. He wasted little time, quickly snapping off lethal rounds. Canton knew there was little to stop the powerful bullet. Hopefully, the big gun's thunderous dispatch would provide some reassurance to McGann and the others.

In his dream, McGann was reliving the events in the Columbian jungle as if he were there again. Sights, sounds, and smells assaulted him. The drumbeat of small arms fire rattled all around him. Then the explosion came and Barker lay trapped on the ground under pieces of debris.

Several defenders ran out from behind the breeched wall. McGann acted on instincts. His legs pounded the ground. He prayed he would not hit a tripwire as he ran to save Barker. His chest heaved, burning with exertion. McGann fired, unleashing a string of nine millimeter projectiles from his MP5. The sight of flailing arms and 'rag doll' bodies crumpling to the ground filled his vision. The soldier's aim was accurate, dropping Esperanza's men before they could end Barker's life.

In the dream, McGann's world moved into a swirling mix of oddities and realities. It was as if there was no end to the drug lord's gunmen. McGann continued firing, sending lethal volleys into endless groups of oncoming attackers. Bullets scoured the ground around his feet. The magazine of his weapon emptied, locking back the bolt. A bullet tore through his shirt without touching skin, although he felt the searing heat of its passing. One of Esperanza's men came at McGann, his pistol shots sailing wide of their mark. The Columbian's lack of training saved the soldier's life.

Bryson McGann dropped into a shoulder roll, as another round buzzed angrily passed his head. He reacted without thinking. His left hand pulled the large curved blade of the Kukura from its scabbard. Rolling into position, he slashed the razor sharp steel effortlessly along the base of his attacker's hamstring. The man shrieked in pain, dropping to his knees. He swung the heavy blade backwards in a deadly arc into the base of the man's neck, nearly severing the man's head. The Columbian fell unmoving to the ground.

The other squad coming to McGann's aid had been effective in overwhelming the *trafficanto's militia*. Accurate small arms fire, grenades, and training provided an impressive display. The rout began, as the special-ops team's battle-hardened edge paid its dividends.

McGann found himself helping extricate Barker from the rubble. Hurriedly, he pulled a container of black pepper from his aid kit. It was a stop-gap measure, but one he knew worked. McGann dumped it onto the sergeant's bleeding wound. Almost instantly, the blood flow stopped. He was pressing a field dressing over the wound when his senses screamed at him. McGann looked up to see the armed figure of a bald headed man, clad only in boots and camouflaged pants. A sheen of sweat bathed the man's white skin. His muscular upper body tensed with surging adrenaline.

Michel Cervanofski's tightened jaw snarled with hatred. Fire flashed from the muzzle as the pistol bucked in his meaty fist. A string of shots created small furrows, plowing into the ground where McGann had been only a moment before. The soldier rolled and returned the fire. One bullet struck its mark, delivering a slug that carved flesh from his assailant's left shoulder.

McGann bolted upright in bed. Sunlight streamed through the window. Sweat soaked the sheets of the rumpled bed. He struggled to clear away the fog from his mind. Then the stark reality struck him full force. It had all seemed so familiar, but just out of his reach. How could he have missed it before? Bryson McGann bristled, reviling at the memory. Now he knew. His ‘would be’ assassin in that dark, Columbian jungle was also the mysterious face in Amsterdam. The same man who nearly took he and Tori Haroldson’s life in the waters off the Nepali coast.

Chapter Thirty-Eight
Potomac - Maryland

FOSTER HUGHES SAT IN HIS OFFICE sipping expensive bourbon from a crystal tumbler. It was early, but the Chief Justice could have cared less. If he wanted to drink, no one would tell him differently. Of course, there was no one except Carmella, his housekeeper of many years. The dutiful woman kept the home immaculate, all except for his office. However, she knew better than to offer innuendo about his disparaging vices and untidiness.

Hughes' private enclave was worn and weathered, fitting of its owner. Nothing in it had changed for over two decades, since the death of his wife. The stale smell of tobacco lingered, oozing from every crevice. Nicotine stained the walls and windows adding to the drab pallor. An ashtray, nearly overflowing, teetered on the edge of his scarred desk, while books and papers lay in disarray scattered across the floor and furniture of the dark library. He placed a finger to his pale colored tongue, moistening it, then continued to thumb the dog-eared pages of a leather bound law book. The justice had taken some time off work, in anticipation of what the day would bring.

After reading several paragraphs, he leaned back in the tattered leather chair, confirming what he already supposed. The ashen-skinned lawmaker stood and walked to the grimy window, surveying the manicured grounds. His family home stood on twenty-five acres of prime real estate in the Maryland countryside in what was once considered horse country. Now developers rapidly devoured the rolling hills with ravenous appetites of self serving plans for upscale suburbia complete with million dollar homes.

Coal black eyes covetously crossed the meadow to the tree line and beyond, momentarily recalling memories of his younger years. A set of bony fingers tapped out a cigarette from the pack and lit it. A flickering yellow flame consumed the brown tobacco. Inhaling deeply, smoke poured rapaciously into Hughes emphysematous lungs, triggering a rattling cough. A harsh testimony to his years of tobacco addiction. The judge's private phone rang, interrupting his thoughts. He moved grudgingly to answer the call. "Hughes," he barked.

"Hell, Foster. You sound like you're going to drop dead any minute." Martin Boggs' voice chuckled into the receiver, his voice digitally scrambled.

Hughes shot back a muffled, "Fuck you," in between urgent breaths. Finally, the searing fire in the Chief Justice's chest subsided, allowing him to speak. "I don't imagine this is an invitation to one of your fancy parties," the raspy voice squawked over the secure telephone line.

Carlton's CEO continued from behind his desk in the nation's capital. "Have you seen the latest news reports from Davos?" he questioned, simultaneously eyeing scenes from a bank of TV monitors.

"I've better things to do than watch all those idiot bastards with their goddamn liberal news reports and sound bites. It's all shit anyway." Hughes slaked his thirst with a long draw of the clear, brown liquid from the crystal tumbler. "Besides, I knew you'd call sooner or later."

"It's begun."

Hughes came to full attention, eagerly listening to what his accomplice had to say. He lit another cigarette with the stub of the first, and pressed the remote. Instantly, the screen filled with a talking head, detailing the highlights of the unforeseen press conference in the Swiss Alps. He turned down the volume to take in what Boggs had to say.

"Simon, along with the other leaders, gave a very solemn outlook to the situation."

"Quit all the bullshit, Martin. Just throw the cards down on the table and give me the skinny."

"You know, Foster," Boggs followed, "you truly are a pain in my ass. Must be why I like you so much. Anyway, everything we've put in place with our Arab friends and with the help of former government officials is paying off. When the world markets heard the news, everything bottomed out. Of course, a vast majority of our interests over the past number of months had been discreetly divested into oil futures and other finances that already have, and will prove to be, even more exorbitantly beneficial. Timelines are such they should avoid any suspicions. If the SEC or anyone else comes poking around, we'll just say we made some good decisions. They may steam but won't be able to prove otherwise."

Hughes listened intently, a wicked smile filling the old man's face. A quick glance from an outsider would have envisioned a skeletal form hovering in the mahogany lined library, until they noticed the person was actually alive. "What about DB? Credit Suisse and UBS?" the justice shot back.

"As you know, we've had operatives in place in all the major firms for a number of years. These men and women were pushing special measures. For the most, they succeeded. They led European banking investments along a convoluted trail that have now cost them billions once this all went down." The CEO smiled smugly to himself, content with the global economic disaster. "Foster, the Swiss and Germans got hit hardest. But none of the banks in Europe saw this coming," Boggs replied. "They got sucked in by an end run, and now the majority of their investments are in the crapper. The EU was hedging their bets on a stable market. The volatility of our actions has created financial havoc and placed us exactly where we wanted to be."

"The indexes?" the chief justice wheezed.

"As expected. A nose dive. The DAX, FTSE, and CAC are in chaos."

"Hell, that means the Nikkei and the Koreans tanked, too." Hughes spit back, relishing the oily nature of the effusive engineering behind the scheming stratagem. "Now that this has swept over the rest of the world, the DOW is got to be going to shit. There's no way for them to maintain stability."

"They're all scrambling to save their asses, as we speak. All except the right people," Boggs intoned. "Our people are ready to implement plans to take control."

"The investment boys with all the big names must be scared shitless. We've got them by the goddamn balls. Now all the major corporations Carlton owns controlling interest in, can gobble up the losers for pennies on the dollar." A throaty chuckle grew from the old man. "Damn, that's good." The old man paused briefly, "Middle class America will be sucking wind. Too bad for all those poor, ignorant bastards with their paltry retirement investments who've listened to all the bullshit. They've got next to nothing now."

"People in this country, hell, around the world, are sheep. Ripe for the plucking," Boggs interrupted. "Shit. Joe citizen will be so desperate to maintain a bourgeois lifestyle, they'll believe anybody who makes the right promises."

"And we've just the right people to spew out all the lies we need," Hughes barked between coughs. "When did our middle eastern friends announce an end to the oil supply?"

"Within the past hour. The entire world's tiptoeing on a razor blade."

"Have them damn Russkies held to their end of the bargain, and shut down natural gas supplies to central Europe?"

"Of course. Same time as the Saudis made the announcement for OPEC. All hell's breaking loose across the pond," Boggs returned.

"What about the Venezuelans and Mexicans?"

"They've been a bit more reluctant. But they don't produce enough crude to make a difference. Besides, with enough arm twisting, they'll fall into line. They're as money hungry as all their other compatriots. The demand for oil has sent prices skyrocketing, and the world's economy is falling to its knees," Boggs remarked flatly, the nasal tone of his Eastern shore accent pouring from the phone.

Foster Hughes sat down and brought the expensive crystal glass to his lips. Satisfaction swelled his chest. The bourbon tasted exceptionally sweet. "A couple months of this and the world will be crying for order." Years of planning were beginning to pay off. His mind wandered, ticking off a list of details. Each was falling smoothly into place. "What about Simon?"

"He performed perfectly, spearheading the leaders into a collective force. Hold on," Boggs paused momentarily, scanning an email that came to life on his computer screen.

"Trouble?" Hughes interrupted.

"On the contrary. Good news," the CEO replied. "Okay. Go ahead."

"Shit, maybe we should give the bastard an Emmy for his acting."

"With only a few more impostors to put in place, all the players who really count are now in our back pocket. Success. You and I'll be rich beyond our wildest fantasies, along with the others, of course," Boggs tossed out.

Foster Hughes waved his hand in disgust, as if the man he was speaking with was in the room. "You dumb shit, Martin. After all this time, and you still don't get it. I don't give a monkey's yellow piss about the damn money. How long do you think I've got to spend it? This is about much more. An ideal. A plan for control in a world where corporate government can rule with authority. Dictated by the privileged, those above and beyond the law. Finally put a stop to all the bullshit from these crazy bastards with their religious zealots and greedy arrogant ways." Hughes blew out a long trail of gray smoke, letting his words knife their way into Boggs. "It's about doing what's best for the world. In the long run, people will be better off."

"Yeah, I do get it," Boggs shot back, irritated by the older man's remark. He knew fully the importance of his ally's connections and the symbiotic relationship with Carlton. Boggs also knew it was a finite situation. It was simply a matter of time before that complication would rectify itself. "Just calm down, Foster. We're on the same page, for Christ's sake."

"You're an impudent turd," the older man's voice rattled with the phlegm living deep within him. "When the world comes to the brink of a global conflict, all the crumb suckers will be siding with anyone they think will help them the most. In the end, it all boils down to who's got the most money, and if need be, the guts to launch a few nukes to get people's attention." Hughes helped himself to another bourbon before continuing. "With Simon leading the charge, we'll position ourselves into a situation where one leader will quite naturally assume control. All the rest of those unsuspecting shits will be clamoring so badly for oil and all the other crap they think they need, they'll do anything to fall in line."

"It's a good deal all the way around," Boggs replied, calm returning to his voice. "The other thing is, we can ruin the Saudis once everything is in place. A few dead sheiks and their house of cards will come tumbling down. Of course, it'll be under the guise of what's best for the world's needs."

"Exactly. People will be shocked at first, but after thirty days most people won't even remember," the Chief Justice wheezed back in response. "Once they tumble, the rest of their greedy oil buddies will fall like a shithouse in a windstorm. Hell, the less anyone has to do with those *rag heads*, so much the better. Somebody needs to bring'em down. They're long overdue for a kick in the ass. Now that the bases are covered, what about the loose ends?"

"If you're talking about our male friend, I've told you before. Don't worry. Solange, on the other hand, is nearing the end of her usefulness. She was kind enough to allow us a place to do our work, well away from the eyes of the world."

"But, Martin..." Hughes voice quieted.

"Foster. Her wishes have been fulfilled. With the collapse of the German bank, those she believed to be responsible for her father's death, have received their reward. Dimitri is vindicated, at least in her mind. What she doesn't know, is who actually caused his death. Won't matter anyway. Besides, there's no way for her to implicate me, or any of the others, in the matter. End of story, Foster."

"I'm still not sure if her disappearance is the best thing to do right now," Hughes wheezed, in the throes of another coughing jag.

"Even you have to admit, her father was becoming a loose cannon. We had to clean up more than one mess he created. However, when he began running his mouth and threatening..." The CEO stopped, letting the memory settle in over Hughes. "Don't get sentimental on me, Foster," Boggs returned sharply. "I know about your cozy relationship with her father. I wouldn't care if she was your daughter. Solange will soon outlive her usefulness. At that point, the chapter ends," he spit back harshly. "I'll be in touch."

A monotone hum filled the earpiece where Carlton's leader's voice had just been. Foster Hughes sat quietly, ruminating over the last words ringing from the receiver. In the end, it was all about the plan. Now that the ball was rolling, no one could stop it. Within a brief period of time, Carlton's subversive stranglehold on the global economy would weave the tendrils of its doctrine into the fabric of every nation. The eventuality of one world government, one currency, would become a way of life. Doing so would finally bring together a plan that had been in the making for many years. Hughes, more than anyone, knew that. Still, the eyes behind the craggy face knew there was also a time and place for everything.

The Chief Justice had not accomplished all that he had without a duplicitous nature of his own. He made a snap decision, confident in its merit. He pushed the dual- scan nano disc into the tray on his computer; at the same time, the justice removed its protective case from the top drawer of his desk. Hughes' hand moved the mouse into the proper position. Just another click and the process began.

Inside the computer, the drives came to life, processing and disseminating information onto the gold disc. The device created a prescribed set of ones and zeros, translating the sordid tale of the past decades. A tale of obfuscation, death, sex, and money: a player's roster of instigators and the hopes of those who meant to see their future dreams come to fruition, no matter the cost, would be digitalized. It was a history that one day would be accepted and viewed in the highest regard. A benevolent gift to society. Now it was simply a method to insure Hughes' safekeeping in the event Boggs decided to take perfidious measures, and stray from the game plan.

The Chief Justice of the United States' bony fingers gently placed the disc in its holder, slipping the package into a diplomatic satchel. He felt confident in his decision. The leather bag would keep prying eyes from reading the old man's sordid tale. Foster Hughes made a discreet call, and within the hour, the gleaming disc was on its way. He hoped it would never be needed.

Chapter Thirty-Nine
Davos - Switzerland

STAN REYNOLDS FOLLOWED closely on the heels of President Richard Simon. *Boxer* was barking out orders, fitting comfortably into the role of the Commander in Chief. Benjamin Wolcott watched curiously as the man he had known and trusted for many years handled the situation with practiced authority and confidence. Still, there was something nipping at him. A prescient demeanor and unfamiliar calm hovered over his boss. The presidential advisor thought he was just getting the wrong read. It was fleeting, nothing he could define. If Wolcott had to explain it, he couldn't. There was a minutely inexplicable variant gnawing at him. Perhaps if he had more time to ponder his misgivings, he could come to grips with it. However, Wolcott's mind was occupied with the oil crisis and its trappings.

The impostor now thought on two levels; one, a conscious process that defined his normal being, and the other, a deeply rooted sinister path, directed by the implant coexisting within him. Simon had been apprehensive at first, self conscious about erring in judgment or actions. Shortly after assuming the role of president, he quickly grew comfortable with the aid from the implanted bio-chip. He knew the others were just like him. The ones to follow would be the same.

The quickly assembled meeting with the other G-8 leaders lasted only two hours. It was meant only as an overview of the direction the decision makers should embark upon. The charade amply fulfilled a need for the free world to see their leaders deeply rooted in finding solutions to the enormous problems facing the world.

The conference leaders unanimously concluded that the People's Republic of China would pose the biggest dilemma. Their demand for oil in an expanding market within their own country would result in the need for diplomatic overtures of a calming nature. The world's leaders harbored no doubts that the communist state would threaten and posture and possibly even go to war. However, its futile attempts would be thwarted by whatever means necessary at the disposal of the free world. Those were terms agreeable to all, in light of the possibilities. Perhaps a few million less people in the world might not be such a bad idea. That was an idea that rested comfortably with the nation's chief executive.

Once the meeting adjourned, Bertoluzzo pulled him aside. "Mr. President, a moment, please," the Italian intoned.

"Certainly," Simon responded. He cast his eyes across the room, the sounds of tangled conversations and high anxieties making a buzzing hum. "Ben, if you'd excuse us for a moment." A raised brow and slight nod of the head followed the request, indicating he would be fine alone.

"Of course. I'll be preparing for our departure if you need me," his advisor answered. Wolcott hesitated momentarily, and then thought better of saying anything else. Something chafed, like the shrieking squeal of fingernails on a chalkboard. He made a mental note to pay closer attention.

From across the room, Stan Reynolds viewed the dismissal of Wolcott warily. The man was trouble. If ordered, the agent would take great delight in making this annoying man disappear. Simon and Bertoluzzo moved off into a private chamber catching the agent's attention. He would stand vigil, protecting the interests of his true employers.

Closing the door, Simon saw his accomplices had gathered for a very private meeting. Smiles filled their faces, while they let nothing go unnoticed between themselves. Each movement or gesture was captured and processed, as if the other were prey for a feral beast.

Haines' voice cut through the dense air between them. "I have word that our newest 'brother in arms' will arrive next week. I've invited the German Chancellor to my estate in Scotland for a private meeting and a bit of relaxation." He eyed the other members of this elite club before continuing. "Replacing him will be easy enough. I have a partridge hunt scheduled to ease the burden of the strenuous demands placed upon us," his smile ebbed and flowed like the changing tides.

"There can be no mistakes," the Frenchman cut in.

"Leave it to me. No reason to worry, Henri," Haines replied.

"Gentlemen," Bertoluzzo interrupted. "Our time is brief. For now, let us concentrate on our strategy for the coming days."

The impostrous cabal spent their remaining moments engaged in conversation about their deceptive schemes. The world held its breath while these men played a game with esoteric desires above and beyond anything of monetary value. Theirs was a nightmarish reality, a treacherous entanglement that would choke life from the world, and eventually bring about the illicit wants of a wealthy class of citizenry. In its wake, the world spiraled into a mire of abject uncertainty.

Chapter Forty

NESSA - Seattle, Washington

MARION TURNER'S FINGERS FLEW across the keyboard, quickly filling her computer screen with the letter Randall Sumner dictated to the Mote Marine Laboratory director in Florida. The proposal to work cooperatively on the Caribbean project in the near future offered advantageous benefits for both agencies. Turner's eyes flew across the words, finding only one mistake. Sumner's assistant immediately corrected it and clicked on the icon at the top of the screen. The machine spewed out a perfect copy on official NESSA letterhead, ready for the director's signature.

Behind the doors leading into Randall Sumner's office, three of the four key leaders in the agency tossed out ideas and direction for numerous issues involving NESSA. A long agenda awaited their collective decision making process.

Carl Steitzer pushed the glasses farther atop his nose, scanning the folder's information, and listening to Kate Harper's evaluation of the European conference. Puzzled, he broke into the conversation, "Kate. Do you think that a collaborative effort will change the political thinking when it comes to global warming when we're still lagging behind the world, even with Simon in the White House?"

"Before you answer that, Kate," Scott Freeman cut in. "Is there any other choice for us to compensate for the past?" The scientist looked like an older model cut from the pages of a men's fashion catalog. Relaxed, but still professional in his attire, the assistant director's qualifications were no less equal to any other in the room.

Harper shot a glance in his direction. The two had developed a close bond in the time they worked together. She found him attractive and much to her liking in men. Perhaps, her mind wandered before answering, more may become of their friendship. Harper snapped back into the moment, brushing back a loose hair over her ear. "In my discussions with various leaders, all gave assurances they were eager to address the issue. A number of them were reticent regarding our past inattentiveness to the situation."

Steitzer leaned back in the plush leather chair, adjusting the ever-present bowtie encircling the blue oxford's collar. "Well," he remarked. "What about the changes that have occurred since Simon's taken the reins? Does that account for anything?"

Randall Sumner always enjoyed meetings with his assistant directors. It seemed as if a part of him always remained detached from the mix while observing their behavior. He often chuckled to himself wondering if they were as interested in his idiosyncrasies. "That's a very good question. Not only one of prime importance now, but the effects of our actions or inactions may dictate the future outlook for global populations." Sumner broke in, bringing the stem of the ornately carved meerschaum to his mouth. As he finished, NESSA's director lit the tobacco in the bowl of an oversized pipe. His fingers wrapped comfortably around the carved clay, enjoying the tactile sensation. He took little notice of Harper's pencil tapping on the conference table. Whenever she was deep in thought, her hand tapped out a rhythmic cadence he found amusing. It seemed to provide her with a sense of calm.

"Actually, Randall," she returned. "That's precisely the point. I believe we need to push harder for changes in Congress."

"How about taking it directly to the people?" Freeman broke in. "Blitz them with a campaign that forces them to sit up and take notice. If you can get people focused long enough on something besides their own problems, change is inevitable."

"True," Steitzer replied. "However, I should think that would require a healthy budget. Possibly, even approval from Washington. Any ideas on that, Randall?"

A long trail of smoke was whisked away by the noiseless filtration system. "I'm in favor of getting people invested in ideas, especially those that have consequences for themselves and future generations. It's imperative that people realize the importance of what we would be attempting to accomplish. With enough push, I think people will wake up. They have to." Sumner sighed heavily before continuing, sawing a thumb and forefinger across his chin in contemplation. "Once we have people turned around, the next step will be convincing big business."

Harper's eyes narrowed. "Won't they be forced into a position if the populace demands change?"

"Good point, Randall," Freeman added.

"In theory, yes. However, there are numerous considerations to factor in. Given the current political climate, I would think that our plan has sound reasoning. As we all know, the president has been adamant regarding his views on the environment in light of the previous administration's negligent behavior. That's a plus. But, there will come a time again when a president won't share our viewpoint on those concerns. Also, big business has to be put to task for doing their share."

"I'm sure their reluctance will increase if they have another friend in the White House sharing their point of view," Stiezer remarked, casting a glance out the window of Sumner's office.

"Then you have the opposite side of the coin," NESSA's female assistant director tossed in. "Those folks on the extreme edge who think no one ever does enough to protect Mother Earth."

"True, Kate," Sumner interjected. "However, I'm of the belief that handled properly, done efficiently, and with the correct amount of prodding, it can be accomplished. No reason not to, if all concerns work together. In all things, a moderate approach to problems with give and take reasoning must prevail."

Marion Turner opened the door to Sumner's office. He looked up in her direction. The director knew her well enough to know whenever storm clouds were brewing. Sumner's eyes tracked his personal assistant as she approached the conference table. Her stride was rigid. The look on her face denoted something seriously wrong. The others caught the NESSA director's concern, turning toward Harper as she neared the other members.

Sumner clamped down hard on the stem of the pipe. Through clenched teeth he called out her name. "Marion." Never one to mince words needlessly, Sumner spit out a very succinct, "Problem?"

She had worked with him since his military days. They had known one another for almost twenty years. She never called him by his first name in public. However, this was different. "Randall. This is bad. First, turn on the news." She stood quietly, poised to continue once the eighty inch monitor came to life. CNN's Vernon Charles was in the midst of a conversation with a government official seeking answers to the same questions everyone had. A split screen showed the news anchor's face and the obviously strained features of a face from the nation's capital. Their conversation continued for several more minutes until the network interrupted with a report from Europe.

The NESSA decision makers sat with their mouths agape, baffled by what they were hearing. Shock whitewashed the faces in the room. "What could spur a reaction like this from OPEC and the Russians?" Sumner asked, barely above a whisper. The obvious fact of what no oil or gas supplies would mean cut deeply into each person there. If nothing was done soon, the world would teeter over the brink of disaster. Sumner had faced the responsibility of difficult situations during his time in the military. As a general, there were moments when he bore the brunt of difficult decision making, and no matter what the outcome, people inevitably suffered. His mind raced with the potential of this overwhelming perplexity.

The implications of such a terrible circumstance branded itself into the mind of each person in the room. The other three member's voices buzzed, filling the air with questions that, at this point, had no answers.

"And the other thing, Marion," Sumner requested, sucking in a sharp breath, feeling the heat from the burning tobacco.

Turner's complexion became ashen. The woman's features were expressionless, yet the pain in her eyes betrayed the forthcoming words. Turner felt her throat catch, from the dryness investing itself. She was barely able to speak. Marion Turner attempted to clear her throat and began again. The wrenching words were forced out past a quivering lower lip, "Joe's missing."

Chapter Forty-One
Pacific Research Center - Hawaii

INTRODUCTIONS HAD BEEN BRIEF when Ashlyn Sanders arrived. The two women struck it off immediately, taking an instant liking to one another. The pleasantries quickly evaporated in the moments that followed. NESSA's Assistant Projects Director filled Ashlyn Sanders in on the recent events in he and Haroldson's lives.

McGann proposed an idea. His notion was simple, but required the assistance of Canton's fiancé, and a lot of luck. Accessing the data banks at NSA headquarters is something that would be frowned upon for a number of reasons. She knew his method was not standard operating procedure. However, it did not take her long to agree to McGann's plan. He felt a rush of anticipation with the realization there was now an opportunity to place a face with an identity.

The trio hurried to an unused office in the complex headquarters. Behind closed doors, McGann quickly logged on to NESSA's computer system. Within moments, the powerful instrument was at the group's disposal.

From there, Sanders took control. Sliding into a back door at the ultra-secret NSA would pose little problem with her knowledge and abilities, although the woman's prodding might arouse suspicions. Ashlyn really had no reason to log into the covert agency's system since she was on leave. If anyone found out, there would be more than a few eyebrows raised as to the nature of her business. Worse, using the NSA as a link to further access FBI data files on noted criminals was something they definitely did not want to be caught doing.

Bryson McGann knew the trick would be to make it seem as if she were in the agency's headquarters in Maryland. Once in the system, Sanders' direction of NESSA's computer infiltrating her own assigned computer would hopefully go unnoticed. As a part of normal routine, the host server at NSA headquarters would assign an Internet Protocol number. An IP number emanating from that source would, theoretically, allow the soft probe to appear genuine. The rub was in the fact that these series of numbers were dynamic, constantly changing every five minutes for security purposes. In addition, the initial assigned IP address had its own sequence for a security source code, readily detectable by the Bureau and its international counterpart, the CIA.

The dilemma, Sanders knew, lay in the design of the agency's computer safety and backup programs, intentionally safeguarded to detect possible scenarios such as this from hackers. It was inevitable that the agency's computers would detect her request for information from another law agency. In and of itself, that would not cause a problem. However, it would not be long before a random check detected that the assigned IP address to Sanders' computer was requesting information from an outside source. Simple and effective. The system would automatically reroute and lock her IP address, after a brief period online, for silent evaluation by the internal workings of the agency's super computer.

Ultimately, it significantly raised the stakes of detection. Since whatever information they hoped to retrieve was considered interagency, perhaps the level of scrutiny would be less. They needed to be in and out in a reasonable period of time. If not, an automatic system scan would signal trouble, raising an alarm due to a static IP address. There was no other choice. McGann weighed the options, feeling confident in his plan.

"You know this really is something the FBI should tackle," the attractive, auburn-haired woman remarked.

McGann cocked his head and flashed a lop sided grin in her direction, "No sense troubling them while you're here," he said, wryly. "Anyway, I'm not certain at this point if I want anyone to know what we're doing. Something about all of this has a bad feel."

Tori Haroldson was puzzled by McGann's remark. "Why wouldn't you?" she said, slightly confused by McGann's statement. Before he had the opportunity to respond, she turned to the woman sitting at the computer, "Can you really do that, Ashlyn?" she asked.

"I'm pretty good at this stuff."

McGann's jaw tightened in response, chewing the words before he spit them out. "There are just too many coincidences, Tori. My gut's telling me there's more to our meetings with our *friendly* boat captain than mere synchronicity."

"Think so, Bry?" Ashlyn replied, interrupting them without looking up from the screen. Sanders' fingers worked their way across the board, filling the air with the rhythmic clatter of keys.

Tori shoved aside an errant strand of blonde hair, amazed by what was developing in front of her. NESSA's powerful computer was more than suited for the task. As quickly as Sanders keyed a command, another set of letters and numbers appeared onscreen. The computer had now been directed to use Sanders' own computer, and route that query through the agency's computer. So far, it appeared as if the search request from the NSA was noted as nothing more than normal workday information seeking.

Suddenly, the FBI logo flashed before three sets of eyes at NESSA headquarters. To Sanders this was nothing new. Her routine assignments often required her to log into their system. She had completed this process numerous times, albeit, most of them, legitimately. "Okay, Bryson. We're in."

"Do a database search. Forget the small time stuff. Go for international felons. Let me give you a profile and see if the computer can match a face." McGann could barely keep up with Ashlyn's keypad wizardry. Within several minutes, they had a list of features. On the screen, a generic image of a face was brought to life.

McGann took his time at this point being careful to remember each detail. Memories from the past meetings with their formidable adversary swirled inside his head. "Ready?"

"Absolutely," the agent responded, looking up at him.

"Tori. If you see something, if anything comes to mind, jump in."

"Got it," she responded, a look of consternation settling over her.

"Let's get started, Ashlyn. First, his complexion should be darker. He's bald. Lose the hair." The prescribed features imprinted themselves on the computer generated face, morphing with each trait McGann offered. "His eyebrows need to be bushier. Lips thinner. There's something about the jaw line that's not right. It needs to be more of a combination of Slavic and Middle Eastern. "

Before their eyes, Ashlyn Sanders transformed the image into what McGann believed would eventually become a visage of the illusive murderer. Painstakingly, characteristics were added and removed, searching for just the right mix.

"Hmm," McGann replied. "The ears are closer to the sides of his head." Several more minutes elapsed while they ticked off a list of features. "Anything else?" Sanders questioned.

Tori chewed her lower lip, contemplating, "The eyes. Darker. Much darker and deeper set. Yeah, that's it."

McGann stepped back from the screen, his gaze fixed on the image. "Looks good. Tori?"

"There's nothing else I can think of."

"Run it," McGann commanded, satisfied with the composite they had made.

Through the computer relays, signals were sent and images appeared in rapid fire order, passing quickly as another took its place. Whenever the computer discovered a like characteristic, a red icon flashed, denoting a match. This was stored and placed with the other memorized bits of information.

Now that the list had narrowed substantially, the flashing faces moved at greater speed across the screen, deleting those that it deemed were not a match. Without notice, the computer screen locked, flashing a green emblazoned icon.

IDENTITY MATCH: CONFIRMED

The image of the criminal was quickly revealed. The features of the man they described stared back lifelessly with the same cold eyes they witnessed on several occasions. Each aspect of the individual appeared in the finest detail. The resolution of the three dimensional image in front of them was perfect. In each of the four corners of the screen, was a different view of the man's face. In the center, a revolving image slowly rotated to display a three hundred and sixty degree view of the culmination of their search.

"What do you think. Is that him?" Sanders asked, waiting hesitantly. She needed no further confirmation other than Haroldson's reaction that the person filling the screen was the perpetrator of the recent events in the lives of McGann and the volcanologist.

"It's him," Bryson McGann answered, reading the name Stephan Kholos on the screen. "Find out whatever you can about him," animosity tarnishing his voice. "Somehow, he's a key that unlocks a door to something greater. I need to know." Sanders knew McGann well enough to sense the urgency in his request.

"I'll have it for you in a second, and then I'll download every detail of this charming man onto a nano disc." The sound of the printer came to life spitting out an abbreviated bio on Stephan Kholos. McGann snatched the initial two page report from the printer. The two women peered over his shoulder at the peccant biography.

"Wow. What hasn't this guy been into?" Haroldson asked.

"Diamond smuggling, drugs, terrorism," Ashlyn remarked. "His profile indicates he's a player. A thrill seeker. Seems a number of his credits had no purpose other than pulling off a crime successfully."

"Not only that," McGann offered, "it's what he's been associated with that's incredible - political assassination, the Chechnya debacle, involvements with the IRA, the possible ringmaster of the Greek terrorist group, 17 November. I'm blown away by our pernicious friend's talents. Stephan Kholos is a man of reckoning."

"I thought they caught the people responsible for organizing that terrorist group," Haroldson remarked.

"A Greek by the name of Giotopoulos was convicted a number of years ago," the NSA agent replied.

"That's if you believe everything you read," McGann interjected. "If you look at the entire list, there isn't much our friend hasn't been suspected of doing. The report also speculates the potential that Giotopoulos was a fall guy. The real mastermind behind the group for the past twenty years was possibly our man. He has a list of supposed aliases and occupations, but no one seems to have the ability to pin him down."

"Incredible. I don't understand how people can live their lives like that," Tori mumbled.

"Evil's exactly that," McGann followed, his eyes never lifting from the report. "Never underestimate its potential."

"Oh, oh. Someone's tracking us," Sanders hurriedly stated, feeling the tension building. She typed in command to attempt to divert the search but to no avail. A red signal continued to flash in the upper right corner of the computer screen.

"Do you have everything on Kholos?" McGann questioned anxiously.

"Should be done in just a few seconds," she responded, tapping her nails on the desk. "Come on."

All eyes focused on the bottom of the screen as a line of small blue segments increased in length, while the information poured in. Time was running out and if they were not done very soon, their game of interagency cat and mouse would be compromised. They each held their breaths, watching expectantly.

"Got it. We're done." Ashlyn brought the keys to life in a staccato tempo. Almost instantly, the screen went blank, cutting the connection.

"Ashlyn," McGann pushed out through a long breath. "Do you think they found us?"

"Maybe, but it's too late now. Anyway, you got the information you were looking for. I hope it helps," Sanders said, sincerely. "Let me know if you need anything else, or if there's something the agency can help you with, officially, of course," she smiled, coyly.

Their discussion was interrupted by the ring of his cell phone. "McGann," he answered. The conversation was not prolonged. He listened intently, discerning the serious nature of the call coming from Seattle.

The sober tone of Sumner's voice resonated gravely. He filled his Assistant Projects Director in on the details as he knew them, although there was not much to tell. "Marion took the call from AGSI. The Narissa went down with all hands except for the ship's captain, Ryan Wyborn, and chopper pilot, John Busby."

"How did that happen?" he shot back, flatly.

"They'd left the ship to attend to some emergent business. About the time of their departure, SEATAC-1 was returning to the ship," Sumner responded. "Joe, Red, and one of the ship's scientists were aboard." He cast a glance out the window into the threatening gray skies above the city, feeling the bile rise in response to his sour mood, as somber as the weather. "There was no reason to contact the ship prior to their return, so it was assumed all was in order. Everyone is stymied by the mysterious disappearance."

"Bad weather?"

"On the contrary, Bryson," Sumner cleared his throat, feeling the pangs of the devastating news. "Calm seas. Clear skies."

"Have they been unable to pinpoint the exact location?" McGann attempted to mask the edge in his voice. He shot a look at Sanders and Haroldson, knowing from their reactions, they grasped the seriousness of his talk with NESSA's director. He felt as if he had been punched in the gut.

"I've sent the last known coordinates and a detailed report as I know it, via email. I'm placing you in charge. Beech and Evans are waiting at the airstrip to take you to Darwin."

McGann hesitated, "Ashlyn's here." He had never spoken any words that sounded as hollow.

From the other end of the line there was momentary silence. "Tell her I'm sorry. I'll call her very soon."

McGann closed the connection, moving towards the computer. He logged on to his email, while he told the women the grave news. Tori Haroldson placed her arms around Canton's fiancé, tears forming in Sanders' eyes. Bryson McGann had no time for grieving at this point.

"Tori. I'm leaving for Darwin to coordinate efforts between AGSI and NESSA. I hope I'm back before the end of the conference." He lifted his eyes toward Sanders. "Ashlyn. I don't have anything to say," he stammered. Something caught McGann's attention in the message Sumner sent. The coordinates for the last sighting of the Narissa struck a nerve. Something struggled to rise to the surface, a hauntingly perplexing feeling.

"What is it, Bryson?" Sanders asked, with tear filled eyes. The shock of Joe Canton's disappearance still had not struck her fully.

"For some reason, there's something vaguely familiar about that location." McGann's eyes widened with the sudden recognition. "Ashlyn, there's no time to explain, but I need your help. I need satellite views of that region. Can you pull them up from NSA while we're in flight?"

"Yes, but I don't understand."

"No time to explain now."

"Oh, no. Hold on a minute," Haroldson interrupted. "You're not leaving me here. Not with Zorba the Greek running around loose. No way," she stated adamantly.

"What about your lectures?" McGann replied, knowing the comeback was weak.

"They can be put off until the end of the conference. Worst case scenario, Dr. Johnson can present them. He has all the information."

McGann took little time in making his decision. "Alright, Tori. I know better than to argue with you. Ladies, we've got a plane to catch."

Chapter Forty-Two
Sula Kai - Banda Sea

THE METALLIC RING OF THE DIAMOND KNIFE striking the floor still echoed in Abram Mossel's ears. He thought his heart had stopped after making the strike on the Oduru diamond. Years of experience had proven invaluable. If he had taken the computer's advice, the gemstone would be of far less value.

The old man knew there would be several diamonds extracted from the gem. His practiced eye scoured the stones. Even under intense magnification, he found no inclusions. The old man's mind could hardly comprehend a stone of this size, completely flawless. What intrigued Mossel even more was the fact that when fully brought to life, this diamond would surpass anything the world had seen. All of the well known gems, from the Crown Jewels to the Hope diamond, would pale in comparison.

Mossel found himself working maniacally since cutting the rough stone. A youthful energy surged through his veins. He thought little of sleep, completely absorbed with the fascination for the Namibian prize. All his life had been a prelude, a preparation for this time. Mossel took pride in knowing his craftsmanship would be responsible for an accomplishment beyond anything anyone ever witnessed.

His aged hands displayed no signs of trembling, moving deftly to cut facets across the rough surface of the gemstone. The diamond cutter meticulously studied his work as it progressed, fully satisfied. His energies were so focused on Peter Oduru's prize, he never noticed the woman standing behind until she spoke.

"You've done well, old man." Solange peered over his shoulder, attempting a glimpse of his progress. "I'm delighted to know that you listened to reason. In doing so, you have prolonged your life." Her words slithered greasily, in an uneasy tone. The Dutchman envisioned the face hovering over him: a creature of the shadows lurking just out of sight, capable of immeasurable iniquity.

He no longer feared her, or the death that he knew would eventually come. Mossel's bravado increased, "Yes, you do need me. If I'd listened to you, this stone would be ruined," he said, shaking a finger of an age-spotted hand in the face of his captor. Solange's eyes widened and quickly settled. The man's thick Dutch accent rang with a tenor of disregard. "No one would even come close to touching this stone. They would know it was stolen." He raised a bushy brow defiantly towards the olive skinned beauty. "It's a shame," he paused, thoughtfully. "A woman as beautiful as you, and look what you're doing?"

"You flatter me, old man. But don't take me for a fool," Solange hissed.

Abram Mossel shooed her away with a wave, turning his attention back to the stone, immediately absorbed by his task. With diligent patience, he worked his magic, bringing to life the diamond the African brought from within the earth, to its full glory.

Solange's eyes seared a stare of loathing into the Dutchman. She despised the old Jew. Yet, theirs was a relationship of need, at least temporarily. "Don't forget," she commanded. "When you're finished today, return the stone to me," she added, sharply. "I'll provide for its safe keeping until tomorrow," her words trailing, as she left the room. She was not clear exactly why the old man irritated her so badly. Her mind wandered across the terrain of possibilities, as she walked down the hallway. When she was through with him, Solange knew she would relish in the delight of feeding him to the creatures swimming in the deep blue waters encircling the island. A glimmering smirk came to life on the beautiful woman's face.

Chapter Forty-Three
Papua New Guinea - Southwestern Pacific

A QUIET SOLITUDE HOVERED anxiously in the cabin of the Gulfstream, forty-one thousand feet above the Bismarck Sea. The bluish silhouette in the distance took shape, outlined by the confines of the aircraft's small window, as the northern coastline of Papua New Guinea grew closer. Below lay the island where some of the world's most difficult and unexplored terrain existed, much of it unchanged by time.

The long flight from Hawaii, normally tedious, was made more so with the added strain of Joe Canton's disappearance. McGann knew Ashlyn was keeping a brave face. He was well aware of how upset she was. It is precisely why he had put the two women to work, seeking any information on Stephan Kholos.

McGann had his own tasks to occupy his time. The coordinates of the missing Narissa had triggered a memory of a news release about the unusual disappearance of a young couple. Sifting through numerous articles about them, he eventually found what he was looking for. Oddly enough, their last known location was in close proximity to the ill-fated, Australian research vessel.

McGann's search carried him through NESSA archives, via a satellite link to its computer data base. As time passed, he waded through maps, articles, and any other information he thought pertinent, before accessing satellite pictures of the area where the Narissa mysteriously disappeared. A number of different images appeared on screen. Bryson McGann scrutinized each one, until he found the specific information required.

"I need to take a break," Tori spoke up, interrupting the protracted silence. "Can I get anybody something to drink?"

"Sure, great," Sanders replied, weakly.

"Be right back." She returned with three plastic containers of bottled water. "What's that, Bry?" Tori asked, handing him a bottle.

"Ladies, check this," he said, moving the laptop into view of the women. "It's a composite shot of search grids. It includes the last known whereabouts of the Narissa. Did either of you hear about Senator Ramsey's son and daughter-in-law, who came up missing on a honeymoon cruise weeks ago? Just a second. Let me tie into the monitor on the cabin wall. We'll get a much bigger picture."

"Yeah, I remember." Sanders stated. The normally affable woman's mood brightened with the fact of something else to distract her. "They came up empty handed."

"The last time they were heard from was a satellite phone call to their families at five-thirty pm. An automatic signal relayed their GPS coordinates to Becca Ramsey's father, an avid sailor himself. He kept up with their daily travels. Oddly, they disappeared within the same area as the Narissa."

"Pirates?" Haroldson spoke up.

"Unlikely. There's been no indication of wrong doing. You can rule out storms, tsunamis, or any other thing that would normally come to mind."

"What then?" Tori asked, taking a sip from the bottle.

The two women listened attentively as McGann ran through a long list of information he had found since leaving NESSA's headquarters. His fingers punched in several commands. "Take a look," he nodded at the forty-eight inch screen. "This grid is at the very edge of the last known coordinates for the ship." Larger and larger composites of the ocean images came to life while McGann worked the control button.

"I'm not following you," Sanders spit back, finding herself irritated.

"Patience, Ashlyn. It's just about ready." A final enlargement appeared before them. "There," McGann said triumphantly, pointing at the screen. "What do you see?"

"Bryson," Haroldson replied, casting an inquisitive glance at Canton's fiancé. "I don't really see anything unusual."

"Exactly. These are NSA images you retrieved, taken the day before the Narissa went down. Now, check this. If you weren't expecting it, you'd never notice," he remarked, his brow gathering tightly. "Look more closely. Do you see that disturbance on the ocean surface?" The two women gazed at the screen. "Let me get a better view of that," he added, making one final adjustment. "NavStar took this image from a distance of eight hundred miles. It was taken within minutes of the time it's surmised the Narissa went down." Both women looked extremely perplexed. McGann continued, "I'm certain this can be the only cause of the missing newlyweds, and our Australian friends. That should be great news for Joe and Red."

"So...what are you saying?" Sanders asked tentatively, ridges of skin creasing her forehead.

"I believe Joe's still alive."

"Methane deposits?" Haroldson blurted excitedly.

"Exactly. The only possible explanation," McGann replied, beaming.

"A pocket of methane trapped below the sea floor has to be the cause of the problem. I don't know why I didn't see it before," Tori beamed.

"Hold on, you two. I'm a page behind," Sanders remarked, now caught up in the intrigue.

Bryson McGann spit out his slant on the incident. "A seismic event could trigger the release of trapped methane gas just below the ocean floor. I searched NESSA's files and came up with this. There were recorded undersea quakes at the time of each vessel's disappearance." McGann took a moment to let the idea jell. "Released gas rises to the surface. The bubbles expand, becoming larger and larger. These enlarged bubbles rocket to the surface, erupting explosively."

"Think of it this way," the volcanologist added. "Shake a bottle of champagne and uncork it. Are you getting a visual?"

"So how does that cause a ship the size of Narissa to sink?" Sanders asked, still mystified.

"The bubbling ocean water becomes less dense," Tori returned.

"With the release of enough methane, most objects floating on the surface become heavier than the water itself. When that happens," McGann paused, sipping the water. "In a nutshell, simply put, you sink."

"I still don't see why that's good news for Joe."

Tori sat back in her seat, listening carefully to a further explanation of McGann's reasoning. "The report from Captain Wyborn indicates that the submersible was tethered to the Narissa at the time the helicopter departed. If so, both the sub and ship would have been sent to the bottom. The depth of the seafloor in that area is well within SEATAC's dive limits. If I can use a phrase from New England whaling days, Joe, Red, and their Aussie friend had a *Nantucket sleigh ride*, only to the bottom."

Sanders' green eyes brightened with the hope McGann offered. "So they should still be there?"

"Possibly, but probably not," McGann came back, already anticipating Sanders' question.

"What then?" Tori interjected.

"I know Joe. If he couldn't release the cable on the way down, he'd cut it using the vessel's mechanical arms, assuming they weren't damaged. They're more than capable for the job. Since the sub hasn't been located, there's only one possible scenario. Something has kept them submerged."

"What about their air supply?" Ashlyn pondered.

"SEATAC-1 has its own air scrubbers."

"So where are they, Bryson?" the auburn-haired woman demanded, her voice filled with frustration.

"Where do the prevailing ocean currents lead?" Tori spit out.

"You're a quick study, and that's the unanswered question. There happens to be some interesting underwater topography in the Banda Sea which greatly affects deep sea currents. I've informed Sumner of the possible scenarios. Unfortunately, the search grid stretches out over a vast area in different directions. Several ships and aircraft are being dispatched. We'll be hooked up with an AGSI research vessel just beginning a new search grid."

"How do we get there?" Sanders asked.

"An Osprey from the aircraft carrier Stennis is waiting for us in Darwin. It has the range to take us out to the ship."

"Sounds like adventures in paradise," the blonde offered.

"Yeah, but not with Gardner McKay," McGann's remark erupted with innuendo.

"Do you really think we'll find them?" Sanders questioned.

"If anyone can figure a way out, it's Joe," McGann replied, pausing. "There's something more," the tone of his voice taking on a flinty edge. "I followed up on that information from NSA about our friend Kholos, soon after we left. In fact a majority of the flight time has been devoted to searching metadata files."

"And?" Ashlyn asked curiously, seemingly calmed by the possibility of finding Canton.

"It seems there's an aura of mystery to our man Kholos. Some we already knew. Some things are sitting on the fringes of plausibility," a wave of concern washing over his features. "I investigated numerous angles, basically exploring any avenue that held promise. Something obscure came up. I found an article in a weekly rag, the Athens News. There was a brief story from a number of years ago. It hinted at ties between Dimitri Pendopolous, a Greek banker and shipping magnate, to the death of a protégé in Switzerland. The Swiss banker was found dead in his apartment. The job was strictly professional."

"What happened?" Tori asked.

"To make a long story short, the mystery was never solved, purely speculation. Some reports indicate Pendopolous was sympathetic to the views of 17 November, at least, privately. However, that opened up another door. Pendopolous was on the board of an international conglomerate, IPI. Curiously enough, Chief Justice Foster Hughes was an active member of that board at one time. Reportedly, there's a friendship that goes back to college days at Georgetown."

Tori raised a finger, "Hold on, Bryson. How does this tie into the sinking of the Narissa and what's IPI?"

Both women listened intently to McGann's tale. Much of what he told them simply seemed unbelievable. He began to outline the conglomerate's intended purpose. "Some say that IPI really stands for *Ignotum per Ignotius*. Loosely translated: *The unknown explained by still more unknown*."

Sanders cut in, "Wait. Are you saying that IPI is in reality some kind of secretive society?"

"At face value. I know it's a stretch."

"This stuff's been shrouded in controversy for years. Does it really exist?" Tori questioned. The skeptical tone of her voice did not go unnoticed.

"Actually, I believe it's the head of a far reaching network. But, call it what you will. There are numerous names. Cogniscente. New World Order. That one was actually used in a presidential speech. The Council on Foreign Relations has been rumored to be part of the cover up. Whatever the name, it really doesn't matter. Supposedly, it all falls under the control of some incredibly wealthy families, who quietly pull the strings. All of which lead towards a behind-the-scenes corporate takeover of world government. Everyone equal. Controlled. Except those with an in, and the means to live the good life. If you believe all that you read, you'll find their snaking tendrils in just about all the major governments around the world."

"Bryson. Do you really think that's possible?" Haroldson asked, incredulously.

"I hope not, but I discount nothing when it comes to greed and power. It's a lustful combination that's tempted more than its share of lovers." Then McGann added a strange twist. "I found a press photo of Hughes and Pendopolous taken six years ago. In the background was a very attractive woman. I noticed her hair was pulled back slightly over one shoulder, revealing what I thought was a smudge on the image. After some enhancement, I discovered a tattoo on her neck."

Haroldson stiffened with the memory from Amsterdam. Her eyes flashed in recognition of the woman lying in the street. "Is she the woman who…"

"In answer to your question, no," McGann tossed back before she could finish, his brow stitching into a line of concern. "Although, the tattoo is the logo for IPI. Apparently, Pendopolous has three daughters. Triplets. One is now in a cell in the Netherlands. The one in the picture, I discovered, is noteworthy in her own right. Her name is Solange. She briefly made the headlines after being blinded in her left eye from a freak accident. With her father's connections and money, she was the first recipient of a powerful retinal imaging implant. The medical accomplishment was swallowed up by other news of the day, perhaps, purposefully."

"So how does all this tie into what has happened?" Sanders asked. "I'm just not getting it."

McGann considered his reply. "I'm not entirely certain." He knew he was knitting pieces of a puzzle together, one with many corners that did not match. Something crawled in the shadows, just out of reach of explanation. Bryson McGann's instincts told him there was more, and he meant to find out. "One more thing to add a little humor to your day," McGann threw out, with a deceptive grin. "Pendopolous' daughters are not only the heirs to his fortune, but they own an island in the Banda Sea. And, it just happens to be in the area we'll be searching."

Chapter Forty-Four
SEATAC-1 - Banda Sea

SHE HAD GONE TO THE BOTTOM bow first. Now the exploration vessel lay on her side, her keel broken. Mangled remnants were scattered across the seafloor. Cold, dark waters harbored the final resting spot of the once proud Narissa. AGSI's pride of the fleet suffered a fate that had captured countless ships since man first set out upon the seas. The ocean avidiously held a quiescent vigil over its captured prizes, and the men who rested eternally in watery graves. Theirs was a tale of eons, a sailor's stock in trade.

SEATAC-1 smashed into the seafloor with a jarring impact, crushing the starboard motor and the mechanical arms. Had it not been for stringent demands placed on her builders, the submersible would have become the three men's tombs. Rigidly constructed, the sub had been ingeniously designed to take just about anything the ocean wanted to dish out.

The events played out so quickly, Joe Canton had little time to react to the strange incident. In fact, none of the men inside the sub knew exactly what it was they witnessed. The tethered, submersible vehicle had been tossed around as the dying Narissa pulled SEATAC-1 into the murky realm deep beneath the surface. One thing the trio did know, they had been unwitting passengers on a wild ride to the bottom of the Banda Sea.

Fortunately, they had been secured tightly in their seats. If not, they would have sustained far worse injuries. Skiddy Pete had taken the brunt, bruising several ribs. O'Brien and Canton came away with a few minor scrapes, nothing that would not heal in a few days.

Inside the sub's command center, pale emergency lighting bathed the men in a haunting glow. Two of the computer console screens remained operable and half of the expected image loomed from the view screen giving them a partial view of the underwater world. Canton tried the communication system with no luck.

Recovering from the uncanny event, Joe Canton and Red O'Brien began a system check of the vehicle. The onboard computer indicated that all mechanical equipment on the starboard side of the sub had been damaged, and was now useless. The port engine could only function at forty percent capacity, and worse, rudder controls were damaged beyond repair. There was no way to steer SEATAC-1.

The mechanical armature on the port side, fortunately, remained intact. Arrays of blinking lights winked in response to Canton's commands from the keyboard in front of him. At his urging, the titanium pinchers on the port side of the hull worked the umbilical cord connecting SEATAC-1 to the ill-fated ship. After some time, the mechanical claw chewed through the steel cable, freeing the men from their underwater captor.

They knew they were still far from safety. Both ballast tanks suffered damage, and because of that, the submersible was tilted on a sixteen degree angle to starboard. It was making their ascent a terribly uncomfortable journey.

All of that had been almost twenty-four hours ago. Now the battered sub limped along on one engine, at the mercy of the currents. Canton yawned, coming awake after a brief nap. "Any idea where we are, Red?"

The Irishman rolled the stump of a cigar from one corner of his mouth to the other before speaking. Facing Canton, his face clouded with frustration. "Hell, no. I can't get a read on the GPS locator. There's more of the director's toys broken in this tub than we thought."

"Depth?" the big man asked calmly.

"That's the good news. We're surfacing. Bad news is, I don't have a clue where."

Joe Canton scanned the console, the lighted displays reflecting in his eyes. "That current's ripping right along," he said, checking his watch and making some quick calculations. "We're a long way from our original site."

"Best guess on our direction," Red asked.

"Toss of the coin, Red. Although if I remember correctly, there's a deep northeasterly current in this part of the Banda Sea. From the looks of things, it doesn't appear that we can pull up any maps to help us out." Canton's agitation simmered, compounded by the inoperable equipment.

O'Brien nodded in reply. "Could be worse, Joe," the gravelly voice returned.

A brief smile rested on the big man's face. "True. I've been in tighter spots. How's Skiddy doing?"

"He's been sleeping for the last couple of hours."

"Good. He needs the rest." The portion of the operating screen in front of the men brightened, indicating they were nearing the surface. "Try the ballast again. See what kind of response you get."

"Aye, aye, skipper," the Boston accent intoned. O'Brien reached for the control and pushed the button. A gurgling sound echoed through the hull while outside a small stream of bubbles came to life, racing for the surface. Both men felt the slight effects as the sub continued to rise. Thirty minutes later the lumbering vessel broke the surface.

"Time to take a look around," Canton smiled. The big man crawled through the exit portal, and released the dogs on the hatch cover. Effortlessly, Canton pushed open the cover as warm air and sunlight flooded the confines of the metal hull. From his position atop the sub, nothing but ocean appeared in front of him. Crystal blue waters, moved by the wind's prescription, stretched as far as he could see. Quickly scanning in all directions, he shouted down to O'Brien. "Must be the luck of the Irish, Red."

O'Brien waited below for his turn to view the outside world. "What's going on, Joe?"

"It won't be long until we're on dry land again." Canton looked down through the narrow opening to see Skiddy Pete's smiling face standing next to the Irishman. "I'm coming down." Canton closed the hatch and slid down the ladder. "Strap yourselves in, boys. Looks like there's a cut in the reef and we're going through. The breakers may get a little rough."

Strong currents pushed SEATAC-1 through the narrow opening, granting it access to the safety of the white sandy beach ringing the tropical paradise. The boat bobbed and rolled, but the men inside experienced nothing comparable to their earlier tumultuous journey. SEATAC-1 came to rest on its side in eight feet of water.

Gathering what supplies they had, the trio of underwater explorers climbed out onto the hull. The swim to shore was uneventful. The Aussie grimaced with the pain from his injury, but never complained. "Well, mates. We're the lucky ones," Pete remarked, finally planting himself solidly on dry land.

"Seems so," O'Brien returned.

"Deadcert," Pete replied, in Aussie slang. "No use dwelling on the negative, boys. Won't bring a soul back."

"Better days," Canton replied, nodding in affirmation. "Right now we need to be concerned for ourselves. Any takers on which direction we should go, gentlemen?" Canton questioned.

O'Brien shook his head as Pete offered, "Up to you, mate."

"I guess we're not in Kansas anymore," Canton joked. "Around that beach head to the left is as good a direction as any."

Sunlight burned from the cerulean blue sky in blazing defiance of the night that would eventually follow. Fortunately, an offshore breeze provided some relief to the humid air. Together, they looked like three tourists strolling the beach; ball caps, sunglasses, and an ever present cigar in O'Brien's mouth.

"Hey," a faint shout boiled up from behind them. "Wait." Each man stopped in their tracks, paralyzed by the unexpected sound of a female's voice. Turning in unison, they took in the form of a bikini clad woman running towards them, with a pony tail pulled to the right side of her head. "Who are you?" she called, as the distance between them evaporated. Barely breathing hard, she stopped in front of the three men. "How'd you get here?" Her eyes scanned the logo on their shirts. "Did Alex's dad send you? I've seen everyone on this island. You're not one of them. Do you have a boat?" she questioned, in a quick staccato.

"Hold on, missy," O'Brien returned. "Take a breath and slow down."

"Sorry. It's just that I haven't seen anyone else for weeks. Becca Ramsey," she said, extending her hand with two bandanas wrapped around her wrist.

"Joe Canton," his massive fingers curling around hers. "Senator Ramsey's daughter-in-law?" he asked, in disbelief.

"The same."

"I believe the world had given up hope of ever seeing you alive," the big man offered, puzzled by the strange encounter. "Red O'Brien and Skiddy Pete," he added, with a nod of his head.

A smile creased her face. "Hi. Nice to meet you. There may not be a lot of time. I don't think anyone followed me, but I can't be totally certain." Without waiting for their reply, she continued, "So, how'd you get here?"

O'Brien pulled the black stump of tobacco from his mouth, grinding out a brief synopsis of their adventure. Pete cut in occasionally, adding some filler to the story as it moved along. Canton listened carefully, cautiously eyeing the beach. From the tone of Becca Ramsey's voice, he knew something did not fit well into the mix. "So we ended up on the beach and here we are," the Irishman finished.

"So what's your story, Sheila?" Skiddy Pete questioned.

Becca Ramsey recounted the harrowing drama, detailing how she and Alex arrived on the island. From that fateful night when they jumped into the roiling waters, until the moment she saw them. "For some reason, the woman who owns the place has taken a liking to us."

"And your husband?" Canton interjected. "Where's he?"

"In our room. Alex says everyone would be less suspicious of me, than if both of us were wandering around. Besides, he's sporting a cast from a broken leg. Compliments from our night in paradise."

O'Brien mulled it over, concurring with her perception. "Sounds reasonable," he replied, casting a glance at Canton.

"I pretty much go wherever I want," Becca quickly followed. "I guess no one considers me a threat. They think I just go out for a walk on the beach. If any of them knew I was really looking for a way out of here, I'd be confined to the grounds. There's not many places I haven't been on this rock, but they don't let me near the boats." Becca chased away a drop of perspiration from the corner of her eye, lowering the tone of her voice. "You've got to find a place to hide, or we need to get out of here quickly. I can go and get Alex and be back in a few minutes. If Solange finds the three of you, she won't be very happy."

"And why's that?" O'Brien grumbled.

"Something's going on," concern etching her tanned face.

"What exactly?" Canton asked, authoritatively.

After filling the three men in on a number of details, Becca added excitedly, "I've overheard a few of the security personnel talking. And you won't believe this, but I thought I saw President Richard Simon yesterday. I was walking through the grounds, and I spotted him being taken under guard to a building."

Disbelief encircled the three newcomers to Sula Kai. O'Brien winced, scratching at the back of his neck, while Skiddy Pete's jaw dropped in disbelief. Joe Canton weighed the possibilities. If it had been someone other than Becca Ramsey, he would have discounted the statement. From what he knew of the woman, she was intelligent and capable. Only two possibilities presented themselves. Either Becca Ramsey was mistaken, or something in the world had gone terribly wrong.

"You have no way of knowing this, but President Simon is probably back from the G8 conference in Switzerland," Canton offered.

"That may be, but I've met him before," she stiffened. "If this wasn't the president, he has a twin. Look, I don't know anymore than you, but I know what I saw."

"Alright. I'll take that. So how do you and your husband plan on getting off the island? Obviously this Solange woman's hospitality won't last forever," the big man stated.

"The only apparent way is by boat. We haven't decided when." Becca Ramsey paused, while her left foot drew circles in the sand and her eyes traveled the distant beach. The woman refocused her attention on the three men standing before her. "I've found a map and gathered up some pieces of equipment. Any of you have any electronic skills?"

"A few," Canton replied. "Why?"

"Radio parts," Ramsey said, hope ringing her voice.

"Okay, missy. What's the quickest way to get to these boats?" O'Brien's gravelly tone spit out, anxious to see their possible means of transportation off the island.

"Just need a bit of time to look around. We'll need something fast," Skiddy Pete added.

Becca Ramsey raised a slender arm pointing in the direction the three men had traveled. "About face, fellows," Becca Ramsey added, evoking a smile from the band of castaways.

The group headed off in the direction they had come from, soaking in all the information the attractive brunette had to offer. Canton knew the odds weren't stacked in their favor, but perhaps with some luck, they could get away undetected. Joe Canton liked the affable demeanor that possessed her. She seemed to be all and more that the magazine articles had mentioned. He could find no reason to doubt anything she told them, and Becca Ramsey might be their only hope for getting off the island.

Their journey back towards the place where Becca Ramsey indicated the boats were moored would have taken them past the stranded sub. Upon rounding the beach-head where SEATAC-1 should have been, only a peaceful stretch of white sand, kissed by lapping waves, filled their eyes. Perplexed, the group looked for any signs indicating the fate of NESSA's submersible vehicle. The group stood dumbfounded on the shoreline watching the breakers rumbling across the outer reef.

"Sweet Mary, mother of Jesus. What the hell do you make of that?" O'Brien frothed.

"Where'd she go?" Skiddy Pete asked, the pitch of his Aussie accent rising with the surprise.

Canton responded in a serious tone, "I think it's more a question of how?"

"Precisely," an unfamiliar female voice seethed. Her menacing tone left no doubt about the potential danger coming from behind the ocean explorers and Becca Ramsey. "Very slowly," the feminine voice demanded. "Turn around."

The small group turned cautiously to find themselves facing the deadly end of automatic weapons, pointing in their direction. Canton instantly realized the serious nature of their predicament. He knew now was not the time to offer resistance. Four armed guards, and two identical, olive-skinned women stood before them. Grim fate was the key waiting in a lock that opened a door to their destiny. Joe Canton knew it was a lock he did not want to open.

Chapter Forty-Five

Sula Kai - Banda Sea

SOLANGE'S CURIOSITY GREW while recounting the instructions from Foster Hughes. The woman wondered exactly what secrets the old man harbored. She had toyed with the possibilities after reading the letter a second time, finally allowing her concerns to slip away. In the end, it did not matter. Hughes had been a staunch friend of her father. That was enough. Besides, the Chief Justice's words had been explicit in their meaning. Under no circumstances was she to open the device and read its contents. Only in the case of an untoward event occurring to him, was she to make use of the information.

The attractive woman walked the hall where glass cabinets housed the cache of stolen treasures. She quickly found the perfect hiding place for the secret information. An automatic sensor underneath a case triggered, allowing the glass to part. Carefully, the woman opened the ancient leather pouch, placing the gold, dual scan nano disc beside the copper ingot and red beads. When she finished, the glass panel slid quietly back into place.

Solange's image stared back at her from the reflective panel. The recent strain of preparing the next candidate for her treacherous plans, and dealing with the old Jew had left her irritated. Carefully she scanned the face peering back from the glass. Her left eye focused in, magnifying the fine lines coming to life under her eyes. Henke had attended to her cosmetic needs in the past. She would see to it that he kept her skin flawless, at least until tiring of him. Nearly thirty-seven, the woman detested her body's degenerative changes. Yet she knew with her wealth, she could look good for many years to come. Hoping to sate her edginess, Solange sat down next to the antiquated looking machine. The instrument had always provided the relaxation she required. Her hands moved over the two antennas sticking out of the device. Solange had become a virtuoso at playing the instrument, originally made by a Russian inventor. Haunting melodies filled the hall, as she closed her eyes, enjoying the sounds of her own music.

"Must you constantly play that damn machine," a mirrored likeness of the musician appeared, catching Solange by surprise.

The distraction annoyed her. "You find it displeasing, Sahtay?" Solange returned.

"Need you ask?" Sahtay waved away her comment, knowing the futility in continuing. "Perhaps we should change the subject. I saw your doctor friend earlier."

"You did?"

"He's leaving for Miami soon."

"I'm through with his services for now. I'll relish the moment more when I'm through with him permanently. Although," she smiled lasciviously, "he's been useful in many other ways."

Pendopolous's daughters were each a replication of the other. Tall. Slender and intelligent. Alike, and yet different in so many ways. Each possessed an inbred confidence that oozed from their beings. The sisters were not only enticing, they were equally dangerous.

Sahtay walked closer to Solange, speaking louder to be heard above the eerie tune orchestrated by her sister. Sahtay gently lowered Solange's hands. The music stopped, and she spoke softly. "Since Stephan's arrival, we've been discussing Sabrah's options. We too will be leaving soon."

"Really?"

"Obviously, our sister's confinement with the Amsterdam *politie* is not something that should be allowed to continue."

"Very true. She knows too much." Solange walked over to a glass case, eyeing an ancient Incan artifact. Removing the piece from its resting spot, Solange watched the reflection of her sister. "Perhaps, an untimely death would be best. That should be easy enough to arrange." She let the silence build until she knew Sahtay would be forced to speak.

Sahtay knew the futility in arguing with her sister. A different tack was needed. She chose her words carefully, treading on a thin edge before continuing. "Death's a possibility. It's not one I've considered. But, it would ensure her silence." Sahtay observed her sister for any hint of anger. "Solange," the woman whispered, moving in closely. Her hand gently stroked her sister's dark hair. "Perhaps in this case, killing her may not be the best idea," she paused, letting the words sink in. "We'll need some assistance to insure her freedom."

"And Stephan's already worked out the details?" Solange inquired, ice frosting the rim of her words.

"A number of them. There are some…"

"Perhaps you would like to join us on our venture, Solange," "The Greek" bellowed, striding into the room, and interrupting the women's conversation. "It'll take some time for all of it to come together. But, I'll handle it. I always do," Kholos stated, confidently. "Your complicity, as well as ours, in this whole affair, must remain hidden."

"Do you think the *politie* will make her talk before you can rescue the poor damsel?" Solange asked sarcastically. "I'm sure Sabrah will be grateful for her release." Sahtay's sister's words were filled with ire.

Kholos laughed loudly. "You shouldn't be so jealous." His eyes grew dark with contempt for the woman who once filled his nights. He had no need for her now, other than being a partner to the collusion hatched in Washington, and receiving a handsome wage for the diamond's theft. Kholos knew that her other sisters amply filled his sexual needs. They had both proven equally exhausting in their desires. Even with that intimacy, there was feigned trust on his part. He knew any one of the three could kill without compunction. They were dangerous women, black widows, and Stephan Kholos never let his guard down. "Don't trouble yourself, Solange. The less you know about Sabrah, the better. When and if the time comes I have need of you, I'll tell you," he added, with a finger wagging in her direction.

Sahtay watched in waning amusement at the game being played between Kholos and her sister. A wan smile faded quickly. "You two bore me with your trivialities." The lithe woman turned and left the room, searching for the warm embrace of a glass of Ouzo.

Kholos began to follow, then stopped, peering over his left shoulder at the sound of Solange's voice. "The deposit's been made." The words were spit out at him venomously, her attitude threatening.

Kholos never assumed anything. He would have been dead long ago if he did. His intense stare bore directly into Solange's face, detecting a slight dilation of her right pupil. The mechanical left eye stared back without response. Behind that lens, lurked a vengeance that simmered just out of sight.

"Don't worry, Stephan," the olive-skinned woman stated flatly. "I told you that your services would be paid in full upon your return. Haven't I always kept my promises?"

"The Greek" nodded silently, satisfied for the moment. "All except one," Kholos mumbled under his breath, leaving the room. "And I've no intention of taking a bullet from you, *mounosporo*."

Chapter Forty-Six
Security Center - Sula Kai

"SWEET MARY, MOTHER of Jesus, what have we gotten tangled around our prop?" Red O'Brien muttered. "We end up stranded on a picture postcard, and then get locked up by two beautiful, crazy ass women."

"Sounds like a bad B flick." Canton attempted to lighten the mood. "I'm surprised we're still breathing. If I was in charge..."

Skiddy Pete scratched his head, wincing at the possibilities. "If I had to bet, I'd say that Solange woman's got a couple screws loose somewhere. Only reason I can think of why we haven't *karked it*. You boys up for having a fair go at getting out of here?"

Canton's face clouded. "There isn't much choice but that. Somehow I don't think the twins plan on keeping us around for long."

"No windows, and we can't get the door open. So what do you propose?" O'Brien tossed back.

"Looks like we're caught between a rock and a hard spot, mates."

"Not exactly." Joe Canton was playing an ace in the hole, and he knew it. He also realized the time frame was tight. The big man had no doubt that by tomorrow at this time they would all be dead, if not sooner. "Well, do you want the good news or the bad news, gentlemen?"

"Might as well keep things on the jolly side," Skiddy Pete spoke up.

"The good news. No cameras in this room. At least none that I can find."

"What's the bad news? Although I've got a pretty good idea, mate."

"First, we don't know if there's a guard on the other side of that door. We could try and break it down, but that would assure us a bullet sooner than expected. Besides, it's probably a waste of time. The door has a magnetic lock, actuated by an ID card. We have nothing to break into the access panel on this side of the wall, so we can't override the circuitry." The three men mulled the facts, realizing their dire situation. "If we stay here, we all know there won't be a happy ending to the story," Canton's voice trailed.

O'Brien clamped down hard on the stump of the Dominican. "Been in some tight ones, but this one's not leaving much room to maneuver."

"We've got one option."

"Okay," Pete shot back. "I'm all ears."

"Becca Ramsey," Canton offered.

"Cutting it a bit thin, Joe?" the gravelly voiced Irishman interrupted. "How's she going to help us?"

"One. We know she's trustworthy. She and her husband want out of here as badly as we do. Two. Becca said she knows this place inside out."

"And your point?"

"That's the point, Red. Plus, she's the proud owner of an ID card that she just happened to *pick up* a few weeks ago."

Skiddy Pete chuckled, "Now that's one resourceful *Shelia*."

"This all hinges on the idea that they haven't locked her up," O'Brien stated, filling his lungs and exhaling a long breath.

Canton smiled. "Gotta have some faith, my friend. Look on the bright side. If she can't get us out, you won't have to listen to Sumner rant about his bruised and battered submarine."

Red O'Brien mulled the response, considering the circumstances. "That's not much of a consolation, Joe. I think I'd rather the old man chew my behind."

☙ ❧

Becca and Alex Ramsey had planned carefully before she slipped from the room. Since there was nowhere for anyone to escape from the island, Solange had never installed visual monitoring devices anywhere on the grounds. That's what offered Becca a chance of hope in her plan. Alex's broken leg would be a hindrance. "I'll be back with the others. Soon."

Her husband's face tried to hide its concern. "Love you."

Clutching her bag of supplies, she moved quietly through the manicured paradise. As she turned the corner of a building, Becca caught sight of a guard. She dropped to the ground, crawling beneath some tropical foliage. The young woman held her breath, hoping she had not been spotted by the sentry ambling by on his rounds. Once the man passed, she quickly hurried on towards the building housing the island's most recent captives.

After a quick glance all around, her fingers slid the plastic card through the slot of the outer door to the containment area. Perspiration gathered along the hairline at her temples, caused by more than the humidity. Becca Ramsey was at full throttle on an adrenaline ride. Her heart felt as if it were exploding in her chest. The rapid rate of her breathing made her feel light headed. From the pit of her knotted stomach, a wave of nausea washed over her.

If there was a guard in the security center, no explanation would prove sufficient for her breaking into the building. The door parted. It was now or never. Becca rushed inside. Her eyes raced along the corridor searching for any signs of detection. Fortunately, the hallway was empty. Becca slumped limply against the wall, the sound of the closing door offering some measure of comfort for her tattered nerves. The muscles in her legs felt rubbery, and the sweat cold and clammy against her back. Wiping away the moisture edging down her cheek, she forced herself to remain calm. Several minutes passed before she finally relaxed.

Once again focused on her mission, another dilemma grew dynamically in front of her. Down the length of the corridor were eight doors. Panic's threads tangled along her spine. Until now she had not given any thought that there might be armed guards in each room. Finally willing herself to stay calm, Becca Ramsey steeled herself for the uncertainty. Her hand trembled as the card slid through the magnetic release. The door opened. Becca Ramsey's eyes grew wide, and a wave of relief flowed over her. The room was empty.

Becca realized the odds were improving. The chances of finding any guards behind locked doors were slim. She took some satisfaction in this. Unfortunately, her next conundrum now lay in not knowing just who or what was locked away in each room. Realizing there was no other approach, she boldly slid the plastic ID through the slot outside the next room.

Darkness welled from the emptiness as she let the door close. The next two rooms were no different. All that changed when the fourth door opened. Becca Ramsey's mouth grew into a circle of astonishment at the sight of the old man. The startled diamond cutter began to speak, but she cut him off. "Listen. No time for explanations. Do you understand?"

The old man nodded in silent recognition, unsure of any other option.

"We're getting out of here. Do you want to go with us?" Becca asked, excitedly.

Abram Mossel replied, "I'm a dead man if I don't. Better to die trying. Yes, I'll go, but they'll be here in just a few minutes to take me to my work area."

"Why?"

"To cut the diamond," the old man responded as if she was aware of his purpose in this tropical paradise.

"Look, I don't have any idea what you're talking about. Just do whatever they say. I promise, we'll come and get you."

"Whose we?" Mossel mumbled.

Becca Ramsey turned as the portal was closing behind her. "No time. When they come, don't say a word."

The old man cocked his head in response, caught off guard. Perplexed by the arrival of the young woman, and even more so by who she would enlist to aid him, a thread of hope enlivened the old man at the thought of returning to his homeland. Mossel knew anything was better than the alternative his hostess had in store.

The next two rooms provided no clues as to the whereabouts of Canton and the others. Becca felt edgy, ill at ease with the situation. Time crawled as the seventh door seemingly inched backward in slow motion.

"Hey mates. Would you look at that," Skiddy Pete's shouted, as the portal opened, revealing the woman.

Canton wasted no time in asking what Becca Ramsey was carrying in the shoulder bag. She held it out for his inspection. His big hands sorted the parts, laying them on the floor. "Where did you find these?"

"Electronics. They had a number of things I thought they wouldn't miss," Becca beamed. "I figured this solder and iron would come in handy. We can make an antenna out of this spool of wire. There's some other things, too. Looks like parts to a portable ham radio unit and a couple of miniature circuit boards." The brunette winced, "The only problem is, I don't know if any of this stuff works."

"How do you know so much about radios, missy?" O'Brien asked.

"You better know a few things if you sail as much as I do. "

Joe Canton continued sifting through the pieces, selecting and discarding items as needed. A smile creased his face when he pulled out several Ultracapacitors. The others watched Canton "Here's the deal. It's rudimentary. Might not work, but I believe I can rig this to send a signal."

"How?" Pete questioned.

"I read an article about a fellow named Graham a few years ago, who created a revolutionary power supply unit for ham radio operators using these same type of capacitors." Joe Canton glanced up from his work briefly. "Actually, he's an acquaintance of Sumner's. Anyway, the guy made it big. His invention just took off. The director tried to get him to come to work at NESSA, but it was no dice."

"You still haven't satisfied my curiosity, mate. What makes them the bee's knees?" Skiddy Pete asked.

"Instead of providing continuous power at a high wattage, which means you need a large power source, the peak power occurs on demand. Something as simple as these batteries will let me send out a signal. We just have to hope they have some juice in them. Hopefully, the nearest relay buoy in the tsunami warning network will pick it up and the relay will get to NESSA or..." Canton's tone grew serious. "There's just one catch."

"What's that?" O'Brien asked, carefully eyeing each piece of electronic circuitry.

"Somebody, somewhere, needs to be listening on the other end."

Almost two hours passed before Canton had created his rudimentary communications device. At first glance, anyone would think it was merely junk, just scraps an amateur pieced together. Joe Canton hoped it would work. Their lives depended on it.

"Well, that's as much as I can do. Let's give it a try."

The trio allowed the door to open as they peered cautiously down the length of the hallway. "Let's go," Canton commanded.

"Wait," Becca shouted.

"What now?" O'Brien spit out, the Irishman's temper rising.

"Can't leave him," Ramsey shot back.

"Who are you talking about?"

"The old man. The diamond cutter. I promised we'd take him. I have to see if he's still here."

"I for one don't have a clue as to what you're talking about, but let's get him and go," Skiddy Pete said.

Becca Ramsey took the card and slid it through the slot to what she remembered to be Abram Mossel's room. As the door opened, Becca gasped, realizing she had the wrong room. Instantly, Canton and the other two men were at her side. Their mouths opened in astonishment. At first, Canton thought it must be a mistake. He had seen his share of unusual things before, but this was beyond measure. It took them all a moment before they recovered, as the man on the other side of the room scrutinized the four strangers standing before him. Canton knew there was no rational explanation for this person to be confined in this room. However, as the man began to speak, they were all certain of his identity. There was no mistaking the voice.

Canton had no concept of how or why the events had unfolded in the manner they did. The perplexity of the situation was nearly unimaginable. However, there was one thing NESSA's Assistant Projects Director knew for certain. Something was terribly wrong.

Chapter Forty-Seven
White House - Washington, D.C.

STAN REYNOLDS PATROLLED the corridor outside the president's office. The agent's eyes missed nothing as he made his rounds. Things were on target, and his controllers were pleased with his performance. The Secret Service veteran had done all in his powers, without arousing suspicion, to keep things on track from his end. The one thorn in his side continued to be Benjamin Wolcott. On several occasions, he noticed the presidential advisor eyeing him suspiciously. Wolcott, he found out, had even lived up to his threat, being brazen enough to demand reassignment for the agent which Simon quickly denied. Reynolds smirked at the reminder of the ass chewing Wolcott received for continuing to push the subject into the middle of the president's plate.

Reynolds' intentions were to avoid suspicion, keeping things low key since returning from Davos. World events had sent the White House staff spinning into overdrive, in prescribed attempts to mollify political issues around the globe, all carefully guided by tutelage of the world's predominant G-8 leader. Right now, the agent did not want to give Wolcott any further reasons for finding cause for problems. Reynolds knew eventually he would have his moment with the *aide de camp*, and he would relish in the satisfaction. There would come a day in the not too distant future when Wolcott's advisory skills were no longer needed. His puzzling disappearance would remain a mystery, and like most things around the Beltway, be quickly forgotten. Reynolds had already planned for the event. He had no sense of remorse when it came to pulling the trigger. After all, there was only one option for anyone not playing on the same team. Elimination.

The Secret Serviceman's thoughts were interrupted by the gentle buzzing of his cell phone. The agent glanced around in all directions, then quickly headed for the nearby exit. Stepping out into the famed rose garden, Reynolds snapped the phone open. "Reynolds."

"Can you talk?"

"Limited," came the agent's reply.

A long pause held his attention before the caller finally spoke again. "We need a face to face."

"When?"

"Sooner than later. Someplace where we won't be given a second glance."

Stan Reynolds moved slowly across the grounds, his features animated as if he were speaking with an old acquaintance. He analyzed the sound of the caller's voice, recognizing the slight change from its normal pitch. Perplexed by the situation, the agent tossed around a number of ideas as to the meaning of this call. Nothing was out of the ordinary on his end, and nothing was buzzing at the White House. If there was, he would know about it. "Lima," Reynolds answered. "Eleven. Upstairs."

The line went dead. Stan Reynolds left the garden to continue his work. He had two hours left before his shift ended. It gave him plenty of time to wonder what precipitated the urgency of this meeting. He did not like unexpected intrusion to his day, especially from this caller. While his shift passed with agonizing slowness, his irritation grew. Reynolds' ability to handle situations when they arose was well known in agency circles. Unusually calm, the thought of this meeting left him out of sorts. He attempted to bury his annoyance in an effort to maintain his normal demeanor.

Reynolds preferred to error on the side of caution, arriving early. It afforded him an opportunity to be seated at the perfect table. A young Chilean hostess with flashing eyes and raven hair saw to that. She had a spicy appetite for what Reynolds offered. She was one of the few he screwed on a regular basis. He had taken his time with her, before revealing the nature of his work. The agent knew he could count on her discretion. Velina enjoyed the sex too much. The woman also realized she had little choice. Reynolds' investigations yielded some hidden secrets about a number of her friends.

Border runners. Illegal aliens was the government's terminology. None had green cards, allowing them legitimate access in the country. The agent could make a lot of trouble for them, and he did not mind bringing it to her attention on occasion. In actuality, Stan Reynolds could have cared less about their illegal status. All of them worked in the food service industry where little attention was paid to one's country of origin. A smirk of satisfaction creased his face. If his threats got him laid, that suited his purposes.

A pulsing bass beat thumped rhythmically from the basement lounge as Reynolds packed away a couple of beef empanadas flavored with fresh lime. Reynolds enjoyed the South American cuisine, particularly when paired with a twenty-three year old Guatemalan rum. A waiter appeared and removed his empty plate, titling his head in response to Reynolds' request for a third round, and a glass of Woodford's finest.

The agent snapped his wrist for a quick check of his watch. His *friend* was a few minutes late. But it was Friday, and D.C.'s streets were jumping in light of the world's problems. The stark reality had yet to take hold in the minds of the capital's younger set. Oil reserves had been released, and for the moment, all was right in their world. Stan Reynolds was in no hurry, knowing that the caller would show.

The agent watched him from above, when the man entered the ground floor of Lima's. Reynolds smiled. The man's attempts at being charming with the lovely Velina yielded little results. He studied her reaction. Polite, yet disinterested. She motioned for the man to follow.

Reynolds riveted his eager gaze upon the temptress, feeling himself aroused, knowing well what lay beneath the tight-fitting black dress. The scooped neckline invited more than a surreptitious glance at her ample cleavage. Shimmering from the overhead lighting, Velina's long hair slid across her shoulders as she guided the man to her lover's table. She offered Reynolds an impish grin, silently hinting at more before she left the two men alone.

"Damn good of you to order me a drink," the man said, raising the glass towards the Secret Service agent seated next to him. He let the clear brown liquid warm his belly before beginning some idle chat.

"Alright, Boggs. Cut the crap. What's so damn important?"

Martin Boggs sucked in another gulp of the bourbon before speaking, all the while eyeing his surroundings to see if anyone was paying attention to their clandestine conversation. The throng of patrons surrounding them were oblivious to the purpose of the two men's meeting. They were wrapped in conversations about their past week's troubles that were quickly vanishing, thanks to laughter and alcoholic libations, like a Caribbean sunset. "It seems I'm becoming disillusioned with an acquaintance," the CEO stated.

"So what did this person do to piss you off, Boggs?" The alcohol was loosening Reynolds' tongue, and frankly, he was finding himself becoming irritated with the man who tried to hit on Velina. "Furthermore, why should I care?" he questioned, words chiming with acerbic curtness.

"Because, I'm the one talking," Boggs flared into a threatening tone. "You dance on my dime. Understood?" The cold words strained themselves through a fraudulent smile, triggering an alarm inside Reynolds that sobered him immediately. "Now, do I have your attention, Stan?" The effusive nature of his subtlety was not hidden from the agent. "IPI has a problem that will need taking care of in the very near future."

"You're the boss," Reynolds acquiesced, visualizing fractures from treading on thinning ice.

"President Simon is about to begin the transition phase of our project. Now that the world is screaming for help from the stranglehold of our Middle Eastern friends, and given the fact that tactical nukes are pieces to be played, the old man is having some misgivings," Boggs lied.

The waiter returned with a refill for Reynolds. He waited until the worker left before continuing their discussion. "If the Arabs are in on the scheme, why do you want to blow them up?"

Boggs cherubic face grinned back at the agent, "Damn, Reynolds. Don't put limits on your thinking. Only selected targets will be hit."

"So what country will top IPI's hit list?"

"Iran. There's no other first choice."

"Why?" Stan Reynolds asked. His eyes grew dark as he mulled the cards soon to be played. It was a game in which the house would win, hands down. Reynolds thought of a couple of reasons, but wanted to hear it from the source. He knew defusing the nuclear equation in that area of the world might bring some stability. The agent returned his attention back to his dining companion, as the devious man began to speak.

"They have plenty of oil. We can very easily remove whoever's in power." Boggs interrupted his soliloquy with a long draw on the bourbon. "By the way, that'll happen soon." Carlton's CEO let his elbow come to rest on the table, rattling the ice and pointing a finger at the man seated across from him. "Once those bastards see we mean business, they'll capitulate."

"What about Korea… China for that matter?"

"Look. Simon has the few remaining original members of the G-8 in his back pocket. We know the others will support the plan. Any threat with North Korea will be dealt with. No warnings. Just blow the shit out of Pyongyang and it's done."

"China will…"

"China will posture. Let'em. They're as fed up with the Koreans as anyone else. They're in no position to do anything. In no uncertain terms, they'll understand that the US and its G-8 allies mean business. Their outlook will change if they know the world has sided against them. Besides, they need oil as badly as anyone, probably worse. We'll offer a deal to keep things settled down. They'll come around. It's that simple," the financial wizard remarked.

"So why's Hughes suddenly so upset?" Reynolds questioned.

"Don't trouble yourself," he responded smugly, waving off the question nonchalantly. "Just know this. He's fallen into disfavor with IPI's controllers. Says he doesn't like the track we're on. Foster Hughes had been instrumental in keeping the dream alive when others were ready to quit. The old man was the needed catalyst to keep the fires burning, reviving the ideals of our predecessors over the years." Reynolds watched Martin Boggs' smiling face evaporate into a mask of clouded darkness. "Stan, the Chief Justice is living in the past." Boggs' hand parted the air in front of him. "You see," he said, after another sip of the bourbon, "Hughes' antiquated ideas for a world government don't necessarily reflect the attitude of today's global needs, or for that matter, ours. When he accepted the responsibility of carrying the torch, his world was a much different place, and now it's pissing the old bastard off."

"So fill me in on the rest of the plan," Reynolds tossed back at Carlton's CEO.

"In a nutshell. Once the events have fallen into place, the conscripted heads of state will push for a world currency."

"And you'll get people to swallow that easily?" he chuckled.

A stern look clouded the CEO's face, letting Reynolds know the importance of IPI's success. "They'll have no choice. If they don't, we'll simply devalue everyone's money worldwide, just to keep a level playing field. Paper currency's already been printed and awaiting distribution. For those who decide that ours is not the best game in town, they'll open the door to their own fate." Boggs buried his face in the menu, searching for a late night dinner. "So, what's good?"

The Secret Service agent gave careful consideration to the CEO's perfidious words. The plan so far had been flawless. He had not anticipated events going as far as Boggs alluded, but he was in it for the long haul. Reynolds had not joined this cabal with thoughts of failure. The agent felt confident. There was no reason Stan Reynolds could think of for everything not to fall into place.

Chapter Forty-Eight

Nerita - AGSI Research Vessel

"MR. MCGANN." THE CO-PILOT'S VOICE erupted from the earpiece of McGann's headset. "Can you come forward, sir?"

"On my way, Lieutenant." McGann shrugged at his two female companions, unaware of the reason he had received a request to join the officers in the cockpit.

The airframe of the V-22 Osprey rattled from the turbulence above the waters of the Banda Sea. McGann moved forward, cautiously. Through the windscreen of the tilt-rotor military aircraft, he caught sight of their destination as he entered the cabin. Naval Lieutenant, Jacob Jones, turned as McGann entered, handing him a headset. "We're three miles out, sir. We're cleared to land on the Nerita," the black officer stated.

Commander Ken Sharp's voice cut in. "Ladies, the landing might be a little rough today with these winds. Strap yourselves in tight. Seas are running around eight feet. Deck's bouncing pretty good." The naval officer's discerning eyes carefully took in the dials and colored screens of the instrumentation before continuing his conversation. The altimeter indicated a gentle descent, leisurely ticking off the numbers as the Banda Sea rose up to greet them. "We will begin transition momentarily." The officer took the time to explain how the aircraft would switch from fixed wing to rotary flight, something many would not bother to do. McGann realized this man was a no nonsense pilot, and obviously loved what he was doing. "Once we lose some more altitude and the engines are fixed in the upright position, the ride will smooth out. We'll be down in no time."

McGann flew Ospreys for NESSA, and was fully aware of the aircraft's peculiarities. However, he was an ardent fan of the multi-use plane, and staunch defendant of its tactical capabilities.

"Captain Sully sends his regards, sir," Jones said. "He'll meet you on deck. By the way, thanks for the tip on operating this crate. That's something they didn't teach in flight school, but I'll remember it."

"When it comes to flying, Lieutenant, it's what you don't know that can get you killed," McGann replied.

Sharp turned again in McGann's direction, peering through his green aviator glasses. "Found that one out myself, the hard way. Good thing is, I lived to tell about it," the veteran pilot smiled.

"Appreciate the ride today, guys." McGann tossed back.

"Our pleasure, sir." Jones flashed a toothy grin from the right seat. "Hey. Good luck finding your friend."

The V-22 Osprey wobbled slightly as Sharp touched down in the middle of the painted red circle at the stern of Narissa's sister ship, Nerita. A golden sunset greeted the three passengers as they disembarked.

A face whose lines carved upon it had seen more than its share of nautical experiences, waited to greet them. Weathered, tanned, and sporting a full salt and pepper beard, the stern-faced Aussie captain spent little time on pleasantries. "Nice to meet everyone," he said, after shaking hands. "I'll make it quick. We're roughly seventy miles from the prescribed coordinates. At top speed we'll arrive at Sula Kai in about four hours. For now, rest and grab something to eat." Captain Larry Sully did not wait for a response. "I'll take you to the galley. Follow me, please."

Time past slowly for them. Sully returned and took them to the chart room. The Nerita's captain wasted no time spelling out his directions, and listened with growing disapproval at McGann's ideas. A stint in the Australian navy gave him the perspective ability to understand the complicated nature of McGann's requests and intentions. Officially, there was little he could do to offer McGann any help in the event of the unknown. He especially disliked the idea of leaving McGann on his own without means for backup.

"I fully understand the implications of my request, captain," McGann's ardent resolve ringing in his words. "But, I don't know of a better way. If the Nerita stays within the island's proximity, it may arouse suspicions. That's something I want to avoid at all costs," McGann said, firmly.

Scratching his beard and weighing the options, Sully grudgingly agreed. He leaned towards McGann and his female companions. "Look," he responded, wiggling a finger toward the newcomers on his ship. "I've no other option than to go along with your plan. My orders are explicit," he said, staring into McGann's hazel eyes. Sully carefully regarded the man standing next to him, realizing Bryson

McGann was not a run of the mill paper pusher. He found it odd that an Assistant Projects Director involved with a reputable scientific agency would possess the steely grit McGann displayed. Instinctively, he began to sense there was much more to this man's makeup than his job title dictated. The captain also understood in that moment, Bryson McGann was not a stranger to this line of work, nor a needless risk taker either. "There's probably not much I could do to stop you," he sighed, resigning himself to McGann's decision.

"Good," McGann responded. He knew the dilemma of sending men into the unknown. He had been in similar positions during his military days. McGann also knew choice was not a word that often fit into trying circumstances.

Pale light rose up from the chart table bathing Ashlyn Sanders and Tori Haroldson in a waxy glow. Both women had expressed their opinions, with Sanders offering a couple of final options that the group mulled and decided upon.

"I don't like the idea of not being able to contact you by radio. What if something happens?" Haroldson asked, pointedly.

"If it does, I'm afraid having a radio won't do me much good. Besides, Ashlyn may need some company." Tori Haroldson was quickly becoming upset by the track their conversation was taking. "You can text message me if need be. It'll come across the screen of my UMPC." McGann tested the miniature computer's functioning, satisfied it was working. After laying out the final details of his plan, the group prepared for McGann's departure. "Listen," he added as an after thought. "All of this is purely speculation. I may end up having drinks with Solange and her island friends. If I do, I'll call and have you join the party." McGann's attempt at defusing the brooding ended with his signature grin.

"Bryson, you can be so damned irritating," Haroldson foamed, storming from the room. McGann felt the pangs of Haroldson's angst, but could not allow himself to be distracted with his feelings for the lovely blonde scientist. Too much was at stake. Deep down her outburst gnawed at his gut. Ashlyn made a move to follow, but McGann interceded. "Let her go, Ash. She needs a few minutes by herself. She's been through a lot lately."

Sully broke the icy moment. "All right, you two. Topside. It's just about time."

The Banda Sea had settled with night's calling. As daylight faded, the winds had calmed and the seas were now running about three feet. Nerita's crewmembers were nearly completed with preparations for McGann's departure. The sea sled McGann would use was to be hoisted over the port side, away from direct view of the island. The underwater craft had two separate enclosed compartments, but McGann was the only one with an "E" ticket that bought him passage to the island.

Four and a half miles off the starboard beam, a faint, shadowy silhouette of Sula Kai's volcanic peak towered above the ocean. McGann glanced into the darkness at his destination, wondering what lay in store. He shrugged it off knowing it wasn't worth the time speculating.

His well muscled body moved fluidly beneath the thin material of the black dive skin as he stowed his gear in the forward compartment. Turning back to Sanders and the Nerita's captain, he slipped into the harness of the compact rebreather. The underwater breathing circuit left no telltale trail of bubbles rising towards the surface, as with typical scuba equipment. It was a coin toss to see if anyone would be waiting to greet him when he arrived on the island. Anything to avoid detection on the final swim to the beach was a plus, and he knew the slightest advantage sometimes made all the difference. Hopefully, no one would notice the uninvited guest, but it was a chance he had to take.

"One more thing, captain. If you keep the ship just over the horizon, your chances of being discovered should be pretty slim. Set a course to circle the island at that distance, and I'll let you know when to come charging in."

The sled was simpler in design than those he had used in his military training, but it basically operated in the same fashion. McGann settled into the cockpit and his fingers punched in the coordinates to carry him safely through the cut in the outer ring of the island's protective coral. Plowing into a brick-hard reef in the middle of the night was not a card he wanted to play. McGann turned, looking out the small sub's enclosed bubble. He gave a two finger wave to Ashlyn and Captain Sully as the sea sled was hoisted over the side. An image of Tori Haroldson flashed in his mind wishing she had been on deck. That idea quickly melted away when the dark waters of the Banda Sea swallowed him, forcing him to focus on the task at hand.

A clicking metallic sound outside the hull signaled the automatic release of the cables tethering the sea sled to the research vessel. Green glowing instruments cast an eerie light within the small confines. McGann flipped several toggles, filling the enclosed space with sharp, snapping sounds. Instantly, the electric motors came to life. His hand worked the joystick control, angling the bow down until he reached one hundred and fifty feet. At this depth, he knew the underwater lights posed no problem of possibly exposing him.

Occasionally, a brilliant streak of silver flashed in front of him. The vehicle's lights would briefly capture a passing school of fish or a deep water predator which quickly disappeared from view. The marine life held little interest in the strange creature invading their underwater habitat. McGann followed the computerized course to the opening in the island's reef. Nearly thirty minutes later, the sea sled slipped through the cut undetected, prowling the inner waters of Sula Kai's coral beds.

McGann let the sled settle on the sandy bottom underneath the protective cover of a magnificent coral formation. Its concealment would make the craft difficult to spot, even in daylight. He shut down the motors and switched off the instrumentation. Pulling the dive mask over his face, he settled into a comfortable position. The odd flavor of rubber sat disquietingly on his tongue, as he slipped the rebreather's mouthpiece into place. In all his years of diving, he had never grown used to that initial taste.

Satisfied the apparatus was functioning properly, McGann pressed another button allowing the craft's twin compartments to slowly fill with water. Once the pressure was the same inside the sea sled as out, the canopies automatically opened. He checked his Breitling and noted the time. He had about four hours to daybreak.

McGann pushed himself forcefully out of the small compartment into the crystal clear waters of the inner reef. Any other time he would have enjoyed a night dive. Tonight, his agenda held much more than a leisurely swim. He still was two hundred yards from shore, and time was not a luxury. An orange glow reflected off his face mask, courtesy of the GPS devise. Bryson McGann brought his left arm up for a look at the instrument strapped to his wrist. He read the information, made a slight course correction, and set out towards the beach.

Powerful legs kicked in rhythmic fashion, propelling him along the prescribed heading. McGann occupied his time with possible scenarios and responses. He did not expect to be greeted with open arms, even if Joe Canton was not on the island. The information he had been able to find on the Pendopolous family left him cold.

There were too many unanswered questions; money, deaths, involvement with what seemed apparently legitimate schemes that with a little bit of digging, held potentially sobering consequences.

Bryson McGann had no illusions as to the nature of uncertainties that lay before him. NESSA's Assistant Projects Director also knew the unexpected waited without remorse.

Chapter Forty-Nine

Beachhead - Sula Kai

TORI HAROLDSON HAD EXPECTED everything that occurred, at least, up until now. Something was terribly wrong beneath the island's dark waters. Subconsciously, her mind sifted through a long list searching for answers as the unthinkable came to life. She was trapped. Struggling to free herself, the scientist realized that her spur of the moment plan may end up costing her life.

Haroldson's mind raced with thoughts of drowning, sending the electrifying effects of adrenaline charging through her system. Gripped with fear bordering on panic, her eyes widened in disbelief. Her lungs began to ache. She tossed her head side to side unable to discover the cause of her predicament. Her vain attempts to free herself used up precious oxygen. As darkness invaded the corners of her mind, the woman realized little time was left.

Somehow, a distant part of her being willed her to attention on the problem. Another part of herself was succumbing to a peaceful bliss. Haroldson had heard stories of near drowning victims and the calm they felt as death approached. That passing thought was enough to make her continue to fight, at least until the end came.

Tori Haroldson remembered the water rising up around her. She had instinctively taken in a deep breath before putting in the mouthpiece. With her first exhalation, nothing happened. Only a trail of small bubbles escaping from the sides of her mouth gave silent testimony to her predicament. Thoroughly familiar with scuba gear, it became clearly evident to Tori Haroldson that stealing a rebreather, without understanding how it worked, had been a serious mistake. The scientist felt desperation's overwhelming grip. She knew it would not be much longer. Part of her wanted to rip out the mouthpiece, hoping to find life giving air. Her chest burned with a ravaging fire, due to lack of oxygen. Burning tears stung her eyes. Strobe colored lights flashed on and off, her brain's final signal before soon lapsing into unconsciousness.

From somewhere in the deep recesses of her mind, an idea welled. The system needed to be switched on. Seventy-five feet below the surface, her hands groped the control panel of the breathing circuit on her chest. Tori Haroldson urgently searched for anyway to turn on the rebreather. Everything her fingers touched in the darkness did nothing to relieve her compelling situation. Death was imminent if she could not manage to activate the circuit. Close to passing out, a slender finger felt an unfamiliar switch on the side panel. Her lungs screamed. Through a deep fog, Tori felt herself pressing it.

She hoped.

Nothing happened.

Her mind triggered in one last act of defiance against death. She pressed the button with her last ounce of reserve. Instantly, the control panel came to life. Her first deep breath burned like a wild fire in her dry throat, sending her into a spasm of violent coughing. Tori closed her eyes, pressing both hands against the mouthpiece, fearful it would slip out. She gulped in volumes of air, eventually sating her body's greedy demands. It took her several more minutes before she recovered her composure.

Now, she began the task of figuring out an answer to her predicament. When she stowed away in the aft compartment, the webbing of the re-breather's harness inadvertently snagged on a small hook under the instrument panel. No matter how hard she attempted to extricate herself, it became impossible.

Tori had only one choice. Releasing the buckle, she slid out of the harness. Her hands followed the strap to the problem, quickly freeing it. Pushing out of the sea sled the woman settled on the sandy bottom. The scientist took in a large breath. Removing the mouthpiece and slipping the rebreather over her head, she readjusted the harness, satisfied everything was in working order.

Fortunately, the water was clear and warm. In the night sky above, a quarter moon and stars gave away their position, pointing her in the direction of the surface. After what seemed an eternity, Tori Haroldson's head rose above the water. She turned in a slow circle searching for the proper direction. She heard the distant surf roll across the outer reef. Continuing the turn, a shadowy outline of the island appeared. The volcanologist let herself sink beneath the water, swimming quickly towards the beach.

Bryson McGann held himself in place, scissoring his legs while treading water. Experience had taught him that rushing onto an unfamiliar beach without precaution was a perilous recipe. Only allowing enough of himself to be exposed so he could eye the shoreline, a number of minutes passed before he moved into shallower water. He took off his fins and rebreather, paddling the last few yards to shore. Wasting no time, McGann ran across the sandy white beach into the edge of the jungle. Crouching, he stopped to listen. Every sound was evaluated. His eyes penetrated the semi-darkness, predatory senses on high alert. When he was satisfied no one had observed him, he placed the diving equipment out of sight. The former special-ops warrior soundlessly blended into the shadows, living up to his Cheyenne name, *Ghost who walks in the wind.*

Tori Haroldson's feet touched bottom and she scrambled up the beach. She pulled the mask up and over her dripping hair, running full speed for the tentative safety of the tree line. The darkness swallowed her form as Tori hurriedly stripped off equipment, concealing the gear as best she could. Realizing she had no idea of where McGann might be, Tori fought the urge to call out his name. There were only two choices when it came to picking up McGann's trail, left or right. The woman chose the latter, moving quickly along the shadowy fringes of the jungle.

Thankfully, her hunch had paid off in dividends. A set of footprints disappeared into the dense vegetation along a small trail. Tori Haroldson took one last look around and set out to find McGann.

Chapter Fifty
Jungle Trail - Sula Kai

TORI HAROLDSON WALKED ALONG THE TRAIL as quietly as she could. The scientist's eyes strained to cut through the night, guided by only the moonlight filtering through the canopy above. Realizing she had no idea of how to find McGann in the darkness, a sense of foreboding crept over her. She now fully understood her strategy was skewed from its initial conceptualization. Tori faced no other alternative than to continue her mission in an attempt to locate McGann. There was no way to return to the safety of the Nerita, and for that matter, did not even know the ship's current location. If she could not find McGann by daylight, then her quest would be compounded by the fact she could be easily spotted. Haroldson also realized that no one on board the ship might know she was gone at this point, which meant McGann had no idea she was missing and lost.

Unfortunately for Tori Haroldson, her movements had been overheard by one of the island's sentries. What she believed to be a set of McGann's footprints had, in actuality, been that of one of Solange's hired guns, who had gone for a night swim in the placid waters of the lagoon.

Ahn Sok had seen his share of battles in the guns for hire world. The Cambodian began to realize he was being followed by the unusual stirring of plants and vegetation behind him. Something was not right. He had come alone to the beach. Quietly, Sok moved off the trail into the dense foliage to play a game of cat and mouse with whoever was coming up behind him. His hand filled with black metal of a silenced pistol. If it was one of his companions having some fun with Sok, he would allow the game. If it was something else, he would end it.

Tori Haroldson continued as the path grew to an incline leading to Solange's compound. Every now and again she would stop and listen, hoping to see or hear McGann moving ahead of her. The scientist heard the rustle behind her and stopped. She turned, filled with relief. "Bryson?"

The woman never had the opportunity to finish her sentence. Three feet behind her, an Asian man suddenly appeared in the darkness. There was no mistaking the menacing gesture of the pistol pointed in her direction. Instantly, her gut knotted. Tori Haroldson did not understand the man's dialect. When she made no move to comply with his demands, Sok stepped forward, waving the Beretta. There was no doubt as to what he meant. Tori dropped to her knees, trying to keep tears from flowing.

Sok was unsure of why this stranger was on the island, but he did know one thing. She had no reason to be there. Feeling uneasy, he quickly glanced in all directions. Scanning the darkness, he also listened for any trace that she was not alone. The guard flipped off the pistol's safety, weighing the idea of just putting a bullet in the blonde's head and getting it over. However, since there were no witnesses, he realized she was in the perfect position for his lascivious plan. Sok stepped forward, the gun pointed at her head. His other hand tugged at the zipper of his pants.

Tori Haroldson's eyes widened in disbelief. A wraith tore from the shadows with lightning speed, making her almost doubt what she saw. The apparition moved with fluid swiftness, silently offering death's greeting. The events were a blur of motion, nearly simultaneous.

Sok's head snapped upwards as a powerful hand clamped over his nose and mouth. His arm holding the pistol was hit with a terribly painful force from underneath, sending it skyward. Solange's guard pushed out a muffled cry. Reflexively, his finger squeezed the Beretta's trigger, sending a silenced slug into the night. Next, the sharp steel of a blade bit deeply into the exposed flesh of his neck, severing the carotid arteries and tearing apart the cartilage of his trachea. Warm blood spilled across the sentry's chest. Unable to breathe and receiving no blood supply, Sok's brain had no time to register the incongruent nature of his dire predicament. The Asian was dead before he fell to the ground.

McGann had moved with practiced ease through the dense foliage. The moon's glow allowed him the ability to see well enough in the darkness. His ears had caught the sound of someone moving off to his left. Needing to know who was there, McGann hurriedly found its source.

Drawing near, he made out the shadowy figures of two people making their way along the jungle path. One suddenly stopped moving, slipping quietly off the trail. The other continued on their approach. McGann spotted her before she called out to him. A normal reaction would have been to call out her name. He knew better. Years of training and battlefield instincts dictated a different course of action.

McGann slid the black metal blade from its sheath. His mind was working automatically, knowing exactly what to do. The man pointing the pistol at Tori Haroldson had but seconds left to live. Bryson McGann moved onto the trail behind the gunman undetected. In a blur of movement, he sprang forward, muscles taut, moving with cat-like agility. His hand clamped across the man's nose and mouth. McGann's vice-like grip forcefully wrenched the guard's neck up and back, exposing the soft flesh under the jawline. His other arm wielding the knife, struck forcefully in a sweeping upward motion. The powerful blow caused a jolting pain along a nerve on the underside of the guard's arm. Reflexively, his finger triggered a bullet into the night sky. It had barely cleared the pistol's barrel when the razor steel of McGann's knife bit through cartilage and blood vessels. He let the sentry drop to the ground, confident the man's life was finished.

"Tori, are you all right?" Urgency stained McGann's voice while he moved quickly to her side.

"Oh, God," she cried. "I can't believe... I'm sorry. I didn't want to leave you alone. I…" Tori's last words came just before she felt the flooding tears, and McGann's arms wrapping around her.

"It'll be alright, Tori," he said, stroking her hair. All the while he kept his senses on high alert, hoping no one was looking for the dead guard. He gave her a few minutes to compose herself. He did not bother asking why she had followed, or attempt to chastise her poor judgment. McGann knew the situation could not be changed. There was no way for her to leave the island. Neither of them felt comfortable with the thought of her being left alone to hide.

"Tori. This is very important. Understand?"

The woman nodded quickly, drying her tear streaked face.

"No questions. If I tell you to sit, stay put. If I tell you to run, don't look back. Got it?" The blonde whispered a raspy response, indicating she understood. "We don't have a lot of time. Once someone finds our friend here, things will get tight." McGann moved the body from the jungle path, doing as much as possible to hide any trace of their existence.

Quickly, McGann explained his plan that he had not bothered to share with the captain of the Nerita. There had been no reason to involve him or his crew needlessly. Besides, with what he believed might be going on with current world events, he had, up until now, only shared with Ashlyn Sanders. If it was not true, it did not matter. The alternative cradled a bleak prospect.

Together they made their way up the sloping path, hiding along the edge of the manicured grounds of the compound. Assured they had not been spotted, McGann pulled two small metal cases from the shoulder bag carrying his equipment, followed by an Ultra Mobile Personal Computer. Haroldson watched McGann curiously as he began his work. Inside the first metal container, a miniature earpiece sat in a carved indentation of protective foam. He placed it in his left ear, and turned on the communication device. "Signal source, 22. Data sequence 11," McGann spoke softly, confirming his identity. "Sequence 11. Activate." A coded script came to life on his UMPC screen. He tapped the face of the miniature computer screen. It sent out an uplink, which then outsourced another signal from the orbiting satellite to its intended receiver, all within seconds.

"You said you couldn't talk to anyone. Who're you talking to?" Haroldson asked.

McGann held up a finger to quiet her as he waited for the reply. "It was a ruse. Give me a second," was all he said. Within a moment, the face of Ashlyn Sanders aboard the Australian research vessel filled the screen of the electronic instrument he held in his hand.

"Signal source, 22. Copy." Sanders' voice replied, in his earpiece. "Be advised that the link is active. Ready to proceed with the operation as planned."

"Roger." McGann returned. The satellite link provided clear reception on the UMPC's color screen. Now it was time to see if his suspicions of the ongoing global mayhem that Dimitri Pendopolous' daughters were involved in were true.

Chapter Fifty-One

Security Center - Sula Kai

"I'M JOE CANTON, Mr. President," NESSA's assistant projects director said, after the initial shock of seeing the unexpected face behind the door wore off.

Richard Simon eyed the group, fully confident they were not a hostage rescue team. However, the President of the United States was as perplexed by their presence as they were by his.

"I work for NESSA, sir," the big man offered. "I believe you know Becca Ramsey."

"Indeed. Becca, it's wonderful to see you. Is Alex…"

"He's alive," the brunette answered before he could finish.

"I know Jason and Olivia will be glad both of you are all right."

"That's if we get out of this alive, sir," Canton interrupted.

Simon had learned a few things during his term, and one of those was that at times it was better just to listen. He made a mental note of a list of questions that grew by the moment. Canton continued the introductions as Red O'Brien and Skiddy Pete shook hands with the Chief Executive. The recollection of Canton's name struck Simon after a moment. The memory of McGann and Canton's involvement with the H.A.A.R.P. situation, months earlier, rose to the surface. Simon took in a deep breath before speaking. "Now I remember," he remarked, pointing a finger at the big man. "Where's your friend, Mr. McGann?" the President inquired.

A grim smile settled in. "I wish I knew, sir."

Simon mulled the events of the past few minutes before speaking again, his brow clouding. "I'd say explanations are in order, although I believe they can wait." He looked at the group standing before him. At least now there was a chance of escaping. Simon's normal take charge abilities fell far short of the predicament facing the group, quickly concluding this scenario was out of his league. "Anyone have any experience at this sort of thing?"

The gravelly Irish accent of Red O'Brien spoke up. "Navy, sir. I seen a few fights in my day." Turning in Canton's direction, he added, "Joe was in special-ops." He rolled the worn cigar to the other side of his mouth and smiled. "We can give it our best, sir."

"Good," Simon affirmed. "I'm in your hands, gentlemen. Anyone have a plan?"

After a brief overview of what Canton hoped to accomplish, the group left the security building. Canton and Becca took the lead, with Skiddy Pete and the president following them. Red O'Brien kept watch for anything unexpected from the rear of the group. Becca led them to an area that offered everything necessary for Canton's scheme.

"This should work." Canton handed the spool of copper wire to O'Brien. "Red, you and Skiddy roll out a piece about one hundred feet long. Becca, take these cutters and clip it in the middle. Then cut me one more about fifteen feet long." Simon watched silently, uncertain as to the big man's plan. After cutting the wires, the brunette handed the longer pieces to him first.

At his request, Becca Ramsey reached into the bag containing the stolen equipment. She filled Canton's hand with a black plastic device. Wrapping the end of each wire around the metal screws in the balun, he tightened them into place. Next, Canton placed shorter pieces of wire into the bottom end of the plastic device. Now the balun and wire formed a rudimentary "T."

Canton nodded in the direction of two trees. "Skiddy, Red, one for each of you. Once you secure the wire, get back here as quickly as possible. I'll take it from there."

"Alright, mate. Let's have a go at it." Skiddy Pete raced from the group's location, scurrying up the tree with Red O'Brien a close second to the other. Both held two equal lengths of copper wire that dragged behind them. Climbing about twelve feet above the ground, the two men secured their wires. Once their work was completed, they made their way back down, sprinting back to the group undetected.

It was now up to NESSA's assistant project director to do his part, while the others scattered into the protective shadows of the ground's foliage. Canton raced to splice together the parts of his jury rigged communications device. He held his breath. The batteries had to work. Each of his hands held a piece of copper wire. Tapping them together in a prescribed fashion, the distress call went out into the night.

Joe Canton hoped it was enough. He knew the chances were slim, but slim odds were better than none. For Canton, President Simon, and the others, it was the only option they had.

Chapter Fifty-Two
Island Compound - Sula Kai

FROM A DISTANCE, THE RUMBLING OF BREAKERS drifted on the still air. McGann's dark clothing was damp from the humid tropical night. Tori Haroldson wiped away a sheen of perspiration from her face, growing uncomfortable at not being able to shift her position. She was steadfastly determined to do as McGann told her.

A very pale light from the UMPC allowed McGann to ready the microelectronics that Gerald Pierson, NESSA's head experimental scientist, had helped develop. McGann's miniature computer allowed him the ability to control only two devices at once, although he could view any one of them at work instantly. That is where Ashlyn Sanders came in. From her quarters aboard the Nerita, the NSA agent could direct all six if needed.

"Signal source 22. Sequence 11, link positive. Proceed," Sanders voiced into McGann's ear.

Tori Haroldson watched on the small computer screen McGann held. It seemed odd to see Sanders speaking, without hearing any sound from her. She still had no idea of what was about to happen.

McGann opened the other metal case revealing six insects, three beetles and three mosquitoes. Carefully, he removed each one and placed them on the container's cover. "Sequence 11. I'll manage two and five. The rest are yours. Copy?"

"Roger, 22."

Nano technology had progressed to the point where micro motors could provide enough power for the man-made miniature insects to fly or crawl for up to three minutes at a time. A brief resting period was all that was needed, in a light filled area, to recharge the photovoltaic batteries. Then the miniature creations could continue their patrol.

Tori eyed McGann's computer screen, watching as the *insects* made their way through the grounds. Suddenly, mosquito number six's screen went blank. "What happened?" she whispered.

"One of two things, a battery malfunction, or something just had a late night snack. Either way, it's a wash." McGann increased the speed of both devices under his control, knowing it would also decrease the time before they needed to be recharged.

Together, they watched the micro-technology in action. The bugs were searching for any evidence that Canton and O'Brien were alive. Both he and Sanders directed Pierson's creatures into cracks and crevices in the surrounding buildings. It was a slow process, but all the areas needed searching. A second screen under Ashlyn's control darkened as the image of a foot appeared above the doomed insect.

"Signal source 22. This isn't looking good. At this rate, we'll never get through everything," Ashlyn Sanders remarked, irritation filling her voice.

"Sequence 11. Understood. Unfortunately, we may lose more before we're finished." McGann noticed a signal that the mosquito under his control needed recharging. It would never make it to a light source. Just below the insect, a guard walked into view, headed for a building not searched before. McGann attempted to land on the guard's shirt and missed. Instead, it touched down on the back of the man's neck. Instantly, it was slapped out of existence. "Damn," McGann grunted.

McGann's beetle scurried along a corridor, keeping close to a wall, in hopes of avoiding similar mishap as happened to number three. He watched the world from the bug's point of view. Steering the device under a crack in a doorway, it roamed forward at full speed, easily slipping under a second door. McGann's command brought it instantly to a halt. The insect's camera captured the image of an old man cautiously working on a diamond of immense proportion.

"Abram Mossel."

"Who?" Tori asked.

"The renowned diamond cutter who came up missing during our weekend in Amsterdam," McGann replied, wryly. "I can bet you it has everything to do with the Oduru diamond." His finger touched the screen sending the insect in for a closer look. "This confirms part of my suspicions. Kholos' link with Dimitri Pendopolous is genuine. He and Solange, and probably both her sisters, are involved with the diamond heist."

"How did they get him out of the country undetected?"

McGann turned towards Tori Haroldson. Pale moonlight bathed half of his face, while darkness filled the other. The woman had grown to know him well enough to understand when something was gravely wrong. His expression filled her with apprehension as he began to speak.

"The stolen diamond was part of a ploy to take away the focus of something far more sinister. Do you remember me telling you about the oddity I noticed when I watched a clip of the English Prime Minister before I left for Europe?"

"Yeah," Tori replied hesitantly. "But what does that have to do with this old man?"

"Everything and nothing," McGann returned, quizzically. "I did some checking on other members of the G-8. I searched recent news clips from the conference in Davos. I also noticed at times, a number of them possessed the same odd characteristic as Haines."

Sanders cut into their conversation. "Sequence 22."

"Go ahead, 11."

"I just received an automatic email relay from my home. Some ham operator named Andreano in Warwick, Rhode Island, just happened to pick up a Morse code signal. He followed the instructions and sent an email to my address. The message gave reference to last known coordinates. Its sender also followed up with a potential position for his current location, somewhere within a hundred mile radius. The sender was asking for help. The message ended with the following numbers, one, four, one, one, zero seven."

"Any significance to those numbers?" McGann asked, casting a wary eye across the grounds in front of him.

"It's Joe," Sanders exclaimed. "We met on the fourteenth of November, last year."

"Great news, 11," McGann whispered in reply. "Joe's somewhere on this rock. Question's, where?"

"Damn. Check four. Now." McGann heard the urgency in Ashlyn's voice, focusing his attention on the screen's images. He quickly enlarged it to optimize the picture. The agent's remote controlled insect hovered above a guard pointing a pistol at three people huddled next to the wall of a building.

The camera zoomed in, panning across grainy images. There was no mistaking the face of Red O'Brien, and another man McGann did not know. Then there was the woman. It took a moment before his recollection of Becca Ramsey bubbled to the surface. The features of the final person with the group startled Tori Haroldson, gasping at the site. The familiar visage merely confirmed the dreadful suspicion McGann had been about to tell Haroldson. President Richard Simon lay on the ground with a pistol pointing at his head.

Without warning, two more people came into the picture. Although McGann could not see either face, there was no mistaking Joe Canton. He towered over the guard. But with a pistol shoved into his back, there was little he could do.

McGann knew the timeline had just deteriorated. His mind raced for solutions. Charging into this situation without more *intel* was the worst possible scenario. Still, he needed a plan. The lives of the five people on his view screen were in immediate danger, hanging from a frayed rope, and the last strands had begun to unravel. McGann knew chances of getting them all out alive were evaporating with each second that slipped away.

The fighter in him would not let himself succumb to thinking about the impossibility of the task that lay ahead. It was not in his makeup. Bryson McGann realized there was no other option than to be willing to sacrifice everything to get all of them, and Tori Haroldson, out of harm's way. If not, their future and the world's threatened to topple into a chasm of chaos of indeterminably devastating proportion.

Chapter Fifty-Three
USS John C. Stennis - Banda Sea

CVN-74 PARTED THE SEAS with her knife-edged angled bow, sending waves of white foam coursing along the sides of the immense gray hull. Behind the huge ship, the waters left by her wake spread out into a flat expanse. The sea was lit with a bluish-green glow, an indication of the presence of bioluminescent plankton, that created a colorful spectacle below a pale moon.

Kendall Stevens bolted upright in her bunk at the sound of the blaring klaxon. "Damn, doesn't the old man ever give up on this drilling crap?" the young officer sounded off to her ship mate, Lt. J.G. Samantha Yates.

Yates, roughly the same age as Stevens, replied through a sleepy yawn, "I don't think that man ever sleeps." She rumpled her fingers through her short red hair, attempting to shake herself awake.

"He's not human," Stevens laughed. The two women hurriedly dressed and left the room, moving on the double to their assigned duty stations.

Heading topside, Stevens ran out across the deck, taking her position with the rest of the personnel who were called to duty. Crews were scurrying over the deck making preparations for the launching of a flight of F-18A/E Hornets. She knew the skipper was observing the night time activity from the bridge high above the flight deck.

The female officer placed her headgear on, hearing the familiar voice of the Air Boss giving directions from his position in "Pri-Fly." On board the Stennis, aircraft were maneuvered into the proper flight sequence and launched as quickly as possible. The flight deck was a maze of activity, each person working swiftly to get the aircraft launched. The deafening thunder of jet engines reverberated out over the waters of the Banda Sea, as their orange tails lit the darkness.

Stevens gave the go ahead for Lt. Casey Slater, call sign Spiderman, to launch. The Hornet catapulted across the deck, rising up into the humid south Pacific air. With his wingman airborne, Black Dog's aircraft moved into position for the final launch. Stevens thought briefly about her invitation to dinner that had been accepted by Ron Wood. She quickly let it pass, realizing her lack of attention could get herself or other people killed.

Inside the cockpit, Wood ran the final checklist of pre-launch criteria and then pushed himself back into his seat. The Lieutenant Commander's right hand gripped the *joystick.* Wood knew Stevens was on duty and the thumbs up signal he gave lasted a little longer than normal. He quickly refocused on the business at hand. Kendall signaled with the go ahead. Wood's jet raced across the deck, disappearing to join the others on the night time exercise.

Kendall Stevens watched the flight group until they were out of sight. Activity slowed, but preparations were under way for the fighters eventual return. She always wondered what it was like for the pilots flying through the skies. Stevens also realized that while they were on duty, anytime planes scrambled, it could be the real thing. There had been nothing out of the ordinary. But Stevens said a quick prayer, hoping all would go well.

Chapter Fifty-Four

Sula Kai - Banda Sea

FROM THE COMPUTER SCREEN, the grainy images of the hapless band of Solange's captives were taken under guard to a room lined with glass cases housing her pilfered treasures. Sanders' *insect* paused on top of one of these cases, recharging its internal battery. While that was occurring, its eyes scoured the room providing details about everything where the detainees were held.

"22. Be advised, I've lost one more. I couldn't get it recharged in time."

"Understood," McGann returned.

"Wow," Tori Haroldson whispered, looking at the room filled with artifacts.

"She has an amazing collection of toys," McGann answered. "My bug's ready. I'm going to take a closer look." McGann worked the control, steering the beetle into Solange's enclave. He took a chance racing the micro-machine past a guard's foot, hoping Canton might recognize Pierson's handiwork. Disappointingly, Canton, or none of the others, seemed to notice. A shadow passed over the beetle and Sanders' mosquito brought to life Solange's digital image stepping in front of the seated captives. Unexpectedly, another man was brought into the room, arms tied behind his back. McGann did not recognized him. No words were spoken as anxious looks were passed around amongst the captives.

"Alex," Solange began, "I'm most disappointed in you and your lovely wife. Unfortunately, you've chosen to ignore my hospitality. That's a very misguided judgment on your part." Her wrathful gaze roamed the collection of faces. "I'm afraid there's no alternative for you, but to face a similar fate as that of your new found friends." An impassionate smirk creased her mouth into a quickly passing bow. "Of course, your death would have occurred anyway. You've just shortened the timeline." Behind her outward sense of calm, a cauldron of emotions swirled in seething contempt. "You've left me no choice." Her words fought their way through clenched teeth. "As for you, Mr. President, you'll accompany your acquaintances to meet their rather grisly demise, beyond the reef."

McGann was torn in his decision. His experience held him in check. He had long ago learned to listen to its call. At the moment, the group was not in peril and the worst mistake he could make was to get himself and Tori captured. He weighed the options, finalizing his decision.

Solange pressed a finger to her lip in contemplation, searching each of them for any sign of fear. She enjoyed the game. "Take them to the boat. The tide will be perfect at dawn. Shoot whoever you wish, and let them bloody the water," Solange commanded the guards. "Breakfast will be served at sunrise. Unfortunately, you'll be on the menu."

Bryson McGann pulled Tori Haroldson along by the hand, stealing through the shadows. His mind focused on the priority of the moment. He kept an eye on his computer screen while moving the insect back towards the location where Abram Mossel was working. Fortunately, they had been able to avoid any further incidents with the guards. Together they made their way to the room where the old man was giving the Namibian gem a careful inspection.

Looking up as they entered unexpectedly, the Dutchman asked quizzically, "Who are you?"

"No time," McGann responded. "If you want any chance of getting off this island alive, come with us now."

"Hurry," Tori Haroldson pleaded.

"Yes, I will come. I must gather my things."

"Leave it all."

"The diamond," Mossel shrugged. "I will not leave it behind."

McGann exhaled impatiently, nodding as the old man placed the stone in a shoulder pack. "Now, I am ready," Mossel declared.

The trio moved out into the outer hallway at the same time a pair of guards escorting a shackled woman rounded the corner. McGann reacted by instinct, his left hand lashing out viciously into the throat of the closest, unsuspecting guard. Immediately, the man fell to the floor clutching his neck, legs kicking in panic from pain and lack of oxygen. Bryson McGann's right hand snapped the barrel of the silenced pistol in line with the other guard's chest, pumping the trigger in a double tap. The man's eyes widened in disbelief, briefly staring at the holes in his torso. He quickly joined his companion in silent sleep.

"We've got big troubles," McGann said. "Their discovery won't take long. Tori, where's Ashlyn's bug?"

Mossel peered over the blonde's shoulder, gazing at the miniature screen. "Still in the room with Solange."

It took a moment before the recollection of the woman's name struck him. Now he recognized the face of the unknown man Solange had been addressing. "Becca Ramsey?"

She shook her head silently, still shocked by the guard's death. He cut the ties around her wrists. Becca Ramsey relayed her tale in a brief synopsis. McGann wasted no time on filling her in on the specifics. "Let's move."

"Where?" Tori asked.

"It's time to take a hostage of our own."

"You must be very careful with this woman," the old man warned. "She's filled with the devil himself."

"That may be, but we have little choice at this point. If the devil wants to dance, he should reconsider," McGann responded with a flinty edge honing his words.

The unlikely foursome made their way to the rear entrance of Solange's home unnoticed. Beyond the cliffs, they could hear the distant ocean's grumbling, washing over the reef. " Sequence 11."

"Go," Ashlyn replied, her stomach souring with the building tension.

"Is Solange still alone?"

"Yes."

"I'm, no, we're going in. We need a bargaining chip. If we don't have some leverage, it may become difficult to get any of us out."

"Understood. But I don't like it. Too many variables."

"Agreed, but that's all we have."

Sanders knew there was little else she could do. "What next, 22?"

McGann whispered into his headset, " Find where they're taking T.C. and the others."

"Affirmative," Ashlyn returned.

"Once we're inside, you take control of my bug. That'll give you another set of eyes. Do a recon of the surrounding rooms. The clock's ticking."

They made their way quietly into the hallway leading into the vast room where Solange was. McGann held the pistol in an upright and ready position. The stakes had been raised and there were no second chances at this point. If any security personnel happened upon them, he intended to silence them immediately.

"This place creeps me out," Tori whispered. "It looks like some kind of macabre art gallery with all these bizarre paintings."

McGann's face twisted, "What's that peculiar sound?"

"Theramin." Tori returned, spontaneously. "Invented by Lev Sergeivitch Termen in the early twentieth century. It was used a lot in horror movies and some rock bands. That's your bit of trivia for the day."

McGann was amazed by Tori Haroldson 's ability to focus on the oddity in the midst of their predicament. They continued to move quietly along the hallway, entering the room behind Solange. The woman had become totally engrossed with playing the instrument and did not hear McGann creep up behind her.

McGann gave little thought to Solange being a lady. Any attempt at disrupting his plan for leaving Sula-Kai, would earn her a bullet in the head. The heavy barrel of the silenced pistol pressed into the soft flesh of Solange's neck. "Keep playing until I tell you to stop," he whispered, a deadly menace creasing his command.

The woman continued moving her hands around the odd machine, bringing forth its unique qualities. She made every attempt to control her breathing, not allowing herself to become outwardly enraged. Solange knew there would be time for retribution. For the moment, she would play along with her attacker's game.

"We're going to take a boat ride, lady."

The ridge of muscles along her shoulders tightened reflexively to McGann's words.

"Turn around slowly. I'll say this just once. Make no mistake. I will kill you."

Turning in response to his command, McGann could not help but notice the striking woman was a carbon copy of the fallen motorcycle rider from Amsterdam. One of three sinister sisters involved in a plot of immense proportion. He could not help but notice the slight peculiarity her mechanical eye possessed. It stared back at him with a chilling quality that seemingly came from the cold, black pit of hell. Solange then focused her attention on the two others with McGann.

Solange smiled, "I see you brought your blonde bitch with you."

Tori Haroldson moved in close to the raven-haired woman. She said nothing. Without warning, the blonde unleashed a punch that knocked Solange to the floor. The woman grimaced with pain as she got back up, startled. "That's to say thanks for your poor taste in hospitality," Tori spit out venomously.

McGann could not help but smile. He held out a hand to prevent the scientist from taking another lick at Solange. Stepping forward, he slid the barrel of the pistol underneath her hair along the right side of her neck. After pushing it aside, he discovered Solange's skin was adorned with the mark of the star cluster and Scylla, like the sister he shot in Amsterdam. "Interesting tattoo," McGann said. "That only leaves the third sister. My assumption would be she's been given IPI's brand also."

Solange was taken aback that the man pointing the business end of the pistol in her face knew the secretive group's name. Her eyes flared briefly. McGann realized he had struck a chord, furthering his theory as to the nature of IPI's true intent. "And Sahtay? Is she close by?"

"You should be careful what you ask for, McGann. Wishes that come true do not always meet one's expectations." Her defiance annoyed him, but he pushed it into a corner. His earpiece filled with Sanders' voice.

"22."

"Go ahead."

"I've located them."

"We'll be leaving shortly with our new friend. Do the passengers have many uninvited guests?"

"For the moment, six. Four appear armed."

"Copy. I'll be back in touch, 11."

Hatred emanated from the woman standing in front of the odd foursome. Somehow she needed to signal an alarm to let Kholos and her sister know of her predicament. Solange had little time left before they left for the boats. Once they were off the island, she realized her chances of freedom dwindled rapidly. "You trouble me, Bryson McGann. Your manner is one of inconvenience. I don't think I'll be leaving with you." She let her voice trail, inching away from the group. "Perhaps a different place or time. But I guess that's not possible at this point." Solange drew in a long breath, shaking back her dark mane. "You do know ambition is the last refuge of failure."

"I've never been much of an Oscar Wilde fan, so I don't buy it." McGann was not about to fall prey to her stalling tactics. His left hand flew up behind her head and rammed it forward, pushing the barrel of the Beretta into the mechanical left eye. She cried out in response. "You've got one choice if you want another breath, Solange." McGann's words flew out in a vehement tone. Abram Mossel looked on with satisfaction, knowing he would not be bothered by the death of this woman who had disrupted his life. "There's no next time. Move."

McGann wrapped his hand tightly around Solange's long hair, pulling it back painfully, letting her know he was in no mood to be tested. McGann scanned the glass cabinets lining the walls, impressed by the precious oddities perched upon the shelves. He realized there had to be a fortune sitting under the lights. As they hurried past the corridor of glass cases, something caught McGann's eye. "Stop. Open that case," he directed, pointing the pistol in its direction. Solange complied with his order. "Tori. Grab that leather pouch and coin. The pistol, too."

Mossel stepped aside to let the blonde remove the articles from their resting place. She pulled them from the shelf. "What should I do with them?"

"Put them in Abram's bag along with the diamond." He directed his words back to Solange. "You've a very interesting collection of artifacts. I'm sure their rightful owners will be delighted to see them returned."

"If you live long enough to see they get them," the olive-skinned woman snarled. McGann yanked forcefully on the fistful of hair, followed instantly by a painful groan.

"I have no intention of not letting that happen. Becca, mind if I borrow your bandanas?"

"Okay," she answered, puzzled.

McGann wadded one up, wedging it into Solange's mouth. He looped the other one over her mouth and knotted it on the back of her head, effectively silencing the woman.

Ashlyn Sanders' voice filled the earpiece McGann wore, providing directions to the entrance leading to the boat dock. The group moved quickly through the house, hoping no one would spot them. McGann knew what the others were feeling. He felt the tension, but was seasoned enough not to let it overshadow the accomplishment of his mission. He hoped Tori was doing alright. With all that she had witnessed in a brief period of time, he knew that stress could have dire consequences. It happened to trained soldiers. Things were critical. He did not need her falling apart under the strain.

ꕥ ꕥ

Dr. Mick Henke could not sleep. He was due to depart the island at daybreak along with Kholos and Solange's sister. Henke had a disturbing habit of being unable to sleep before any trip, always finding himself restless and frustrated by his quirk. Henke decided that if he could not sleep, he might as well drink. He slipped on a tee shirt and closed the door behind him. A gin and tonic on the veranda might ease his foul mood. Henke rubbed the back of his neck, padding barefoot across the bamboo floor. He rounded a corner and was startled by the sight of a man with a gun pressed into the back of Solange's neck.

He almost shouted and then stopped himself. Part of him wished the man would silence Solange permanently. Ending the relationship would get him off the hook. However, there was her sister to deal with and the fact that if Solange talked, his life would live under an unwanted scrutiny. He did not relish that idea. Flying under the radar suited Henke's purposes. The doctor remained silent, letting the group disappear out into the coming dawn. Mick Henke realized he was in over his head. The physician only knew of one person who could help. "The Greek".

Chapter Fifty-Five
Boat Docks - Sula Kai

MICK HENKE'S PROFESSION gave him an edge at reaching decisive conclusions. He wasted no time after making his decision. Henke found himself breathless as his fist pounded forcefully upon the entrance of the secluded bungalow. A sleepy-eyed copy of Solange with rumpled hair peered out from behind the crack in the slightly opened door. She stared back in disbelief, wondering why he was waking her at such an early hour. Henke attempted to catch his breath, juiced up from the booze and exertion. He spit out Kholos' name between ragged breaths.

Sahtay rubbed away the sleep, realizing something was wrong, "It better be good, Henke. Stephan will be in no mood to be awakened." His presence cut like a jagged edge into her mood.

"It's already too late," the husky voice called out from behind the woman. "What is it?" he demanded, his words edged with a menacing challenge.

The doctor was finally able to speak in sentences they could understand. Kholos listened intently, scowling with the news. "Did they see you?" the assassin cut in.

"No. I don't think so."

"There are only two places they could be heading. Get dressed, Sahtay. Check the helicopters. I'll take the boat docks. It's the more likely place for them to be. No sense taking chances. If you find nothing, come to me. Two more things," he dispatched with authority. "Arouse the guards, then wake up the other pilot. Tell him to ready both helicopters. We may need them," "The Greek" ordered.

"What about me?" Henke asked.

Kholos had no use for Henke. He despised the man. "The Greek" carefully considered his question before speaking. "Do you know how to use a gun?"

"Yes," the physician returned tentatively, stumbling over his words.

"You must kill with it," Kholos stated with a detached chill. "Are you capable?" he asked flatly. Henke's gut was spinning with fear at the thought of murder. Although, he was intelligent enough to know that things were taking a wrong tack. If the hostages got away, it could spell the end of his lucrative medical career and more importantly, his life. He would learn to live with himself later, if it came to that. Henke nodded, taking Kholos aback.

"You surprise me, healer," Kholos returned, staring into the doctor's eyes, seeking the blackness he knew so well that allowed a man to take a life with calloused abandon. "Come. I'll give you a weapon." Henke walked into the room, following the heavily muscled killer. He took in the tempting treat of Sahtay slipping on a pair of jeans over her naked form. She returned his stare with a feral sneer of animosity.

"Take this," Kholos said, returning Henke to the troubles at hand. An H&K nine millimeter pistol was tossed in his direction. The weapon was quickly followed by two extra magazines. "Go with Sahtay. Doctor, try not to kill yourself."

Kholos slipped into a pair of shorts, leaving the two of them behind, as Sahtay finished dressing. Seldom had Kholos been forced to deal with attackers on his turf. Hurrying off at a run as dawn's gray light came into the world, the sound of his own breathing filled his ears between footfalls.

His mind conjured up the possibilities. Interpol? Mossad? A long list of international law enforcement agencies? "The Greek" dropped all those to the bottom of the pile. He continued to process the information, discounting the possibility of a military strike. No one knew he was here, of that he was certain. His trail had been well covered.

The two men from NESSA and the Australian. How did they figure into the equation? Who could be audacious enough to attempt a rescue on the island? NESSA continued to be the broken spoke in the wheel. He thought back to that day, reliving the moments. His mind replayed a movie of the event along the sun drenched Hawaiian coast. The thunder of the boat's powerful engines. The sharp, splintering crack of fiberglass against the hull. He could feel his strong hands gripping the wheel, turning the craft on a heading away from the scene. There was nothing he overlooked, except the ultimate mistake.

Confidence.

It struck him that he never looked back over his shoulder. His stamp had always been to confirm the outcome of his deadly work. The certainty of McGann and the woman's death now lay in question.

It was a tactical error he had never allowed himself to commit, and somehow, he slipped. Up until now Kholos had been sure. Uneasy tendrils of doubt began to weave themselves into his mind. It seemed an impossibility. Instincts he had learned to depend on were suddenly the compass rose pointing in that direction. Could it be? Had he failed again to put an end to his nemesis? As far as Kholos was concerned, if it was McGann, he would savor the pleasure of watching him die. This time there would be no mistakes.

Kholos turned his attention back to matters at hand. Mentally, he worked his way around the docking area; its hiding places, advantage points. He knew them all. Whoever was on the island could prove to be a very formal adversary. The man from Sibenik would have to be very careful.

"There's an elevator down to the docks," Becca whispered as they stood at the concealed entrance in the rock face. She quickly detailed the layout of the docks where the hostages had been taken.

"Bad choice," McGann replied. "Any other way in?" he asked, handing each woman a weapon. Both Tori Haroldson and Becca Ramsey felt uneasy with the thought of using their pistols. However, they realized the grave consequences of inaction. Their eyes met, each quietly steeling themselves to the possibilities.

"There's a spiraling set of steps cut into the volcanic rock," Becca added, ending their tension. "It's steep. Poorly lit. I'm sure they don't know I'm aware of it. "

"Good. My bet is they won't be expecting us to come that way." McGann outlined the plan to the group. "We know Ashlyn spotted them being taken down this elevator." McGann turned, quickly surveying the area. "There's no reception from her surveillance device. We'll be going in blind."

The pistol bucked in McGann's hand. Two silenced slugs drilled into the elevator's control box. Now whoever followed them had no choice but to use the tight staircase. It gave them a slight advantage. "Becca, take the rear. Give me a heads up if anyone comes down those steps. Tori, stay behind me and keep Mossel safe. If I go down," he paused, looking away. "Just do your best."

McGann and the others made their way down the steep stairway chiseled from volcanic rock. Damp stone walls gathered in around them. It was obvious its builders never meant for this to be used except as an alternate exit in the event of an emergency. The dank odor of mildew clung heavily inside the narrow passageway. The steps were steep and slick from the thick, humid air. Mossel nearly lost his footing on more than one occasion. Each mishap cost precious moments McGann knew they could not afford.

Finally, a light from the entrance spilled into the passageway. McGann held up a hand. He crept forward soundlessly, peering into the dock area. Red O'Brien was being forced at gunpoint onto the speed boat tied to the dock. Two of Solange's guards were already on the boat, while a third oversaw the boarding. That left two workers and a fourth gunman unaccounted for, and no time to find out their location.

"We're out of time," McGann said, returning to the group. "They're all on board the boat." The rumble of inboard engines reverberated from the dock inside the massive sea cave.

"What now?" Tori whispered, excitedly.

"Time for the cavalry," McGann spoke through a lop-sided grin. His hazel eyes gave no hint of joviality to their predicament. The muscles in his jaw flexed with grim determination knowing full well the stakes. "Do what I told you."

McGann was on the run, eyes scanning the interior of the cave, hoping he could get much closer before the gunfire began. Without warning, the fourth gunman appeared around the corner of several large wooden crates. Bryson McGann leveled the pistol. He triggered the handgun, dispatching a deadly round. The man was only fifteen feet away and by the time he looked up, the bullet cored through the bridge of his nose, erasing a good portion of his face. He dropped instantly.

McGann never gave the man a second glance knowing his shot had been accurate. Sprinting toward the boat, each stride brought him closer to the impending gun battle. He was thirty feet away when both Canton and one of the guards heard the footfalls. The guard standing on the dock turned, momentarily unsure of what was happening. It took him a moment to realize his mistake. Those precious seconds cost him his life. McGann sent a double tap into the man's abdomen and chest. Two red blotches stained his uniform, signaling his death.

Canton realized the situation was not in his favor. He had been the next one to climb aboard the boat. "Everyone down," the big man cried out. The others with him reacted immediately, falling down, in an attempt to get out of harm's way. Joe Canton launched himself at the two guards, sending the full weight of his two hundred and fifty pounds crashing into them. The snapping crack of bone indicated that at least one of the men was injured. One guard managed to extricate himself from the jumble. A limp arm hung painfully by his left side. Fortunately, it did slow his response in bringing his gun to bare on McGann when he jumped over the side of the craft.

McGann dropped and rolled onto the deck. Two bullets sailed past. Rising up on a knee in a doubled handed grip, he squeezed the trigger twice. The hired gunman fell limply. McGann was up immediately, running to the aide of Joe Canton. The guard struggling underneath him was punching Canton ineffectively with his left hand, while the big man's full weight rested on the guard's other wrist, pinning the pistol to the deck.

Canton's bindings hindered his movement, but he was finally able to maneuver and deliver a debilitating blow. In a blur of motion, Canton planted both elbows into the guard's chest, expelling a painful gush of air. The Asian guard writhed in agony from the broken ribs, punctured lungs screaming for air. McGann hurried over and kicked the pistol from the man's fingers. Yanking the smaller man up from the deck, McGann pitched him into the water. The guard sank immediately, unable to swim.

Relief washed over everyone's faces with McGann's unanticipated arrival. He quickly cut T.C.'s wrist restraints, and then Canton took care of the others. McGann called out for the two women hiding with Abram Mossel. Running as quickly as possible with the old man in tow, their feet drummed an unsteady rhythm on the long wooden dock. They cast nervous glances behind them, unsure of what to expect. Canton revved the engines, and Tori Haroldson felt her mouth go dry. She tossed Mossel's bag to McGann, and they jumped into the boat.

Kholos stopped on the stairs, frozen in place. In the distance, he heard McGann's voice. It spurred him onward. He entered the cave just when the boat pulled away from its slip. The growling of the powerful boat's engines was not enough to cover the sound of the gunshots unleashed by "The Greek". Too far away to be effective, his bullets sailed wide.

McGann's laser-like stare tore across the water with a menacing wrath. The two men's eyes collided. There was a tab to be paid. Bryson McGann meant to see it was paid in full. But for the moment, it would have to wait. His mind tumbled with what came next. He knew the small group of refugees had to put some distance between themselves and Sula Kai. The group's immediate safety lay in great jeopardy.

With throttles pushed to full, Canton steered the powerful boat through the channel, racing for the open ocean in hopes of escaping any plans "The Greek" had of retribution. Both McGann and Canton knew that when the dice tumbled, the odds of rolling a seven or eleven were slim and none.

Chapter Fifty-Six

Outer Reef - Sula Kai

JOE CANTON BROUGHT THE BOW up on plane long before it exploded from the darkened entrance of the sea cave. The hull tore through the clear blue waters of the lagoon heading straight for the cut, on a plumb line for the sea beyond. His one hand gripped the twin throttles, while the other held the boat on a steady course as it rode the relatively calm waters of the protective reef.

"We've got troubles, T.C. The heat's just been turned up," McGann hollered over the sound of the twin motors and rushing wind.

"Besides the possibility of losing life or limb, that's a bit of an understatement, little brother." Canton knew exactly what his friend was eluding to, as his vision filled with the whitecaps rolling in the nearing distance.

"Look at it this way, T.C. Since the president's decided to join us on our South Pacific cruise, you can add co-captain of the presidential yacht to your resume," McGann quipped, knowing full well the harrowing nature of their predicament. "It'll look good if you ever need another job."

"Irony at its finest." Canton's words were quickly lost on the wind.

The craft left the lagoon in its wake. McGann eyed the speedometer, its digital readout wavering around the fifty mark. Solange's sleek-hulled boat flew across the wave tops in a bone-pounding ride. Seated in the cockpit, McGann turned back in the direction of the boat's passengers. They all sat rigidly silent, holding onto anything to keep them from being tossed from their seats. Stress scarred their features with distant looks and fear of the unknown. Wind blown hair danced wildly around masks of vague uncertainty, in spite of their recent freedom from their captive's talons.

"I've got questions, Bry," Canton shouted, as the first hints of orange sunlight burst forth from the eastern sky. Golden rays spilled out onto the expanse of blue water, marking the new day.

"Bet you do," McGann shouted. "Columbia." He searched the big man's face for recognition of the culprit to their current troubles.

It took a moment before the mask of puzzlement evaporated from T.C.'s face. "That drug dealer who escaped?" Canton asked, in disbelief. "You sure?" His life-long friend shook his head in reply, confirming the answer. "Bry, you really do know how to piss people off." T.C. turned his head in McGann's direction. "Wouldn't you think by now he would've forgiven that minor indiscretion? There's no sense holding a grudge," Canton remarked, before letting his features cloud with the serious matter. "What's he got to do with this?"

"Plenty, but it's complicated, T.C. I'll explain later. Oh, one more thing. Just in case you didn't know, I don't think you made his 'A' list either," McGann quipped.

"I figured you'd say that." Canton turned his attention on guiding the craft through the rough waters. "Any ideas?" he shot back.

"You know me, T.C., I've always got a back up. Trouble is, this one's marginal. Time's the problem. I'm sure there're other means of transportation off that rock than those boats tied up in the cavern."

Canton nodded in response. "Well, for now, Bry, sit back and enjoy the ride," sarcasm ringing in his words.

McGann reached for the radio. "I'm going to try to get hold of the Nerita."

"Narissa's sister ship?"

"None other, T.C."

"What's she doing here?"

"That's how Tori and I got here. Ashlyn's on board. And hopefully in fairly close proximity. We all thought you were dead, T.C.," he shouted. "Ashlyn will be delighted to see you. If we make it."

"Your ability to get straight to the heart of things offers an enlightening outlook on life."

McGann pressed a button moving through the radio's digitalized frequency indicator until the one prescribed by the Australian captain came into view. McGann cradled the mike in his hand and keyed the button. He sent a rapid fire message detailing the problems, requesting Nerita's current location.

"McGann," the Aussie captain's stressed voice spilled from the speaker. "Where the hell are you? We don't show you on our radar."

"Leeward side of the island."

"We made a run in before dawn when we didn't hear from you. We're on a heading making for the southern tip of the island."

McGann tapped Canton on the shoulder pointing at the direction he should turn the boat. The watercraft heeled to port, slicing through a tight turn that sent a towering sheet of white spray into the air off the starboard side of the boat. "We're headed your way and probably bringing trouble with us."

"Couldn't think of better news," Sully remarked dryly, seriously concerned for the group's safety. "Keep me advised and get here in one piece. Anything I can do in the mean time?"

"Pray," McGann replied.

Red O'Brien looked up, pondering the twin black spots moving through the sky in their direction. It took a moment to register. He nudged Skiddy Pete. The two men confirmed each other's suspicions, knowing that the helicopters coming towards them were not there for a rescue mission. "Hey, Mac," the Irishman hollered, instantly capturing McGann's attention. Turning at the sound of the voice, McGann followed O'Brien's finger pointing skyward past the stern. A flash of sunlight glinted off the windscreen of the lead chopper, winking mockingly at them in the morning light.

"T.C." McGann tossed his head toward the back. Canton instantly responded to McGann's subtle direction, spotting the aircraft heading their way. "Should be a fun party, little brother."

"That's what I'm afraid of." He moved toward the back of the boat giving the group commands. "Tori, Becca, Alex. Go below and search the cabin. If you find anything that resembles a weapon, bring it up. Red, you and Skiddy search those compartments along the gunnels. See if there's anything we can use." McGann moved quickly back to where President Simon sat, taking in the events playing out. "Mr. President. You and Abram might be safer down below."

Simon looked at the older man, reading his thoughts and carefully considering McGann's offer before declining. "Can't imagine that'd be the case, Mr. McGann. I appreciate the offer." Simon smiled grimly, extending his hand. "It's a pleasure to finally meet you."

"Kind of you to say so, sir. Thank us later if we get out in one piece." The president clearly understood the gravity in McGann's tone.

"Why don't you two give Red and Skiddy a hand? A couple more people will cut down the time."

"What about her?" Mossel questioned, waving an aged finger at the dark-haired woman.

"Trust me," McGann replied, "I have plans."

The sound of the approaching aircraft was barely heard above the twin engines. Closing the distance, McGann and Canton could clearly make out the aircraft and the chain gun hanging below the belly of each one. The two men eyed one another knowing their chances had just been whittled down to a thread. "Time to send out a May Day, T.C. All channels," McGann commanded.

They knew they might be able to out maneuver the helicopters once or twice, or with luck, make it to the Nerita. But either way, the firepower of those weapons would be devastating for anyone within range. Unfortunately, they were the target and the cross hairs were centered on them.

From inside the cockpit of one of the helicopters, Stephan Kholos glanced in the direction of the other craft. Its pilot knew the stakes and what was required. "The Greek's" finger rested on the weapon's control button. "Where's you doctor friend?" he asked, his voice ringing in Sahtay's headset.

The woman flashed a wicked glance in return to his question. "I left him on the island. He would be of no help to us. Besides, I despise him."

Kholos smirked. His thoughts of the physician harbored the same cold edge. Something about the man with his arrogant brandish turned his stomach. For the moment, the doctor was still of paramount importance in the completion of Martin Boggs and IPI's plans, until he heard otherwise. He toyed at the possibilities. Once there was no further need of Henke's services, a feral sneer erupted at the thought. "I'll make a pass." Kholos spoke into the headset, directing the other pilot. "Fire a warning shot across their bow. Give them some time to think about it. If they don't stop, then we'll blow them out of the water."

Chapter Fifty-Seven
Sortie Squadron - Banda Sea

"STRIKE TEAM LEADER, do you copy?" The voice from the Stennis sounded inside Wood's helmet. He pulled the dark visor down to shade his eyes from the assault of the orange fireball rising up over the eastern horizon. The naval pilot always enjoyed air time in the early morning, but as the flight group headed back for the Stennis, something in the urgency of the voice required his full attention.

"Roger that," Black Dog responded, listening intently to the command and a repeat of the message the carrier had picked up. Lt. Commander Ron Wood was curious about the order to check out a May Day signal coming from a NESSA employee a short distance flying time south of the air group's current location.

"Proceed on vector one, niner, zero from your current location. Air space is free. No other aircraft in your location."

"Roger. Vector confirmation." His gloved finger punched in the coordinates on the aircraft's colored control panel, taking in the low reading on his fuel gauge. There was a little room to play, so he acknowledged the request from the air control officer on board the carrier. "This is Black Dog," he spoke into the mike, calling out to the other pilots of the tactical fighter group riding the jet stream thirty thousand feet above the Banda Sea. Lt. Commander Wood ordered the main body of the group back to CVN-74, and kept Lt. Casey Slater as his wingman. Wood guided the stick and let his Hornet roll right, mirrored by the other aircraft close on his wing. Sunlight glinted off the aluminum airframe as Spiderman followed suit. Together, they dove for the deck, dropping their altitude until they were three thousand feet above the sea.

"What do you make of it, Black Dog?"

"Not sure. But it won't be long before we find out. I've got us about seventy miles out. Should be fairly routine. I'll go in first and you ride my tale," Wood added. "Besides, with our fuel levels, that's about all we can do. It might give them some hope."

"Copy that, Black Dog. Unless there's a surface ship close by, there's not much chance of a rescue. It's too bad most of their transmission was garbled."

"Would be nice to have a heads up. We'll just play the hand we're dealt, Spiderman."

The Hornets hurtled through the morning skies at over five hundred knots. From their vantage point inside the cockpit, there was no sense of speed with the vast ocean below and nearly cloudless sky surrounding them. The pilots' heads up display indicated they were twenty five miles out on their inbound run. A couple more minutes and they would arrive at their destination.

"Spiderman. You should have visual acquisition of the target shortly."

"Affirmative."

"Drop your air speed to two five zero as we make our approach. We'll do a pass at five, zero, zero feet." Wood's hands reached out, engaging the radar and immediately three blips showed up on the screen. He was puzzled by the unexpected sight of two other aircraft. He glanced out the canopy at Spiderman who returned his quizzical expression. Ron Wood knew Slater well enough to know he was having the same questions. Black Dog acknowledged his wingman's puzzlement by unforeseen radar contact. "I know what you're thinking. No answer, Spiderman. Let's go and find out."

Both aircraft slid in to a steep descent, their altimeters displaying the loss of altitude. Wood watched the air speed indicator on its downward run. It registered the decrease in the jet engine's output as the fighter slowed to the prescribed air speed. At one thousand feet above the deck, Wood and Slater caught a glimpse of the target in the distance. The jets closed the gap rapidly. Both pilots were confused by the presence of the helicopters following a short distance behind the boat.

"Looks like they have assistance, Black Dog." Slater commented.

"Confirmed. We'll stick to the plan. Let'em feel the love," Wood chuckled.

Five hundred feet above the Banda Sea the Navy's fighter planes leveled out. Inside the cockpits, attitude indicators gave them a perfect read, nose up and wings level. The pilots were making their initial approach from behind and to the right of the helicopters. Closing the distance on their inbound flight, both men would soon realize the situation would be anything but routine.

Chapter Fifty-Eight
Showdown - Banda Sea

"HURRY," MCGANN SHOUTED to the three people in the compartment below. "Get that stuff up here, we're running out of time." He turned towards Canton shouting, "Keep it redlined, T.C. We need everything this boat's got." The grim hard set jaw and black eyes of Joe Canton did not go unnoticed by McGann. He tossed a wary look over his shoulder, spying one of the helicopters dip its nose and increase speed. "First one's on its way in. Everybody down."

The helicopter attacked, unleashing a hail of twenty-five millimeter projectiles that stitched a line of small geysers across the waves. The thumping beat of the rotors and the buzz saw staccato of the helicopters chain gun cast an ominous pall over the group. It passed over them at full speed and circled back to its original position.

Both McGann and Canton knew that the first helicopter's initial pass had merely been a warning, the opening chorus for a deadly show. The next, was another story, one with intent. Canton knew what to do. The big man could not help but wonder if it would be enough to buy time until the Nerita arrived. The second chopper came with guns spitting flame from the end of the revolving barrel tucked underneath its fuselage.

"Hang on," was all McGann had time to say as Canton pulled back on the throttles, wheeling the boat hard to starboard. The sky was filled with the terrifying buzz of the automatic weapon. Canton's maneuver saved all of them, although several rounds struck the boat, sending splinters of wood and fiberglass into the air. Flying debris stuck Mossel, Skiddy Pete, and Becca Ramsey. The windscreen blew apart, sending shards of glass in all directions. Both McGann and Canton were recipients of stinging cuts, but fortunately, no one had been injured seriously in the assault.

"Now," McGann shouted, his shirt stained with crimson spots. All the men leaped up, careful not to fall in the bouncing craft, while the women and Mossel went below. O'Brien and the president grabbed Solange roughly, pulling her up from the deck. They worked quickly as the second helicopter circled back, teaming up with Kholos and

Sahtay. They held back, keeping pace with the boat before the third and final run.

Thankfully, the cabin below had been filled with some supplies that McGann thought would at least give them some hope of fending off the attackers. Hurriedly, the heavy duty bungee cords were wrapped around Solange's body and attached to the transom and sides of the water craft. McGann wasn't sure how long they would hold. He wondered if it would buy enough time to reach the Nerita which just appeared in the distance.

The edge was slim.

Time was short.

Their chances were dwindling with each moment that went by.

If their survival was not measured in seconds, the scenario had to appear almost comical. Solange had been strapped in place on the stern rail of the boat. Her arms and legs were splayed, appearing like DaVinci's anatomical depiction of man. The woman's black hair whipped wildly about in the wind. McGann was counting on the deceptive ploy to buy a few more precious seconds. At this point, he would take any advantage that came his way.

"*Kopritis*," Kholos shouted into his headset.

Sahtay peered at the spectacle open-mouthed, befuddled by the sight of her sister being used as a deterrent to the next attack. "What do we do?" the woman asked. Her eyes wide with disbelief at the words "The Greek" spoke into the headset.

"I have no love for your sister. And I believe she planned to have us killed. Fuck her. She needs to die."

Sahtay was not shocked by what she heard. Frankly, she hated Solange, but had no wish to be an active participant in her own sister's murder. Kholos' cohort turned her head away, looking out the glass of the helicopter's window. "Stephan," she cried out.

Her call captured his attention. And what he saw raised the hair of his neck. Behind them, approaching from their right side, two jet fighters were closing the distance at a very low altitude. Kholos was not a man given to paralysis from fear. He had seen far too much in his lifetime. "The Greek" was galvanized to action, quickly formulating a plan. He called out to the other helicopter pilot, quickly detailing the events that were going to occur.

From the deck of the boat, a hand flew up, followed by a cry from Alex Ramsey pointing at the pair of Hornets headed directly at the group. Three heads peered out from below as McGann tapped Canton on the shoulder, shouting over the roar of thunderous engines. "T.C. The cavalry's arrived. At least we've got a few more moments."

"I'll take whatever we can get, little brother. Engine's heating up. Two choices, Bry. Drop speed and hope it cools down, or run her 'til she quits." Canton already knew what McGann's decision was before he heard the words.

"Take everything this crate can give until she rips apart at the seams, T.C." Determination set itself in his hazel eyes. There was no part of him that allowed himself to think they would not make it, especially now that the flyboys had arrived.

The pilots came in low and slow above the water confounded by the spectacle. Two hundred yards to the stern of the boat the black helicopters kept pace, but held themselves in check. A woman was trussed up on the stern of the boat. Both men were confused as they flew past the small group flailing their arms at them from below. "What do you make of that, Black Dog?" There was no time for a response as the situation deteriorated. Both pilots became part of the unusual events being witnessed through binoculars from the ship's bridge, by Ashlyn Sanders and Captain Sully.

Kholos put his plan into action knowing that if he didn't make the first move, they would lose the advantage. His estimation of the pilot's confusion was accurate. "Engage," he commanded to the other pilot. The tracking array of each helicopter's radar found their respective targets, as the fighters passed directly over the speeding boat.

Instantly, alarms rang out inside each fighter's cockpit. Furiously blinking lights on each aircraft's instrument panel signaled the serious nature of their predicament. Wood could not believe he had led both himself and his wingman into this dire situation.

"Break right. Break right," Wood screamed into his radio. "He's got a lock."

A cacophony of twin buzz saws ripped through the skies as a hail of twenty-five millimeter projectiles followed the radar tracks, tearing into the bodies of both aircraft. Under normal circumstances with faster speeds and a greater distance, the chain guns would have been ineffectual. However, at the present range of a few hundred yards, they found their marks quite effectively. Both pilots had been sucked into the ruse, snared by "The Greek's" trap.

"Black Dog," Spiderman hollered above the sounds of the alarms filling the cockpit. "I'm hit. I'm hit." Smoke poured from the port engine in a thick trail, the ominous result of accurate fire. "I took hits up the pipes. I'm losing power. I can't control it."

Lt. Commander Ron Wood struggled with his own dilemma. Several heavy rounds had shredded a hydraulic line, and it was becoming increasingly difficult to steer the craft. He pushed the throttles to full and cranked back on the stick, hopefully averting any further damage from the deadly volley of fire. The airframe of the Hornet shuddered in response, making a valiant attempt to respond to his commands. The naval pilot stole a quick glance at his wingman's futile attempt to gain altitude. Smoke and flame now streamed from both engines. The aircraft succumbed to its fate. The out of control fighter rolled to the right. It nosed down, preparing to crash into the sea. Wood yelled into his radio. "Eject."

Black Dog doggedly determined he wasn't going down without a fight. He focused his concentration on activating his missiles. He had but seconds for the aircraft's radar to lock on to one of the helicopter's heat signature. Satisfied he had target acquisition, the pilot launched the Sidewinder missile. Springing to life from its resting spot beneath the left wing, the missile pursued the prescribed trajectory with lethal purpose. A scream from the rocket's engine whistled wickedly through the air as the weapon flew toward its computer driven destination. There was no chance for the chopper as the Sidewinder fulfilled its devastating purpose, tearing the helicopter to shreds in a pyrotechnic display and thunderous explosion.

On board the boat, the group watched the catastrophe unfolding. It was if a Hollywood movie had somehow taken a wrong turn. Shock filled their faces. One of the Hornets crashed. The Nerita was still two miles away. And now the second navy fighter was flying erratically.

Wood was in serious trouble. Black Dog called upon all his experience to keep his Hornet airborne. The pilot had no further chance to retaliate. He attempted to put some distance between himself and the remaining helicopter, hoping to avoid any further damage from the chain gun's assault.

A flashing array of warning signals lit up the instrument panel. Angry alarms sounded unceasingly. His chest tightened. Nerves were grated raw. Each breath caught in his throat, making it even more difficult to put out the urgent call to the Stennis.

His opportunity was measured in seconds.

Then, time ran out for Ron Wood.

Chapter Fifty-Nine
USS John. C. Stennis - Banda Sea

"ATTENTION ALL HANDS. Battle stations. This is not a drill. I repeat, this is not a drill. Battle stations," the officer of the deck called out over the ship's PA system.

Lt. J.G. Stevens had watched the last of Black Dog's group touch down safely when the alarm klaxon rang out. The call to battle stations had been frequent since the inception of the skipper's around the clock, never know when training. However, this was the real thing. She knew Wood and Slater were still out there. Stevens felt a lump growing in her throat. Her mind ran wild with concern.

The deck filled with personnel racing to scramble a flight of fighters from the carrier while it turned into the wind, racing up to full speed. Within minutes, the first aircraft leaped skyward, waiting to be joined by several others. Two Sea Hawk rescue helicopters came to life. The sound of their whining turbines cutting the air steered her eyes in that direction. Stevens observed the first one lifting off the ship's deck, followed closely by its twin. Both turned and headed out on the same course as the fighter squadron.

Stevens was a bundle of nerves not knowing if the two pilots were still inbound to the carrier. She realized they were long overdue, and their fuel levels had to be dangerously low. The call to arms and the fact that rescue choppers had been sent out, could only mean one thing. Disaster. Something must have happened to one or both pilots.

Stevens felt her eyes misting. She turned away from the other crew members, fighting to hold back the tears. The last thing she wanted was for them to see her crying. The young lieutenant knew the dangers. Until now, the naval officer never truly considered the fact she would ever have to face the end result.

The ship bristled with pulse pounding bravado by many of the crew. Whatever happened, they knew their boys could take care of it. The U.S. Navy was the best in the world. Yet, none of it provided her any sense of confidence. Her gut churned, contemplating the harsh realities.

A weighty veil of foreboding hung heavily over the young woman's shoulders. Kendall Stevens drew in a deep breath. The nauseating, painful ache in the pit of her stomach left a telling weakness. Part of her wanted to scream, while the other half attempted to hold herself in check. Stevens was forced into a situation she never wanted to imagine, and certainly did not want to think about now.

With no answers, she was left in limbo. There was no one she could turn to at the moment. Even though she was a female, there was no special treatment. Stevens attempted to put all of the emotions in her back pocket. There was more than just her personal concerns to worry about. Lt. J.G. Stevens had a job to do. Lives depended on it. Nothing less was expected, or acceptable. Duty was inscribed in her job description. The military code was an expectant master, with little concern for affairs of the heart.

Chapter Sixty

Nerita - Banda Sea

STEPHAN KHOLOS' FACE FLUSHED. Every fiber of his being seethed with revenge for the destruction of the other chopper. It did not matter to him that they had shot the two fighters out of the sky. There were now other concerns. He knew a very real possibility existed that the pilot of the second jet aircraft had ample time to send out a distress call. That message spelled danger. The next wave of aircraft would not be as foolish. Sand in "The Greek's" hour glass was running out. His margin of safety diminished drastically. Time had just become a very precious commodity.

This was not a chess match. A slip in this game meant his life. "The Greek" had no intentions of letting that occur. Peering through the helicopter's windscreen, Kholos eyed the distant ship pursuing a direct course for the boat below. He figured McGann for one wily enough to have some type of backup plan, but this time, there would be no second chance.

The rational part of him dictated he finish what he started. The dark, malicious aspect of his soul sought fulfillment of his murderous desire to see everyone aboard the boat torn to pieces in a glorious vendetta. A simple vengeful caress of the trigger would do the trick. He relished the anticipation of what was to follow. Kholos did not hesitate any longer.

"What are you going to do, Stephan?" the woman demanded.

"Shut up," he shouted, casting a set of burning eyes in her direction. "Don't ever question me again."

Sahtay let her own anger quell, retreating into silence. The woman learned long ago not to argue with the man when he was engulfed in a fit of rage. She had seen the effects. It was nothing she wanted to experience personally.

The Greek dipped the nose of the chopper, making a run for the boat. Kholos quickly closed the distance. His finger toyed with the button, ready to unleash a withering hail of fire on the people huddled below. In a moment, any traces of life on Solange's boat would be erased.

Kholos let his rage build to a crescendo. It was enough. "The Greek's" meaty fist gripped the stick with a vengeance, his thumb pounced on the chain gun control. Screams of terror rose up from the boat's passengers. A deadly hail of projectiles tore through Solange's body, ripping her to pieces as blood and gore sprayed the air.

ꕤ ꕤ

McGann hollered. "Get ready. He's just about here."

Canton eyed his friend cautiously. "This better work, Bry."

"Has to." The familiar lop-sided grin came to life, doing little to defuse the stalwart resolve shooting from McGann's eyes. "I'm out of tricks, T.C. Hope I'm reading him right." He turned, pausing to gauge the helicopter's distance. "Guess it won't matter much if I'm wrong."

In their earlier quest for weapons, they had found a long section of thick rubberized tubing and a discarded piece of bent chrome railing. It had given McGann an idea, which they were about to unleash. Each end of the rubber tubing had been securely attached to the compartment walls below.

McGann's words were lost in the cacophony of rotor wash from the helicopter. Kholos moved in over the wounded boat, now spilling wispy gray smoke in its wake. McGann could easily see "The Greek" and Solange's sister glaring through the chopper's glass. Hovering above them like a menacing creature waiting to pounce on its prey, the helicopter was about forty feet over head when McGann shouted, "Now."

ꕤ ꕤ

From the wheelhouse of the Nerita, still over a half mile away, Ashlyn Sanders and the captain felt the pangs of anxiety. They were too far away to be of any help. Both had witnessed the destructive powers wielded by the helicopter. Each knew the people aboard the boat would be chewed apart by the powerful automatic weapon. Ashlyn Sanders felt sick, a wave of nausea passing over her. There could only be one result of what was to come next.

ꕤ ꕤ

In the compartment below the deck of the fleeing boat, Tori Haroldson, the Ramseys, and O'Brien placed the chrome railing over the thick band. They grasped the ends of metal tubing, pulling back with all the strength they could muster. Together they strained, coaxing every inch out of the thick rubber tubing. Their arms ached from the tension. Beads of sweat poured from their reddened faces. Upon hearing McGann's command, they released their grip, collapsing to the deck and praying the wild plan would work.

Kholos began walking the gun across the deck, punching holes through fiberglass that offered little resistance. Below deck, the engine seized from the effects of the powerful slugs. Flames erupted in a fiery dance from the stern. The boat's speed dwindled rapidly, heralding its death knell. "The Greek" was having his moment before turning to run. He smiled with satisfaction at his handiwork. He was enjoying the carnage. Next, he turned his attention to the others onboard.

Kholos only saw the projectile at the last moment. His hands frantically worked the controls, in an attempt to avoid being hit. Both of them heard the terrifying sounds of the rotors splintering, as pieces flew out in all directions. The blades catapulted the tubing through the windscreen, nearly decapitating Sahtay. Broken rotors jeopardized the helicopter's ability to stay aloft as "The Greek" fought to regain control of the wildly bucking chopper. Stephan Kholos had no alternative. If he or the woman had any chance of surviving, they needed to get back to the island. Kholos only hoped the aircraft did not tear itself apart before that happened.

In the midst of a thick cloud of billowing black smoke, greedy flames were devouring the remains of the sinking boat. Those on board the AGSI research vessel no longer needed binoculars to see firsthand the terrifying drama unfolding before their eyes. The Australian ship struggled valiantly, her engines pushed to the limits. Ashlyn Sanders held her breath, praying for time, hoping for the impossible. Only two hundred yards away, they were helpless to prevent the explosion that ripped across the ocean.

Chapter Sixty-One
Rescue - Banda Sea

MIRACULOUSLY, MCGANN'S PLAN WORKED. The heavy tubing rocketed skyward, tumbling end over end, fulfilling its purpose. Flying erratically above the sea, the wounded chopper's engines screamed in protest. McGann wondered if their assassin's piloting skills would be adequate to prevent a deadly crash. In the end it did not matter. It was enough of a distraction to save their lives, at least temporarily.

Only two life jackets were in the boat. One for the president - even though he declined, and at McGann's determined insistence put it on - and the other for Abram Mossel. McGann and Canton worked feverishly to get everyone into the water. Swimming for their lives, they each set off in the direction of the Nerita, putting as much distance between themselves and the burning boat as possible.

Leaking fuel erupted. A ball of flames shot from the stern. Roiling clouds of choking smoke fanned out across the sea. It was only a matter of seconds before the main fuel tank exploded into a hellish inferno.

The rapid current quickly scattered the hapless band of individuals valiantly struggling to stay afloat. Assured everyone was off, Canton dove into the water. McGann was close on his heels, until he realized there was something he desperately needed. He flew down the ladder, rummaging through the compartment below until he found the waterproof container. Scooping it up, he bounded up the steps two at a time, never breaking stride. Two more quick steps across the deck, and he hurled himself over the side. McGann dove deeply, slicing through the blue water with powerful stokes.

The ensuing explosion reverberated in a thunderous clap over the water. Shards of Solange's boat scattered in all directions, while a fireball eagerly devoured what remained. Within minutes, it was over. Any traces of the blackened hull were settling to the bottom of the Banda Sea.

The helicopter's airframe shook violently from the stress of the out of sync rotors. "I can't hold it any longer. We're going to crash," "The Greek" shouted. "Get out." Both he and Sahtay undid their belts, kicking open their doors. Pitching violently to the right, Sahtay was flung out of the aircraft. Kholos followed her into the sea below. They hit the water hard from sixty feet, sinking heavily. The chopper spun haplessly out of control. They both surfaced just in time to watch the black helicopter nose dive into the Banda Sea.

No one on board the rescue ship had seen them jump. Neither of the small rescue craft even bothered to see if they survived the accident. The strategist in Stephan Kholos could not have planned it better. The long swim back to the beach had left both of them exhausted, and lying in the sand.

"We made it, Stephan," Sahtay called out, rolling over on her back. Something in the distance caused her to give a second glance. She raised a hand to shield her eyes from the glare as the specks grew in size.

"Get up now," she shrieked. "Run."

Closing the gap at a rapid rate, a flight of Hornets from the Stennis descended upon the island of Sula-Kai.

Kholos did not bother to ask. The urgency in her voice clearly dictated the need to comply with her demand. "The Greek" was up, running for the cover of the jungle. Sahtay stumbled. Reaching out, his muscular arm pulled hard, half dragging her through the sand until she regained her footing. They ran deep into the thick vegetation, taking cover below the trunk of a fallen palm.

Within moments, the screaming sounds of engines passed overhead. The sortie continued to circle, searching for any signs of life on the island below. Finally, the fighters broke off, leaving behind eerily silent skies. Kholos' mind raced to formulate a plan.

In the ensuing melee, Sully had given the command to launch the rescue craft. Racing across the surface, two rigid-hulled, inflatable boats darted out, picking up the wet, but happy survivors.

Once aboard the ship, medical teams quickly surveyed each individual. Everyone had cheated death from the initial blast, but not everyone came through unscathed. Skiddy Pete had taken the worst of it. A jagged piece of flying metal sliced into his leg. The bleeding wound required the immediate attention of the Nerita's medical officer. O'Brien had several burns that bought him a short stay in sick bay.

Both Ramseys suffered minor scrapes and burns, fortunately nothing more. Abram Mossel was near exhaustion when they pulled the old man from the water. He required rest and oxygen due to the exertion and emotional stress. Minor lacerations and burns kept the medical staff busy with the others for a brief period, but miraculously no one faired any worse.

McGann felt an overwhelming relief knowing Tori was alive. A nurse was stitching up a small cut along the hairline on her neck when he caught up with her. Her blue eyes cast a weary glance in his direction, followed by a withering smile spilling past the sooty, black smudges on her cheeks. "That's a little more than I bargained for."

"Not exactly a day at the beach," McGann returned. He put a finger under her chin and raised her head slightly. Bryson McGann kissed her softly on the lips. "I'll catch up with you a little later. Get some rest."

Tori Haroldson nodded, offering no resistance to his command. She was bone tired and knew some sleep was the perfect prescription.

After receiving some cursory medical attention himself, McGann found Canton and Sanders. Together they met privately with Richard Simon. The president appeared puzzled by the fact of Sanders' presence. "I should probably ask what the NSA is doing here, but we can save that for later."

"Fortunately, no one's recognized you yet," McGann began. "We'd like to keep that under raps for the moment. And we need to let Captain Sully in on what's going on. He's trustworthy," McGann offered. "Plus, we need his help."

Richard Simon quickly weighed his decision. "I think you're right. Those responsible for this must believe that I've been killed. The ruse needs to continue, at least for now, until we can figure a way out of this predicament."

"Not only that, sir. You're not in the best position to do anything about it," Canton interjected.

The president's concern grew with his nod of affirmation. "Suggestions?" Simon sat back, intertwining his fingers behind his neck, followed by a weighty sigh.

"Mr. President. I've not had time to fill Joe or Ashlyn in on what's taking place. What I do know will shock you. The scope and magnitude of this operation is far reaching in governments and the private sector throughout the world." McGann paused briefly, letting them contemplate his words. "I'll be able to shed some light on the intricate details of this operation, if you'll bear with me."

Canton threw a glance at McGann, unsure what exactly his friend was talking about. McGann left it at that. He would divulge the final details later. Once he had the opportunity to work his way through the data crammed onto the nano disc he found inside the ancient Viking pouch, McGann was certain the missing pieces of the puzzle would come together.

Ashlyn Sanders and the four men met privately in Sully's quarters. In the midst of their discussion, a knock sounded on his cabin door. "Enter," Sully boomed.

Tally Smyth, the ship's junior officer, thin as a stick and just as tall, walked in and informed the captain in a heavy down under accent that the U.S. Navy had arrived. "We've apprised them of only the bare essentials, skipper, just as you ordered."

Sully's craggy features seemed to deepen with the burden of the unforeseen circumstances. NESSA's alliance and keeping quiet about harboring the U.S. president onboard his ship, had become much more than he ever counted on. The captain cocked his head, indicating that Smyth should continue.

"A bird just lifted off with the pilots we fished out of the water."

"How are they?" Canton interrupted.

"One's a little rough around the edges, but nothing he won't get over," Smyth remarked. "The other's still touch and go, mate, but he's hanging in there." The officer turned his attention back to Sully. "Skipper, there's a Commander Nash who's been giving me a bit of a *bloody earbash*. The bloke's not any too happy about their airplanes taking a dip in the drink."

"No…I don't imagine he is."

"He wants answers."

"Take him to the conference room. Tell everyone to keep a tight lip and we'll be there shortly." Sully turned to the other four at the table after the junior officer left. "Since I'm at your disposal, Mr. President, if we all came up with the same story, perhaps it would be beneficial for everyone." The captain's eyes roamed the faces of those seated around him, searching for agreement to his request.

"Ladies and gentlemen," McGann began. "Before we introduce ourselves to our guest, let's deal the cards like this."

Navy Commander Earl Nash was in no mood for anything less than what would satisfy the commander of the Stennis. So far, he had not heard it. Nash was a hardball, no nonsense, square-jawed lifer. The navy man was not afraid to ask questions, fully expecting answers that fulfilled his requirements.

McGann admired the man's determination, but was unfazed. He knew the story the four of them concocted left a lot of holes. After a ninety minute grilling by Nash, the commander left with the promise of an imminent return. His intimation clearly defined the need for more thorough explanations. The Commander left no doubt in anyone's mind about his and the U.S. Navy's intentions.

A less than congenial face flashed with the mention of officious reports to the Australian government and AGSI. "You have my promise of the State Department's involvement in this." Like a scolding parent, with a finger waggling in front of them, he continued his tirade. "There will be a forthcoming Pentagon inquiry. Before this is all said and done, you will become intimate with every other entity in D.C. that will take delight in crawling up your collective asses searching for answers." He personally assured them of the jarring reality that would make their lives more than miserable. For now, that was all he could do. Nash stormed out, very disgruntled.

They watched with relief as the Navy chopper lifted off. The pilot made a beeline on a heading for the carrier group. "Do you have any other ships nearby, captain?" McGann asked.

Sully grimaced and rubbed the back of his stiffening neck. "Let's go have a look at the charts."

"Sounds like a plan," McGann said. "I think the time line's wearing thin. Our friends from the Navy will be back, and we need to be long gone."

☙ ❧

Kholos meant to insure the remaining guards' eternal silence. Both he and Sahtay quickly gathered them together. Those who were still alive listened intently to "The Greek's" ploy. He watched them for any signs of suspicion regarding his plans. *Simple sheep for slaughter*, he thought.

Kholos and the woman unleashed their automatic weapons, riddling the bodies with a life ending hail of gunfire. Sixty rounds of copper-jacketed slugs cemented the certainty that Sula-Kai would remain the guards' final resting spot.

Sahtay never gave their deaths a second thought. "What about everything here?" she questioned, before the gun smoke cleared.

"Forget it." Kholos fired back, his eyes searching for signs of life. He slapped in a fresh magazine and released the bolt, in the event of anything unexpected. "Solange kept no paper trails. When they come, they'll find nothing more than some high-tech surgical equipment and dead bodies." His cold words delivered a chilling punch in the face of the steamy tropical climate. "Now where's that fucking Henke?"

The doctor had spotted Kholos and Sahtay from the cliffs after making their return to the island. He had considered calling out, but decided it was not a good idea. After witnessing the murders from his hidden location, the physician was confident he made the right decision. Sahtay and "The Greek" made a cursory effort to find him. Neither knew how much time was left as precious minutes ticked by in their futile attempt. Being on the island in the midst of a search was something neither one wanted. Their safety was in jeopardy. After an unsuccessful quest to find the doctor, the two made their escape.

Mick Henke let the boat carrying Sahtay and Kholos disappear into the distance. Relief washed over him. His legs felt rubbery. He wanted nothing more to do with either of them. Mick Henke knew that luck had been on his side. It was not his day to die. The physician worked rapidly, gathering needed supplies - food, water, and a bottle.

He hurried down into the cavern where the final two boats in Solange's fleet awaited. After filling the fuel tank along with a number of extra containers, Henke refigured his calculations a second time, checking the charts. Traveling alone across open water, even for a competent sailor, was fraught with danger. With any luck, he might make it, but that was in light of anything unforeseen occurring. However, he knew the option Kholos and the woman offered would have made for a very bad day.

Mick Henke steered the boat, engines screaming, as he tore through the cut, leaving Sula-Kai behind like a bad marriage. He never wanted to see the place, or mention its name again. The eminent physician decided he needed some time off after returning to Miami. Unscrewing the cap off the Sapphire, he took a long slash from the pale blue bottle. He never even felt the bite of the clear liquid, invigorated by the promise of better days. From his chair in the boat's cockpit, his mind weaved itself around a web of future plans: his checklist for the tomorrows to come. Get out fast. Tap into off shore accounts. Spend money. Go some place where no one cared what the hell your name was, as long as you paid with greenbacks. Plenty of booze. Hot women.

"Shit, yeah," he yelled, words lost in the wind. He eyed the GPS coordinates while his other hand worked the wheel. Henke pushed the sunglasses up into place in an attempt to keep the invading sun from burning his eyes. Nothing could stop him now as the streamlined hull skimmed over the tops of the blue swells. The familiarity of his own deluded arrogance surged through him, bolstered by the effects of the intoxicating gin. His white teeth sparkled radiantly from behind a full-faced smile, one of self-indulgent confidence in knowing there was nothing he could not do. No one was going to stop him or get in his way. "Mick Henke's back," he shouted for all the world to hear. "Shit, yeah."

Chapter Sixty-Two

NESSA Pacific Headquarters - Hawaii

"I CONCUR, RANDALL," President Richard Simon said, emphasizing his understanding of the need for absolute silence. "We're faced with a dilemma of incredible magnitude and profound connotations. Each and everyone who knows about this must be sworn to secrecy. Nothing can be divulged." The president continued on, looking directly at John Beech and Pat Evans. "Your involvement makes you a potential target also, gentlemen. I can't thank you enough for your part in this tangled web."

"No thanks necessary, Mr. President," John Beech returned.

Randall Sumner had known Simon for many years, and felt comfortable with admitting Noel Johnson, one of NESSA's upper echelon, into the small sphere of individuals that knew the president had been smuggled inside the compound. It was the director of NESSA's responsibility to make sure no one else would ever know of the closed door meeting.

It had taken two days, several different ships, boats, and airplanes for the unlikely band to make their way to the relative safety of the Big Island compound. There had been a few minor glitches and a couple of near misses with the U.S. Navy, but McGann and Canton had managed to outwit them. He knew if the military found out where they were, not even Sumner's status would cause a moment's hesitation in coming after them.

The group had become close in a short period, something that often happens after witnessing traumatic events. They were on a voyage that each would share, one that against all odds called for success, or if not, their lives held little value. Thrown into a dilemma none had ever asked for, they waited to see what hand fate was going to deal. Their only advantage lay in the fact that the world thought each of them was dead.

"Mr. President," McGann began.

Tori Haroldson drew in a deep breath. She understood the weight he felt obligated to carry, and let her hand come to rest on his shoulder. He turned and flashed her a fleeting grin.

"Please, I don't wish you to think me so pretentious that I need to be addressed formally. As a matter of fact, it's probably best if none of you did."

"As you wish." McGann felt no need to argue, and agreed with Simon's reasoning. Any slip of the tongue overheard by the wrong ears could spell disaster and probably cost them their lives. "Is there anyone you can trust, without a doubt?" McGann asked.

"There are a few people," Simon responded. "But, only one that I would think of involving at this point."

"Who's that, sir?" Canton asked.

"Benjamin Wolcott."

"And you believe he had nothing to do with this?" Sanders hard lined.

McGann watched Simon's reaction. The president stiffened with the possible thought of his friend and advisor being an accomplice in the turn of world events. In another moment, Simon put it to rest, letting the intimation recede like an outgoing tide.

"Forgive me for asking, but he certainly has the inside track and would be a perfect candidate for involvement."

"A point well taken, Ashlyn," Sumner tossed back, releasing a puff of gray smoke from the bowl of his pipe. "But I do have to agree with Richard. I think he's the man."

"What about my father?" Alex Ramsey asked, interlacing his fingers in Becca's hand.

"A good choice. But, no. His life could be put in jeopardy," McGann interjected. "His close relationship with the president scratches him from the list. I do believe he will be a much needed ally at some point down the road."

After several more minutes of discussion, McGann revealed part of his plan for getting the president back to his rightful office. "What I have to say obviously stays within this group. There's no turning back. None of us are afforded that luxury."

The gathering grew quiet and attentive. Abram Mossel nodded solemnly in agreement. Several puzzled faces pondered what was coming next. Red O'Brien chewed the ever present stogie and looked across the room at Skiddy Pete, giving him a thumbs up.

"I retrieved a leather pouch from Solange's enclave." He lifted the water tight container it had rested in since their hasty departure from

Sula-Kai, and unscrewed the lid. Carefully, he removed the Oduru diamond and the ancient bag. "Abram. I'll give this back to you for safekeeping." The old man coddled the massive gem tenderly in both hands, as if holding his own child. "This pouch belonged to someone the past has long ago forgotten, or more aptly, most historians choose not to believe existed." McGann opened the bag and palmed an immense copper ingot. Several peculiar red beads rolled out onto the table, along with a titanium housing holding a gold, dual scan nano disc. Two more things followed from the container - an old revolver, worn with age, and a brilliant gold coin.

"What does all of this have to do with the problem at hand?" Sumner asked, between puffs on his favorite Peterson pipe. A hint of cherry flavored the room from the tobacco curling its way toward the ceiling in a grayish cloud.

"Most of it's a matter of synchronicity. For me, purely a case of being in the right place at the right time. From a gun collectors standpoint, I've found a gem." McGann picked up the model 1910 Browning. "This was used by Gavrilo Princip in 1914."

"To assassinate Arch Duke Ferdinand," Alex Ramsey blurted out.

"Precisely," McGann answered. "You know your history. The serial number is a match to the original. Either this is a fake, or Solange orchestrated an elaborate exchange with the military museum in Vienna. Knowing our friend, I believe the latter." He flipped the twenty dollar gold piece into the air. "Now this coin can be returned to its rightful owner."

"Oh, my, God," Tori said, wide-eyed, catching the gold piece. "This is the coin you were telling me about. The one stolen from Duncan McGann." McGann's familiar grin erupted on the heels of her exclamation.

Canton did not give his friend a chance to elaborate. "Is that the missing pouch from the Viking site in Vermont?" he asked, incredulously.

"One and the same, T.C. Solange was a collector. When she heard about the find, she sent her sister to steal it. But all of that's another story." He stopped, eyeing the group and added, "If we get through this." McGann held up the dual scan nano disc for all those in the room to see. "I didn't say anything before because I wanted to be sure. What I've seen confirms my suspicions. I had the opportunity to sift through most of the information on our return flight."

"So, Mac, what tipped you off in the first place?" O'Brien cut in.

"Geoffrey Haines."

"The English PM?"

McGann nodded. "I caught a glimpse of a news piece a while back. I remembered a very odd peculiarity during a speech. It was almost imperceptible. Somehow it stuck. When I found the nano disc and discovered the players, I went back and searched recent news footage of the G-8 leaders. I found a number of them possessed the same quirk. That and all the other craziness, it's far too unlikely to be coincidental."

"So what's on that disc that's going to change the world?" The Irishman's words ripped through the mounting tension.

"Probably more than any of you want to hear, but something each of you needs to know." McGann cut to the chase, rather than giving the opportunity for questions. "For the moment, we're presumed dead. Once the echelon of decision makers realizes Solange is fish food in the Banda Sea, they'll safeguard their plans at all costs. I'm afraid the old axiom rings true. It's going to get worse before it gets better."

Tori Haroldson shook her head in disbelief. "I've got to say, Bryson McGann, you sure know how to show a woman a good time." Tori's blue eyes softened, "You think maybe dinner and champagne would be too much to ask?" The levity lightened the mood of everyone gathered in the conference room.

Laughter was incapable of lingering once McGann began to detail the methodology spearheaded by Carlton Trust. Forty minutes elapsed before he finished the complicit tale in a bullet pointed presentation of the major items; the purpose of Solange's island retreat, Stephan Kholos' involvement in the diamond theft, its intention of deflecting media attention away from Davos, Simon's replacement as well as other world leaders, Martin Boggs and the IPI connection.

In a final note, McGann wrapped up the loose ends, tying them all together with a common thread. "The archivist, who was looking for insurance with his neat little gift to his long time friend's now deceased daughter, Solange, is none other than Chief Justice, Foster Hughes."

A quiet fell across the group. All of them understood the world had changed, never again being what they once knew. They could only hope and pray for better days. The enormity of the struggle which they were undertaking seemed nearly insurmountable. Freedom from the iron talons of clandestine control, by the greed mongers of the world's elite, was paramount. At stake was not just their own lives, but that of the world and future generations.

Chapter Sixty-Three
Camp David - Maryland

"I'M RELIEVED TO KNOW that our Deutsche friend is settling nicely into his role." Comfortably ensconced in the plush leather of the armchair, Simon let the crackling fire and crystal tumbler's single malt contents ease away the burdens of the day. "Might as well take a free ride on the taxpayer's dime and drink only the best, hey, Martin?"

Martin Boggs face stared back impassively from the video screen hanging above the fireplace. The screen doubled as a television when not in use for conferencing. A secure line was hard wired in as well, along with the capability to scramble both men's voices. No one outside the soundproof room new of their treasonous discussion.

"That leaves only three compatriots who have not, shall we say, been defaced," the CEO chuckled, amused by his own words.

"I've been in contact with the other leaders. I've convinced them. They concur. The idea of a preemptive strike is palatable," Simon stated smugly. "The military's on alert in the region, and they've been told to keep it buttoned up. A scripted diversion in Paraguay should keep the press busy right up until game time." The president stole a glance at his watch. "It'll all go down in less than 48 hours. Everyone's agreed on the finer aspects and ready to take the flack, parlaying our game plan to the world." Simon sat his drink down, wiping his moist fingers along his trousers. "This stranglehold that you've masterminded will undoubtedly be the most incredible turn of events the world's ever known. I'm amazed how quiet you've kept everything." Simon peered from under a hand, rubbing the skin above his brow. "So where exactly is my counterpart?"

"Let's just say he is safely tucked away. Other than that, you should have no concerns, trust me."

"Then I guess no one will ever have any reason to come knocking on your door, Martin." The impostor's expression signaled doting approval of the CEO's plan. "You're to be congratulated."

"No mistakes. No options other than complete success." Boggs' cherubic features turned sour. "There'll be those who'll oppose this. Probably become quite vocal. They must be disenfranchised quickly. Labeled traitors. Precision military assaults from selected squads of contracted mercenaries at our disposal, will see to their end." Boggs stare bore directly through the screen, imprinting itself on Richard Simon's retinas. "Not a problem, right?"

"Murdering fellow countrymen? None whatsoever," the president replied. Inside his brain, the miniscule chip placed by Mick Henke became more a part of him each day. Sending out signals, it directed his thoughts and actions, like his *cohorts* in the world's political arena. "It's the patriotic thing to do."

"Good. I'm putting some safeguards into place of my own."

"Oh?"

"Don't trouble yourself with wondering what, Richard. Just know this. It will be a benefit to you as well."

"I like the sound of that." Simon smiled, picking up his drink and swallowing greedily.

"Once the world is tumbling end over end, no one will bother with the obituary," Boggs said, flatly. "Frankly, his death will be made to look quite natural. Actually, the process is rather ingenious."

"I'd expect nothing less, Martin."

"I'll be in touch."

Simon tapped the disconnect, staring into the darkened screen. Pondering the weight of the Carlton's leader's words, the new and improved Richard Simon decided it was time for a refill. Another nightcap before bedtime, why not? After all, he was the president.

He found the prescribed duties a burden, reports and conferences, timetables compressed to minutes on a series of matters, day after day. He knew that soon enough, much of his world would change. Most of the daily crap he was required to accomplish would be tossed out the window. Once the world settled down and fell into line, life would at least be better, if not, very good. The president rifled through the last report finishing it along with one more drink than he had intended.

Sighing heavily, he turned on the television to catch the latest reports of world chaos before he retired. Pandemonium had dug in its heels, imbedding its spurs deeply into the world's flanks. The desire for the viscous, black liquid that had stopped pumping from wells throughout the Middle East had escalated to the breaking point. Oil reserves were dwindling.

Sound bites offered proposals of remediation with OPEC, but so far nothing surfaced. Glad-handing by administration officials and false smiles did nothing to resolve the burgeoning crisis. The news networks showed rioters in the inner cities burning cars and looting, in reaction to their plight. Promises to end the current situation had drawn to a stalemate, with neither side willing to give any farther. Simon even caught a piece about himself, urging the nation to remain calm. The way he figured it, his Emmy award winning performances dictated the need for another scotch, which he poured from the decanter next to his chair.

He found himself laughing, thinking of how gullible people had become. Tell them anything with the appearance of sincerity. Lie in the face of facts. Stamp it with the seal of the president's office, and nearly anything was possible. Why not? The chief administrator prior to the real Simon's election had doled out far more than his share of self-serving lies during his tenure; adding to the coffers of his cronies, as well as his own. Even worse, his legacy had left behind a mire of debt and doubt about the true intentions of the United States. It was a shadow the real President Simon had worked hard at remedying.

By the time he emptied his glass, Simon was prepared for a good night's sleep. He tossed the remote onto the table, and stacked the official reports into a neat little pile. Pushing himself from the comfortable leather, he left the room.

Close on the heels of the president, Stan Reynolds followed, speaking into his microphone. "Command post. *Boxer's* mobile. Ready to be tucked in for the night."

A set of eyes followed the Commander in Chief on a screen from the command center down a long hallway, picking up his image as he rounded the corner. The president stopped in front of his suite. Simon turned the handle and nodded at the agent. Stepping inside, he quietly closed the door behind him.

"*Boxer's* secure." The agent did not need to look at his watch. He was due to go off shift momentarily. Everyone who worked for him knew of his penchant for punctuality. One ass chewing from the boss was all it took to never be late again. Reynolds smiled to himself, at the sound of his replacement's footfalls rounding the corner a short distance away.

Stan Reynolds reported off to Ron Abernathy. The young agent had recently been assigned to the Secret Service detail and was looking to make good with his boss. Reynolds was feeling jubilant, and decided the kid needed a break. He complimented his punctuality. He was playing the younger agent, because the following night, he needed the rookie to cover for him.

Another task awaited Stan Reynolds. It was one not sanctioned by the Secret Service. In fact, they would be highly displeased if they knew of his involvement in the forthcoming chain of events. What he had in mind was a punishable offense with serious consequences. Reynolds understood his assignment. It was simple enough. His handiwork would, in effect, make it look like his victim suffered a massive coronary infarction. No one, not even the coroner, would have the slightest inkling. The effects of Stan Reynolds' visit would be untraceable, permanent, and above suspicion.

Chapter Sixty-Four
Continental Divide - Colorado

HIGH ABOVE THE ROCKY MOUNTAINS, the Gulfstream, piloted by Beech and Evans, streaked through the night sky, on a course for the nation's capital. The plight of the unlikely travelers thrown together by circumstance and bound by the need of survival, hung precipitously on a thin strand of hope and a lot of luck. If the man they would soon be placing their trust in was complicit in the Carlton conspiracy, they had but a short time to live. The pendulum of the clock was swinging and fate hung in the balance.

"Benjamin Wolcott?"

"Yes," the presidential advisor answered, leaning back into a leather chair behind his desk. A pale yellow light illuminated the darkened office of his Georgetown residence. Who's this?" the presidential aide questioned, perplexed by the unfamiliar voice.

"Ashlyn Sanders, NSA."

"Do I know you?" he asked hesitantly, annoyed by the intrusion.

"No. But you're the one person, I'm told, that he trusts completely."

"Miss Sanders, I don't wish to sound rude, but it's late. I've had a very busy day. Frankly, I'm exhausted." The president's advisor felt his ire rising. "To be truthful, I'm not really in the mood for games. Good night." Wolcott's finger reached for the disconnect button when he again heard the woman's plea. Something pulled him back. Reluctantly, he told her to get on with it. "You have one minute," he added sharply.

"This is of the highest priority," Sanders returned with forceful confidence. She didn't give a him chance to answer, knowing the stakes would be raised with the mention of the commander in chief. "It concerns the president."

"Who the hell is this?" Wolcott demanded of the unfamiliar voice. "How do you expect me to verify…?"

"I don't," Sanders fired back. "However, Richard Simon is in danger. That should be your prime concern. Now, do I have your attention?"

An extended pause waited impatiently as Wolcott wrestled with the turn of events. "I'm listening," he replied, tentatively, after careful consideration.

"Are you on a secure line?"

"Of course. Digitalized random sequence voice scrambling. I think even your outfit would have a hard time breaking this. So, what's so urgent?" he demanded, irritation encompassing his words.

"Now that I have your attention, I'll put you on speaker phone."

"Benjamin." The familiarity of the voice took him by surprise.

Benjamin Wolcott's mind raced with multiple scenarios, upset with all the possibilities. "Mr. President. Are you alright? Where are you?"

"Yes, I'm fine for the moment. In response to your second question, I believe we're over Colorado."

"You…you can't be. I just spoke with you a short time ago," Wolcott stammered. "You're at Camp David. I watched you get onboard Marine One myself. No one's notified me of any change in plans. You're slated to spend the entire weekend at the retreat." Benjamin Wolcott's temper flared. "If this is some type of..."

"I can assure you it's not," Randall Sumner cut in. "Mr. Wolcott. This is Director Randall Sumner of the National Earth Seas Science Agency, and I'm with the President of the United States. This is no ruse. In fact, you can check the flight plan our pilots filed with the FAA." The director let the authoritative steel of his words cut through Wolcott's hardened veneer, until the realization struck the man fully. "I'm here with a number of other individuals, along with Becca and Alex Ramsey."

A long pause ensued before he spoke again. "Jake Ramsey's…" he asked, astonished. "I thought they were dead."

"They're very much alive. I also have three other NESSA employees with me, and Dr. Tori Haroldson, a member of the Australian Geological Survey Institute, and a Dutch diamond cutter."

"I won't even begin to ask."

"Ben," Simon interjected. "I'm going to turn this over to Bryson McGann. He's an Assistant Projects Director at NESSA. You may recall his name from the H.A.A.R.P. debacle."

"Yes…yes, it does rings a bell. I remember now."

"Mr. Wolcott," McGann started.

"Please, Ben," the voice sounded over the intercom.

"Okay. What the president and Director Sumner have told you is true. Currently, we're headed to an airfield in Virginia to meet with you. However, since the man who is acting as Richard Simon is at Camp David, we need to shift gears."

"Whoa. Hold on. Are you saying there's an impostor posing as President Richard Simon at Camp David?"

"Absolutely. Make the call and see if the president's there." Several minutes passed before Wolcott returned. "The agent on duty indicated the president was asleep in his room."

"It's a long story, Ben."

"I've got time."

McGann replayed the events regarding the abduction of RED 7 from the G-8 conference, giving the president's trusted friend a very brief run through the ingenious plan to gain control of world governments. "There's much more. Once we're on the ground, you can confirm the president's identity through a retinal data base link. Ashlyn can get you connected on board our plane."

"Fair enough," Wolcott replied.

"Two things. The easy part first. Transportation. We need you to bring another driver. Someone you trust without fail. One who'll not arouse any suspicions. Lives depend on it," McGann stated, leaving no room as to the serious nature of his request. "Any problem?"

"No. I can do that," Wolcott returned, confidently.

"Next, you'll have to get us into Camp David without alarming anyone. "

"That's a tall order. Security's tight. Do you think they're just going to let us stroll on in, McGann?"

"I'm counting on it."

"And what if your plan fails, Mr. McGann?"

"I don't think in the negative, Ben. The rest of it, I'll explain after our arrival."

"Bry, I've got the name of the closest airfield to Camp David," Joe Canton cut in. "It's a private strip with about five hundred feet to spare. Beech said it's no problem."

"Tell them it's a go. Get an ETA, T.C."

Canton didn't bother to answer. Within a moment he had disappeared through the door into the cockpit. Evans entered the data into the on board computer which spit an arrival time back almost instantly.

Joe Canton returned quickly, "The boys have the engines pushed to the limit. We'll be on the deck in two and half hours." Bryson McGann relayed the information to Wolcott. They agreed on the details and the presidential advisor signed off.

Benjamin Wolcott's duty under normal circumstances would have been to inform the Secret Service immediately. The incredibility of the situation dictated another route. Pulling open his desk drawer, his hand pulled a forty-five caliber Colt from its resting spot. His practiced eye carefully inspected the weapon, slapping seven rounds into the well. Satisfied, Wolcott's index finger speared the keypad, tapping out the numbers he knew well.

Chapter Sixty-Five
Thurmont - Maryland

THE TEDIUM OF THE TWO AND A HALF HOUR FLIGHT took its toll. The group had slugged down some coffee and sandwiches, staving off the hunger. Still, everyone was edgy, not knowing the future's expectations for their lives. In the back of the plane, Abram Mossel slept soundly. McGann gathered the others, filling them in on his plans for what came next.

"This is how it goes down. Red. You're with me."

"Understood," the Irishman replied.

"The president and Randall will ride in the first vehicle, along with Tori. Wolcott will be with us."

"T.C., you and Ashlyn will be in the second vehicle along with Wolcott's friend. The Ramsey's, Skiddy Pete, and Mossel will ride with you, too. If anything looks suspicious, smells bad, or just doesn't sit right with you, get everyone out. Don't let anyone or anything get in your way. "

Ashlyn squeezed Canton's hand, turning to meet his gaze. "Right. By the numbers, Bry," the big man affirmed.

McGann stared directly at Richard Simon. "We've no way of knowing if Wolcott's involved. Until that bridge is crossed, and since we don't know who he's bringing, we're flying blind. No offense, sir, but all the bases need to be covered."

The President held up a hand stopping McGann, "None taken. I'm out of my territory on this. It's your game."

"T.C., Ash, do whatever the situation dictates. There may be Secret Service involved in this." McGann's hazel eyes burned with an intensity that provided a testament to the seriousness of the forthcoming situation. His natural abilities provided him with the talent for leadership, but he realized the odds were not in their favor. No matter how good you were, it did not matter. Their lives could end in an instant from a well placed hollow point. Bullets never asked questions or harbored grudges. They simply did their job, efficiently, without compunction, and caring little for the recipient of their lethal gift.

None of it was enough to stymie the granite resolve within Bryson McGann. He lived his life with a fierce determination for doing what was needed when the call came. This was such a moment, and it was a challenge he had no choice but to tackle.

"Okay," McGann finished, stealing a glance at his Breitling. "We'll be on the ground soon. Any last questions?" All eyes focused on him, providing assurance of their understanding without saying a word. "T.C., give me a hand. Thanks to Director Sumner, we'll have a few unexpected surprises to bring to the party."

The Gulfstream taxied to the end of the runway where two sets of headlights illuminated the fuselage emblazoned with the NESSA logo. The pilots turned the aircraft back around with its nose pointed toward the far end of the runway, just in case. McGann and Canton peered from the cockpit into the night, finally deciding everything was in order.

"It's now or never, Bry. Feels like we're playing cowboys and Indians again," Canton joked.

"Yeah, but who's the good guys?" he quipped. "Split and go wide when we hit the tarmac."

"I know the drill, little brother." Deep resolve overshadowed Canton's normally jocular manner.

The cabin door opened and the steps unfolded. Both McGann and Canton operated with lightning precision, moving in opposite directions with guns drawn, pointing at Benjamin Wolcott and the female standing beside him.

"Arms above your heads," Canton yelled, running toward them. Stopping in front of them, he kept the pistol barrel pointed squarely in their faces. Joe Canton was prepared to do whatever circumstances required. McGann made a quick inspection of the twin black Suburban vehicles and the surrounding area. Once things met with his approval, he returned.

"Quite a greeting," Wolcott offered. "For the record, I would've done the same. May we put our hands down?"

After patting them down, McGann nodded his head. Satisfied, he and Canton holstered their weapons.

"Gentlemen. Andrea Buckler." Five feet nine inches tall, the attractive red head looked lean and fit in the black jumpsuit. Her grip was strong. Buckler's eyes did not back down when his gaze bore into her. McGann got a clear read that Ms. Buckler could handle herself in most situations.

"Academy grad. I'd trust her with my life."

"You may have to, Ben, " McGann said grimly, a steamy cloud following each of his words into the chilly air.

"Let's get on board. You can authenticate the president's retinal image. Once you're satisfied, we'll review everything and head out."

"Agreed," the president's advisor replied.

Together, the small group made their way onto the plane. In a few minutes, Wolcott had his assurances that the man he was speaking with was indeed, Richard Simon. Final plans were made. Sumner decided that Beech and Evans would fly to D.C. and wait until he contacted them. If anyone suspected their involvement, or asked too many questions, they would have to make the best of it. The details were hashed out one final time before the unlikely group departed.

McGann watched the Gulfstream streak upwards into an obsidian sky. From this point on, there was no turning back. This group's destiny was being forged in the fires of the unknown. The list of uncertainties in the equation continued to multiply. Answers lingered in darkened realms, enveloped in shadowy expectation and fear. However, the only question that truly mattered at this point, was if they all would be alive to see the sunrise.

Chapter Sixty-Six

Camp David - Maryland

MARINE SERGEANT, BARRY COOPER, pulled up to the main gate, strictly following his duty schedule. He had just rolled up and parked his truck, when a black sedan with government plates sped past the sentries. The vehicle's engine growled, as its driver punched the accelerator. Fishtailing onto the road, the vehicle narrowly missed McGann's Suburban, and disappeared into the night.

"Somebody's in a hurry," McGann said, watching the automobile speed past. His concerns grew with the tail lights growing smaller in the Suburban's side mirror. "I don't like the looks of that, T.C.," he voiced into the thin wire microphone at the corner of his mouth.

"Too coincidental?" Canton tossed back.

"You know me and my hunches."

"I know enough that it usually means trouble's riding shotgun, and the fun's about to begin."

"Show time, T.C.," McGann answered, wheeling the heavy vehicle up to the checkpoint at the main gate. Lowering the window, McGann did not give the sentry a chance to speak. The military's hierarchy required those of lesser rank to listen and obey. So McGann took the lead and fired off a few lines about official business.

A young marine corporal was nonplused by McGann's officious attitude, barely able to ask for credentials and the reason they were there. Sergeant Cooper approached the sentry, concerned by what was unfolding. So far, McGann's tactics were working. He figured the shock value of the president not being where he was supposed to would deliver an unexpected punch, causing enough confusion to help orchestrate their entrance into the compound. Sitting behind the driver's seat, Richard Simon waited impatiently to play his part, along with Benjamin Wolcott. Bryson McGann lowered all the windows.

"Mr. President," the stunned sentry said.

Cooper interjected, "Excuse me, sir, I wasn't told you'd be off site, and I didn't know Mr. Wolcott would be with you." The inquisitive marine continued his grilling, but only briefly. He had barely finished his first set of questions, when he demanded to know who the other two passengers were.

Simon rose to the occasion. Throwing open the door, the president launched himself from the passenger compartment, ridiculing the marine guards for not knowing of his whereabouts. He launched into a tirade about the inadequacies of the marines guarding the presidential retreat, demotions, and a laundry list of discrepancies that he would personally pass on to General Mowry at the Pentagon.

Cooper was no 'wet behind the ears' recruit. He had seen more than his share in sixteen years, and all of this was beginning to leave a bad taste in his mouth. "Mr. President, please return to your vehicle," the sergeant asked politely, but with an air of authority. Simon failed to comply. After a more stern command, Cooper stepped backward. "Sir, if you're the president, my apologies. However, I will not ask you again to return to your vehicle."

The sentries were unaware of Canton slowly inching the Suburban closer to the one in front. He felt the bumpers touch, and threw the lever into park. McGann read the situation, knowing what would follow. He did not give the guards the opportunity to proceed to the next step. Cooper's hand reached for the holster containing the sidearm and the two other marines guarding the entrance made a move to bring their M-16's into a defensive position.

McGann jumped from the front seat, pushing the barrel of his pistol into the sergeant's forehead. "My apologies, sergeant. Tell your men to disarm. This man is President Richard Simon. The man inside the compound is an impostor. You'll have to take my word for now." McGann's eyes bore into the marine, leaving no room for anything other than complying with his directive. Canton, O'Brien, and Andrea Buckler moved with efficiency in coming to McGann's aid. With the business ends of their weapons directed at the guards, Cooper nodded reluctantly and they dropped their weapons. The trio wasted no time handcuffing the cadre of camouflaged sentries, locking them in the guard shack.

"Gentlemen, we probably have very little time. Someone at the command center will be monitoring the video feed," Wolcott spoke up from inside the truck, tucking the hidden pistol inside his jacket.

"No time like the present." McGann turned in the direction of his friend, knowing that a breech of the presidential compound called for asking questions later, but only if anyone was alive to answer. "You ready, T.C.?"

"*Oh the wild charge they made! And all the world wondered,*" Canton responded.

"Yeah, I know the rest of it, T.C.," McGann replied, remembering the outcome of the Crimean War's British brigade. "Hopefully, we'll fair better than Tennyson's ill fated warriors."

The two vehicles, filled with anxious occupants, roared along the roadway as quickly as possible. Canton was glued to McGann's tail. He knew the others were relying on both men to get them through another difficult situation. Hopefully, fate would be kind. Canton's gut knotted when he tossed a glance in the rearview mirror. A set of headlights appeared in the distance. "We've got company, Bry. Humvee."

"Wolcott says we're almost there. Get everyone out and inside as quickly as possible."

The massive vehicles skidded to a halt on the damp pavement. Their occupants ran for the cover of the presidential quarters. Closing in rapidly, the sound of approaching vehicles signaled that time was a premium.

"Richard, you first," McGann ordered. "The sight of the president ought to distract anyone inside, momentarily."

Richard Simon strode briskly through the corridors he knew so well. McGann and Canton followed a few steps behind with the others in tow. Red O'Brien and Andrea Buckler kept a close watch, in case anyone attempted an assault from their rear.

Ron Abernathy was alone. The young agent's oath called for protecting the president, even the ultimate sacrifice. His earpiece rang with voices from the command center, detailing the security breech. He was processing the information when the president opened the door to his suite. "What the hell's going on?" he barked. "I just received a phone call saying…"

"Yes, sir. I'm aware of the situation. At the moment, I'm the only person you've got until we get some help." Abernathy spoke into his mike, "Abernathy. Boxer is mobile. Let's go, Mr. President."

"Stop," a voice bellowed from behind them.

The agent threw the president to the floor, wheeled and pointed his gun at a twin of the man he was protecting. His mouth hung limply at the sight, attempting to make sense of the situation with several pistol barrels pointed back in his direction.

"Don't shoot. You might kill the President of the United States," McGann shouted. "We're putting our weapons down," he called out, further confusing the agent. "What's your name, agent?" McGann queried.

The impostor squirmed beneath the weight of the Secret Service agent. "Shoot the damn bastards, you idiot. Can't you see they're going to kill me?" Inside Simon's head, the neural signals fired off at an incredible pace. The artificial intelligence was prompting *the president* to regain control of the situation, doing anything to preserve the ruse.

From behind the group, McGann heard the sounds of pounding footfalls closing in on their location. "Red. You and Andrea fire off a few rounds," he whispered into the mike. "Then drop your weapons and hit the deck. That'll slow them down." Several bursts of gunfire rang out in the corridor, providing the momentary distraction they needed. He knew the time was short. "Everyone else on the floor now."

Sweat gathered on Ron Abernathy's face. None of this made any sense. He could not understand why someone attempting an assassination would give up so readily. Nothing in the manuals covered this situation. Simon heaved upward with all his might catching the agent by surprise. Attempting to regain his balance, Abernathy fell backwards. His pistol slipped from his grasp. The presidential impostor snatched the weapon from the floor.

McGann watched helplessly. Nothing could have anticipated this outcome. His plans were heading south by the change of events. Things were now totally out of control. In the midst of the melee, shouts bellowed from the group of Secret Service agents and Marine guards. Their intention was to save the life of the president, at all costs. Their weapons came to bear on the intruders as they rounded the corner. Shock etched their faces at the sight of the Commander in Chief, armed, with his finger on the trigger.

In the next instant, the enclosed hallway came alive with the deafening ring of gunfire. When the thunderous explosions faded, the President of the United States, Richard Simon, lay dead.

Chapter Sixty-Seven
Presidential Suite - Camp David

BODIES FILLED THE HALLWAY. The president lay in a pool of his own dark red blood. "No one move," screamed the agent in charge of the assault team. Everyone in McGann's group knew better than to even flinch. Nervous eyes looked up into the business end of numerous weapons. It would not take much to restore the tension that hung in a malignant veil only moments ago.

The assault team moved cautiously. There was no mood of congeniality as they roughly yanked each person to their feet. Each individual was checked for weapons and cuffed. Abernathy rose to his feet, detailing the impossible scenario to one of his fellow agents.

"Where the hell's Reynolds?" the agent asked.

"Told me he had to meet someone," Abernathy sputtered. "It was urgent. Asked me to cover for him. I said, okay. I didn't know…" His sentences were chopped, the effects of the gunplay surging through his veins.

"I'm Richard Simon," the President stated with authority, being pulled up from the floor.

"You'd better be, or you're in a world of shit, mister," a vehement marine with a blistering scowl spit back.

"It's Benjamin Wolcott," another one of the marines shouted, rolling the limp man onto his side. "He caught a round." The sergeant quickly pressed his hand onto the wound. "Someone get a doctor."

The building was overflowing with agents and military personnel when a marine officer spitting nails pushed his way through the crowd. "Somebody tell me what the fuck's going down in here. Get this place locked down now." Major Burroughs hollered, capturing everyone's attention. "Somebody check with the command center and see if the perimeter's intact. I don't want anyone getting cozy with my ass that I don't know about." A blackened scowl hovered menacingly. "I want some goddamn answers now," he demanded. "You people got thirty seconds to come up with a story that makes me happy, or I'm going to jack all of you up."

"Randall Sumner. NESSA," the director spoke up. "Major," the former general said, nodding with authority, "that's President Richard Simon."

"A retinal scan will prove that," McGann offered, drawing a sharp look from Burroughs.

The marine did not answer. Burroughs quickly made a decision. Within five minutes the scan was completed, and the entire group were taken to a meeting room for a debrief on the perplexing situation. Hitting the highlights, McGann finished his part of the tale in a rapid fire account. Finally, he asked the president to order someone to crank up Marine One.

"Hold on just a damn minute, McGann," the officer growled authoritatively. "You're not going anywhere. Guards," Burroughs hollered over his shoulder. "See to it that this gentleman doesn't get out of this chair unless I authorize it," the officer commanded. "He can shit his pants for all I care, but he doesn't move. Understood." The major's words were followed by a withering glower directed at the NESSA employee.

"Stand down, Major," Simon commanded sternly, before the guards had time to respond.

"But sir," he protested, wearing a veil of astonishment.

"Enough."

McGann spoke up, "Time's of the essence. I think I know where our friend was headed. The one who was in such a hurry to leave as we arrived. He's got a good jump on us, but Joe and I should make it," his voice trailed.

"Whatever you need," the President returned.

"As for the rest of us, Major," the President began, "I believe a little hospitality's in order for our guests. Will you see to it, Major Burroughs?" Simon stood and faced the group. "I know each of you has been through a lot. If you'll follow me, I'll find us a more comfortable setting," Simon offered, wearily.

"Bryson." Tori Haroldson rubbed her thumb and forefinger together in nervous anticipation. He turned towards the soft voice. The doctor threw her arms around his neck and planted a kiss fully on his mouth.

"That was nice, but not nearly enough."

"You'd better get back here in one piece."

"Do I have a choice?" Then he and Canton went racing for the helipad.

Chapter Sixty-Eight
Potomac - Maryland

AN UNEASY STILLNESS rested on the night, while the conspiring darkness bore witness to the actions of the intruder. Gaining entrance to the old man's house had been little problem, especially with the forehand knowledge of camera locations and the main control panel. The wiring had not been updated in years, and the man easily circumvented the system. Skillfully, he tapped into the cable providing a digital feed of all the rooms. The only difference lay in the fact that now nothing was live - only spooled, pre-recorded images played - just in case someone checked.

Moving silently through the darkened house with the aid of the night vision optics, Stan Reynolds smiled to himself at just how easy this would be. A quick in and out. Once he completed his task, not even the coroner would suspect anything. Only a few people would know the true nature of the man's demise, and they had no intention of telling anyone.

Reynolds' hand gripped the knob, quietly turning the handle. The stale scent of tobacco assaulted him in an overpowering wave. The room stood in juxtaposition to the rest of the immaculate home. Dust and overflowing ashtrays, along with stacks of leather bound law books, were strewn about the judge's private enclave. At first, he was taken aback by the disgusting conditions. He quickly shook it off, knowing that in a matter of moments, it would be a forgotten memory.

Stan Reynolds walked over to the cart holding a decanter of the judge's prized bourbon. He paused, listening purposefully for any hint of detection, before beginning his murderous deed. Removing a small glass vile from his jacket pocket, Reynolds carefully emptied the container of the white crystalline powder into the decanter holding the judge's liquor. Swirling the liquid until all of the powder dissolved, he knew the old man was as good as dead already, and replaced the stopper.

The government agent's silhouette passed in front of the large bank of grimy windows overlooking the vast expanse of the tree-lined property. Moving in behind the judge's desk, Foster Hughes' worn leather chair protested adamantly in response to the unfamiliar person taking a seat. Reynolds' extra weight drew forth a long, strident squeal that he hoped went unheard.

Stan Reynolds snapped the release and opened the laptop. With a push of a button, the computer screen came to life. Fortunately, the chief justice had never taken the time to enter any pass codes. After booting up, he was in. Simple. Reynolds beamed with smug satisfaction.

Through the powerful lens of the rifle scope, "The Greek" spotted the image of his target. His fingers adjusted the dial of the infrared thermal settings, outlining the heat signature of a man in different shades of red, yellow, and blue. State of the art optics delineated the different parts of his target's body by its temperature. Kholos was certain the trespasser prowling through the old man's office was none other than the man he had been sent to kill. Martin Boggs had personally assured him of it.

Concern grew momentarily, when the assassin caught the sound of a large helicopter passing in the distance. After realizing it was not headed in his direction, he once again focused attention on the prescribed task. Kholos had been in his sniper's position in the tree, over three hundred and seventy-five yards from the house, for more than two hours. He had found a suitable spot to wait, concealed in the branches of a large maple tree. Even though it had shed its leaves, the tree offered a discreet hiding place in the midst of a set of tangled limbs. Conveniently, the same branches provided a stable resting spot for the large caliber rifle and its eighteen inch silencer. From this distance, it was an easy shot for Kholos.

"The Greek" switched the scope's setting to night vision mode and a ghostly apparition of the Secret Service agent replaced the colorful image. Gluing his right eye to the scope, Kholos' brain processed the fact that the crosshairs of the expensive laser optics were now centered squarely on the base of the man's neck. The heavy slug would sever the spine and tear apart the neck and upper torso. The bullet would also leave the man's face intact, instantly identifying the judge's murderer.

The gunman's ears echoed with the metallic snap of the safety being undone. Automatically, the assassin's right hand slid into place, passing his index finger through the guard, and letting the cold steel of the finely knurled metal caress his skin. Drawing in a slow deep breath of chilly night air, "The Greek's" finger tightened on the trigger.

Hughes' diseased lungs erupted into a congested fit of coughing, catapulting him from his sleep. Several minutes passed before the episode faded. Doubting he could return to sleep, his withered, well-practiced fingers pulled a cigarette from the pack and lit it. The smoke burned as it traveled down his windpipe, but the nicotine craving far surpassed any discomfort.

The sound froze him in his tracks. The years had not tampered with his hearing. He left his room, armed with a revolver nearly as old as himself. Unfortunately, for whoever decided to break into his home, the revolver functioned as efficiently as if it had just come out of the box.

Hughes entered his office through a side door, fighting the urge to cough. He could not tell from the dim light of the computer if the man's face was familiar. It really did not make a difference. The individual sitting at his desk was an uninvited guest.

"I wouldn't move a hair on your ass, you son of a bitch," the old man wheezed.

Reynolds jumped slightly, eyes growing wide in response. He had been so engrossed in his work, he overlooked the other entrance into the room. Stan Reynolds' mind rapidly sifted through all the training scenarios over the years. Nothing was a match. The agent was on his own, and it wasn't looking good. Turning slightly in Hughes direction, he eyed the business end of a barrel pointing at him. The hand that was holding it, did not tremble. This was turning out far from his expectations.

The unexpected tinkle of breaking glass, and what followed, occurred nearly simultaneously. The event played out in slow motion before the judge's eyes. "Holy Christ." Foster Hughes hollered, paralyzed by the utter shock of what just happened.

Stan Reynolds never felt a thing. The sniper's bullet accomplished its purpose. What had been his neck blew apart in a gruesome spray of blood and tissue covering Hughes' desk and the floor beyond. The heavy bullet ripped its way through the agent's upper chest. The now jagged projectile, distorted into a mushroom shape, continued its destruction. The bloody lump of lethal metal collided with the laptop screen. Shattered plastic flew in all directions. Kholos' bullet ended its assignment by coring into the library's far wall with a heavy thud.

The old man's body trembled uncontrollably. Hughes' heart pounded with jackhammer speed, threatening to explode from his chest. Leaden legs were incapable of responding, nearly buckling beneath him with any attempt to move. The heavy revolver slipped from his grasp. Gripped by the unforeseen event, it took the Chief Justice a moment before the shock of what happened dissipated with an agonizing slowness.

The limp torso slumped to the left side of the chair, dripping thick, red blood into a pool on the worn wooden floor. Reynolds' bloody head hung precariously, attached by a few strands of exposed muscle and pale skin. The distinctive coppery odor of blood and death filled the room.

Finally, the old man crept towards the window, peering cautiously around the dusty curtain's edge. His eyes strained into the darkness, desperately searching for any signs of the gunman. Unable to see any movement on the grounds, the hollow feeling of spent adrenaline squeezed in on him. He ran the bony fingers of a hand through his thin white hair, exhaling forcefully.

Foster Hughes' thoughts scattered. The judge was on edge. Thinking irrationally. He badly needed a cigarette. A bourbon, too. Hughes sucked in the smoke. He averted his eyes from the dead man, quickly walking around the desk. His fingers fumbled with the switch, and a pale yellow light cast a surreal glow from the dim bulb. It was enough for him to pour a tumbler full of a much needed drink.

Chapter Sixty-Nine

Marine One - Maryland

"TAKE US DOWN," McGann spoke into his headset. The Marine pilot responded to his command.

Joe Canton shown a pale red light across the map, pinpointing their location. "That should put us a quarter mile from the house," he spoke into his mike, peering up at his friend. "Once we're on the ground, we'll move along the tree line and enter the side of the house."

"That'll work, T.C. What about alarms?"

"Presidential powers were enough to persuade the security company to provide the access code. The cover was some song and dance about protection, the justice department, U. S. marshals..."

"Never hurts to have friends with connections."

The helicopter touched down heavily and Canton threw open the door. Both he and McGann hit the ground running, covering the quarter mile to Foster Hughes' home in just minutes.

"Plans indicate the front door's on the south side of the house, Bry," Canton voiced softly, from their position in behind a row of hedges. "Garage is out. There's a service entrance on the west side. Looks like the best bet."

"Can't imagine Hughes would be too excited about a couple of late night travelers knocking on his front door," McGann added, his words followed by a cold steamy vapor. "No lights. That's a good sign." Bryson McGann gave the house a going over once more from their position. "Let's do it, T.C."

The two men were up and running. Their military training had given them the skills they needed to do the job. Moving as one, they made their way around the immense brick house undetected, stopping by the service door entrance. McGann tested the knob, surprised to find it turning in his hand. "What are the odds? You think the judge left the door open for us?"

"He's either overtly hospitable, or the rest of the story, I don't think I'm going to like, little brother."

McGann slid the pistol from its holster underneath his arm. "You're never too old to rock and roll, T.C." He was through the door with Canton close on his heels.

McGann and Canton were in the process of searching the first floor of the judge's home when they heard him cry out. Not knowing what to expect, they moved swiftly, ever mindful of the unknown. The door to Hughes' office stood ajar. Both men listened from the hallway.

With their guns pointed, McGann went in first, throwing open the door. The room was silent except for the old man's raspy breathing and the sound of liquid splashing into a glass. McGann's voice echoed with a menacing timbre as he commanded the judge not to move. Hughes' nerves had been on such a sharp edge that the stranger's voice did not even startle him.

"Come in, gentlemen," Hughes extolled.

"Put your hands out in front of you," Joe Canton ordered.

Hughes chuckled, "Surely you're not afraid of an old man. Besides, I've got my hands full. The perfect combination, a drink and a smoke. Anyway, I'm doing better than my friend over there," Hughes indicated, with a gnarly finger.

Both McGann and Canton turned toward the grizzly sight. "Someone's had a bad day," McGann offered.

"Looks like a .308, possibly bigger," Canton suggested, alluding to the destructive bullet's caliber. They had seen enough not to be shocked, although the gory scenario firmly imprinted itself. Both men turned their attention back to the other living member in the room, lifting their eyes from the pallid corpse.

"Let me pass on some more good news, Judge," McGann began.

The old man, appearing more frail in the withered light, blew out a long trail of smoke. Shrewd eyes belied the apparent lack of concern. "Get on with it. Better make it damn quick."

"Solange is dead." The words hit the old man hard. He nearly fell to the floor, teetering against the liquor cart. Before he had a chance to recover, McGann struck again. "Does this look familiar?" he asked, holding up the dual scan nano disc.

"Your team's lost again, Hughes," Canton followed.

"It's over," McGann spit out between clenched teeth.

Hughes recovered quickly. "You bastards break into my home and come up with some damn bullshit you're going to try and pin on me?" Hughes coughed out. "You two are dumber than dried dog shit," the Chief Justice added, indignantly. "This goes beyond whatever you think you know. Besides, I'll be long dead from these cancer sticks before anyone finds me guilty. Immunity is a more realistic option," he sneered. "Bottom's up, fellas. And by the way, go fuck yourselves," the judge expressed with a raised hand. Hughes took a long swallow of the satisfying liquid.

The old man's body began to convulse uncontrollably. His hand became incapable of holding the crystal tumbler. It crashed in a splintering display. The judge followed, falling heavily to the floor. The synaptic process between nerve endings, responsible for controlling his muscles, failed. His lungs screamed for air. Hughes' heels tapped out a disjointed rhythm as the seizure increased in its intensity. McGann and Canton eyed the event with uncertainty, knowing it was beyond their control. A spew of frothy blood foamed from his mouth. The yellowed sclera of his eyes rolled upward, while the old man's ravaged heart was pushed beyond the limits.

McGann chewed his lower lip, turning to his friend, "I can think of better ways to start the day, T.C."

Canton winced, "I'd have to agree with you, Bry."

The gunman had viewed the entire event. Anger clouded his judgment. The gray light of dawn was erasing the last of night's shadow. Reason demanded his escape. Kholos' ire dictated more. No one had ever defied him like the image of the men in the rifle scope's lens. This was the perfect opportunity. Stephan Kholos meant to see it end now.

Bryson McGann caught a glimpse of an intense beam of scarlet light passing across Canton's shoulder, searching for its intended target. Instantly, he knew its meaning. McGann reacted. Leaping forward with incredible swiftness, he shoved Joe Canton out of the way. The sound of breaking glass from the large window resonated once again in the office of Foster Hughes, as both men fell to the floor.

EPILOGUE

"RANDALL, WE'VE KNOWN EACH OTHER for a long time. I won't lie to you," the President stated flatly. "There's no room for error in the chess game that's being played. This country, for that matter, the world, can't afford it." His words were followed by a steely-eyed resolve that complimented his no nonsense attitude.

Randall Sumner wielded the Micro-Sun above the bowl of his pipe, rekindling the dying embers that sent a puff of smoke swirling into the air. He listened intently as the rightful president, Richard Simon, filled him in on all the details, at least the ones he was allowed to know from this point forward. The former military man, and NESSA director, knew the score. Already, there had been heavy pressures applied to certain players on the world stage. Sumner also knew enough to surmise much of what was to come. When it came to the security of the United States, there was no option but play to win. "I agree and certainly understand."

"I'm sure you do. I thank you for that support." The President let his fingers fold together slowly before speaking again. "Let's just say there'll be instances in the very near future that capture the headlines. Much of it will be a diversion for what happens behind the scenes."

"And for the part that's not?" Sumner interjected.

"For the public's good, it must stay that way."

Sumner acquiesced, contemplating the President's words as he chewed the stem of his pipe. Simon did share with him that the Saudis had agreed to sway the other OPEC members to follow a more logical route of thinking. Their compliance had been sealed when they were informed as to just how close they came to nuclear devastation within their borders. He made it implicitly clear that card was still on the table in the very near future. The United States would use every means at its disposal if steps were not taken to increase oil output immediately. Once word leaked through the appropriate channels, the Russians grudgingly allowed natural gas to flow again into Europe.

"Foster Hughes' death played quite well on the news." The NESSA director tossed in, sawing his thumb and forefinger across his chin. "If McGann and Canton had not found the small bit of residue that Reynolds spilled, no one would have suspected thiophosphate. Smart move on someone's part to use insecticide."

"My understanding is, it mimics a massive coronary infarction."

"And it's nearly undetectable," Sumner added. He let his gaze wander the room. "It's a terrible business, this business of government."

"At times it can be, Randall. I'm afraid there'll be more shocking revelations in the near future. The proper people have been contacted to discreetly manage things. One of the impostors involved in this subterfuge, Henri Becque, has agreed to quietly remove himself from office. All for good reasons, of course, and under our strict guidance."

"The others?" Sumner asked.

The tone of the President's voice lowered, "Time's not on their side."

"Boggs. Any word on his disappearance?"

"At the moment, unknown." Richard Simon pushed himself back from his desk and stood. He took in the picture of Abraham Lincoln hanging across the room. "What do you think he'd do?" he asked, tossing a glance at the former president.

"Different place, different times," Sumner volleyed.

"You'd make an excellent politician, Randall."

"My job keeps me close enough," he replied, the corners of his mouth bowing.

Drawing in a deep breath, the President turned and stared out the window of the Oval Office. "It's my firmest belief that the world will return to order, at least a semblance of it anyway. We've rooted out several others, higher up in the pecking order. They've already been secretly taken into custody. One of the local players, Congresswoman Gail Littleton, was found this morning at her residence. The FBI's discovery reveals another tentacle in the conspiracy. She left this world with a finger curled around the trigger of a pistol. Killed herself. I guess she decided it was the easiest way out," Simon said, attempting to inform his friend, as much as understand himself.

Sumner sat quietly, taking in the conversation. What followed exceeded his expectations. The chilling words Simon tossed out bit into him. "We've confirmed that IPI is behind this scheme. Unfortunately, on the surface, it's a legitimate entity. They have positioned themselves to be untouchable. Above the law. Made up of the super elite. There is an echelon of men and women with great power and wealth." Frustration continued to cloud Simon's words. "They occupy positions of vast importance in many different arenas. Individually, they can claim ignorance. Nothing is traceable."

The President turned back towards Sumner and let his hands grip the top of his leather chair. The recent events had taken its toll, fatigue staining Richard Simon's features. Lowering his head, he continued. "They're the puppet masters, Randall. They lurk in the shadows, pulling strings that the world dances on. Any traces to Foster Hughes were erased with his death. Rest assured that news spread like a malignancy, long before the networks ever got a hold of it. Sure we'll catch some more. They will be tossed out as bait. Anything they tell us we probably know, or their information will lead nowhere. Anyone willing to testify with relevant information will probably end up with a bullet in their head long before we get a hold of them. But the shadowy figures behind all this, will remain just that."

"Richard," Sumner interjected. "This sounds terribly like what happened in nineteen thirty-two with Marine General, Smedley Butler. Are you aware of that incident?"

"Yes. I have a recollection. Don't remember all the details."

"He had been contacted by a group of wealthy business men. They wanted the general to spearhead an attempted coup on Roosevelt's administration." Sumner's mood darkened. "Fascist ideals, all self-serving, of course. Their hope was profiteering by maintaining the economic plight of the Depression. What they hadn't counted on was Butler's love of country," Sumner added. "He dropped the dime and provided a Congressional testimony."

"Fortunately, he stood up and they listened."

"True. Unfortunately, it was mostly forgotten after Congress sided with him. No one was ever prosecuted. Talk about people pulling the strings. There's an all too haunting theme regarding these circumstances, Richard. The foiled plot involving Hughes' father in November of sixty-three, and now this."

"Randall, most people probably wouldn't believe you, or care if you told them. They're clueless. Anyone who touts that type of doctrine gets labeled. You know the story."

Sumner indicated his answer by peering out from under the junction of a furrowed brow. "So the snakes simply crawl back under their rocks, until the time is right to strike again? That's not a very pleasant scenario."

"Zealots are all the same. They'll cower and plan. Use any means at their disposal. Lay low until the time is right." Simon paused briefly, choosing his words carefully. "For the moment, I can only tell you this mess is being handled as neatly and with the highest priority as possible."

"It's not pretty, Richard," NESSA director's barb implied much more.

"Never will be," the President shot back.

Something stirred in Richard Simon, a renewed defiance riding to a crest as it welled upwards. "Time is on their side, my friend. We as a nation must be vigilant. Get people to shed their complacency and realize their liberties have a price. If we let those things slip through our fingers, or be taken for granted, there's no return. Not only will we have failed, but we will have failed the world." Richard Simon inhaled deeply.

Sumner added, "Similar words were spoken by another president when he left office. It seems as if very few have listened to Eisenhower's words."

The President pulled himself up, ramrod straight. "It may be another forty years. Shorter. Longer. It doesn't matter. What does matter, Randall," Simon voiced, with a finger pointed at NESSA's director and determination gripping his jaw. "It won't happen on my watch."

☙ ❧

Sunlight cast an iridescent turquoise glow to the water as Lt. Commander Ron Wood watched the morning surf break along the Hawaiian shoreline. A couple of die hard boarders were already testing their skills, searching for the perfect wave. The pounding rumble brought back the haunting engram he experienced over the Banda Sea. Wood's thoughts were invaded by a reflection of his narrow escape from death at the hands of Stephan Kholos. He also knew it would be some time before he buried that bitter memory.

According to Captain Culpepper, the preliminary investigation into the unanticipated outcome of 'splashing a bird' had not jeopardized his flying career. Wood believed that as tough as the Stennis' captain could be at times, he was, if nothing else, a straight shooter. Culpepper was well aware of the traumas involved with just such an event. He had ordered the pilot to take a leave. Get some rest. Find some place to regroup and recoup. That's the way the skipper put it.

Ron Wood's wingman, Casey Slater, was still in the hospital. Even though the pilot was feeling better, he admitted to being unsure if he had the taste to be a fighter jockey any longer. Wood understood. All the bravado in the world soured quickly when death's shadow hovered over you. If he lost Slater as his wingman, he only hoped the next pilot to fill those shoes would be as good. Replacing Spiderman would be tough, but life goes on. He made it a point to visit him again in a few days.

His eyes followed the attractive brunette walking in his direction. She stared at the surf, alone with her own thoughts as she approached. "Hey sailor," she called out, her voice filled with laughter. Her fingers traced a soft line down his cheek. "Come on," the woman taunted. "You've been sitting here way too long. Besides, I'm hungry," she added. "Buy me some breakfast?"

Wood stared into her soft brown eyes. It had only been a couple of days, but they each felt comfortable with the other, as if they had known one another far longer. He enjoyed her laughter, and the quiet moments, too. Whatever haunting thoughts possessed him melted away as he stood and let his fingers intertwine with the woman's outstretched hand.

She walked closely by his side. They talked of hopes and dreams, wondering about possibilities that life offered. There were so many things she wanted to tell him, but for the moment, Lt. J.G. Kendall Stevens, simply smiled.

Inside the hospital room, coarse fluorescent lighting glared above the bed. A steady beeping signaled the beat of the patient's heart, a steady sinus rhythm. IV's hung at the bedside, dripping at a metered pace. An intermittent *whooshing* sound erupted each time the vacuum triggered, pulling the blood-tinged fluid from his gut through the tube in the patient's nose. The Navy doctor's labors at Bethesda had successfully removed the bullet that nearly cost the man his life.

After some time he awoke. His tongue felt thick, his mouth dry and pasty from the oxygen tubing in his nose. He attempted to speak and found his voice hoarse. Swallowing hard, he forced the words. “You’re still here,” he croaked.

Andrea Buckler peered over the top of William Beck’s latest best seller, and closed the book. “Of course,” she replied. “Where else would I be?”

“So, what’s the verdict?” Benjamin Wolcott questioned, his mind clouded by the narcotics keeping him comfortable.

“You’re too damn ornery to die.”

“Feels like I already did.” His eyes closed and it took a moment before he spoke again. “It’s funny, Andie,” Wolcott’s words were slurred, compliments of the drugs. “I’ve been in combat. Bullets, bombs everywhere. I never even got a scratch. Hell, then I get shot by the man I think I’ve known for years. Nuts, huh?”

“No, Ben. It’s irony. Bad karma. Call it what you want. What matters to me is that you’re still alive,” Buckler said, affectionately. “In a few months I’ll have you back in shape. Five miles, no sweat,” the woman chuckled. “Besides, I have a few other enjoyable plans for you during your recuperation. Now, shut up and get some rest,” she added, her eyes returning to the book.

“I’m at your disposal,” Benjamin Wolcott whispered, letting the fatigue carry him away. His eyes closed in needed sleep.

The tropics were ideal this time of year. Warm winds and hot women. Mick Henke had a passion for both. Nobody really knew the man who claimed to be from somewhere far north of his current latitude. None of them cared. He spent money, and that made them happy. Everyone knew him simply as Mick.

Henke’s ardor for women was only outweighed by his love for gin. The rich, expatriated American was enjoying the party life. His new yacht lay anchored on the placid waters outside the harbor of Basseterre. St. Kitts offered a back drop of lush green hills, providing the perfect setting for a waning sunset. It also held the promise of a long night with a wealthy thirty-something blonde. The attractive Swede from Helsingborg found Henke engaging and liked his style. What appealed to her even more was his wallet. A few nights of good sex before heading home whet her appetite. She decided to make her holiday a memorable one. It soon would be.

Both lay sleeping soundly, spent from their vigorous exploits and the booze. Neither heard anything as the man dressed in a black wetsuit climbed aboard. He pulled a small pistol from a water proof bag and racked the slide. His eyes roamed with the well practiced skill of a predator from behind the black balaclava. The man's ears registered every sound. He searched the boat finding what he wanted, and after accomplishing his task, followed the sounds of heavy breathing to his intended target.

A remarkably attractive woman lay naked next to Henke. Her blonde hair was woven into a tangled nest. Moving soundlessly, he placed his hand over her mouth. The blond's startled eyes flew open in wild panic. He shook his head, indicating to her that she should not make a sound. Tears welled in the corners of her blue eyes. The man pulled her from the bed. Henke never stirred. He took the woman on deck and tossed her a robe. "Name," he demanded, sharply.

"Sassa," she squeaked out in a timid reply.

"Take the dinghy. If you don't know how to row, now's a good time to learn." The man's eyes bore into her with purpose, delivering a dreadful chill through her bones in the warm night. "In case you're wondering, I've disabled the engine. One more thing, Sassa," he paused, with a menacing air. "Don't look back."

She wondered what Henke could have done. Tears streamed down her face in a silent cry. Sassa pulled the oars with every ounce of strength she possessed, hoping to put as much distance as possible between her and the boat, in case the man in black changed his mind. Once she had rowed a sufficient distance away, he returned to the master suite to finish his business with Mick Henke.

The excruciating pain in Henke's forehead from the steel barrel jolted him awake. A blinding beam from a flashlight clawed at his eyes. His pupils constricted, tears followed as he attempted to blink away the pain. Disorientation from the alcohol and rude awakening filled Henke with abject fear.

"Who are you?" Henke questioned, his voice strained with confusion.

"Does it really matter, Mick? Now get up," the flinty voice demanded.

The bore of the pistol centered itself on the plastic surgeon's chest. "Hey, come on, give me a break. What do you want to bother me for?" Henke's gut turned cold. His lips dried as he felt the tendrils of fear weaving through his system. "Look, I've got money," the surgeon offered, hoping its enticement would be enough.

"Mick," the voice cajoled. "Don't need your money. But you've caused enough problems with your avaricious deeds. Profiting from deceit and being responsible for the death of others exacts a price." A hint of moonlight escaped from the cloudy sky, casting deathly shadows onto the teak deck. "I'm giving you a chance, Mick."

Henke leaped at the hope the opportunity presented him. "Sure. What. What can I do?" he asked, nervously. "Anything."

The black clad intruder offered a grim smile. "Water's warm. Put on the scuba gear." Henke eagerly agreed, donning the equipment. "Tank's full, Mick." The physician licked his lips, nodding repeatedly, understanding that his chance of survival just increased. "Sit down." Henke complied, eyeing the roll of duct tape the stranger pulled from his bag. The black-clad man jammed a small piece of metal into the regulator's mouth piece. It would cause the mechanism to free flow once the tank valve was opened. "Stick out your tongue. Put the regulator in your mouth." Reluctantly, Henke complied.

"This'll give you a good seal." The tearing sound of duct tape seared the night, as the intruder finished winding it around Henke's head and mouth, covering the regulator's exhalation ports. The doctor's muffled cries were dismissed by his assailant. He grabbed Henke's arms, pulling them painfully behind his back, binding them in tape. "Here's your chance, Mick. Water's about a hundred feet deep. You make it to shore, you're a free man."

Mick Henke's insides recoiled in horror, his eyes widened. The unknown intruder wrapped the heavy weight belt around him, cinching it into place. Between the tank and weights, Henke was now over a hundred and twenty pounds heavier. "Here's the deal, doc. You're going to sink like a rock. Then your ear drums will rupture. But that's the least of your problems. Good news? You'll have a continuous air supply." The man's voice hardened into steel. "Problem is," he continued, "I'm going to shove a plug up one of your nostrils."

Henke's eyes widened at the thought. He could take air in, but only a limited amount would be exhaled.

"Even though the air will compress in your lungs the deeper you go, at some point, it will become too much. And Mick, you're a smart guy. I think you can figure it out. Your only hope is getting to shore before it's too late." The intruder painfully shoved a plastic plug into Henke's nostril, taping it into place. Dragging the struggling doctor to the stern, he whispered, "Nice night for a swim."

Henke hit the water hard, eyes stinging from the salt. He felt himself rapidly freefalling in the liquid environment. At thirty feet, pain shot through his head when his eardrums burst from the pressure. He struggled vainly, unable to free himself from his bonds. Breathing became difficult. His heart increased into a galloping drum beat.

Mick Henke hit the sandy bottom hard. Something innate took over. The will to survive drove him onward. With great effort, he managed to stand, but without fins he was unable to swim. Henke was capable of walking across the bottom, but it came at great cost. His breathing became labored after about ten yards, and a fire burned in his chest. The input from the tank was becoming more that he could exhale. He felt dizzy, his chest tightening. He hollered in fright, the sound all but lost in the black darkness of the waters.

A small stream of bubbles left a trail from his nose, but it was not enough. The regulator was simply doing what it had been called upon to do. The building pressure in Henke's chest became unbearable. Gripping panic seized the doctor in a vicious talon. His over inflated lungs ruptured painfully, filling with blood. Mick Henke's final act in life was registering the moment of his death.

The excruciating torment was a fitful retribution for the doctor's unprincipled deeds. The intruder did not bother to erase any evidence of his presence. He slid soundlessly into the water, evaporating into the night.

Mick Henke's yacht blew apart in a thunderous, fiery eruption, callously displaying its orange colors over the face of the water. The rumble rattled windows in Basseterre. Sassa decided to take the unknown man's advice. She did not look back.

In the background, music played. The smoky bar in Darwin reverberated with the sounds of raucous laughter and clinking glasses. Boasts, enhanced by the pub's refreshments, were spilled out by sailors from around the world. Red O'Brien and Skiddy Pete, along with the remaining two members of Narissa's crew, Ryan Wyborn and John Busby, raised their glasses in salute to the lost crew of the sunken ship.

"They were all good mates," Skiddy Pete said.

A resounding chorus of, "Here, here," sprang to life from the other three.

"I'm looking forward to getting this project going again," the Irishman said. He pulled the cigar from his mouth. "Here's to better days."

☙ ❧

"Looks like our friends are quite a hot item," Tori Haroldson remarked, tossing the popular magazine down onto the table. The smiling faces of Senator Jake Ramsey's son and daughter-in-law beamed silently underneath the headlines. Tori let her arms encircle his neck, breathing in his scent. "I wish it hadn't taken you so long to get here."

"I had to return an overdue favor. I know Joe and Ashlyn have taken good care of you. Anyway, it was only a few extra days."

She closed her eyes and drank in the moment. "I'm glad Randall told you to take some time off. If I didn't know better, I'd say we're staying at a plush resort. Private beach. Beautiful home. It was nice of your father's friend to offer."

"It was, and I plan on enjoying every moment. I've got a few ideas in mind," McGann returned.

"Okay, I'm ready for breakfast," she said, sitting down beside him.

"Can't wait for T.C. and Ashlyn?" McGann asked.

"No. You made me ravenous this morning," she mused playfully.

In the distance, the blue waters of the Pacific rolled onto shore. The golden yellow sunlight of morning added an artist's touch to the postcard vision spread out before them. From the patio's vantage point, they watched with fascination as a breeching humpback whale shot out of the ocean, sending geysers of water skyward, after it fell back into the sea.

"I found a couple of internet news articles of interest while you were in the shower."

The blonde scientist rested her arms on the table, folding her hands underneath her chin. "Oh?"

"One was about Abram Mossel," McGann began.

"What'd it say?" she asked, her curiosity aroused.

"Obviously, Mossel was happy to comply with the president's need for secrecy regarding the situation. The story they concocted for him seems to have worked as well as the one for Becca and Alex."

"I'm hooked. Go ahead, tell me."

"His disappearance was a marketing ploy by the diamond company to add an aura of mystery to the Oduru diamond."

"Creative capitalism," Tori remarked. "And the other?"

McGann's reply came under the covering of an arched brow. "A brief paragraph about a woman escaping from the Dutch police on her way to prison. Seems our friend, Sabrah, is on the loose..."

"Hey, you two, you're up early," Ashlyn Sanders interrupted, walking onto the sunlit patio. Joe Canton followed closely, with four mugs and a carafe of coffee.

"So Bry, how was Vermont?" Canton asked.

"Very cold," McGann returned, staring directly at his friend.

Canton understood the reference.

Quickly changing the subject, he continued, "That Brutsch fellow's a nice guy. He was happy to hear about the artifacts and wants to donate them to a museum. Our names, and NESSA, cropped up in a news report. They interviewed some professor talking about the importance of the copper ingot and other items shedding a new light on our look at history."

"Sounds great, Bry. The archeological team is making preparations to remove the boat from the cave. And, Sumner's already making plans for NESSA's credit at the Smithsonian display."

"Nothing like a little self-promotion."

"Never hurts. Hey, you never did say how you thought that Viking ship ended up so far from home. The answer is?" Canton asked.

Both women turned their attention to the conversation, swept up by McGann's explanation. "Simple. I can't believe it was overlooked." Perplexed stares followed. "I did some research, pulled up some satellite imagery, did some computations, and came up with the answer," McGann shrugged, letting the suspense hang in the air.

"Okay. What?" Sanders questioned, feigning annoyance.

"There's a fault line running along the New York and Vermont border. Actually, in 2002, they had a relatively large disturbance that did some damage in Plattsburg. The shock waves radiated well into Vermont."

"So?" Haroldson asked, intrigued by the unfolding drama.

"I believe a major quake took place somewhere around a thousand years ago. It changed the entire course of, what was then, a route from the St. Lawrence through Lake Champlain and eventually into Lake Bomoseen." The group listened intently, somewhat unsure of what seemingly was the improbable. "Give me a minute," McGann said. He returned shortly. He held a file brimming with maps and other documents. Spreading them out onto the table, his finger traced a path from Canada into Vermont, as he began again. "The Vikings left Canada on this tributary which, at that time, was connected to the waters of the St. Lawrence. Eventually, their southerly course took them into Lake Champlain. At the southern end of the lake, they made their way along this river, the Poultney. Prior to the earthquake, it was much broader and deeper. Eventually, the boat wound up in an ancient sea cave on Lake Bomoseen."

"This map doesn't show anything like that," T.C. remarked.

"True. However, after studying this satellite photo…"

"It's well documented that seismic activity has created major changes in topography in numerous areas around the world," Tori interjected. "It's a very interesting theory."

McGann continued, "This shows a faint outline denoting topographical changes in the terrain. I believe these areas were once part of a river bed. Look at this overlay I've made."

"Can you prove that, Bry?" Joe Canton questioned, eyes still tracing a path along the proposed route.

McGann returned quickly, "Not fully. It's somewhat speculative. But, I defy anyone to prove it's not true. There's simply no other explanation for the Viking knarr ending up in some place it shouldn't be."

"And the beads in the leather pouch?" Sanders cut in.

"After doing further research, I'm convinced they're Phoenician," McGann replied. "Positively, no doubt about it."

"How's that possible?" Sanders asked, in disbelief. The trio stared at one another, even further confounded by McGann's newest revelation.

"The Phoenicians were ancient seafarers of incredible talent…" McGann paused, as a small Hawaiian boy unexpectedly ran up the steps leading up from the beach below.

McGann curiously observed the child with large brown eyes peeking out from under a thick crop of dark hair. Reaching the top of the steps, a small hand holding an envelope of very expensive stationery, shot out in McGann's direction. He took the card. Without a word, the boy turned, running quickly down the steps. They called out to him without success.

"You want me to go after him?" Canton asked.

"Don't bother." McGann opened the envelope, pulling the card from inside. To his surprise, he discovered a handwritten note. He quickly processed the Greek wording.

There will be a time for you and I to meet again, Mr. McGann.
I am a man of my promises. Ask all the dead men.

Bryson McGann looked up, eyes warily surveying the coastline in all directions. He came up empty.

"What's up, Bry?" Canton asked, puzzled.

"An invitation?" Sanders questioned. "Someone having a party?"

"Who's it from?" Tori Haroldson asked excitedly, trying to get a look at the card.

"Hmm," Bryson McGann mumbled. The signature lop-sided grin belied the consternation burning within his hazel eyes. Folding the card, he shoved it into his pocket. "Just an old friend."

About the Author

William Beck currently resides in the Nashville, Tennessee area. When he is not writing, he enjoys spending time between New England and Florida. Beck served with the United States Army and has an extensive background in the medical field. William Beck's varied interests contributed greatly in the creation of this work. He is a certified scuba diver and underwater photographer. He holds the rank of Sho Dan, first degree black belt in Go Ju style karate. Pistol marksman, culinary specialist, and aspiring pilot are but a few attributes on his list of accomplishments.

William Beck is now at work on ***Caribbean Agenda***, the next book in the adventure-packed series of Bryson McGann novels.

You can find out more about William Beck at http://www.booksbybeck.com.

Printed in the United States
200733BV00004B/55-69/A